MW00872478

NOTHING TO REPORT

Mr. Patrick Abbruzzi

NYPD Lieutenant's Shield used with permission of the New York City police Department.

© 2012 Patrick Abbruzzi. All rights reserved
No portion of this book may be stored for retrieval, reproduced, or transmitted by any means without the written permission of the author.

This story is a work of fiction. Names, characters, businesses, places, events and incidents are either the products of the author's imagination or used in a fictitious manner. Any resemblance to actual persons, living or dead, or actual events is purely coincidental.

ISBN: 1494738074
ISBN 13: 9781494738075

Forward

"I am the Officer"

I have been where you fear to be,
I have seen what you fear to see,
I have done what you fear to do -
All these things I have done for you.

I am the person you lean upon,
The one you cast your scorn upon,
The one you bring your troubles to –
All these people I've been for you.

The one you ask to stand apart,
The one you feel should have no heart,
The one you call "The Officer in Blue" –
But I'm a person, just like you.

All through the years I've come to see,
That I am not always what you ask of me;
So, take this badge... take this gun...
Will you take it... Will anyone?

And when you watch a person die,
And hear a battered baby cry,
Then do you think that you can be,
All these things you ask of me?

(Author unknown)

Dedication

This book is dedicated to Dawn Urcinoli, my life-long partner and best friend, who has inspired me to persevere and finish this novel.

It is also dedicated to police officers everywhere, especially those of the New York City Police Department, who daily place their lives on the line for the citizens of our great city.

Finally, it is also dedicated to Nay Nay Bear. Thank you for being there.

CHAPTER ONE

Part of the never-ending duties of being assigned as a chauffeur or driver for the sergeant or lieutenant was the simple task of making the much needed coffee run. It probably dated back to the times when men made their rounds and trod their beats on the old Bowerie, which stretched all the way from the tip of Manhattan to the grassy farms of what we now call Soho, the area just south of Houston Street. The men likely drank their tea from heavy metal flutes they stashed in their call boxes that were affixed to the gas lamps along Broadway.

Lt. A. remembered when, as a rookie assigned to the 1st precinct on Old Slip, he had found an old, musty blotter and read an entry likely written with a feathered quill pen. If his memory served him, the entry was dated in the early 1890's. Although smudged, it was beautifully written and took up much of the waterlogged page. The first letter, which was a C, took up three of the log's lines.

*"Cries for help on the old Bowerie reported. Police officer McShane will tender report at end of day."*_

Charlie had to wait for the sergeant to finish the roll call and when the eager troops of the first platoon turned out before taking the coffee order. The chauffeur would grab an old, yellow piece of scrap paper and quickly jot down the requests from the house brigade and then be on his way.

The Platoon Commander or Lieutenant would also get a quick cup even though he could just as easily go out into the tar and brick laden streets to get his own brew. Then the Lieutenant would finish any last minute paperwork that the 3rd Platoon Lieutenant hadn't been able to finish or simply left hanging.

1

The chauffeur would also bring back coffee for the desk sergeant, who surely would die quickly and with much fanfare if he did not get his injection of caffeine along with the rest of the troops.

The list would also have orders from the cell attendant who was affectionately called 'the broom,' the 124 man, and the telephone switch-board operator.

The assignment of cell attendant stemmed from police houses in the past in which policemen were actually assigned to sweep the floors and empty garbage cans filled with stained coffee cups and as well as endless volumes of Guinness Stout bottles. The broom would make sure to keep a wary eye on the teletype machine and whenever the pages and pages of paper covered the filthy floor, he would rip them off and file them appropriately in the teletype logbook. In this day and age, the broom was not allowed to leave the cell block area. As a result, he could not even join in on the loud and vulgar bullshit session that was now taking place behind the desk.

The 124 man was the precinct's clerical man. He would type all the reports, such as aided cases and accident reports, as well as assign numbers to complaints or U.F. 61's. He would also assist the desk sergeant in any way he could.

On this particular night, Charlie Goodheart was the Lieutenant's driver and would make the coffee run. Lt. A. had offered to buy for the entire house. The Lieutenant was not a millionaire, far from it, but he would have still offered even if he were just a regular cop. It was just the way he was. The other sergeants wanted to contribute, too, so they would buy on alternating nights.

Charlie took the list and walked through the rear door into the back yard of the precinct. The rear lot was well lit from the full moon, which actually was so bright it caused eerie shadows to form around him. Thanks to a cloudless sky, he was able to spot the RMP immediately.

The RMP, also known as auto 2231, was the Lieutenant's official method of transportation. The old blue and white was dirty and had seen plenty of action in its short lived but full life. Charlie could imagine how a fair number of perp's had bled sticky, red blood in its back seat over the years. He'd heard the stories about a few Puerto Rican babies saying hello to the world there, being delivered en route to hospitals in the cavity between the aged vehicle's back doors. He could also safely wager there had been more than one boss' pointy toes curled up all the way to his nose on that seat as they got a blow job from some female officer who chose to suck her way up the ladder of success.

He got into the car and right off the bat was almost succumbed by the sexy and delectable aroma of Shalimar.

"That new policewoman, Pastore, must have been a boss' driver on the 4x12," he thought with a smile.

The entire precinct had turned out with bells on its toes and fingers to welcome the newest addition to the hallowed halls of the 120th. Adele Pastore had only been in the precinct for two weeks and already the old fort at St. George was bristling alive with ripe and rampant rumors that she had the plushiest and sweetest tush on this side of Jersey Street. It was also said that she had learned quite quickly who to shake it at.

As he started up the car, Charlie noticed Pastore had left the gas tank bone, fucking dry. He made it to the side lot where the gas pump was on fumes alone, then went back into the house and retrieved the gas log and pump key. The bullshit session was still going strong and a small cloud of smoke hovered over the participants, created by those in the group puffing away on cigars, cigarettes and pipes. Charlie simply walked behind the desk and took what he needed, not surprised in the least when the conversation didn't even break a stride.

After he gassed up the car, he pulled out of the lot onto Wall Street and made a right turn onto Richmond Terrace. He then headed south to Victory Boulevard and headed west on Victory until he reached the Dunkin Donuts on the corner of Victory and St. Paul's Avenue. This local coffee shop wasn't good to the precinct and absolutely nothing was on the arm, but it was convenient and they made good, fresh coffee every day and night. They also had their own private security force comprised of square badges so they did not depend on the local constabulary for help; hence, the full price was in effect.

Charlie pulled into a spot directly in front of the joint on a fire hydrant that still bore the red, white and blue leftover from the bi-centennial hoopla of the seventies. He didn't like to make a habit of parking on johnny plugs but this area of the precinct, as well as much of the north shore, had a blight cast on it. In addition, the local clientele had a disdain for law enforcement officers, or 'pigs' as they loved to shout, with an oink, oink here and an oink, oink there.

He walked in and spotted some locals sitting in the colored booths in the back of the room. The wooden, carved cubicles wore the scars of overuse and lack of cleaning. The phone on the far wall was being used by a local bookie. Charlie knew it had to be a personal call because no action was ever taken that late at night.

He glanced to his right and was struck by a Sicilian thunderbolt.

She was a pretty, young thing with long, straight, black hair that stretched down the entire length of her back. He could tell she was wearing a bra but figured she had to because she was built like the proverbial brick shithouse. He also noticed she had on an ebony black apron and when she turned around she displayed the cutest and tightest ass Charlie had ever seen. He fell in lust with her right there on the spot. He knew, without a doubt, that he had to get into this chick's panties. She smiled at him with a set of pearly white teeth that would put Farah Fawcett's shiny whites to shame. This chick was clean.

"Do you work in the 1-2-0?" she asked.

"Yeah, but I've never seen you before. Are you new here?"_he shot back.

"Yeah, I started yesterday but I still have to get used to these hours," she answered.

Charlie understood this all too well. Working late hours year after year sapped the very lifeblood out of one's soul. It was almost as if an invisible Dracula rode with you in the RMP and helped himself to a pint of your most precious fluid night after endless night. Charlie didn't even dwell on this anymore, however. He just accepted the fact that he felt perpetually dog-tired, looked ten years older, and felt more ragged than he really was.

For a young girl as attractive as this waitress was it probably meant she either went to school during the day, so she would not have to work in a sleazy coffee joint at ungodly hours forever, or she had a kid she had to care for during the day. When she worked she probably left the kid with a teenaged babysitter who ate non-stop and ran the Con Edison bill up with the stereo blasting. If the waitress was lucky, the kid was left in her parents' care instead, but would probably grow up to be a spoiled brat.

Charlie didn't want to scare this fox off so he played it cool with her and simply told her he would probably stop back during the night if he had a chance. He wisely added that if she were to encounter any problems at all, she was to call him right away, and he furnished her with the precinct phone number and his first name.

He said goodbye and gave her a long look with a smile that hopefully told her he wanted to eat her from top to bottom, but he did not say the words. Instead, he left it as a mystery for her and a growing lasciviousness for him.

He returned to the station house but did not blab about her like some mischievous high schooler who couldn't keep his tongue in his mouth or his cock in his pants. Charlie also knew, in sure and certain time, that every male on the late tour would find out about her and every slippery snake with a gun belt on would begin scoping her out as if she were a piece of delectable cheese on a mousetrap.

Once he turned out onto the street with Lt. A. Charlie mentioned the girl but the lieutenant played it cool and did not ask Charlie to pass by so he could get an eye full, too.

Part of the Platoon Commander's duties on the 1st platoon was completing the nightly visits to cooping prone locations. Some cops were notorious as well as ingenious in avoiding work. They would park their RMP's behind gas stations, in parks or generally anywhere hidden away from the public eye, and these visits by the Platoon Commander had to be done twice during the shift, with one of these visits being made after 4:00 a.m. The other visit could come at any time. Lt. A. knew no one would be in the heave at 1245 hours so this was when he chose to make his 1st visit and the men loved him for it. The men on the 1st platoon in the 120th knew that cooping was futile anyway because it was always so busy. Besides, you couldn't make any money sleeping on your back in the coop and most collars made on the late tour allowed them to attend court for drawing up affidavits and arraignment garnishing them time and a half in overtime.

Lt. A. also helped the men get collars. He had been a cop himself prior to leaving when he made sergeant having served there seventeen years. He knew the precinct like the back of his hand and was familiar with where all the crime happened.

The lieutenant and Charlie had a fairly busy night but it was mostly run-of-the-mill family disputes and aided cases. There had been no felonies or 49's (forms which had to be completed regarding serious, past crimes) for the lieutenant to prepare, and they surprisingly hadn't even run into any Puerto Rican mysteries for Charlie to get some summons activity.

Puerto Rican mysteries were usually difficult to solve but were a good way to fulfill the much dreaded monthly quota of summonses that the Commanding Officer demanded and extracted from each cop on patrol. Quotas were the unwritten and unspoken part of the job that everyone knew existed privately but which were vigorously denied by the brass as well as City Hall.

The typical Puerto Rican mystery would involve a Chevy being driven by a non-English speaking Puerto Rican. The registration plates wouldn't belong on the car and the vehicle identification sticker and plate would be long gone or defaced. Usually, the car would be uninsured and uninspected. After determining the car wasn't stolen, tickets could be written, and it was not uncommon to give the driver five or six moving violations. In mysteries such as these, the car was usually owned by a cousin twice removed or any other person the driver could conjure up in his brain.

6

A good patrol cop could complete his monthly quota with one Puerto Rican mystery. Men of the 120th were lucky because the Hispanic community did not learn from their mistakes; either that or they just did not give a good, flying fuck about the whole matter. They just kept on driving those 'chebbies,' much to the pleasure of the entire 120th patrol force.

Charlie was tired when he signed out at 0757 hours. The hours were crazy but the police department had to justify their productivity give-backs for the last big raise of $3\frac{1}{2}\%$ which had been graciously bestowed on them by the city's fathers.

He began to think about the strength of his will power. He had not visited his brunette beauty once during the night, not that he didn't want to. Although he had fantasized about her many times during his shift and since he didn't even remotely know her, he valiantly fought off all temptations that haunted his mind as well as his cock, which he felt stiffening every time he pictured her tight ass.

He slipped out the back door of the precinct and made his way up the steep, grassy embankment to his car where it was parked on Stuyvesant Place. To his left was the Health Department, a building resembling a fortress, and to his right was the Staten Island Museum, which all area residents cursed.

Daily rituals brought busloads of kids on school outings, with bus drivers who double-parked then left their buses without leaving any type of note signaling their destination. These uncaring bus drivers were forever blocking in residents, attorneys and judges as well. The local area surrounding the 120th housed the Supreme Court, Family Court, and the Grand Jury rooms as well as the Supreme Civil Court, so parking was always at a premium during the day. Charlie was grateful that he worked midnights because parking was always available.

He wearily climbed into his car, a yellow Subaru station wagon which he loved. The car had pep, was great on gas mileage, and he could carry anything in it. He bought it a local Subaru dealership on the Island and got a great deal because the salesman was a cop in the precinct and worked there as his 2nd job.

Charlie started up the Subby and drove home to the island's south shore. Everybody was driving to work towards the St. George ferry area as they traveled to their nine-to-five jobs, either in St. George or Manhattan, but since he was going against the traffic his trip home was a breeze.

He lived in a duplex with a neatly manicured lawn in a quiet neighborhood with a mix of Irish, Italian and Polish who took care of their property. He liked the gay couple next door and often invited them over for barbecues.

He stepped through his front door just in time to give his wife, Annette, a goodbye kiss before she left for work. She spent her days in an insurance office, going through her nine-to-five ritual every day.

Annette Goodheart was just three months older than Charlie and, for an old broad of forty-six, she still had a pretty good body and took care of herself. She had deep blue eyes and ebony black hair and at 5'9" was tall for a woman. She was Italian and a fantastic cook, having been taught by both her mother and grandmother. She could throw together a meal in no time and was famous for her Spaghetti Putenesca.

They had met at an outdoor concert at Silver Lake Park when they were both nineteen years old. Charlie still vividly remembered seeing her for the first time that wondrous and beautiful night twenty-seven years ago. She was with a girlfriend and he was with an old college buddy named Eddie.

Charlie and Eddie had been looking for some action and the concert was one big pickup zone. They wanted to score, like most guys that age, but the night quickly passed and things did not look promising. Then, Charlie had spotted Annette at almost the same time she saw Charlie.

She had on a pair of white Bermuda shorts, which allowed the outline of her black panties to be visible. They were tight enough to accentuate her beautiful ass but loose enough to show she was a lady and had some class. She also had on a yellow, silky blouse that showed some cleavage and really outlined her beautiful breasts. Her hair was dark and shoulder length and she had such a truly beautiful face. Charlie had felt as if she was an angel sent down from heaven just for him.

Both guys approached the girls and before long they found themselves enjoying the concert and talking the entire night. They wound up going to a local malt shop but the night ended there. There had been no sex.

Their kids were grown now and Charlie and Annette had been married for almost twenty-five years. He thought they would have grown closer with the kids gone but it just hadn't happened. Once Charlie Junior had left, Charlie had really tried. One day he put a sexy flick in the VCR and he and Annette had tried to make love right on the living room rug, but she had not been aroused. He was ready to do anything to please his wife but, for some reason, had been unable to. This was one of the last times that Charlie and Annette had been together sexually.

He really didn't think his wife was cheating on him but she did dress attractively to go to work. He had tried desperately to dismiss those crazy, insane thoughts from his mind. He was faithful to his wife and had been for his entire marriage, but he was a man who was horny and wanted to get laid. He was a regular guy and even though he often found himself lusting after women he met at work, he didn't come onto them, even though they were often abused by their husbands or boyfriends and were vulnerable and starving for the least bit of affection.

He settled down with a beer and the remote, flipping through the channels as he wound down from his long night. When he found nothing interesting on the tube, he went to bed and fantasized about the waitress, jerked off to get a release and soon fell fast asleep.

The next night he stopped at the coffee shop on his way to work. Most cops usually stop somewhere to bring in the first cup with them and they were notorious for getting to work early. With that first cup they walk into their muster rooms and peruse their roll calls to see their assignments for the tour. Then they sit and bullshit for a while before heading to their locker rooms to put on the blues.

As soon as Charlie walked in, he realized the waitress was there. She spotted him and almost did a double take. She had never seen Charlie in civilian clothes before so she looked at him as if to say, "I know you from somewhere." It didn't take long for her to remember.

"Hi. How are you? Remember me? I came in last night with the list from the precinct," he said.

"Yes, I remember you. I thought I would see you again during the night but you never came back," she responded.

"Yeah, I know. It was kind of busy and I drive the lieutenant so I have to go where he tells me to go," he explained.

Charlie hoped she would buy his lame excuse and decided to put on a pair of balls and ask for her name. He had nothing to lose.

"What's your name? If you don't mind my asking," he said.

"I'm Terry," came her willing response, "and yours?"_

"It's Charlie, and actually, I need to head in to the station now but I'll probably be back later with another list."

He asked if she wanted or needed anything from another store on the way back, since he knew the girls who waitress at night usually didn't go out to other places on their breaks.

"That's really sweet of you, Charlie. I really could use another pack of Marlboro cigarettes. I really don't think I could last the night with what I have in my pocketbook. Let me get my purse and I'll give you some money," she said.

"We'll straighten it out later when I come back, okay?"_he replied as he turned and walked out to his car which was parked in a legal spot. He never parked on a hydrant with his private car. Although he knew lots of cops who violated traffic laws while off duty, he was not one of them. His head was swimming. Not only did Terry look great but she smelled great, too. She wore Shalimar. It was his favorite perfume and drove him crazy.

His mind was racing a million miles an hour and he knew had to slow himself down and focus. He had a night ahead that might require him to use every bit of concentration his mind and body could muster.

He drove to the precinct and decided to stop at a local bodega, which was directly behind the station house on Stuyvesant Place and across the street from the Staten Island Museum. The store was open twenty-four hours a day and depended on the cops, especially at night. They were a local numbers joint but weren't bothered by the local uniformed force. The plain clothes cops were the ones who serviced this joint and most likely were on the pad. The nearness to the St. George ferry terminal afforded the local stores with plenty of customers, twenty-four hours a day.

Often people of all races, creeds and opinions who were filled with curiosity got off the boat and wandered the local decaying neighborhood to see what Staten Island had to offer. It was too bad that all they saw was the sleazy squalor of the north shore. Some were just lice-ridden skels and bums, some were experienced thieves just looking for fresh, virgin fields to steal from, and some were bleeding heart hippies and young yuppies trying to escape the soaring rent rates of Manhattan.

When Charlie walked into the bodega he saw a long line at the counter which meant business was good, especially for 11:15 at night. Juan Diaz was the night manager on duty and was good people; he worked hard and told no lies. He was born in the south Bronx and migrated to the lower east side when he was a teenager. When crime forced him and his family from Rivington Street, he settled in St. George and worked in the bodega where he was now manager. Juan hoped he would own it one day and Charlie hoped it would happen.

Juan had a Wilson baseball bat under the counter that Babe Ruth would have found difficult to lift. He would not hesitate for one iota of a second in using the wooden weapon to bash someone's skull if he thought he was being robbed of his night's receipts.

Charlie got in line with the rest of the paying customers, noticing that everyone almost always bought the same things at night – beer, cigarettes and pampers, although every once in a while someone would buy the roll ups makers used for marijuana cigarettes. Those little packages were kept out in the open so people would not even have to ask for them.

When it was Charlie's turn at the counter, he asked for a pack of Marlboro red for Terry and a pack of Vantage regulars for himself. He gave Juan a five dollar bill and received five singles in change. It was always done that way when Charlie was in uniform because the patrol force never knew when some nosy shoo fly from the Ivory tower's Chief of Departments office would be watching. Money was tendered and money was received, plain and simple.

Charlie said goodbye to the man behind the counter, knowing he would see him again during the night. Juan was good and the men of the 120th were going to keep him that way. This meant stopping by often to make sure he was alright. It also meant stopping at other food joints where cops got food on the arm. One team stopped at a KFC every night and always brought Juan back some chicken for him because they knew he loved fried chicken.

Charlie walked to the front entrance of the old precinct but before he entered he slowly glanced up at the decaying gargoyles which bravely stood silent watch and guarded the old fortress. On either side of the pigeon-stained lions were the ever-burning green lanterns that adorned all precinct houses throughout the city. Of course the lights here hadn't been burning for years and were probably two years older than dirt.

It's believed that the Rattle Watchmen, those who patrolled New Amsterdam in 1650's, carried lanterns with green, glass sides at night as a means of identification. When the watchmen returned to the watch house after patrol, they hung their lantern on a hook by the front door to show people seeking them that they were inside the watch house.

Today, either green lights or lanterns are affixed outside the entrances of police precincts as a symbol that the "watch" is present and vigilant.

Charlie opened the massive and heavy wooden front doors and stepped up two wide and grimy marble, permanently blood-stained, steps. No one knew where the blood came from, however. It could have come from a perpetrator or from an injured officer.

Directly in front of him now were yet another wide set of doors, but these were made of glass. If Charlie had earned a single dollar every times a perp's head went through these familiar panes, he probably could have put a down payment down on the new car he wanted.

He opened the doors and stepped into the station house. His destination led him directly to the front desk, which was the very heart and soul of the precinct. As he approached the area directly in front of the desk, Charlie saluted sharply. The 4x12 lieutenant glanced up and gave Charlie a little acknowledging smile.

Saluting the desk was something all the old timers did. It was part and parcel of being a cop. It was tradition. It was love. It was in your blood, never to be lost. It was respect for everything that came before and everything that would ever be. Although Charlie hadn't seen any of the younger members do it, he quietly hoped with the passing of time that they, too, would learn and gather the meaning of that first salute.

He entered the rear muster room and saw that some of his fellow cops were already there, nursing their important first cup of coffee. They were busy discussing the latest rumor that Mayor Rudolph Giuliani was going to bounce Police Commissioner Bratton.

Bratton had been the brain trust of the department and had been responsible for lowering crime in NYC with innovative crime fighting techniques. However, everyone knew Mayor Giuliani would not allow Bratton to accept the credit for it. The Mayor was self-centered and wanted the spotlight only on himself.

Bratton also liked the limelight and loved to frequent New York's trendy watering holes where he could hob-knob with the city's rich and famous. In fact, Commissioner Bratton was a frequent visitor of Elaine's, a very upscale establishment. The collision of their wills was an accident waiting to happen.

Bratton's wife was a famous newscaster in her own right as part of the Channel 7's Eyewitness News team. Cheryl Fiandaca was married to Bratton, although it had been rumored that their marriage was headed south.

From out of the blue Police Officer Vito Madoni stood up and placed his hand over his heart, which was difficult for him because he had about six pounds of shimmering gold dangling from his neck. Vito had sworn he was going to snare the new waitress at the Dunkin Donut shop and had warned everyone to stay clear from her, signifying that she was his and that there would be deep trouble if anyone interfered.

Vito was married and a Guido Italian, which is what the Italians who were born on Staten Island called the Italians who had traversed the Verrazano Narrows Bridge. Guido Italians brought with them crudeness, disrespect and two tons of gold per family member.

Vito was also a typical Brooklyn cop. He had transferred from Brooklyn's 68th precinct in Bay Ridge and thought the 120th was still Brooklyn. He was boisterous, painfully brutal to all his prisoners, and generally disliked by the entire late tour crew. He hesitated in picking up his jobs and tried to talk his way out of most of his collars. Most of the men and some of the women called him a coward but he didn't seem to give a flying fuck. What did matter was that he tried to do as little work as possible. In doing so, he jeopardized everyone on the force.

Lt. A. had Vito's number right away. After Vito warned everyone to stay away from Terry, Lt. A., who was also sitting in the muster room having his coffee, approached Vito with a question.

"Vito, are you telling me that I can't talk to that pretty young thing? I saw her the other night. She's a doll," Lt. A. coyfully exclaimed.

"No, not you lieutenant. I mean all these other guys," Vito stammered.

"Now, Vito, all is fair in love and war. Did you ever hear that?" replied the lieutenant.

Not to look any dumber than he really was, Vito answered in the affirmative.

When the conversation ended, Lt. A. gave Charlie a wink out of the corner of his eye and went up the rear stairs to the lieutenant's locker room, which was on the second floor facing the front of the station house. There was a magnificent view of New York Harbor from this room and, in the distance, the lights of the famous New York City skyline glimmered.

The locker room was fairly sparse and painted in the pale green which seemed to cover most precinct walls in almost every station house throughout New York City. Paint was peeling in some places, however, laying bare the plaster hidden beneath. There were two neon ceiling lights overhead, one of which continually flickered on and off, and approximately fifteen full lockers reaching from ceiling to floor. There was one wooden bench mounted to the floor between the lockers which enabled the lieutenants to sit while they changed into their uniforms.

Lt. A. kept most of his uniforms for all seasons handy in one of the dented, metallic cabinets. He had his black leather jacket, which was only waist length and really didn't keep him warm but was suitable enough for riding in the RMP, as well as his knee length winter coat, which hardly anyone ever wore, tucked behind the scratched, metal door. The latter he'd had when he was a rookie in the 1st precinct and kept it more as a memento than as an article of clothing to wear.

Along one locker room wall was a single desk with a lamp which furnished just enough light in case anyone wanted to read or finish any reports. On the desk was an old, black phone, used only within the station house to warn the lieutenants of any unwanted visitors from the Chief of Department's office. A few feet away was a single, comfortable chair frequently used to grab forty winks if one so chose. The final piece of décor was a torn calendar hanging on the wall, courtesy of some scotch tape and two push pins.

Charlie headed for his locker room and on the way he used the male bathroom which was adjacent to the muster room. You could walk through the bathroom to another door leading to the rear stairs which then led to the third floor officer's locker rooms. Many a female cop often forgot to knock on the bathroom door by mistake, or perhaps it was intentional, and more than once some female officer caught some good looking stud of a cop with something more than his summons book in his hand.

There were several locker rooms available for the officers in the station house, and Charlie's locker was on the 3rd floor. When he reached it, he opened it and immediately saw the picture he had taped to the inside of his door. It was a photo of his wife and kids. Most cops hung pictures of their wives and girlfriends inside their lockers in the same way, while some hung Penthouse beauties in all their full nakedness. Many cops even carried photos of loved ones inside the lining or pocket of their uniform caps.

Charlie quickly changed into his uniform, securing his shield on his shirt. Then he grabbed his briefcase, which was full of various forms he knew he might need during his shift with Lt. A. Often, when it was busy Lt. A. was assigned jobs and Charlie was his scribe as well as driver. He was also responsible for filling out the reports.

He went down the front stairs, this time passing the telephone switchboard operator en route to the muster room.

The cop assigned to the T.S. called him over and handed him a folded piece of paper. Those who were assigned to the T.S were a special kind of cop. They were the go-between for single cops, married cops, girlfriends and mistresses and always had to be discreet. They were forever delivering messages to the guys and many times were forced to lie to wives who were trying to reach their husbands. These T.S. operators had special talents for lying and it was not uncommon for the snakes to grease their palms once in a while.

Some cops actually went away for days at a time with their girl-friends, having told their wives they were on special assignment or had made large busts and were going to be tied up in weekend court for extended periods of time. Two things might have been true; they probably were involved with large busts and they were also probably tied up in some way.

Charlie took the piece of paper handed to him and opened it right away. It was from Terry. It simply said, "Thanks, Terry." He smiled knowing he was in her thoughts because God knew that she was in his.

He glanced at Terry's note again and felt frightened all of a sudden. He didn't want to lie to Annette yet felt as if he just had to pursue this. To him, this was more than his wanting sex or an urge to get laid. Sure, Terry was younger than he was, and sure she had a great body, but he really felt as though he wanted to get to know her and get closer to her emotionally.

Christ, who was he kidding? Charlie wanted to fuck the living daylights out of her! As he read the note a third time, he thought perhaps she was just being friendly.

"Yeah, that must be it," he rationalized out loud. After all, she could have any guy she wanted, he thought silently.

After roll call was completed and most of the troops had hit the bricks, the coffee list was compiled and, as usual, Charlie got to make the coffee run. Lt. A. even told him to take his time because there were enough sergeants working and the lieutenant wanted to catch up on his paperwork.

After some brief chit-chat, Charlie took the list and drove over to the Dunkin Donuts shop. As usual, he parked right in front then walked in with a shit-eating grin on his face, fully expecting to see

Terry. Much to his chagrin, she was nowhere to be seen anywhere behind the counter.

He wanted to be cool so he walked up to another waitress and ordered his coffee and donuts. In the middle of his order, another waitress walked over to him.

"Are you Charlie?" she politely asked.

"Yeah, I'm Charlie."

"Terry had to leave on an emergency. Something came up and she wanted you to know that she was sorry she didn't get a chance to see you tonight," she said.

The waitress had sort of a mischievous smile on her face as she spoke.

Charlie thanked her and walked out of the joint, almost forgetting to take his order with him.

He got in the RMP and began the five minute long ride back to the barn as his mind filled with questions. What was the emergency? Did she have sick kids at home? Maybe she had to go care for a sick husband.

He felt the onset of a fit of nausea stirring deep down in the pit of his stomach as another thought suddenly occurred to him.

"Did she even have a real emergency?" Perhaps she met someone else and went to a motel with the guy.

His stomach was in knots and he was angry for allowing himself to feel this way. He had an entire night ahead of him and could not afford to fall apart now. Thankfully, as he neared the station, he began to get his emotions under control.

He did not even know this girl. He was much older than she and the entire thing was absolutely fucking crazy, yet he would have to go through the entire shift, day and evening, before he could see her again. He wondered if he would be able to even fall asleep when he got home.

He tried to think cleverly and logically as he sorted through the questions in his mind. As he did, he wondered why Terry would go through the trouble of telling another girl to watch for him and deliver such a personal message.

It was driving him crazy, not knowing the circumstances surrounding her absence, but he knew he had to calm down. By the time he got back to the precinct, the boss had finished his paperwork and they headed out to the streets. Lt. A. was in a talkative mood, for which Charlie was eternally grateful. His mind had been reduced to liquid Jell-O and now he wouldn't have to spend the night thinking and imagining weird things about Terry.

CHAPTER TWO

L t. A. had many wonderful war stories, which he thoroughly enjoyed sharing with his driver. He was especially fond of his days when he was also a cop in the 120th. The lieutenant's partner back then had been Frank Brownell and they had been partners for twelve years.

"Charlie, Frank and I were together for twelve fucking years. It was busy as hell but we loved every minute of it," Lt. A. said with a reminiscent smile.

That's when the boss began to tell Charlie about a family dispute on Sand Street, just off of Bay Street in the Stapleton section, which was located in sector Eddie.

Stapleton and St. George began to have a big influx of Albanians as well as Yugoslavians in the seventies and eighties. Most of them were either afraid of the police or simply held no trust in them, which could be traced back to their roots in the old country. Many of the men carried concealed weapons and took care of business in their own way, while the women were cleaners who worked in Manhattan at night servicing the high risers, generally from 6:00 P.M. until 2:00 A.M. They would often be seen walking from the ferry, right up Victory Boulevard and along Bay Street, saving the bus fare.

Anyway, one day Frank and I were doing a day tour and we got a job from Central directing us to respond to a family dispute at an old wooden framed, two-story house on Sand Street. As soon as we pulled up in front of the home we noticed pretty yellow flowers that had been planted along the crumbling edge of the ancient sidewalk. The front yard was small but well-kept and had a religious statue adorning it. To the left of the statue were several plastic Disney characters which had obviously been repainted. It was very apparent that the family who lived here at least tried to maintain some neatness to the neighborhood.

This area that had been taken over by the Albanians was a welcome change. Previously it had been inhabited by mostly blacks. In those days the yards were untouched and the household garbage barely made it outside into pails. More often than not the garbage was just flung out to the yards and street.

Lt. A. continued with his reminiscing and Charlie listened attentively.

Because of all the chicken bones and ribs which littered the streets and yards on Sand Street, the guys in the precinct used to call it "chicken bone alley".

We approached the front door and gave it a few raps with our night-sticks, and after several seconds, a woman who was probably in her late thirties or early forties greeted us. She was wearing an old, blue house dress that reminded me of something my seventy year old grandmother would have worn. It was tattered and covered with stains. The woman's face was weather-beaten and the wrinkles on her brow hid a multitude of pain and sorrow. It looked as if she had been crying because her left hand clenched a snot-laden tissue and her eyes were as red as beets. She kept turning around and looking behind her as if she expected a fire breathing dragon to suddenly appear and drag her away.

Eventually she motioned for us to come in and led us to a front parlor. Close to one wall was a table with a dirty lace doily. In the center of the table was a cracked flower vase with no flowers in it. A mirror hung on one plaster wall, deep cracks running across it in all directions. The room was fairly clean even though it was sparse. To this day I still remember the aroma of cooking cabbage that filled the room; it smelled good. After several long seconds, the woman began to speak to us with a broken accent.

Lt. A. paused to take a sip of his coffee then continued.

The woman's voice was aged and tired.

"Please to sit down, here. My husband... he has been drinking the vodka for two days now. He become very mean when he drink the vodka," she moaned.

"Where is he now?" asked Frank.

"He is basement with dogs," she answered.

Both Frank and I were concerned about their dogs so we asked her what breed they were.

"We have two Rottweiler. They are friendly. Not to worry, ok?" she offered as if reading our minds.

"Does your husband have any guns in the house?" asked Frank.

"No. He have no gun in house. That I am sure," she said.

Frank and I were curious as to why she had called the police. Searching for one of the many puzzle pieces, Frank asked, "Did he hit you?"

"No. It is not for me. I call for my daughter," she explained.

"Your daughter?" Frank asked with surprise. *"Where is she? How old is she?"*

Lt. A. glanced at Charlie with a brief smile, his eyes bright with the memories.

"Frank came out with so many questions all at once. He was good at that."

"My daughter is in attic. She is fourteen-year old and she come home from school with bad report card. My husband punish her."

The woman fell silent as she began to cry again.

"What did your husband do? Did he lock her in? Is her room in the attic?" inquired Frank.

"Yes, he lock her in attic and she is screaming," sobbed the mother.

"Why didn't you go and unlock the door?" asked Frank.

"Then he would surely kill us both," she answered. Although her tone was matter-of-fact, her eyes dropped to the floor.

"This was the first time this woman even hinted that the man in the basement with the dogs was could be violent," Lt. A. said as he glanced at Charlie.

"What is your husband's name?" asked Frank.
"His name is Rejic," the woman responded.
"And what is your daughter's name?" asked Frank.
"Her name is Barbara."

"The American name was typical of immigrants trying to blend into the culture," Lt A explained. "The parents who immigrated to this country usually kept their names and had a tough time with the language barrier. Those same parents most often gave their children American names so they would be easily accepted by other kids."

Lt. A. described how he and his partner Frank made their way up to the attic, guided by the mother who was now visibly trembling. The stairs were very narrow and dimly lit with only one bare bulb at the base of the stairs. Each step creaked and felt as if they might collapse under the weight of both men, who were both laden down with sticks and lead.

As they approached the top landing the mother turned on a light switch and soon the hallway was illuminated by a single bulb which sat in a wall fixture that was missing its glass enclosure.

As they neared the attic door, both officers heard moans coming from the other side. Although they were alarmed, it was not the screams the mother had described earlier.

"Open the door!" Frank demanded.
"I have no key. My husband, he have key," the mother stammered.
"Oh, Christ! What do you want us to do? Break in the door when your husband has the fucking key?" Frank yelled.

"Frank was the type of individual who had an extremely high boiling point, Charlie," Lt. A. explained. "It usually took a lot for him to lose his temper, but at that moment, he was furious!"

"What do you want us to do?" Frank asked again. "We can break it down or we can go down to the basement and drag his ass up here. But if he starts any shit with us, I swear he'll go to St. Vincent's Hospital first before we lock him up and take him to jail! Do you understand that?"

The woman nodded. "I give permission to break door," came her meek response.

"Okay, stand back," Frank ordered.

Lt. A. took another swig of his coffee and looked at Charlie as he explained what he'd seen that night.

"It was an old wooden door and very likely the original one that came with the house. In spite of this, it looked sturdier than the pieces of crap that builders put in new houses today.

"Frank took out his memo book and made an entry attesting to the fact that she had given her permission for us to kick the door in. He asked her to sign it and she did. Frank and I both knew there was no sense in the department getting sued later.

"When the formalities had been taken care of, Frank kicked the door once. Thankfully that was all it took. It flew off its hinges and landed several feet inside the darkened attic."

Lt. A. shook his head with the memory and his eyes clouded over with sadness.

"Neither Frank nor I expected to see what we did when we entered the eerie, grave-like darkness of the secret laden chamber. It had an old, damp musty smell that most attics acquire after so many years, yet this one was somehow different."

Charlie was all ears as he maneuvered through the quiet streets. When the lieutenant fell silent, Charlie glanced at him but the man in the seat beside him was staring into the distant past.

"The initial odor that viciously attacked our nostrils the instant the door was off its hinges was one of human excrement," the lieutenant said quietly. "Not long after that, the woman who accompanied us into the room began to scream."

Lt. A. took another drink of his coffee and ran a trembling hand through his dark hair. He sighed quietly then continued.

Hanging from the huge, blackened, middle rafter by a rope, which was tied around her bleeding ankles, was the crying woman's daughter, Barbara. She was completely naked, her clothes in a rumpled pile several feet away. Human feces covered her back and hair, which was heavily matted from a combination of excrement and urine. It didn't take long for the stench to flood into our noses, attacking us without mercy. Small, liquid piles of feces littered the ground directly below the young girl's head, which hovered about two feet above the urine-soaked floor.

The nearly unrecognizable girl was moaning softly. She sounded like a dime store mama's doll but only much, much weaker. As I stood there watching her, I realized this young girl who had made the monumental error of bringing home a bad report card was completely unaware that her salvation for such a grievous sin was almost at hand. It was almost surreal.

She was actually quite beautiful in a weird, disgusting way. She had huge, bulbous breasts, but even though she was hanging upside down like a pig after slaughter, her breasts did not sag from the gravity being exerted upon them. The way they protruded through the air was amazing and truly inexplicable. Both nipples were hard and erect and looked like a pair of very wide, thick buttons. She had one of the largest pubic hair areas that either Frank or I had ever set our eyes on. Although we had both heard stories about how Eastern European women from the Slavic countries never shaved under their arms, neither of us were prepared for the massive bush jutting out from the region just inches below this young girl's belly button.

Lt. A. took another drink of his coffee, now getting cold, and grimaced before he went on.

I found a chair in one of the attic's corners. It was old but sturdy enough to accomplish the rescue at hand.

As we looked around the rest of the attic, Frank and I slowly realized it resembled a medieval torture chamber. There were chains, whips, ropes and leg irons scattered throughout the room. Barbara's mother found another light switch and soon there was enough light for the three of us to cut down the bound young woman. As Frank grabbed the girl's body in an attempt to steady her, I stepped up on the chair and cut the rope which bound her ankles together. The sobbing mother cradled her daughter as if she was a newborn infant and we gently lowered the girl to the dingy, wet floor. Barbara's mother quickly covered her with an old, dusty quilt she had found in an old chest of drawers, probably left behind from a previous family years before.

The mother began speaking in her native tongue and it was easy to guess that she was cursing her husband. We listened to her for a minute or two then Frank quietly explained that he was going to go down to the floor below and use the phone to call for an ambulance. Thankfully, the mother quietly acquiesced. After a nod to me, Frank quickly descended the steps, found a phone and called 911 to request that a bus respond immediately.

While Frank was calling for the ambulance, I tried to explain to Barbara's mother that her husband was going to have to be placed under arrest. This might be hard to believe, but after everything this poor family had been through, the mother was reluctant to press charges against her husband.

Lt. A. paused as he looked out the window for nearly a minute before he added, "This is when I realized that the monster below really ruled the house with fear."

He described how he found it necessary to explain that they were still going to place Barbara's father under arrest, even though her mother was reluctant to press charges. They knew they could arrest the man based upon their own observations of the abused girl and that, coupled with the wife's previous statements, would be prima facie.

Frank came back into the attic after completing his call to 911.

"Well are we ready partner?" he asked.

"Let's get that mother fucker," I answered.

We began the walk down to the basement, leaving the mother to tend to her daughter who, thankfully, was quietly speaking now. As we approached the cellar stairs we withdrew our service revolvers from our holsters and quietly began the descent to the room below. It wasn't long before we began to hear the dogs barking.

"Rejic! Rejic! Are you there?" asked Frank.

"Lock those dogs up now if you don't want them to get shot," I ordered.

We immediately heard a man calling the dogs and in less than a minute, a door slammed shut. The barks were more muffled now and we assumed Rejic had put the dogs in another room. As we made our way down the rest of the stairs, we saw a male figure standing in the rear of the cellar.

Looking around, it was obvious that this room was a man's domain; there was nothing feminine about it. It was dirty and cluttered, with vodka bottles, old pizza boxes and overflowing ash trays strewn all around. No part of this room had seen a dust rag or mop in a long time.

Although there was a small work shop area on one end of the room, it was clear that neither this man nor any other had built or repaired anything there in years. A calendar from the previous year hung on the wall near the door.

As far as the man himself was concerned, he seemed small and diminutive. He appeared to be the type that was probably wimpy around other men but mistreated smaller men and all women. He was wearing a clean dress shirt and jeans, likely thanks to the woman upstairs who probably toiled day and night for the bastard. He had about three or four days' worth of growth on his face, which was certainly not an uncommon sight on foreigners.

"Turn around and put your hands on top of your head. Do you understand what I'm saying?" Frank asked in a serious, resounding tone.

At first the man in the cellar was unsure on his feet and almost tumbled backwards, but after several seconds he regained his stance and followed Frank's directions. Rejic turned around and quickly placed both of his hands squarely on the top of his head.

Frank and I quickly approached Rejic and, while I covered him, Frank holstered his revolver and cuffed the man's hands behind his back. Thankfully, Rejic offered absolutely no resistance at all.

28

The lieutenant glanced at Charlie and nodded.

"As you can imagine, both Frank and I silently hoped the prick would have resisted or even tried to get away. We both wanted an excuse to beat the shit out of him for what he had done to his daughter. Unfortunately, it didn't go down that way.

Frank gave him a quick toss but didn't come up with any weapons or contraband. Glaring at the man, Frank then sat him down in a chair before bringing him upstairs.

"How could you do such a thing to your daughter?" I asked.

"She bring home bad school," the father replied in broken English.

"Well, if she doesn't do well in school, you get her some fucking help. You don't torture her like a stuck pig. Are you fucking crazy? That's your little girl!" screamed Frank.

"Don't you know that you're going to go to jail now?" I asked, even though I knew this question was futile. How could you talk sense into a man who had just stripped his daughter, tied her up by the ankles and hung her up to dry just like a bundle of helpless grapes in a wine cellar? This was more than child abuse. It was also felony assault and possibly even sexual abuse or worse. He may have even raped his own daughter for all we knew!

Rejic gave us no answers. Instead, we would have to wait for the final medical report once it was obtained from the hospital.

The ambulance arrived and both mother and daughter were transported to St. Vincent's emergency room over on Bard Avenue. Without a word, Frank and I took our prisoner to the 120th for processing in central booking.

Charlie was glad the Lieutenant told some of his war stories. Not only did they keep him entertained, they were also quite informative. Sometimes they were sad and sometimes they were so funny that he would have to park the RMP in a deserted area just to get out and take a piss in fear that he would wet his pants.

On this night Charlie was glad that Lt. A. was occupying his mind, because he was trying very hard not to think of Terry. He had conjured

29

only about a million reasons why she'd had to leave the coffee shop in such a hurry. There was no doubt that he really had to ease up on his emotions.

Lt. A. began to tell Charlie another story but they were both interrupted by a job on Bay Street near Canal Street. Some fool had placed a briefcase with exposed wires in the doorway of the Staten Island Savings Bank and a Good Samaritan saw it and called 911. The job turned out to be an all-nighter and was boring and tedious. The briefcase was found in a business area that bustled during the day but had no residents living within at least six blocks of the bank in all directions. The only concern was for the transit authority bus routes along Bay Street and the traffic, which was handled quite nicely by a few other RMP's directing it on a detour pattern. A call had been made to the local transit authority garage that dispatched its own supervisor to handle the detour. The NYPD emergency service unit responded and requested the services of the bomb squad which had to respond from Rodmans' Neck way up in the Bronx. The bomb crew soon arrived with the containment vehicle as well as a robot with its own X-ray attached.

After roughly seven hours of standing on the sidelines and letting the pros do their jobs, it was finally determined that it was a hoax with no explosives whatsoever.

CHAPTER THREE

The lieutenant and Charlie signed out of the precinct at 10:00 A.M. When Charlie arrived home, he expected to walk into an empty house since his wife usually left for work between 8:00 A.M. and 8:30 A.M. He saw Annette's car in the driveway when he pulled up in front of his house, which should have tipped him off. After entering the house, he headed for the kitchen.

Annette was the sort of housewife who could not tolerate clutter, or what she considered clutter, anywhere on the counters. Charlie vividly remembered how difficult it was for her to concede just to allowing an automatic coffee maker to remain out in the open.

He noticed that the coffee maker was still on but Charlie saw no sign of Annette. He thought perhaps she had left her car home and gotten a ride to work. Without thinking about it any further, he decided to go upstairs and hit the hay. He was bushed.

As he made his way into the bedroom, much to his amazement, he found Annette on the bed wearing a very sexy teddy and nothing else, including panties. She also wore the sexiest makeup he'd seen on her in a long time. She looked sexy as all hell.

Although he was tired, he loved sex in the morning. It seemed he performed better in the morning than at any other time of the day, and although he was never one to say no to a good session of lovemaking, at this moment all he wanted to do was fuck her brains out.

He grabbed Annette roughly and kissed her fully on the mouth. He then lowered himself down to her stomach and began to lick her pubic area. He forced open her inner and outer lips and began to lick and suck roughly on her vagina.

He could hear his wife moan as she grabbed his head and thrust his face deeper into her pussy and Charlie suddenly found himself fantasizing about Terry. He actually visualized Terry and imagined it was her pussy he was eating. He raised himself up and forcibly entered Annette with his swollen member. He wanted to come inside Terry but knew he could not come inside Annette without protection, so he pulled out at the last minute and ejaculated all over his wife's breasts. Although Annette didn't say anything, her eyes told him that this was not the Charlie she knew.

He knew he had used Annette and was obviously disappointed in him. For that matter, he was disappointed in himself. He hadn't spoken one word to her, not one word, telling his wife how beautiful she looked. He hadn't said a single word of thanks to her for staying home today, not one, single word. He had been a heel.

He could have pleased and satisfied her; hell, he *should have* pleased and satisfied her. Instead he had only thought of himself and his needs. Even worse, he thought of another woman.

Annette knew something was wrong.

"Charlie, are you okay?"

Before he answered, she continued.

"Look, I'll be honest with you. I've been planning this for a while and then you don't even call me to let me know that you're going to be late!"

"Honey, at 8:00 A.M. I was still out on the street. I would have called you had I known you weren't going to work," Charlie offered.

"Look, sweetheart, I'll be honest with you. I was looking forward to a great orgasm," she blurted out.

Charlie was taken back. In all their years together she had never actually come out and said anything quite like this. He knew Annette was good in bed but coming out and saying it so boldly was bewildering to him. He was also a little bit afraid.

32

Although he was really tired, he didn't want to disappoint his wife so he started to kiss her again with the intention of really pleasing her this time. He decided to please her orally and, as his tongue approached her vagina, she began to moan and writhe as if she were a snake on fire. A few minutes later Annette experienced an explosive orgasm the likes of which Charlie had never seen. The wetness and heat from her body aroused him even more now than when he first saw his wife in her teddy.

Charlie was amazed that she was still wet and moist after all these years and it was evident. His wife knew he was aroused again and grabbed his swollen member and drew it into her mouth. She played with him for a while but when she sensed he could no longer hold back, she allowed him to explode into her mouth and swallowed him as she had from the first days when they had begun dating.

Afterwards they both lay in bed together enjoying a cigarette. They engaged in small talk but really did not say anything of importance to one another. After they extinguished their cigarettes, Annette got out of bed and kissed Charlie goodnight. She drew shut the room darkening shades they had purchased together when he began working the late tours then walked out of the room, softly closing the door behind her.

Some people could fall asleep with the morning sun streaming through the windows, but Charlie was not one of them. He needed darkness. It was almost noon and he was exhausted after first being up all night, then the lovemaking session, but he was glad Annette had decided to stay at home and wait for him. He wanted to be honest with her and tell her about the stupid childhood crush he had on some strange girl at work, but he could not bring himself to say it. He swore to himself that nothing would ever happen between Terry and himself then fell asleep quickly and easily.

While he slept, he dreamed of Terry.

CHAPTER FOUR

Although Charlie and Lt. A. both had Sunday and Monday off, Friday nights were always busy in the 120th. They would finish up on Saturday morning at 8:00 A.M. then not have to return until Monday night at midnight. It was a steady 64-hour swing. The advantage of steady days off afforded one the opportunity to plan one's life.

Charlie decided to go straight into work and bypassed the donut shop. He began to feel stupid because he did not even know this girl and she didn't know him.

As he drove through the city, his mind once again began to play twenty questions with him. Why had she called? Why did she leave a message at the precinct? Was she attracted to him?

Before he got to work he stopped elsewhere for the coffee he so desperately needed. When he arrived at the station house, he parked his car at the rear of the precinct on Stuyvesant Place.

The precinct was located at 78 Richmond Terrace. The surrounding area was the hub for the entire criminal justice department and parking was a cinch on the late tours. There were no judges, lawyers or Probation Department people to fight over parking spaces with. Directly adjacent to the precinct at 100 Richmond Terrace was the Family Court, and one block south of the precinct were the buildings that housed the Supreme Court, Borough Hall and the District Attorney's offices. Everybody who was somebody had a reserved spot or parking privileges.

Charlie walked into the precinct and strolled into the muster room as usual. He perused the roll call to see the nightly assignments then glanced at the area below it, where there was a series of wooded slots labeled A through Z. Personal mail as well as departmental mail was diverted into these slots and served as the mail boxes for the uniformed force of the 120th precinct.

Charlie looked into his and retrieved two envelopes. One contained a copy of an accident report which he had been expecting. The other contained a written message from the T.S. operator.

Charlie began to read the piece of paper and once again was astonished by the words which appeared before his eyes.

"Terry called. Call her at 390-1275," the message read.

His heart began to race, just as it had on the previous night, and his stomach was churning in overdrive. He walked over to the clerical man at the 124 desk and retrieved a phone book.

He began looking up the phone number of the Dunkin Donuts shop where Terry worked. As the pounding of his heart beat so loud that he wondered if anyone else could hear it, he seriously questioned what in God's name he was doing. Hadn't Annette pleased him the other morning?

He told himself to put the phone book down but he didn't listen. The phone number of the Dunkin Donuts shop was not the same number as in the message. He wanted to call the number written on the small scrap of paper but he would need complete privacy if he did. He didn't want the entire precinct breathing down his neck while he was on the phone.

The room opposite the telephone switchboard was the SP 10 operator's room. The SP 10 operator was a civilian employee who took police reports directly over the phone from complainants, which saved time as well as police manpower. Police presence was not always needed at certain past crimes because most reports of minor thefts and damage were required for insurance purposes only. However, if a complainant actually wanted the police to respond, they did so regardless of the crime.

Every cop who had a girlfriend or mistress used the SP 10 room. Charlie did not want to fall into that category so he quickly went up to his locker room and changed into his uniform. As soon as he opened his locker door he saw Annette's picture. It was one he had taken at one of their children's graduations. Again, he felt like a heel.

Feeling Annette staring at him, he changed quickly and closed and locked his locker, spinning the combination tumblers several times before walking away. Without a glance back, he made his way down the rear stairs on his way to the muster room. When he got to the ground floor he passed the rear clerical office and noticed it was empty.

He walked in and sat at one of the desks to make his phone call, feeling as nervous as he had been when he first called a girl for a date during his teen age years. He stared at the phone on the desk, frozen in doubt. He could not throw the paper away, which was what he wanted to do and knew he should do, yet he could not dial the number, either.

He finally mustered up enough courage and picked up the receiver. He dialed the number and silently prayed that Terry would be the one to answer the phone. A female answered but it was not Terry's voice.

"Hello?" answered the voice on the other end of the line.

"Hi, my name is Charlie. May I please speak to Terry?"_

"Hold on one minute," the voice responded.

It seemed like an eternity before anyone else spoke into the phone.

"Charlie? Is it you?" the sweetest, most heavenly voice answered.

"Yes, it's me. Terry, are you okay?"_he asked, but before she could respond, he began to ramble.

"I got your notes, both of them. I spoke to the other waitress and I have been beside myself for two days, worried about you."

He was frantic but honest. When he finally fell silent, he heard Terry giggle a little on the other end of the line.

"Charlie, I'm sorry. I didn't mean for you to go crazy," she insisted.

"Listen, I want to apologize for anything I might say that may offend you, but I want to be up front with you, okay?"_Charlie said, his voice even and serious.

"I understand," she said.

"Terry, I don't know what it is but you have been in mind since I saw you. I think about you all the time and I have found myself missing you," he blurted out.

"Oh, Charlie, that is so sweet! You have been in my mind, too. That's why I left those messages with Irene," she admitted.

"Who's Irene?"_he asked.

"Irene is the other girl I work with at the coffee shop. She's a good friend and is discreet," she answered.

"Where are you now?"_he asked.

"I'm home. That was my mom who answered the phone. I have a son who has asthma and when he gets a bad attack I usually stay home," she said.

"Is there anything I can do for you?"_

"You already have. Believe me," Terry offered. "Look, Charlie, I know you are married. I want you to know that I would never hurt you or do anything to jeopardize your marriage."

He didn't know how she found out he was married but could only assume she had spoken to some of the other guys in the precinct.

"I wanted to let you know that," she said quietly, "and I would like to see you again whenever it's good for you; that is, if you want to see me again."

She had given him an out right there. He could have said no to this whole crazy idea and still felt like a man, but he could not resist the excitement. He felt desire growing deep in his groin.

"What night do you come back into work?"_he asked.

"I'm on my days off now. My next shift is Sunday night," she said.

"Okay. Listen, I won't be back until Monday night but I'll be honest – I don't think I can last until Monday night. Can I call you before that time?"_he asked.

"I would love that, Charlie," she murmured.
"Okay. I'll call you,'" he said.
"Goodnight, Charlie."

The conversation ended and he smiled as he made his way back to the muster room for the roll call, feeling as if a great weight had been lifted off of his chest. A shadow of guilt was mixed in with his relief because of the things he'd told Terry, and because he'd been given an opportunity to end this before it started but he chose not to. So much for a Catholic upbringing and the guilt it produces.

CHAPTER FIVE

As usual, Charlie was assigned to make the coffee run and he was almost glad that Terry was not going to be there. He also felt like a rubber band being stretched from one end of the emotional spectrum to the other.

He decided to release the entire matter from his mind and give himself a much deserved break and figured he would call Terry sometime during his swing of two days off. He returned back to the station house with the coffee order and felt worry-free for the first time in days.

Before long he had finished all his routine work and he and Lt. A. finally made it out to patrol. Charlie hoped the lieutenant would have another good story to tell but he also knew it would likely get busy soon. Either way was good for him.

Lt. A. had been a cop on patrol for eighteen years and was also a member of the Street Crime Suppression Unit. He was good at observation and making arrests. Although the department frowned on supervisors making arrests, because they were supposed to supervise and not spend time in court, the lieutenant frequently asked the guys if there was anyone who wanted to get on the sheet and make an arrest. Late tours were good for overtime because most family disputes required the arresting officer to be present in court in the morning. Dealing with drunken drivers was also good for overtime. If the lieutenant knew who was catching he would ten-eighty-five them to the scene and give them any collar he observed.

Most RMP teams handled their jobs quickly because they wanted to be available later on during the tour for the real heavies they knew were going to occur. If a sector got a radio run and Lt. A. was in the vicinity, he would direct Central to have the unit remain available and he would handle the assignment. All the guys knew the lieutenant was a working boss and would be out there like all the rest of the men on patrol. The difference was he just didn't ride around and give orders. There weren't many like him left.

As Charlie and Lt. A. began their patrol, they soon found out that this night was like any other Friday night. There were bar fights, vehicle accidents, phony gun runs and disorderly groups everywhere.

The radio dispatcher called 120 sector F-Frank to handle a dispute at Van Duzer Street and St. Paul's Avenue. Charlie and Lt. A. had been sitting on Van Duzer Street in the parking lot of Taco Bell adjacent to St. Paul's Avenue looking for red lighters. When the call came through, the lieutenant acknowledged it instead of Sector F and asked the female dispatcher if she had any further information. She radioed back with a specific house number on Van Duzer St. and Lt. A. quickly reminded her that there were two different intersections where Van Duzer Street and St. Paul's Avenue intersected, which not many people knew except, of course, for the regular sector teams. Lt. A. had been assigned to sector F for twelve years when he was a police officer in the 120th, so knew the precinct boundaries like the back of his hand.

"Charlie, you don't mind if we handle the job, do you?" asked the boss.

"Lou, you don't have to ask me," was Charlie's polite response.

They pulled up to the side of the building roughly one hundred feet from where they had been parked and both men exited the vehicle after notifying Central they were on the scene. They slipped their night sticks into the metal ring on their gun belts, specifically made to secure the batons, then the lieutenant approached the entrance with caution. He knocked heavily upon the thick, wooden door and Charlie noticed that, even with all the time the lieutenant had on the job, he still remembered to stay to one side of the doorway as he knocked. After what felt like an eternity, a woman answered the door. It was obvious she had been crying.

"Come in please. Close the door behind you."

As she turned around, she screamed, "It's the police!"_

As soon as she spoke Charlie knew she was from the deep south. She had an accent so thick you could just picture her on a rural farm in Georgia.

She had on a pair of velcro hip huggers that were about two sizes too small. As a result, they accentuated her obesity, which was sickening to look at. Her long blonde hair was very matted and in dire need of washing and brushing, and she had some scars on her face but none that looked recent. The woman led the officers into a small kitchen area where they observed a man sitting at a small wooden table which only had three chairs instead of the customary four. The dirty white cabinets were covered with at least several months of grime and grease and, like the woman's hair, were also in need of a good cleaning.

The sink was full of dirty dishes covered in caked on food from who knew how long ago. Food was scattered all over the small kitchen area and there were several pieces of broken dishes and plates also covering the bare linoleum floor.

The lieutenant walked over to the stove and removed two large cast iron pots and placed them into the sink. Charlie knew this was the sign of an experienced cop. A good cop removed any and all signs of anything that might be used against him during the worst of all police assignments, the family dispute. He recalled that several years earlier a police officer actually lost his life when he was pushed and fell into a large broken mirror that had been used between a husband and wife during their argument. Theirs had been a real whopper of a dispute, with dozens of broken items littering the floor and counters.

The tall, slim man at the kitchen table had not spoken a word. His hair had been pulled back into a pony tail and tied with a rubber band,

and he was wearing a pair of overalls covered in dry paint. There were so many colors on the overalls that it seemed as though the unidentified man might have painted a rainbow somewhere. His face was pock marked and had at least three days' worth of growth on it. Tattoos covered his forearms with what appeared to be crosses and numbers, and a tattoo of a devil could be seen on the top portion of his left hand.

"What's going on here?"_Charlie asked.

The woman explained how the man never gave her enough money then would come home and beat her if dinner was not on the table. While Charlie was asking questions the lieutenant was walking around surveying the place. Before long Charlie noticed the lieutenant speaking to a teenage girl who was sitting on the kitchen floor adjacent to the stove. He didn't think anything of it and continued asking questions. After a moment or two the lieutenant jumped up and began screaming at both the father and mother at the top of his lungs.

"Who the fuck is responsible for this?"

Charlie knew the lieutenant had a temper but wondered what he had heard to make him react this way.

"Where the hell are you fucking people from?"_the lieutenant bellowed.

The husband became noticeably uncomfortable at the lieutenant's use of language and Charlie began to wonder if they were going to have trouble with him.

"We just moved up from Georgia," the man replied in his southern drawl.

"Yeah, well tonight you're both going to jail," Lt. A. exclaimed.

"What the fuck are you talking about?"_asked the father.

"Charlie, look at this. Look at this fucking shit," ordered the lieutenant.

Charlie walked over to where the young girl was sitting. It didn't take him long to realize that the girl, who must have been all of thirteen or fourteen years old, was tied by a piece of rope to the pipes at the rear of the stove. As he looked closer he saw she was wearing a simple cotton dress which was wrinkled and smeared with grime. Her hair had not been combed and her face was dirty. As far as he could tell, she hadn't bathed for several days at least.

What Charlie next observed was something he had not expected to see in a million years. The girl was not wearing any panties. There was caked blood on her inner thighs and dripping spots on the dirty linoleum floor directly beneath her. It was her time of the month.

The lieutenant was livid.

"Who the fuck tied her up like this?"_he bellowed.

"Oh shit, Officer, that's nothing," the father explained, his tone matter-of-fact. "We have to tie her like that every month. When she has her monthly, all that damn fool girl wants to do is go out and mess with boys. She becomes a regular little slut."

A closer look at the teenager's wrists revealed scars and lacerations of varying ages, alluding to the fact that she had been tied up before.

"Charlie, if you don't want this collar, I'll call for another sector," said Lt. A. in a hushed tone.

"No, Lou. It's okay. I'll take it," answered Charlie.

Lt. A. called for another car to transport the young girl to St. Vincent's emergency room so she could be checked out completely. He didn't like the jealous tone the father had shown when he spoke about his daughter fooling around with boys. Sexual abuse by this father, upon his own daughter in this case, was entirely possible.

The girl mentioned she had an old aunt in the St. George area that had moved up from down south years before, so Lt. A. arranged for the aunt to care for the girl after her release from the hospital and until the courts could decide what to do with her.

Charlie went into the precinct with his collar and began the arrest procedures while the lieutenant went back to the muster room and worked on his own paperwork until Charlie was finished.

Charlie eventually went to court with the collars and learned some months later that the girl had eventually been returned to her parents.

He didn't see the girl again for six years. She must have been nineteen or twenty and was working the street near the Bay Street strip bars as a prostitute. After that he periodically read her name in the Staten Island Advance saying she had been busted for hooking, and a few years later he read that she had been found in an abandoned alley two blocks from where she lived. Her throat had been slit. Her killers were never found and Charlie believed no great effort was made to do so. After all she was just a local prostitute, so who cared?

CHAPTER SIX

Charlie went home after he finished his arraignment at Criminal Court at 67 Targee Street. As usual he picked up the New York Daily News as well as some fresh bagels at his local Bagel Bistro. He knew today his wife would be home because she had Saturday and Sunday off.

He pulled into his driveway and saw his neighbor Mike in his own front yard. Mike had been on the force for about sixteen years but then was involved in a pretty serious RMP accident, and every time he saw Charlie he wanted to bullshit about the job. Although Mike had not been the operator of the vehicle involved in the accident, he had still sustained some serious injuries. The RMP was totaled and Mike eventually retired on an accidental disability pension. Eventually he had gotten himself a small part time job off the books to keep himself busy.

Charlie really never understood why some guys got off the job if they were still able to work in some capacity. He reasoned that the tax free disability pension was just too much to say no to.

He had also been involved in a serious RMP accident where the car had been totaled, but luckily he had been uninjured. In spite of this, everyone told him to start reporting sick and to claim pain in the head and neck but he just couldn't do it. He loved the job and loved being a cop.

He got out of his car and spoke with Mike for a while, then went inside. Annette had the coffee on and welcomed him home with a good morning kiss then asked if wanted any breakfast. He declined food but read his paper while he enjoyed a fresh cup of coffee. After a while he decided to lie down but set his alarm for 12:00 noon. This was now the start of his swing and he just wanted to take the edge off his tired feeling. He would get up at noon, shower and start his projects.

He planned to make a trip to the local Home Depot and knew he could use the pay phone there to call Terry.

He made his way to the bedroom and Annette followed. When they entered their bedroom, she drew the shades for him as usual. Charlie was always horny in the morning but he did not say anything about it and neither did Annette. After a while, he fell asleep and did not dream.

To Charlie, sleep was what death was all about. Death was probably just an endless, dreamless sleep. He thought about all the so called religious people who say they believe in God, yet he knew that when asked how they wanted to die, those same people would invariably say they wanted to die in their sleep. Whenever he would ask them why, he always got the same answer. They chose this way so they would not know they had died. He always loved to play the devil's advocate with these holy rollers. He would argue that, if they believed in God and an afterlife, shouldn't they wake up at the moment of death and realize they were dead?

He got up at noon and showered. Although he was still tired, he wanted to do some chores around the house. Surprisingly, he felt good.

He needed some paint and rollers so he got into his car and headed to the Home Depot on Forest Avenue, where he bought what he needed and headed back out to his car. He placed his material into the trunk then headed back to the front of the store. There he found a phone booth which had the accordion type doors that afforded privacy. He dialed Terry's number and felt the nervousness coming back over him.

The phone rang and Terry answered.

"Hello?"

"Terry, it's Charlie. I hope I'm not disturbing you," he said.

"Oh, Charlie! I knew I would hear from you today. Where are you?"_she asked.

"I had to go to Home Depot so I decide to call you from there," he answered.

"Charlie, I miss you. I can't wait until Monday to see you. Do you think you might be able to come over to my house now? We could have a cup of coffee here," she said quietly.

"Is anyone home with you?"_Charlie asked.

"My mom is visiting some friends and will probably stay for dinner which means she won't be home until later tonight. My son is in the living room watching his morning cartoons."

Charlie thought about it and was a little hesitant about going. He really wanted to get started painting but it didn't take him long to rationalize how one lousy cup of coffee could put a dent in anything.

"Sure, you know I would love to see you," he said.

Terry gave him her address, which was in the confines of the 123rd precinct. He was glad about this because it meant he would not run into any guys on patrol in the 120th precinct.

He said goodbye, headed back out to his car and began the drive out to Terry's place. He was on Forest Avenue already so all he had to do was head out to South Avenue and get on the West Shore Expressway. He got off at Bloomingdale Road and drove a few blocks to Foster Road. The drive took him all of fifteen minutes. It was a rural section of Staten Island and was probably farm land years before.

He spotted the house but did not want to park directly in front. Instead, he drove past it and found an empty curb about a block away. It was a beautiful day.

As he approached her residence he noted it was a small ranch with a neatly manicured lawn. It could use a paint job but it still wasn't that bad. There was one car parked in the driveway and Charlie surmised it was Terry's.

He rang the bell and, after a few seconds, she answered the door. She was wearing jeans and a white cashmere sweater that accentuated her breasts. She looked absolutely beautiful.

Charlie said hello and she welcomed him into her home. She led him into the living room where her son was quietly sitting on the couch watching television.

The living room had wall to wall carpeting and the color of the room had a blue motif. The couches were a deep sea blue while the rug was a light, pastel sky blue. The lamps seemed to be French provincial and matched the walls, which were painted in the hue of a robin's egg. It was so clean that you could have eaten off of any table or even the carpeted floor itself.

Her son was a good looking boy with dark hair and blue eyes. He was still dressed in his pajamas, the top half of which had the Superman insignia on it. The young man looked up when they paused in the doorway and Terry introduced Charlie as a friend from work. Her son politely said hello and quickly diverted his eyes back to his cartoons so Terry took Charlie by the hand and led him into the kitchen.

"I think we might have a little more privacy in here. I hope you don't mind just sitting at the kitchen table, Charlie," she said quietly.

"I'm just happy to see you, Terry," he answered.

He had arrived at Terry's place shortly after 2:00 P.M. and it was almost 5:00 P.M. when he left. While he was there they talked about everything and he enjoyed being with her so much that the time just flew by. When he did leave, Terry walked him to the door. Once there, they just seemed to stare at each other for the longest time before she finally spoke.

"Don't you want to kiss me goodbye?"_

"Terry, I want to kiss you so much that I'm shaking," he replied. Charlie was filled with desire. Without waiting for her response, he gently took Terry's face in his hands and kissed her softly on her lips. They were soft and smooth and the aroma of her perfume drove him wild. Their first kiss lasted roughly three seconds and afterward, they looked at each other in silence, neither wanting to break the spell. He took her in his arms and kissed her again, fully and hard on the lips, and quivered as Terry inserted her tongue deep into his mouth. He heard her gently moan with pleasure as he sucked on it and, as he pulled her closer to him he felt her nipples harden as they shared multiple kisses. His excitement continued to build as he pressed his body toward her so she, too, could feel his growing desire for her.

Although they were both quite aroused, Terry pulled away first. After she caught her breath, she said it was not the time or place. Charlie agreed intellectually of course but would have taken her right there on the doorstep. After sharing a few more, less intense kisses, they said their goodbyes and he told her he would call her.

He walked to his car and took a long careful look around just to make sure no one familiar was nearby. When he was satisfied that no one saw him, he got into his car and started the drive back to his home on the south shore. As he drove away, he felt a sticky wetness near his crotch and looked down to find a stain in his trousers caused by his embrace with Terry.

He arrived home in time for dinner but avoided his wife, lying on his way to the bathroom as he explained he had met an old friend at the store and decided to stop for coffee with him. Once in the bathroom, he thoroughly washed Terry's perfume off, quite relieved to know he had gotten away with his little rendezvous with her. Thankfully, the subject did not come up again and Charlie spent the next day painting.

Monday night finally rolled around and Charlie could not wait until he went into work so he could see Terry. Roll call came and went as usual then he and the lieutenant went out on patrol.

Lt. A. wanted coffee so Charlie decided to drive over to the Dunkin Donuts shop where Terry worked. Charlie wanted to go in but so did the lieutenant and he couldn't very well tell his boss to stay in the car, so they both went inside. As they stared at the menu board over the horizontal racks of donuts and muffins, he realized Terry was not there and he wondered if she or her son were sick again.

This time he could not wait until morning or for the next night, for that matter, so he told the lieutenant he had to make a phone call and remained in the joint to use the pay phone in the back. With a nod, the lieutenant went out to the RMP with his coffee and donuts to wait.

Charlie felt funny and a little guilty about dialing the number Terry had given him, especially considering what time it was, but he had to do it for his own sanity. He dialed the number hesitantly and after a few rings, Terry finally answered the phone.

"Terry, are you okay?"_he asked.

"Oh, Charlie. I have such a bad cold. I must have caught it from my son. He's always bringing something home from school. I certainly hope you don't catch it from me since we did get intimate in a nice kind of way the other day," she said, almost purring like a cat.

"How could I forget?" Charlie asked in a reminiscent tone. "I would catch a cold from you any day of the week. You kiss so nice and your lips were so smooth, pretty lady."

"What did you call me?"_she asked.

"I called you pretty lady," he repeated.

Silence followed for several long seconds.

"I like that," she finally said. "I wish you were here right now. We could sit on my couch and just cuddle all night long."_

He wanted so much to ask the lieutenant for some time off but he knew it was not just possible on such short notice.

"Well, maybe you could stop over in the morning. My mom will be leaving early and my son will be in school," she hinted coyly.

Even though he was a little hesitant, his heart skipped a beat. He knew he probably could, but doing so would mean he would have to lie to Annette and concoct some story. He hoped he wouldn't have to make a collar and go to court.

He also had no doubt that if he did go to Terry's, they would very likely wind up making love.

"What time should I get there if I can?" he asked.

"How does 9:00 A.M. sound? Is that too late for you?"_

"9:00 A.M. it is." His reply was quick, without hesitation.

They said their goodbyes and Charlie walked out to the RMP, where the lieutenant was just finishing up his coffee and French cruller, which was his favorite. Thankfully he didn't ask Charlie for details about his phone call.

"Charlie, I would just like to take a ride and keep moving for a while, if you don't mind. You can go anywhere you want but I just feel like going on patrol."

"Are you catching tonight?"_asked Lt. A.

"Not tonight, Lou, if it can be helped. If you run short, of course, I'll be there for you, but I'd rather not tonight. Okay?"_

The lieutenant nodded and Charlie began to drive up Victory Boulevard. As he did, he felt relief wash over him. He had told Terry he would be there in the morning and he definitely didn't want to take a chance winding up in court with a collar.

He continued his drive up Victory Boulevard passing Silver Lake Park and the Silver Lake reservoir. Although the reservoir was completely fenced to keep out swimmers, every summer at least one poor family was notified that a son or daughter had been lost in its deep water.

Lt. A. was in a talkative mood. As they roamed through the streets, he started on another war story. Charlie was all ears.

"Charlie, you have two grown children, right?" asked Lt. A.

"Yeah, Lou, I have a boy and a girl. They're both away at school."

"I thought so. You know, I have a boy and girl, too. Mine are a little older of course, and I wouldn't hurt them for the world," Lt. A. said quietly.

At first, Charlie thought the boss was going to lecture him on the evils of adultery. Not that Charlie didn't need lecturing but he did not want to preached to, either.

"You know Charlie, it's funny what we choose to remember or what we effectively block from our memories.

"I can remember even the smallest details about my kids from back when they were toddlers, and I can reach back into my memory and see when my daughter was just six years old. If I close my eyes, I can still see her wearing those little white dresses my wife used to make for her. I remember the little black satin shoes she wore and I can see so clearly the pink ribbons we lovingly tied into her golden, blond hair," reminisced the lieutenant.

Charlie sensed that this next war story was going to be about either the lieutenant's kids or someone else's, so he decided to turn right on Clove Road and follow it all the way to Richmond Terrace before turning left and heading out to Mariner's Harbor. The route was a fairly straight one and would afford Charlie greater concentration in listening to the boss tell his story. After a few seconds of silence, the lieutenant began.

"I remember one particular Easter Sunday. I was still a footman in the squad and had not been assigned a seat in any sector yet so I was basically a fill-in to any empty seat. I had not even met my future partner Frank yet.

"Until then, Frank had been in another squad and worked with another cop. As a fill-in, I walked foot posts, flew on details, and often was assigned the dreaded switchboard. On this particular day I was assigned to Sector K, which was a solo, also known as a one-man car. The 120th had one-man cars back in those days, even though we were a considered a busy house, although those same one-man cars were not the one-man report cars that exist today, and we responded on all kinds of calls, including gun runs as well as family disputes.

"On this particular day I had to respond on what I thought was a routine fender bender but it turned out to be one of the most horrifying calls I have ever handled,"_ said the lieutenant as he stared at the road ahead of them. After hesitating a moment, the lieutenant reached for yet another cigarette and glanced at the man beside him. This was when Charlie suddenly realized the lieutenant had been chain smoking ever since he said he was going to tell his story.

They passed the old Weiss Glass Stadium on Richmond Terrace and the boss told him to pull in and drive underneath the deserted bleacher stands.

The stadium itself had been dismantled years before but the old dilapidated bleacher stands were still there. The area junkies used the place as a local shooting gallery and prostitutes brought their Johns there for their quickie lays and blow jobs.

The lieutenant was killing two birds with one stone on this location. He had chosen to make a visit here because the area had been classified as a cooping prone location. The other reason, Charlie soon found out, was the lieutenant had to take a leak. The boss urinated while staring at the center of the arena, which had held wrestling cards long before the World Wrestling Federation was even dreamed about.

With a reminiscent gaze, the lieutenant told Charlie how, as a kid, he remembered seeing the world champ, Antonino Rocca, fight for his title against Gorgeous George in the same arena.

It was a different world back then.

The lieutenant got back into the car and Charlie put the car in drive, taking them back on patrol.

"Where was I, Charlie?" the lieutenant asked.

"You were going to handle an accident," Charlie replied.

"Oh, right."

It was about 11:45 A.M. and I had just finished my third cup of coffee down by Sailor Snug Harbor. I wasn't in the coop but it's quiet down there and always a good place to do reports or crosswords.

Easter Sunday in the 120th usually meant a fairly quiet morning, but I have never been lucky with Easter Sunday in this precinct. The radio dispatcher called me first not only because the job was in my sector but because it was a perfect job for a one-man car.

"120ʰ King," called Central. I answered the call by stating I was standing by.

"King, respond forthwith to Castleton Avenue and Clove Road on a report of a vehicle accident. Injuries may be involved," the dispatcher from Central directed. Without hesitating, I turned on my lights and sirens and headed west onto the Terrace, turning left on Clove Road when I reached it.

The lieutenant hesitated before adding, "I don't think there's a cop alive who enjoys going to vehicle accidents. At least I know I don't."

When I was heading south up Clove Road I received yet another disturbing call from Central stating that numerous calls were coming in and for me to put a rush on it.

As I approached the busy intersection, I saw flashing red and white ambulance lights reflecting off of store windows. There were also crowds of people everywhere, both lining the streets as well as on street corners. Most were civilian bystanders who were totally useless and not assisting in any way. I maneuvered the RMP into the Gulf gas station so as to not block any emergency vehicles that were responding. I also didn't want to get blocked in if I had to move out of there in a hurry.

Before I got out of my car, I saw the blood and bodies strewn everywhere. It looked more like a train wreck than a vehicle accident. Blood was on the sidewalk, the street pavement and sprayed all over the storefront windows and facade. It looked as though the B.F. Goodrich tire store on the corner had gotten the brunt of the splattered blood and the scene reminded me of grotesque photos I had seen of the St. Valentine's Day massacre. The EMS team from St. Vincent's Hospital was there, too, doing their best to attend to the more serious victims. One of the EMT's was on his radio calling for more buses to respond to the scene and I quickly called for the sergeant, asking him to have the Accident Investigation Unit also respond ASAP. It was pretty evident that this was a very serious accident and the possibility existed that someone was injured seriously and very likely might die. The next thing I requested was for additional sectors to respond to assist me with traffic and crowd control.

I walked over to the EMS people for an update. They informed me that they were going to transport two victims immediately to the emergency room and two additional ambulances were en route to the scene. Then they asked me if I could transport another victim in my RMP. I explained to them that I was a solo operator but they said another technician would ride with me while I drove. I walked over to my car and moved it until it was adjacent to the ambulance, then I reached over and opened my right front passenger door.

The technician got in while cradling a little girl who looked to be about seven years old. She was wearing what once was a beautiful white dress but was now splotched with large, crimson blossoms. On her hands she wore matching white gloves which were totally smeared in blood. Looking at her from head to toe, I noticed she had on a single, black satin shoe on one foot and her curly blond hair was caked in blood which was beginning to coagulate. She was barely alive.

Lt. A. sighed. Charlie glanced to his right, not surprised to see that the lieutenant was visibly shaken. The boss's eyes were beginning to well up but Charlie didn't know what to say or do.

"Lou, do you want coffee or anything," he asked quietly.

"No. I'm okay," Lt. A. answered, his voice low and husky with sadness.

After an endlessly long minute, he seemed to compose himself and lit another cigarette. After a few deep drags, he continued with his story.

The injured girl had gotten to me, but I swallowed my emotions and floored the gas pedal to get her to the hospital. I must have been doing 100 miles an hour on the straight away. When we arrived at the loading dock of the emergency room, the technician next to me asked me to carry the little girl while he ran in to prepare the hospital staff for her.

For a time Charlie didn't think the lieutenant would finish his story, but after a while, he continued.

I gently took her in my arms and carried her in. Before I got through the doors, her head shifted and I realized that the under part of her head was almost totally gone. As I made my way into the brightly lit building, that little angel opened her beautiful blue eyes for just a second. That's when she found my eyes. I would swear she looked at me, right at me, but looking back now, especially after all these years, I don't think she was actually looking at me; I believe it was some kind of reflex action. That night though, right then and there, just seconds after the gaze which filled my soul, I saw that little angel's eyes roll back into her head just like I've seen so many times when someone is going out of the picture. I have no doubts that she died on the spot, right there in my arms.

He took another drag of his nearly demolished cigarette.

Oh, they worked on her for a long time, for such a very long time. They'll do that if the victim is young. Those doctors took that little girl's heart right out of her chest and actually massaged it with their hands. They tried everything, but everything wasn't good enough. She died that night, and I truly believe I was the last person she saw on this fucking earth. Me, some fucking stranger in a blue uniform who did not even know her name!

The lieutenant's body shook as a sob erupted from somewhere deep in his throat. His eyes fully welled and the tear drops began to fall, leaving crooked, shiny trails on his cheeks. He fell silent and turned his head towards his window, eventually using his sleeve to wipe away the tears. Charlie respected Lou's need for silence as Lt. A. lit another cigarette and drew in heavily, taking the acrid smoke deep into his lungs. The cigarette seemed to calm him down a little and finally, after several long minutes without words, he began speaking about the little girl again.

"You know, Charlie, I never even got a chance to talk to her and tell her that everything would be okay. When it was over and she was declared deceased, I went out to the ambulance loading bay and bawled my eyes out. We were all crying including the nurses and even some of the doctors. That innocent, little angel made quite an impact on many of us.

"One nice nurse walked over to me while I was in the loading bay and asked if I was okay. I explained to her that I had a little girl the same age and with blond hair, too. Charlie, that night it was like carrying my own little girl into that hospital and watching her die," sobbed the lieutenant again.

He lit another cigarette and inhaled deeply, held it in for a while then slowly exhaled through his nose.

"The agony of that Easter Sunday will live with me forever," he said quietly.

"I learned about the details of the accident when I returned to the precinct at the end of my tour and, believe it or not, there was only one car involved in that awful, bloody accident. A black woman was learning to drive. Can you believe that? She was learning how to drive on fucking Easter Sunday morning! She just had to have lessons on Easter Sunday! Damn, she didn't even have a learners permit! The fucking car was unregistered and she had no insurance. The fucking schmuck teaching her didn't have a license, either. He'd also been drinking and was as high as a kite.

"The driver had come down Clove Road, headed for Castleton Avenue. A beautiful, innocent family with a mother, father and seven children, all dressed in their Easter finery, were walking to church along the sidewalk adjacent to the B.F. Goodrich tire store. According to eye witnesses, the woman had a red light but must have stepped on the gas instead of the brake pedal because she shot across the intersection, pinning the father and three of his kids up against the side of the building.

"Both the father and one of his innocent little boys died. They were the two that were rushed first to the hospital. Three more people died that Easter Sunday morning, including my little angel. I absolutely hate Easter Sundays in this fucking precinct and I'll tell you why someday.

"When I got home from that Easter Sunday shift the first thing I did was grab my daughter and give her such a big hug and a kiss. In fact, I held onto my baby girl so tight that my wife thought I was going to crush her. Her little mouth was so sticky from eating chocolate the Easter Bunny had delivered the night before in so many beautifully wrapped baskets. I cried and thanked God for that moment and, believe it or not, I never told my wife about the accident," admitted Lt. A. as his story concluded.

The remainder of the tour was fairly busy but the lieutenant remained quiet after reliving his Easter Sunday tragedy. He seemed to smoke more than his usual amount, especially once his story was told, lighting one cigarette after another the entire night.

As the silence surrounded them during their tour, Charlie thought about Terry, searching for an excuse to tell Annette why he wasn't coming home right away when he got off work. After he and the lieutenant had signed out, he went directly upstairs and changed into his civilian clothes. As he listened to some of the guys talking about how they were going to stop at old man Harry's bar on Van Duzer Street, Charlie had to purposely avoid looking at his family's pictures that were taped to the inside of his locker. Although he was guilt ridden, it didn't stop him from thinking with the head between his legs instead of the one on top of his body.

CHAPTER SEVEN

Old man Harry's place opened early and the guys on the late tour liked to stop there once in a while to have a few brews before going home. Cops who did 4x12's stopped after work and so did the 12x8 crew. The beer they consumed always helped them sleep during the day.

Charlie could have called Annette and explained to her that he was just going to stop off for a few with the guys but it meant he would have to come home smelling like a brewery. Instead, he decided to tell her he made a DWI arrest, which was a good excuse because the *Staten Island Advance* never published particulars about drunk driving arrests, unless there was a fatality involved.

He called Annette and tried to be as nonchalant as he could but was still nervous. He thought he sensed that she perceived he was lying; at least his guilt led him to think she did.

He finished his call as well as could be expected for a family man so laden with guilt, then decided to contact Terry to confirm their morning meeting. He called her from a phone booth located on the corner of Wall Street and Stuyvesant Place, directly behind the 120th station house. As he approached the phone booth he suddenly recalled that he was in the same one Albert Finney had used when he was filming the movie *Wolfen on* Staten Island. He was amazed at what was going through his mind.

He held his breath as the phone rang in his ear but it didn't take long before he got lucky and she answered.

"Hi, Terry. It's Charlie. I'm just touching base to see if everything is okay?"_

"Oh, Charlie, you scared me! I thought you were going to tell me you couldn't make it. I just took a bubble bath and can't wait until I see you. My son is fine and went to school and my mom is already gone for the day," she said.

"Do you want me to stop and pick anything up?"_he asked.

"No, but am I still your pretty lady?"

"You know you are," he cooed with excitement.

"Then I just want you to come over, Charlie," she whispered, her voice low and inviting.

"I'm on my way," he said, his tone husky. He wasn't surprised to notice he was becoming aroused.

He hung up, made his way to his car and began the drive fantasizing about her all the way to her house. He was quivering with desire as he wondered what she would be wearing.

Traffic was quiet as he headed out to the other side of the island where Terry lived. Everybody was always headed to the Ferry or the Verrazano Narrows Bridge at morning rush. He pulled up to Terry's house, forgetting to park in a less conspicuous spot. He tried to be casual as he walked up to her front door because he didn't want nosy neighbors to think something mischievous was going to take place. Charlie rang the bell and Terry answered it almost immediately.

The first thing he noticed was her hair. It was sparkling and still a little wet from her bath. She was wearing a white silk robe that was open just a bit, allowing an enticingly small amount of Terry's cleavage to spill into view. Charlie took a step inside the house and before he could say anything, she placed her hand over his mouth, motioning for him not to speak. He wondered what in the hell was going on. Had her family returned?

He did not make any attempts to say anything but began worrying about what might happen. Under a blanket of silence, Terry took him by the hand and led him into what appeared to be her bedroom. Two windows, each on separate walls, were covered by long, pastel curtains. Through small gaps in each set of curtains he could see blinds had been drawn. As a result, the room was veiled in cool, dark shadows. On matching small tables on either side of the bed a small group of tall, thin candles with blinking flames illuminated the room while soft music filled the air around them from a radio on her dresser.

She led Charlie to the bed and beckoned him to quietly sit. He found he was under her spell and could only obey, even if he didn't want to. She knelt before him and slowly removed his shoes one at a time, placing them partially under the bed. Next, she unlaced Charlie's ankle holster and gently put his weapon to the side of the night stand. When that was done, she removed his socks and tucked them into his shoes.

Satisfied with her progress, Terry stood up and began to undo Charlie's belt. She pulled the belt through its loops and undid the button on his pants. She slowly unzipped his fly and brushed her hand against his penis, which was hard and erect and would soon break through to freedom. During all of this neither of them spoke a word.

Next, she slowly slid his trousers down his legs. Once they were removed, she moved to his boxer shorts, gently sliding them downward until they, too, were lying in a small heap on the floor. His eyes closed, Charlie thought this was a perfect example of what his mother used to tell him about always wearing clean underwear in case you were in an accident. He almost laughed to himself, but somehow managed to remain silent.

He was now naked from the waist down. He felt silly when he realized the only things he still wore were his tee shirt and outer jacket. Terry beckoned him to stand up with one motion from her velvet hands which apparently had lotion on them. She removed every other stitch of clothing he had on with gentle, expert hands. She smiled as he stood before her, stark naked and with an enormous hard on. Without a word, she stepped back and removed her robe, dropping it to the floor in a whisper of soft fabric.

Her breasts were beautiful and huge. Her areolas were darkly pigmented and her nipples were hard and the size of buttons. Charlie had never seen nipples such as these. They were flat and wide but so hard. Her pubic area glistened with silky black hair. He took her into his arms and they embraced. They kissed fully and deeply, each sucking the other's tongue.

Terry moaned loudly and grabbed Charlie's penis, stroking it with slow, expert movements.

He picked her up and gently placed her on the bed, still kissing her but deeper and harder now. He began to explore her vagina with his hand, rubbing her clitoris gently at first but faster and harder as each moan from her throat urged him on.

"Oh, Charlie! I'm going to come! You're driving me crazy. My God, what you do to me!"_she screamed.

With that, she came as her body jerked and quivered in ecstasy.

Her head moved violently back and forth from one side to the other as she whimpered in pleasure while her vagina became a faucet of fluids, and Charlie found he could no longer contain himself. He knelt before her, thrusting his mouth and tongue deep into her vagina, licking and sucking in a frenzy of movement.

She quickly came again and begged him to stop, whispering to him that she was going crazy. He did as she asked, watching her as she closed her eyes and lay still, catching her breath, a huge smile of pleasure lighting her face. When she finally looked at him, her eyes were filled with mischief.

"This is only the beginning, Charlie."

She got up, gently pushed him back onto the bed, and climbed on top of him. Smiling at him, she grabbed his penis and inserted it into her vagina. He immediately felt how tight she was and wondered when the last time was she'd had sex. That thought quickly disappeared as his full attention turned to the pleasurable feelings below his waist.

She began to move her hips and thighs up and down, slowly at first but quickly escalating her movements until she was riding him like an untamed bronco. Her scent, her taste, everything about her was driving him wild. He could have come right away but wanted to prolong his hardness for as long as he could for her.

"Oh, Terry, you're driving me crazy. You feel so good. You're so wet, so hot and so deep. Your pussy is on fire. I want to stay hard for you all day. I want to make you come again and again," he hissed as a moan of pleasure consumed him.

"Does it feel good, Charlie?"_she panted, her breasts swaying and bouncing with her movements.

Before he could answer, she ground her pussy down even harder on his swollen, stiff member.

"Tell me how it feels, Charlie. Tell me! I want to hear you say the words," she growled as she ran her hands through her damp hair.

"You're setting me on fire! You're pussy is on fire and it's so fucking tight," he said through gasps of pleasure, fighting his impending release. He wanted nothing more than to make this feeling, this oneness, last forever.

"Do you want to come inside me, honey?"_she asked as she slowed her movements, her voice seductive.

"Oh, I want to explode deep inside of you, baby. I want to give you every drop of me that I possess. Oh, baby, drain me dry! Don't leave a drop for anyone else," he nearly screamed.

His moans of passion drove Terry deeper into a frenzy. Without another word of encouragement, she began to grind her body even harder on his thoroughly engorged penis until he vaguely thought it might snap off, but he didn't care. His senses were overloaded. Her breasts bounced and swayed in the flickering candlelight as she rode him and the scent of her perfume, mixed with the aroma of her snatch on his face, filled the air. Her tight pussy, wrapped around him like a second skin, sent tingles from the top of his head to the ends of his toes. It was all too much, yet would never be enough. He couldn't hold it any longer. A few seconds later, Charlie came like he had never come before in his entire life. He exploded deep within Terry and felt as if he would come forever. She slowed her movements and lowered her upper body toward him until they were face to face. He raised his head and they kissed deeply, even as Charlie continued to spurt within her vagina.

After a short time she climbed off and they both held each other for what seemed like an eternity. They lingered that way for a while, basking in the afterglow, both gently stroking the other. Eventually they relaxed their grips and lit up their cigarettes. They smoked while they spoke about Terry's son and their respective jobs.

Before long, Charlie extinguished his cigarette and felt himself getting aroused again. He took her face in his hands, enjoying the silky smoothness of her skin. He brushed her forehead with gentle, tender kisses then moved to her eyes and nose. He was being playful as well as romantic. He began to nibble on her ear lobes, first with soft butterfly kisses, but soon thrust his tongue deep inside her ear, which nearly drove her wild. She began to twist and turn and thrust her ear harder against his wet and exploring tongue. After several long seconds, Charlie withdrew his tongue from her ear and tilted her face toward him, thrusting into her open and waiting mouth. She began to suck on his tongue frantically, almost as if she were trying to swallow it. He felt himself drowning in her passion and wanted every part of her. She was moaning loudly now and he couldn't help but wonder if the neighbors could hear everything happening behind the closed shades.

He didn't care.

"Charlie, please take me! I need fucking so much," she begged. "Please, Charlie!"

He rolled her over onto her stomach and placed both hands on her hips. She knew what he wanted. Without a word, she moved her buttocks upward, ready and waiting. As he looked down at her, eager to be inside her again, he saw her hand moving between her legs. With a moan of anticipation, he watched as she spread apart the lips of her vagina, welcoming his swollen staff of hardness.

He entered her, first with slow, gentle movements which soon grew into hard, urgent thrusts. The sight of her ass and his penis pounding in and out of her was more than he could stand. He gripped her hips, rocking her back and forth, as he continued his attack on her like a wild man who was getting laid for the first time during the last minutes of his life. His eruption into her was everything he was and ever would be. They would forever be connected by this act of love and lust. He held tightly onto her thighs as he exploded deep within her, emptying every last drop into her for a second time. Afterward, he did not pull out of her right away but gently lowered her stomach down onto the bed and allowed himself to soften inside of her.

He lay down next to her for a while then she got up and went into the bathroom. He checked his watch for the time and was surprised to see it was almost noon already. He had been there almost three full hours in which time seemed to stand still for him.

After a few minutes, Terry came back in with a pair of silky black panties on. She blew out the tapered candles which had practically burned down completely and they cuddled on the bed. After a while, Charlie asked her if she had any misgivings for what they had done but Terry assured him solemnly that she did not. Before he knew it, it was his turn to enter the bathroom and he showered and dressed. He felt somewhat depressed that he was leaving her and told her he would miss her. She replied by saying she did not want to think about him leaving but only to concentrate on when they would be together again.

She walked him to the door where they embraced and said their goodbyes then he walked to his car and got in. Neither of them had said the word love.

When Charlie got home he was relieved to see that Annette had already left for work. He was exhausted from his love making session and decided to go straight to bed. Sleep came easily.

When Annette arrived home from work she woke Charlie at his usual time. He was glad she never once mentioned his DWI arrest.

Before she could ask him questions, he jumped into the shower, shaved, and left for work.

He wanted to stop at the coffee shop and spend time with Terry but he also knew he had to be discreet or else the entire precinct would ride him.

Charlie was assigned as chauffeur, as usual, to Lt. A.

CHAPTER EIGHT

H e felt great. In fact, he hadn't felt this good at the start of a late shift in years. The lieutenant, not surprisingly, was also raring to go, and Charlie sensed it was going to be a busy night.

"Charlie, are you ready to work tonight?" asked the boss.

"Yes sir."

"Good. We're going to have the borough Task Force meet us at those kiddie bars down on Bay Street," Lt. A. explained.

The kiddie bars were a series of bars along Bay Street as well as certain side streets. In the early seventies the United States Navy decided that Staten Island's north shore ports, with its easy access to the Atlantic Ocean, were perfect for harboring parts of the North Atlantic fleet. Much effort and money were put into dredging efforts to make the existing ports deep enough to sustain and berth the naval armada that soon would call Stapleton, New York, home. The United States Army had moved out of Fort Wadsworth at the southernmost tip of Bay Street and the United States Navy had moved in. Millions of dollars were spent building homes and quarters for all the naval personnel soon to arrive and businesses of all kinds began to pop up along the waterfront and the adjacent neighborhoods. Bars and restaurants, such as delis and grocery stores, sprang up and proliferated. Where there used to be one Chinese restaurant in the space of two miles there were now a dozen. Stapleton, Rosebank, Fort Wadsworth, Tompkinsville and Saint George all wanted the Navy's business before they made it into Manhattan and the great white way.

After a few years of dredging and around-the-clock construction, the Navy families moved in and, wouldn't you know it, the Navy changed its mind and went elsewhere. The families moved away and their housing became quiet, abandoned shells. As a result, the bars that would have become havens for dry-throated naval personnel transformed into asylums for teens from Brooklyn and New Jersey. They became drug emporiums and soon were the base of operations for gangs, such as the Bloods and the Crips, to exercise their will and muscle. It was not uncommon to have one or two shootings each and every weekend in one of these bars.

Lt. A. made it crystal clear to the officers at roll call that he was going to make collars and check I.D.'s. He enlisted the assistance of the Patrol Borough Staten Island Street Crime Suppression Unit, which would be working at least until 2:00 A.M., as well as the Borough Task Force. They would all remain there until needed.

Lt. A. knew and had worked previously with the commanding officers of those units who were also lieutenants. He had worked under them as a police officer but, after making Sergeant quickly, had risen to Lieutenant and now relished calling his previous boss' by their first names.

At approximately 1:00 A.M. and after all units had consumed at least one cup of coffee, they met in the parking lot of the Western Beef supermarket on Bay Street. This location was several blocks away from the main drag of bars.

One bar in particular, the Wavecrest, was known for allowing its rowdier patrons to fight with weapons as well underage patrons to both enter and consume alcohol.

The Lieutenant's plan was simple enough. First, the unmarked cars would pull up and the plainclothes officers would enter and strategically position themselves inside. At a given signal within a given time frame the interior lights would be turned on by those officers and the uniformed officers outside would enter the location and block the exists, allowing no one to exit or enter.

At 1:15 A.M. the plainclothes officers entered the Wavecrest and at 1:20 A.M. the uniformed force went in. The lieutenants of all three units entered together.

"Nobody move a fucking muscle!" shouted Lt. A.

People tried to shove their way past the three bosses but were quickly stopped by the officers guarding the doors. The sound of metal hitting the floor was so obvious it was almost funny. The plainclothes officers who had entered first arrested everyone who discarded a weapon. There were knives, guns and even brass knuckles. Patrons who seemed underage were asked for I.D. and several arrests were made for forged driver's licenses.

The Lieutenant personally gave the bartender a summons for operating a disorderly premise, which hopefully would lead to its closure by the State Liquor Authority. The arresting officers who made the collars at the Wavecrest removed their prisoners to the 120th and began their paperwork in the 2nd floor arrest processing office. Any and all arrests made on Staten Island were taken to the A.P.O., which served as the borough's central booking location.

The lieutenant and other bosses grouped outside the bar and, after a brief conversation, dismissed several units to return back to their commands to either sign out or finish up the remainder of their tour. Lt. A. had several of the 120th precinct units remain behind on a side street, which really threw Charlie for a loop. After several minutes the units waiting with the lieutenant heard what sounded like gunfire and saw several youths running down Bay Street. Lt. A. had all those waiting converge from all sides and the rowdy teens were grabbed and placed under arrest without incident.

Upset that some of their fellow gang members had been arrested in the earlier raid, the disgruntled teens decided to shoot out store windows in the area. During the arrests, several guns were confiscated. Naturally, the store owners were elated and, as a show of thanks, they often invited the officers and their families to come to dinner. However, the borough Commander would have personally lynched the first cop who partook of a free meal or handout.

One might often wonder what the difference is between all the testimonial awards and dinners that top officers receive for the work the beat cop does for them as well as the free cup of coffee that same beat cop has to hide from the brass. It was no secret that the borough Commanding Officer, Assistant Chief Carmine Dragonetti, didn't want anyone to make waves in his borough or upset his apple cart of ruling with an iron fist. He was dead set against vehicle pursuits and emphatically stated there would be none in his borough, intentionally forgetting the fact that they were allowed in other boroughs as well as the written guidelines for those pursuits. Dragonetti didn't care if the pursuit was to apprehend a traffic violator or a cop killer. He threatened every single officer and supervisor with a transfer out of Patrol Borough Staten Island, which meant a transfer off of Staten Island. He frowned on unorthodox police work and actually called men on the carpet for reducing crime and removing guns of the street.

The man had no balls and everyone knew it. As a result, they ignored his ranting. Lt. A. and the other bosses had no doubt that they would eventually have to face the chief, but they didn't care.

Dragonetti was a little man with a hook nose who smoked a cigar that was as big as his ego. He used too much black hair coloring in a vain attempt to appear youthful, but it didn't work. There was also a rumor that he had lied about his age to remain on the force. He spoke a language called profanity because every other word out of his mouth was fuck and cocksucker. He belittled men and supervisors without care of their rank. He had no shame. It had been more than one cop on the late tours in the 120th and 122nd who had chased a speeding, dark Chevy over the Verrazano Bridge in the wee hours of the morning only to sadly find out that they were chasing a speeding Chief Dragonetti coming home from a late night poker game at Police Headquarters in Manhattan. No one dared to pull him over once they realized it was a department car with the chief inside.

Dragonetti had been a sergeant during the time that Lt. A. was a rookie cop in the 120th and he broke Lt. A's balls at every opportunity. In spite of his lesser rank, Lt. A. wasn't afraid of the chief and Dragonetti knew it.

***

It all came to a head one night when Lt. A. practically accused the Chief of being a liar. The men in the precinct had not heard much about it but Lt. A. filled Charlie in later with many of the sordid details. It was a long story that began with one of the late tour sergeants, who frequented Harry's place while off duty, with his squad of men. The rule book emphatically stated that a supervisor should never socialize with his men because he might find himself in a work situation where he would have to discipline them.

It's the old saying that warns how familiarity breeds contempt. Sergeant Kellin always stopped at Harry's after work with the guys and seemed to be well liked by them. He wasn't a rookie sergeant but a veteran cop with good supervision time under his belt.

"One day while Sergeant Kellin was working his late tour in Zone 1, which covers Jersey Street, he saw one of the men in his squad who had reported in sick. As you know, the rule book says if you are out on sick report, you must remain in your residence," Lt. A. explained to Charlie. "The cop took his chances but was observed by his squad sergeant in his very own precinct. He had been visiting his girlfriend on Jersey Street and should have been more careful."_

"What did Kellin do?"_asked Charlie.

"Well, the Sergeant had several options available to him. He could have ignored it, chosen to quietly speak in private to the offender at a later time, or written him up. Sergeant Kellin chose the latter."

The offending man was an officer who was off duty as well as a cop in the sergeant's own squad. He had never been called in on the carpet for any infractions and was considered a good producer. He was also someone the sergeant hung out and drank with on occasion.

"Sergeant Kellin became a rat to each and every man on the late tour, Charlie."

The Lieutenant could not and would not outwardly agree with the men but Charlie knew the boss would have never written up one of the guys who wasn't even working the tour and had not interfered with any police operations of the night. The offending officer eventually got transferred out of the borough, but for the men of the late tour it meant that headquarters brass would now turn on the heat and increase outside supervision.

At one of our roll call meetings, with Sergeant Kellin present, Lt. A. addressed the troops and explained how he was concerned about the situation. He reiterated that he was not one to pull punches or to draw things out, and that, for whatever reason, the heat was being turned on and it was going to feel like hell out there for a while. He also stressed that, for what it was worth, he would be the target. He was the late tour Platoon Commander and the buck stopped there. The bosses from the ivory tower in headquarters would be looking for the smallest infractions, so he emphasized to the troops to have their memo books up-to-date and be careful with their radio dispositions. He said to them, "If they get you, they've got me." He reiterated that Sergeant Kellin had made a decision and, right or wrong, it was his job to make decisions, like it or not. Now they had to stick together until they were out of the spotlight.

"The majority of the men knew it had been their own Sergeant who had brought down the oncoming wave of supervision that might get even more of them in trouble," Lt. A. explained. "They also knew that this same Sergeant, the one they had broken bread and drank with, had first come to me for my opinion. Scuttlebutt had it that I had explained how to handle the incident in a positive way and with minor discipline but with nothing that would have included outside brass from headquarters."

Charlie knew the Sergeant had not taken the Lt. A.'s wise advice and now all the late tour had to suffer, especially the lieutenant, who would be directly responsible and held accountable for any violations uncovered by the brass. The men knew they would all have to play by the book for a while.

All except Officer Jack Donnelly.

CHAPTER NINE

Police Officer Jack Donnelly had been best friends with Officer Jamal Green, the officer who had been visiting his girlfriend on Jersey Street after calling out sick and who was subsequently transferred because of Kellin's action.

Donnelly took it one step further. Most of the men heard him making threats about Kellin, saying he vowed to get him, but everyone thought it was just careless talk. No one thought he would ever follow through with any of those threats, but he did.

It was the cell attendant's responsibility on payday to maintain control over the little metal strongbox which held the entire command's paychecks that had been delivered earlier in the day by messenger for the borough command. Also included in this box were the sign off sheets. Each member of the command had to sign next to his name to validate that their check had been received.

On the following payday Sergeant Kellin arrived for work at his normal time, which was approximately 11:00 P.M. As was usual custom for a payday, he made his way over to the cell block to get his paycheck from the cell attendant, but the cell attendant could not find it. When checking the sign off sheet, they quickly realized a signature was affixed next to Kellin's name, albeit forged.

The sergeant was livid! Now the precinct had an internal theft to investigate, which meant Internal Affairs would have to be brought into it. As a result, the precinct went from the frying pan right into the burning fires of hell.

Lt. A. went bug fuck and spoke to the troops that very night.

"As you all know and are very much aware, we have been undergoing a lot of shit and heat from headquarters. Our original watchdogs came because a supervisor made a decision to take action. Right or wrong, it was his right to do so. Jamal Green was not the innocent victim here. Whether or not common sense was used in the decision making process is not my call. Green was out on sick report and in his own command fucking around. Sergeant Kellin didn't tell him to violate the procedures, Green did it all by himself and he got caught. As a result, he was written up and got transferred.

"Now Green is probably making overtime up the fucking ass in Manhattan while we all fucking suffer here! Like it or not, Green was wrong and Kellin was right. I told every damn one of you to drop the shit you were playing with Kellin, didn't I? Of course, now some fucking scumbag had to go and steal his fucking paycheck, and whoever did it is a fucking, scumbag motherfucker! If you had any balls at all, you would admit it now!" Lt. A. bellowed.

Frowning at his men, he waited for a few minutes to see if anyone would admit to the theft and wasn't surprised when he was answered with a deadly silence.

"What are you, a fucking chicken?" he roared. "Don't you know that within twenty-four hours another check will be cut? You all know me. By now you should ALL know I would walk through fire for a fellow officer! I would not hesitate to back you up to the fucking Police Commissioner if you're in the right. I would do that in a heartbeat for a good cop though, not for the lowlife scumbag who is hiding among you. How do you know that Kellin's wife or kids didn't need that money right away? Maybe they needed it to buy medicine."

He paused as his eyes scanned the faces staring back at him.

"Cops' wives really don't know what we do. They read the biased newspapers and see bleeding liberal hearts on TV describe what an officer does in such a biased slant that it almost always seems as though we are judged by Monday morning quarterbacks who don't know a fucking thing about police work. We bust our balls every damn night, putting our lives on the line, and now we have some fucking scumbag cop, here on my late tour, hurting a fellow officer's family."

Lt. A's face was flushed with anger.

"Damn you! If you're so angry at Kellin then approach him like a man and duke it out, you fucking, yellow coward! I swear to fucking Christ that if I find out who did this, I'll break your fucking face and then put the cuffs on you myself! You had better put in for a transfer now because in my eyes, you're a dead motherfucker!" he yelled.

None of the men in the room had ever heard or seen their beloved boss yell so loud or become so irate. The troops all knew the Lieutenant loved his fellow officers as well as how very much he despised dirty cops. Everyone at roll call was silent and had no doubt at all that the boss meant every word he spoke.

"If there is one among you who is decent, step forward and tell me if you know who it is. If you're not comfortable doing that, then for God's sake at least call Internal Affairs anonymously and report it. Whoever did this should visit the Wall of Honor at One Police Plaza and read about real cops who have given their all. Those were, and always will be, heroes and great men."

Lt A's voice was solemn as he slowly began to calm down.

***

No coffee run was made this night as Charlie and Lt. A. continued their tour of the streets. After telling his story, the Lieutenant didn't waste any time in asking some questions.

"Do you think I was too hard on them, Charlie?"

Charlie didn't know what to say. He tried to place himself in the boss' shoes but it was difficult. He just didn't have that awesome responsibility.

"I'm not a boss, Lou, so I can't really say one way or another," he finally answered, trying not to make that decision.

"You're missing the whole point, Charlie. It's not about being a boss. It's about being a cop, a good cop. People shit all over cops all day long, from the skels on the street to the bleeding liberal hearts, both in the media as well as those inside the ivory tower of police headquarters. Someone has to stick up for the good cops. Someone has to support the cop who does a dirty and distasteful job day in and day out and then gets shit on by his own kind. If someone stole your check and you had no doubt that your fellow officers knew who did it, wouldn't you want them to help you out?" the lieutenant asked.

Charlie knew Lt. A. was right but he didn't want to be a rat either. The blue wall of silence was entrenched deep, even in good cops. Nobody wanted to be a rat no matter what the cost. Charlie also knew that the boss was right about a cop's family, even though he didn't like that part.

"The fucking coward who stole Kellin's check has accomplished one thing and one thing only. He's succeeded in bringing down the late tour just like Truman destroyed Japan. We are going to be decimated and the heat will last for God knows how long. Your buddy, whoever he is, hurt an NYPD supervisor. Do you think this is going to go away by some miracle?" asked the lieutenant as his eyes flashed with anger. "It probably will mean my transfer out of this precinct that I love and that I wanted to retire out of."

"Why would you get transferred, Lou?"_asked Charlie.

"They will hold me directly accountable for this one. It's almost tantamount to a mutiny on the high seas. The theft of a supervisor's check is a theft from me as well as them. If I can't come up with the responsible scumbag, I'm gone. What's worse is they will replace me with the hardest and meanest lieutenant they can find."

Charlie didn't want to lose his beloved Lieutenant. He had to figure out some way to get the men together and help the boss solve the problem; well, everyone except Donnelly. Although his desire to help was strong, Charlie really didn't expect too much from his comrades.

Once again he knew that the blue wall of silence was solid, especially on the late tour.

One might often wonder what the difference was between police officers or doctors who refused to testify against their comrades who made life threatening errors in operating rooms. How does a police officer who goes out on patrol night after night with his partner expect to turn in his partner to whom he owes his very life? It's not easy; in fact, it is one of the hardest things imaginable for a cop. It's not as if men who sit at desks all day long are expected to turn in tax cheats. Police officers depend on their partners eight hours a day, five days a week. Their very existence is based on trust that their partner will not let them down and stand toe to toe with them when they face the grim reaper in the form of a six foot giant who refuses to move when directed.

The blue wall is as complex as it is controversial.

CHAPTER TEN

The effects of the looming threat of transfer for Lt. A. became obvious when he started to reminisce about his appointment to the force.

"You know, Charlie, I came on the job in 1965 and graduated from the Police Academy in July. I can remember it as if it were yesterday. It was a sweltering day with weather reports calling for record breaking temperatures and high humidity. Not surprisingly, Macy's department stores were reporting their highest ever sales on air conditioners and fans.

"I was a just rookie back then. It was so hot that the pavement on the streets made you feel like you were in an oven and the black tar oozing off the street stuck to our brand new Knapp shoes. Five hundred of us were ready to graduate from the academy and take our positions as probationary patrolmen. That was the polite name for us – Probationary Patrolmen – but everyone in the department called us Rookies. That's all we heard for the next twelve months.

"Our graduating class was so big that we had to use the 59th Street Armory as the site in order to accommodate friends and families for our graduation. Each one of us had on our brand new, never worn before uniforms. Our hats were navy blue with black felt that formed a band above a shiny black visor. Our shirts were also navy blue, not at all like the sky blue shirts we wear today, and they had brass buttons, held on by a metal clasp that were actually removable. This meant you had to take them off before you either washed the shirt or brought it in for dry cleaning.

"Graduation was an official department ceremony which meant we had to wear the summer blouse. The term blouse was a misnomer because it really wasn't a blouse; it was more like a blue sports coat with brass buttons. It's similar to what we wear today but much heavier. The department allowed it to be worn at any event it deemed fitting regardless of what season it was. I actually had to wear it one Christmas Eve when the temperature was hovering around eight degrees. Some things change and some do not."

Lieutenant A chuckled as he continued.

"We still had to wear our white gloves back then with the summer blouse, just like we do now. They were normally held in place by little clasps and buttons at the wrist, but the ones I wore the day I graduated were totally different from those we wear today. Although they had them back then, we didn't need the snaps that particular day because the high humidity made the gloves stick to our hands like cotton candy.

"I was 21 years old and I remember it like it was yesterday. We were all idealists about to make New York City a safer place to live. We were husbands, fathers, sons and some of us were Veterans, all of us looking for a secure job.

"Freddie Bock was our company Sergeant. He wasn't really a Sergeant, though. He was really just another cadet like the rest of us. Since he was the oldest and had been in the service, he was given that dubious distinction. The company Sergeant was the point of contact between the administration office and our individual company of recruits.

"On graduation day, Freddie had been given our field assignments before the actual ceremony but he was told not to tell anyone anything until after the event. We all badgered him but he held his ground and didn't say a word. After the ceremony our entire class surrounded him; photos with family and loved ones took a back seat to Freddie. Hell, we all wanted to know where we were going to be assigned!

"The roster was in alphabetical order and, of course, I was first," Lt. A. said with a smile.

"Audenino, the one,"_Freddie said.

"If he were to say that today, naturally he would have said the 1st, not the one," said Lt. A. "As you should already know, cops address precinct designations in a certain jargon. For example, the twenty fifth precinct is the two-five. The one hundred and twenty third precinct is the one-two-three."

It began to make sense to Charlie. He remembered being told that Lt. A. had been born Giovanni Audenino. Giovanni is Italian for John, and the Lieutenant had been named after his mother's father.

Lt. A.'s grandfather had been born in a little town in Italy called Turin, located somewhere in the northern Alps. He came to America in the early 1900's and settled on the lower east side. He was a baker by trade but the Irish influence in New York at the time prohibited him from following his profession. As a result, he found himself in construction and worked on the building of many projects that were underway in New York City at the time.

Eventually, the Lieutenant's grandmother and grandfather moved to Staten Island in Sunnyside. Clove Road was the main thoroughfare dividing the wasp end of Sunnyside from the section where his grand-parents settled.

"That area was called nanny goat town because most of its inhabit-ants were Italian who had goats, chickens and other types of animals," Lt. A. explained. "The White Anglo Saxons on the other side looked down upon the 'Guineas,' whom they considered inferior. The Anglos strove to buy big houses with huge pieces of property.

"My grandfather, whom I affectionately called Nonno, had a green thumb and grew anything and everything from tomato plants to fruit trees. He used to take me on walks through the woods where we would search for mushrooms after a rain. Thankfully, he taught me how to distinguish poisonous ones from edible ones.

"Those same woods are now where the Staten Island Expressway stands."

When Lt. A. graduated he was assigned to the 1ˢᵗ precinct in lower Manhattan, which was located on Old Slip. Today the building is used as the New York Police Department Museum. Before it was re-configured to be a showplace for police archives it was used in the filming for the motion picture *Serpico*_starring Al Pacino.

Lt. A. and his entire class of recruits were assigned to subway platforms on the newly created 4ᵗʰ platoon. Their shift was from 8:00 P.M. to 4:00 A.M. and was boring and monotonous to say the least.

"After I finished my stint in the confines of the subways in downtown Manhattan I was given the opportunity to be a foot patrolman in the 1ˢᵗ precinct," Lt. A. continued, "and it wasn't long before I learned why the 1ˢᵗ was called the 'flying first.' As one of three brand new rookies, I was lucky if I worked once a week in my own command. I always worked my first tour in the 1ˢᵗ before I 'flew'_ to other commands for the rest of the week. The various commands of the city had ongoing details and there was always some group or organization demonstrating or protesting something which required a police presence.

"The rookies in the first began wearing wings over their shields, just like men in the Air Force. The wings were definitely not part of the uniform but most bosses never made an issue of it. I began to look forward to the first day of each week because I got to work in my own command. Most of the time it was a foot post but once in a while I got to ride in a patrol car with other members of the command."

Lt. A. seemed as if he was in deep thought as he reflected on his early days as a footman.

"You know, Charlie, I truly believe that the first person you work with has a definite bearing on the kind of cop you turn out to be," he said quietly.

Charlie was getting a little tired from driving and asked if it was okay for him to pull over for a while and rest. Thankfully, Lt. A. had no problem with his request. After finding a quiet place to park, Charlie turned off the car and took out a cigarette. He lit it and inhaled deeply as the lieutenant began describing one of the first cops he worked with.

"I will never forget one particular day in 1966 when I was assigned to a radio car in Sector D-David. This sector's boundaries included the southern tip of the precinct, essentially South Ferry and all of Battery Park, as well as lower Broadway, Wall Street and Trinity Church.

"My partner on that tour was a ten-year veteran named Joe Kehoeth. Joe had been dumped into the 1st precinct from the far reaches of the Bronx where he lived and had been assigned to a Bronx command. He had gotten himself in with the ladies and wound up being transferred to the southern tip of Manhattan as punishment. It was always reassuring to know that the majority of cops on the force considered my very first command a dumping ground. Even though Joe was still known to have a reputation with the ladies, any lady other than his wife actually, he was a good and knowledgeable street cop.

"As you know, there are certain tricks and techniques one learns from a good street cop that simply can't be learned in the police academy. The academy can teach you to write a ticket but they can't teach you how to control your fear when the person you are writing the ticket to says he is going to shove it up your ass when you give it to him. We really can't go around shooting everyone who speaks nasty to us and gives us shit, now can we?" laughed the lieutenant.

Charlie laughed along with him and thanked God he had not met that person yet.

"Like it or not, Charlie, we have to learn that John Q. Citizen has a right to voice his opinion. What a good cop must learn is that the law is on his side. The good cop must learn when to write the summons and when to stop writing and place the son of a bitch under arrest. Remember, the summons is in lieu of arrest. We shouldn't go around and lock up every one who goes through a red light but we could if we had to.

"Once we decide to make an arrest, we enter into another phase of the process and other factors come into play, giving us the right to use force if necessary. The bottom line is that a good street cop learns to be in control of his emotions and, more importantly, how to use those same emotions effectively in many different and varied situations.

"Joe Kehoeth was the type of teacher I needed at this very early stage of my career," Lt. A. said. "He taught me about family disputes and how important it was to not trust the wife when she asked you to lock up her husband, even if you saw and heard her screaming. Most of the time that same wife or girlfriend would have a change of heart after she saw you putting cuffs on her bread-winner husband. And that," warned Lt. A., "was when you had to be mighty careful, because that same wife or girlfriend might be coming straight at you with a frying pan."

Joe taught Lt. A. about car stops and how being in control meant telling the person stopped to remain in the car forcefully, thereby increasing the safety area. The lieutenant then told Charlie about one particular tour he did with Joe.

It was a mild, quiet day and they were doing a four to twelve shift. They were assigned to the 1st precinct, also known as the financial capital of the world, and the first hours of the tour were slow moving. Several hundred thousand people work downtown in office buildings that comprise much of the 1st precinct and there were always hundreds of pedestrians out on the sidewalks. Patrol speed in the 1st was no more than 5 mph.

Joe and John had their share of assignments or "jobs,"_ as Joe taught John to call them. There were all kinds of disputes with street vendors who proliferated the area like stars filling the sky. Taxi passengers were always relying on the police to settle fare disputes with dishonest cabbies that overcharged or simply failed to turn on the taximeter. Crime in the 1st precinct was really unheard of except for an occasional burglary on the midnight tour or an assault stemming from fights in some of the bars down near the pier areas. However, on this night with less than one year under his belt, John was about to see some real action.

"Remember, this was in 1966 and some of the laws were different than what they are today," Lt. A. explained. "In those days we could use deadly physical force. If necessary, we could also use our guns to shoot at fleeing felons."

"What if the guy was unarmed? Could you still shoot at him then?" Charlie asked.

"You could shoot at any fleeing felon. It didn't matter if he was armed or not," Lt. A. said.

On this particular night, John and his partner Joe were on Radio Motor Patrol on Broadway near Wall Street. Most of the pedestrian traffic had dissipated and the 1st was starting to look like the ghost town it was noted for. They were headed down to the Battery Park area where Joe wanted to stop at the Bean Pot, a place in Lower Manhattan that was well known for its bar fights on weekend nights. It was frequented mostly by residents of "the dog house," which was an old seaman's home a few blocks away that had been nicknamed by local residents who were very much aware of the squalid living conditions those old salts lived under. Even so, they could be found drinking it up on Friday nights at the Bean Pot, which was not a skel joint. When those old sailors fought, they fought hard and meant to kill, and when they were sober they were perfect gentlemen.

Although many in the area called the Bean Pot by its actual name, the 1st precinct old timers called it something different - they called it "a bucket of blood."

Joe wanted to check out the new barmaid, who supposedly had huge breasts and was friendly to the cops. She was from Ireland and had red hair as well as a thick, Irish brogue.

As they were heading down Broadway, he spotted a young kid he believed was too young to be behind the wheel of a Pontiac GTO. John was the recorder that night so Joe asked him to contact the radio dispatcher and run the plate to see if the car was stolen. The dispatcher responded by saying the car was hotter than the noon day sun so Joe turned on the light and siren and directed the kid to pull over to the curb.

Not surprisingly, the kid took off down Broadway like a bat out of hell, trying desperately to avoid capture. As luck would have it, there wasn't much traffic except for cab traffic and the usual amount of sightseers for that time of night was minimal. In spite of this, the kid tried to mount the curb to avoid the cab traffic.

He was not a good driver.

As soon as he realized what the kid's intentions were, Joe stressed that they had to either terminate the pursuit or stop the boy quickly before he killed someone. John thought Joe was going to end the chase and let that be the end of it, and he was right. Joe ended it by taking out his gun and letting rounds fly while driving with one hand. Amazingly enough he got the young driver. The GTO crashed into a fence at a construction site on lower Broadway.

Joe quickly jumped out of the RMP and rushed over to the completely totaled vehicle. It was leaking green antifreeze from its demolished radiator and gasoline from its damaged fuel tank.

John thought there might be danger from a fire starting so he notified the dispatcher to have one piece of fire apparatus to respond for a wash down. This would assure that any leaking gasoline would be washed away into the sewers and diluted.

While John called that in, Joe grabbed the kid out of the wrecked GTO. The boy was semi-conscious but Joe placed him into the rear of the squad car without calling for an ambulance.

John's next call was for another sector to respond to safeguard the GTO, which wasn't going anywhere. The assisting sector would await the department tow truck and have it removed to the police pound as evidence and safekeeping.

Joe was anxious to get back to the station house so he could begin his paperwork and make night court. When they arrived at the precinct they carried the kid in. He was bleeding from the shoulder as well as his wrist so the desk officer, an old Irish boss, directed the switchboard operator to have an ambulance respond to the station house when he saw the boy's injuries. The desk officer directed Joe to lay the kid down on the floor, away from the desk area. The kid was conscious enough and smart enough to not answer any questions without a lawyer present, which made it all the easier for Joe.

When the bus finally got there it was determined that one of Joe's bullets had entered the kid's shoulder and exited at the wrist, but absolutely no one came to question Joe about the shooting. They had to send his gun to ballistics for examination but that was it. The rest went smoothly. Joe finished his paperwork and the kid went to the hospital. Joe made Manhattan night court and drew up his affidavit.

***

Eventually John was re-assigned to a foot post in Battery Park, which was an easy post. One of the last people he worked with in the 1st precinct before cleaning out his locker and transferring to the 120th was Police Officer Joseph Patrick MacGovern.

Joe was a twenty-year veteran and a gentle giant of a man. He was 6'5" and weighed in at about 240 pounds. He had silver gray hair and spoke with a brogue. His parents had come from the old sod and he was the first in his family to enter into Civil Service. He was a gentleman and a good old time cop to boot. He had entered the police force when John had been all of three years old.

One day when John was in the muster room of the precinct, Joe approached him.

"I hear that you've been transferred to the boondocks of Staten Island, kid," said the older man.

John was surprised that Joe talked to him because most old timers didn't waste too much time with probationary officers. It was probably out of some fear that they could have been rats sent out from the Academy to uncover corruption, which was rampant in the 1st precinct. There were so many opportunities for cops on the take in the 1st precinct to make a buck. They got dirty money from the vendors, the bars, and other shop keepers. John was glad he was being transferred to the 'boondocks,' as Joe called Staten Island.

"I live there, Joe, so it won't be so bad. Look at all the money I will save by not having to commute over the bridge," John said.

"Kid, remember one thing. If you can write 'nothing to report' in your memo book each day for the next twenty years then you've got the job by the balls," Joe said, smiling from one ear to the other. Then he laughed and both men shook hands. John never saw him again.

John did not realize it then but there would never be a day during the next seventeen years, while he was assigned to the 120th, that he would ever write 'nothing to report' in his memo book.

The last tour in the 1st was a sad one for John. He was leaving his first command as well as two of his best friends, Bruce Price and Willie Lytell.

John, Bruce and Willie had been Academy classmates and were assigned to the 1st when they graduated. They commuted together from Staten Island, all being assigned to the 4th platoon. Bruce and Willie had not requested the transfer to Staten Island, thinking they would not get it, but they were wrong.

While driving home after his final day at the 1st, John thought of his comrades and swore he would keep in touch. Sadly, they never saw each other again.

CHAPTER ELEVEN

John looked forward to his new command and was assigned to the 2nd squad.

Members of his new squad ended their work week on Sunday and were not due back until the 4X12 tour on Wednesday so John decided he would use his days off to travel to the precinct to pick out a locker and stow all his gear. When he entered the station house he noticed that the lieutenant on the desk was writing in the command log, also known as the blotter, where the desk officer noted all the daily activity of the shift.

John learned early on in the 1st precinct not to disturb the lieutenant when he was writing in the blotter. He had gotten his ass chewed out in front of the entire platoon by Lieutenant Dubrow, who reamed him out for doing just that.

The Lieutenant looked up and saw John, then looked down and began writing again. John stood silently, waiting patiently. A few minutes passed before the lieutenant looked up again.

"Yes?" the man behind the desk mumbled in an agitated tone.

"I'm Police Officer Audenino. I've just been transferred in from the 1st. Can you direct me to the locker rooms, please?" John asked quietly.

"Third floor," answered the Lieutenant.

"Thank you."

The lieutenant did not acknowledge him any further and kept on writing in the blotter without breaking stride. John found a staircase but it only went as far as the second floor, so he decided to walk down this second floor hallway where he eventually found another stairway which led him up to the third floor. There he found several locker rooms used by the patrolmen. He walked into one of the rooms which faced the rear of the station house. It had three aisles with lockers about twenty deep in each row. Most were occupied but several were not. None of them were new.

He immediately found a cluster of empty lockers and picked one that looked very secure. He opened it and surveyed the inside, not surprised to find the usual wire metal hangars still dangling from the single metal rod that spanned the inside of the locker.

There were old inter-departmental envelopes on the bottom of the locker that dated back several years but were empty. In a rear corner there even was a pair of old dirty socks. He cleaned out all of the refuse and placed his own wooden hangars on the metal bar. Next, he placed his police hat on the top shelf after making sure it was clean and dust free, then set a plastic jar next to his hat into which he dropped his new 120 insignia as well as his brass buttons. He hung his gun belt on one of two large hooks affixed on either side of the interior of the locker then neatly hung his trousers and shirts on the wooden hangars.

Next he placed his memo book and as well as his rules and procedures manual inside a plastic waterproof case, as well as an attaché case, which contained many of the forms he would eventually use while on patrol.

He closed his locker and secured it with his combination lock then affixed his name and squad number on the outside according to police department regulations. John knew that placing his name on the locker was the most important step because brass from the Chief of Patrol's office could come up at any time and request to do an inspection. Although this wasn't something that was ordinarily done, it could be.

"Charlie, when I go back and think of my first days here in the 120th, I find myself remembering the lessons learned from my grandfather. I know I've told you a little bit about him, but there is so much more.

"My grandfather was sort of a hoarder, a pack rat if you will. On our many sojourns into the woods of Staten Island he would collect old nuts and bolts he found as well as odd lengths of wire and string.

"At some point in his life he built a shed in his back yard that was really a small house. It had two levels, windows and a fantastic work shop. During those trips into the woods, he would even bring burlap bags to shovel up any horse manure he found, left behind by horses privately owned or rented from the Franzreb Stables on Clove Road and who had ridden up there.

"My grandfather taught me so many things but the most important one was a love of nature and respect for all living things. He taught me to enjoy watching the wonder of the sun coming up in the morning, and on many a day we would set out for the woods before daybreak so as to get a head start on collecting.

"I miss him, Charlie, and I wish more than anything that he could have been there at my graduation from the police academy. I know he would have been so proud of me because I was the first in our family to enter into civil service."

The lieutenant became a little teary-eyed as he spoke so Charlie asked if he wanted to grab a cup of coffee. The boss declined the offer and continued to speak about his grandfather.

"Sometimes I feel as though he is with me, I mean right beside me. I know it sounds weird but I just feel it."

Lt. A. paused for a moment, lit a cigarette then continued.

"When I made Sergeant it was like a miracle. The sergeant's list had expired and I had given up all hope of promotion. I had nineteen years on the job and had passed every sergeant's exam I took. This was during the fiscal crisis of New York City, and either they froze the list or I didn't score high enough. I decided to take one last shot and I passed it but once again everyone said the list was dead, so I gave up all hope of ever being promoted.

"Then, one day I was in my basement doing laundry and, out of the clear blue sky, I heard my grandfather's voice. It wasn't as if I heard it in my thoughts; I heard it through my ears loud and clear. He spoke to me in Italian and it scared the shit out of me!"

"What did he say?" Charlie asked.

The lieutenant chuckled and said, "He told me I would be promoted in two months."

Lt. A. took a long drag on his cigarette, held it, and let it out slowly.

"I stopped doing the laundry and went up and made myself a stiff drink. Two weeks later there was an ad in *The Chief*, the civil service newspaper, stating that the sergeant's list would be re-opened because they had an immediate need for supervisors. I was a Sergeant six weeks later."

The lieutenant smiled and glanced at Charlie.

"I miss him, love him and know he will forever be with me," he said with a sigh.

CHAPTER TWELVE

N ow that he seemed more relaxed, the lieutenant continued his story about his graduation from the police academy.

"After Freddie Bock finished giving us our command assignments, we all promised to keep in touch. That night, our entire company agreed to meet at the Colonial Inn on Richmond Road for a dinner party with our wives and girlfriends. That was the beginning of all of our war stories. Next, we were instructed by Freddie to call our new commands and ask for the roll call office.

"I was scared shitless but was fortunate enough to have two class-mates, Bruce and Willie, with me. When we got to our new precinct, no one spoke to us unless we asked a direct question. No one said hello or goodbye. No one gave us advice as to where to eat or where to go if we had to take a dump. It was sheer hell," explained the lieutenant.

"Today it's a different world for rookies. When they get assigned to a precinct they are practically taken out by their hands to their posts. Their training sergeants do everything for them, which seemingly includes wiping their asses dry. The veterans of yesterday were prob-ably testing the rookies to see if they were worthy of their attention."

"I was assigned to the 4th platoon along with Bruce and Willie. We carpooled and worked together every night.

"I will never forget the day I made my way into the sitting room of the 1st precinct. I walked around and looked for anything that might have reminded me of the academy but saw nothing. There was an old shoe shine machine with worn out bristles and a brush holder with no brush. There were two metal containers of black shoe polish but they were devoid of any polish," the lieutenant said quietly.

"There was a coffee machine dispenser that was empty and probably used by the 4X12 shift, and I suddenly felt like I was an orphan with no home or country. On one wall stood a large, wooden cabinet which had about forty to fifty slots in it. A big, tattered sign hanging over it read: 'Forms - Please replace what you use.' A closer look into the slots showed that it was used as a huge garbage disposal. There were cigarette and cigar butts as well as chewing gum remains in almost all of the slots. Any forms still inside were torn or had coffee stains on them.

"The windows in the sitting room were almost eight to ten feet high with metal gates on the inside and bars on the outside. They were completely covered with filth and soot. There were two long wooden tables with strong cast iron legs, and scattered around the room were metal chairs with torn, green, vinyl padded seats. An old sergeant appeared out of nowhere and bellowed an order for us to fall in. The three of us stood in a row at attention, not moving a muscle or saying a word.

"The sergeant glared at us as if he was actually pissed that we took him off patrol for this 8:00 P.M. roll call. We probably interrupted his free dinner that he was either getting or going to get. As a result, he didn't welcome us on board or wish us luck. He just called out our names and gave us our assignments. Then, speaking with a very thick Irish brogue, he finally asked us if we had any questions," said Lt. A.

"Do ye have any questions, lads?"
Willie was the first to speak up. "How do we get to our posts, Sergeant?"_
"Lads, you use your feet that the good Lord gave ye. Anything else?"

"We three rookies had no further questions and walked out of the station house just as fast as the Sergeant had appeared. We were all so eager on that first night that all three of us broke the cardinal rule of all cops," the lieutenant said as he stared into the distance.

"What was that, Lou?" asked Charlie.

"We all went directly to our posts without stopping for coffee," the lieutenant said with a laugh.

During the mid-sixties crime in the subways skyrocketed so much that the lieutenant's entire graduating class was assigned to platforms in every borough. John and his fellow officers, Bruce and Willie, found themselves attached to the platforms in the 1st precinct. They were assigned to Whitehall Street, Wall Street, Bowling Green and the South Ferry station.

"My tours in the subway system were boring to say the least, Charlie. We all wanted to hit the streets and ride in the RMP's because subway duty was an endless round of rowdy drunks, panhandlers, the homeless and sexual deviants. In those days there weren't many tourists to give directions to, especially between the hours of 8:00 P.M. and 4:00 A.M. and especially in the 1st precinct, which became a graveyard between those hours. Sometimes I would come across a drunk or wino on the platform and hold him until the next train pulled in. When it did and the doors opened, I would shove him inside. The drunk then became the responsibility of the Transit Authority cop assigned to the train.

"Those T.A. cops weren't slackers, either. For every wino I placed on their train, they would throw two off onto my platform. It was a fucking game of musical winos," laughed the lieutenant.

***

The lieutenant and Charlie decided to grab a hamburger at the Clipper on Bay Street near the overhang. The night short order cook was a good guy who liked cops so they and their fellow officers stopped there at all hours of the night just to check up on him. Gene was his name and he even was invited to join the police bowling league, which he did and really enjoyed himself. A few years later he opened up his own little coffee shop on Stuyvesant Place and called it Gene's Luncheonette. He opened up at 3:00 A.M. and guys on the late tours stopped in to get coffee and visit while he pre-cooked all his hashed brown potatoes and bacon for the morning rush.

Charlie and his boss took their burgers and decided to park in the gas station at Bay Street and Vanderbilt Avenue. It was close to the busier areas and would make for a quicker response time if they were needed in a hurry. The lieutenant wolfed down his burger and coffee and began speaking about his days in the 1st precinct again.

"The worst detail for me in the subways was checking out the bathrooms. I didn't want to do it but they were part of the post and had to be checked several times a night.

"I'll never forget the first time I entered one of the toilets because I had to actually use the facilities. The first thing that hit me square in the face as well as my nostrils was the extreme heat of the air mingled with the stringent odor of urine and feces. Most of the bowls were not even operable; some did not flush and some did not even have water in them. The standing urinals, which were stained and grimy, worked but the flow of water was so weak and slow that they did not even wash the urine down the drain. There was feces in some of the bowls that had never been flushed and in some places it was caked on like dry cow dung forgotten on the prairie.

"None of this stopped the winos and deviants from using these restrooms. Even worse were the condoms still filled with ejaculated fluids left behind by the perverts who wandered through the subway system. If aids had been a household word back then I would have quit on the spot. Those deviants and sexual predators were called 'chicken hawks' because they preyed on young boys and men and often times forced themselves upon unwilling victims. I didn't have to travel to 42nd Street to find any midnight cowboys; they were right there in the confines of the 1st precinct," Lt. A. said.

Having finished their burgers, both men lit up cigarettes and just relaxed in quiet for a few minutes. Charlie wondered if his lieutenant was finished with his war stories for the night, but after a slight pause, Lt. A. began speaking again.

"I'll never forget my very first aided case that I handled by myself. I had just finished eating and was walking my post on the platform of the BMT line at Rector Street. In the weeks that I had been assigned to the 1st I had found a little Greek coffee shop above ground right at Rector Street and Broadway. I made friends with the night crew there because I spent my meal hour bullshitting with them. They liked my company as well as the extra coverage I provided, so naturally I didn't have to pay for my egg sandwiches and coffee that were the best I had ever tasted.

"I decided to check the bathroom at the northern end of the station just to get it over with and as I approached the toilet I heard faint moans coming from inside the facility. I thought I was going to catch two queers doing their thing with the one-eyed worm but when I opened the door I saw a body sprawled on the urine soaked floor roughly half way inside one of cubicles that had no door.

"Before I could even get to the guy, he stopped moaning and with a final gasp for air, he seemed to stop breathing completely. His pants and underpants had been pulled down below his knees. His scrotum and groin area were smeared with blood, as well as his face and mouth. Several of his teeth had been completely knocked out of his mouth and were lying next to him in a separate puddle of yellow piss mixed with blood. I also noticed blood underneath him but didn't know where it was coming from. I turned him over and saw right away that its source was directly out of his ass. There was an empty, cardboard toilet paper roll core extending from his bleeding anus.

"I ran out of the room and went over to the token booth where the clerk was stationed. I had to rap on the window with my night-stick because he had fallen asleep, which was not unusual for many of those underpaid clerks. I told him to call an ambulance for what I had found then ran back to the toilet. Thankfully, the victim had begun to breathe on his own but was still unconscious.

"I tried to revive him by talking to him. When that didn't work I grabbed some used paper towels and soaked them with water from the standing urinals. At least the water was cold. I applied the wet towel to his mouth in an attempt to stop the bleeding from his jaws. I tried to stay calm and remember what I had been taught at the academy. I knew I had an aided case but I also knew that this guy didn't slip on a fucking bar of soap. I had a crime victim and a crime scene. He had been assaulted and was likely to die, so I knew I had to preserve the scene at all costs.

"Charlie, I'm sure I don't have to tell you I was scared shitless. All I knew was that it was my totally awesome, fucking responsibility not only to tend to this bloodied mess of a victim, but also somehow guard this scene by myself. I knew I had to keep the restroom free of outside contamination from anyone who might come strolling in, especially the nosy, busybody news hounds.

"I remembered that I also had to make the required notifications to the patrol sergeant who would probably arrive first, then I would have to notify the precinct detective unit. I suddenly remembered I hadn't directed the clerk to call the precinct so I ran all the way back to tell him to do so. When I got there and saw the clerk, he explained to me that, thankfully, he had already called the precinct for me. He said he was told to tell me not to let anyone enter the bathroom until the sergeant arrived, which I already knew.

"I realized that the clerk was probably an old timer and had seen his share of life in the sewer. I ran all the way back to the toilet. Luckily, no one else was there. As for the victim, he was still out cold but still breathing. The blood around him had started to congeal and it looked as if he had stopped bleeding. Soon I heard the sound of footsteps and when I looked up I saw one of the 1st precinct sergeants approaching with his driver. The sergeant was an old timer and, according to scuttlebutt, was a real prince of a boss. His name was Sgt. Burdick. He spoke to me first," Lt. A. said as his eyes glazed with the memory.

"Charlie I was so nervous. I didn't want to come across like a rookie, which of course I was, but rather like a veteran, a hair bag."

"Whatta you got, kid?"_Sgt. Burdick said nonchalantly.

"I think I have an assault, Sergeant," I tried to say as calmly as possible.

Burdick's driver spoke up, laughing, "You think you have an assault, kid? This ain't no fucking dentist office. This is a fucking shit hole! For Christ's sake, the guy's teeth are scattered all over God's creation and you think you have an assault? Maybe the fucking tooth fairy visited him while he was taking a dump, right?" The driver stared at me, his voice mocking.

"Leave the kid alone," interjected the Sergeant.

"It seems the Sergeant was a prince after all, Charlie. He told me to make out the aided card as well as the complaint report, which I later found out is referred to as the '61.' He told me to refer it to the 1st precinct detective unit under the heading of Investigate Aided, then he instructed me to list the victim as a John Doe so the news media would not get his name later on at the station house," said the lieutenant. "When I asked him why we had to list the victim this way, he gave me an earful of an answer."

"Kid, did you notice the toilet paper core stuck up his ass?"_asked the Sergeant.

"Yeah, Sarge. Why?"

"If his attacker really wanted to hurt him he would have shoved a broomstick up his ass instead. This was a sex act gone wrong that turned ugly and violent. I'll lay two to one odds that when they get him to Beekman Downtown Hospital, they'll find the remains of a hamster or gerbil in the guy's rectum, or some kind of proof that one of those little creatures had been there paying a visit very recently. It's the latest fad for these fucking queers and one of the newest ways they get each other off," explained the Sergeant.

"Charlie, this guy was a great boss. He explained to me that he was going into the station house and said he would let the desk lieutenant know what I had and say I would be coming in with my paperwork.

He also explained that he would direct the 124 man to make all the required notifications for me as well. I thanked him and off he went," said Lt. A.

"The ambulance arrived and I assisted the attendants with getting the victim onto the gurney and into the awaiting vehicle, then it roared away with its red lights flashing and siren blaring. I walked over to the coffee shop and got two regulars to go then made my way back down to the platform and offered the clerk one of the coffees. He was grateful and invited me into the booth to sit and relax for a while. After some friendly chitchat, I finished my paperwork.

"Around 3:30 A.M. I decided to take a slow walk back to the precinct. The night air was cool and refreshing. It was quite a change from the stale metallic atmosphere of the subway system, especially since I still had the aroma of blood and urine still entrenched deep within my nostrils. I stopped and inhaled deeply as I tried to cleanse my nose and lungs of the putrid smell that was becoming part of my very being. As I did so, I looked up at the twinkling stars and felt good, Charlie. I had effectively handled and preserved a crime scene, my first, and communicated with my patrol sergeant, who found no fault with my police work. Better than that, though, I had helped a fellow human being. I was on top of the world in this, our chosen profession."

The lieutenant smiled proudly.

There would be bad days ahead and the lieutenant knew it, but on that historic night in his life, so very long ago, he was proud to be one of New York's finest.

CHAPTER THIRTEEN

*M*y walk back to the barn only took about ten minutes. I entered and saluted the desk then walked over to the 124 man's room and gave him all the paperwork I had completed. The 124 man assured me that he would take care of everything for me, so I thanked him and walked over to the desk area where the return roll call sign out sheet was kept. I signed out and walked up the two flights of stairs to my locker room, locating the metal coat hanger which was used to open the door at off hours. There was no handle or knob on the door but it could be locked from the inside. When it was, the coat hanger was the only way it could be opened short of kicking it off its hinges.

I was careful not to make any noise because I knew there would be cops sleeping in the dorms directly across from the locker room.

"You see, Charlie, in those days all of the precincts maintained dorms for cops who made arrests on the 4X12 tour or even late on the 8X4 tour. Those guys were required to be back in court at 8:00 A.M. and some of them lived in Nassau and Suffolk counties. Some even lived upstate in Orange County. They could never make the drive home and be expected to make the drive back and be on time the next day. The dorms were maintained by the PBA police widows fund and staffed by women who had lost sons, husbands or brothers in the line of duty. The linens were changed weekly."

I started to fool around with the wire hangar when the door opened suddenly. It was Willie who had heard me and opened it. He and Bruce had been in for a while and already were dressed in civvies. Willie noticed I was beaming and I explained my night for them both, then we rode home in Willie's VW Beetle and swapped war stories as if we were old hair bags."

Lt. A. smiled at this.

"You know, Charlie, I told you before that it was a requirement to affix your name and squad number on the outside of your locker. I can honestly say that I never saw or experienced firsthand anyone from headquarters opening anyone's locker because of wrongdoing, although we did have an officer who died in the line of duty and his locker had to be opened to give any personals to his family.

"My initial tours in the 120th were fairly good," said Lt. A with a nod of satisfaction.

He then explained how he had walked foot posts quite a bit but was glad to be outdoors considering he had walked those subway platforms for almost three months while assigned to the 1st precinct. Because he was assigned as a footman in the 2nd squad, he became a fill-in for the regular sector car teams and rode in a car if the regular guy was out sick or on vacation. He liked it that way because he got to learn the entire layout of the precinct and the sector boundaries.

Winter came and he found himself riding more. He now had almost three years on the job and was liked by his peers as well as the station house brass.

One night he was scheduled to work a midnight tour in sector Q as in queen which covered the Clove Lakes section of the precinct. It was also an early car, which meant it turned out thirty minutes earlier than the actual 12:00 A.M. cars. This assured that there were some cars available to handle assignments while the 4X12 sectors were heading back to the barn for end of shift.

John turned out at 11:30 P.M. and waited for his vehicle, sector Q, to pull up in front of the precinct, its usual relieving point. The car was late getting in, so late in fact that the 12:00 A.M. cars had turned out and already left for patrol. He found himself alone waiting for his sector car to show up.

At approximately 12:45 A.M. he saw a radio car headed his way on the Terrace coming from the direction of Jersey Street. The police cruiser had only one headlight operating and when it pulled up in front of the station house, John walked down the steps to relieve the operator. He did not recognize the officer behind the wheel which was understandable because sixty new men had recently been transferred into the precinct. Working in a 20-squad duty chart meant it was entirely possible that you never worked with many of the men.

The operator got out and spoke.

"You have some damage on the right side of the car," he mumbled.

"What do you mean, 'damage'?" John asked.

Instead of answering, the driver walked up the steps and disappeared into the vestibule of the precinct. John surveyed the damage and noticed a dent in the right front fender. He knew it was not unusual for vehicles with slight damage to be used for patrol as long as it had been reported and was scheduled for an appointment at the police repair shop in the borough.

He took his place behind the wheel of the vehicle and shoved his night stick down into the seat, then tossed his memo book up onto the dash. He placed his cigarettes up over the visor, lighting the one he had removed. He decided he would need a cup of java soon because he was tired and cold. He started the engine and put the vehicle in drive then pulled away from the curb. As he drove, the car seemed fine on the straight away but as soon as he made an attempt to negotiate a right turn, he heard a loud screeching sound and felt the car shaking. He realized that the fender was rubbing into the tire and he could not safely operate the vehicle so he decided to pull over and made some entries in his memo book. He wrote down the time that the 4X12 operator pulled up in front of the house and described the damage to the car as well as what the cop had said to him, word for word.

That having been accomplished, he heard a transmission from Central Dispatching being broadcast over the police radio.

"All 120th early units, ten-two your command. Repeat, all 120th early units, report back to your command!"

Following orders he headed back to the precinct with the thought of quickly getting another replacement vehicle so he could get back out and make a collar early which would result in some overtime.

When he got back to the house, he saw roughly ten squad cars parked and idling in front of the precinct. The next thing he saw was all kinds of brass standing outside on the front sidewalk freezing their butts off.

"What the fuck is going on?"_he mumbled to himself as he made his approach.

As he negotiated the car into a parking spot at the curb, he could hear the bare metal of the fender screeching against the tire.

"Here it is," said a Sergeant to a Lieutenant.

John got out of the car but before he could open his mouth, the Lieutenant began to ream his ass like a John Deere harvester.

"Get in the fucking station house and throw your shield on the fucking desk! You're on your way out of this fucking job, kid!" screamed the Lieutenant.

John did not say a word but went into the station house as he was ordered. Another Lieutenant was sitting behind the desk and several sergeants were standing behind him. As he stood in front of the desk, the Lieutenant seated behind it looked up and asked him what he wanted.

"The boss outside said I should come in to see you," John replied very quietly.

"You must be the kid with the damaged car, huh?" asked the Lieutenant.

"I guess so," John answered.

"Go sit in the back room, kid. The Duty Captain is on his way in," ordered the Lieutenant.

John went into the back room, found a chair and sat down. He could feel the dread rising in his stomach, subduing him. He removed his hat but decided to keep on his winter blouse because the Captain would soon be arriving. He now realized that everyone thought he was the driver who caused the dent in the RMP. He was surprised to see so many bosses getting involved in such little damage. As he sat there he had a sudden urge to use the men's room but decided against it. He didn't want to miss the Duty Captain and before long, an old timer approached him.

"What's the matter kid? Can't take it?" asked the veteran.

The vet's name was Joe Nunzio. He had about twenty-two years on the job and was considered a lifer. He was also the broom in the precinct – a teat detail that was usually reserved for old timers or anyone that wanted to get off the streets.

"Who are you?" John asked warily. At that moment he felt as if he could not and should not trust anyone.

"Just call me Joe, kid. I'm in your squad. How the hell did you fuck up that car?"_the veteran asked, never at a loss for words, especially when it came to the F word.

"I didn't damage it. I got it that way from the 4X12 cop," John answered.

Joe stared at him incredulously.

"Holy fucking shit. Every fucking boss in this precinct is going around thinking that you did this!"

Joe told him to sit tight while he went out to the desk and explained what had happened to the Lieutenant. A few minutes later the desk lieutenant as well as the lieutenant who was outside walked into the back room.

"Look kid, I'm sorry I screamed at you outside. I thought that you were the 4X12 operator," said the first lieutenant.

John was instantly relieved that they now realized he wasn't the responsible party. He was also advised that an RMP, his RMP, left the scene of an accident after striking a private vehicle, leaving the RMP's hubcap at the scene. He might as well have left his fucking name and phone number. Eyewitness accounts also saw a police officer exit a bar in full uniform and enter a police cruiser. One of the eyewitnesses had the brains and foresight to jot down the RMP number, which was 1215. It was the same car that John had entered at the relieving point.

The Lieutenant told John that the duty captain was now present in the command and had already called the home of the 4X12 officer and ordered him to return back to work for an interrogation. The lieutenant was honest with him, saying John was not out of the woods yet then wanted to know why John had not come back into the station house to report the damage. He also asked if John knew the 4X12 officer. John responded by saying he had assumed that the vehicle had been given a green light for patrol and he would have never guessed in a million years that the damage had just had happened.

"Lieutenant, as far as the officer goes, I have never seen him before tonight," John said.

The boss knew it was entirely possible. There had been a mass transfer into the 120th recently, and he had not even met all the new men yet.

"I have memo entries concerning this incident," John offered.

"You do?"

Lou handed the Lieutenant his memo book after flipping to the page with the information about the damage which he had written just hours earlier. The boss read it silently.

"Well, I guess if you were trying to cover something up, you would never have written this," said the Lieutenant.

John felt very much relieved after hearing what the Lieutenant had to say, and after a moment the Lieutenant told him to sit down again, explaining he would get to John after he finished interviewing the civilian witnesses as well as the 4X12 officer who was responding from home. The Lieutenant walked back to his desk and Joe walked back to where John was now sitting.

"How about a cup of coffee, kid?"_asked Joe.

John said he would rather wait until the Duty Captain was finished with him and looked at his watch. It was 12:50 A.M. It didn't take him long to realize he should have taken Joe up on his offer.

At 2:30 A.M., Joe walked in and told John that the Duty Captain was going to Saint's Vincent's emergency room to interview the 4X12 cop who had been ordered back into work. The cop had received the message to respond back to the precinct but had gotten into another accident on his way in. He struck a utility pole and was taken by ambulance to the hospital.

When the duty captain heard this, he became enraged! Now the department would not be able to administer any breathalyzer test because of any medications the doctors might have given the cop.

Before he knew it, it was 6:15 A.M. and the day tour crew was beginning to come in for work. These men were wide awake and ready to take on the day while John could barely keep his head from bouncing off of his chest.

"Audenino, report to the Captain's office, forthwith," blared the overhead loudspeaker.

John buttoned up his winter jacket and placed his hat squarely on his head then walked over to the shoe shine machine and gave his shoes a quick buffing. This machine, unlike the one in the 1st precinct, had polish and worked well. When that was done, he made his way out to the desk area and the Lieutenant pointed to the Captain's office, making a motion with his fist as if he were telling John to knock. Standing before the door, John knocked twice and heard the Captain voice, telling him to enter.

John suddenly remembered one of his first lessons he'd learned while in the police academy. When you walk into the Captain's office, you remove your hat and stand at attention. The police department was, after all, a semi-military organization.

"Sit down, Audenino. Get comfortable," said Captain Levin, a thirty-year veteran of the department and was said to be a pencil

111

pusher. It was also said that he did not know how to deal with people but he did know the book backwards and forwards.

John knew that the Captain had been awake just as long as he had, but the Captain showed no signs of weariness. He was impeccably dressed and every silver-gray hair on his head was in place. His white shirt was starched and looked as if he had just put it on and his captain's bars shone in their epaulets upon his shoulders. He wore a pair of horn rimmed eyeglasses that made him look more like an accountant than a police captain.

"I've spoken to all the civilian witnesses who were willing to come forward, as well as Police Officer Cooke in the hospital," said the Captain.

John had not even known the 4X12 cop's name until now.

"I also spoke to our lieutenants here in the precinct and I know you were not the one who operated the vehicle or caused the damage. However, I want to be sure that there is no collusion or cover-up. Do you understand?"_

"Yes, Sir," replied John.

"Let me have your memo book," ordered Captain Levin.

John handed him the memo book and the Captain began making copies of John's entries. Then he sat down and began asking relatively easy questions about John's time on the force. The Captain wrote all of John's responses down into a notebook of his own then excused him. After John thanked the Captain, he walked out of the office, tending a salute.

"How did it go, kid?" asked Joe.

"Okay, I guess."

"Those entries you made in your fucking book saved your fucking ass, kid. You did good." Although it was a compliment, Joe's tone was serious.

John's first brush with the department's disciplinary process was enlightening. He learned that it paid to document your actions. The department could find fault with you for not being correct with some fact but they couldn't accuse you of a wrongful omission. It was a valuable lesson learned for the years ahead.

A few weeks later, John learned that Police Officer Cooke had been transferred out of the 120th and sent to the 4th precinct, which was adjacent to the Holland Tunnel on Canal Street in Manhattan. Surprisingly enough, Officer Cooke once again crashed his RMP while he was under the influence of booze, this time running into a private vehicle. The Police Commissioner terminated Officer Cooke after Cooke refused to admit he had a drinking problem. The Commissioner wanted to send him upstate to the farm to dry out but he flatly refused. As a result, he lost his job.

"So, Charlie, that's basically how I started out on the job and how I got to the 120th," Lt. A. said. "I wound up staying at the 120th for almost seventeen years before I made Sergeant and got shipped out to the 62nd precinct in Bensonhurst, Brooklyn."_

"I used to hear stories of how the bosses on the desk were years ago. I guess they're all true," said Charlie.

"Back then the Sergeant was your boss and the Lieutenant was the 'Captain_ of the ship.' The Commanding Officer's word was gospel and was untouchable. He came and went as he pleased and you rarely saw him unless he was inspecting your uniform or you really fucked up in spades.

"Today things are much different. The Patrol Sergeant is just another radio car answering calls with a little power and the Lieutenant is bogged down with so much shit and paperwork it's not funny. The Captain has so much more responsibility these days that he can't even handle because it's physically impossible. I mean the poor slob has to actually respond to RMP accidents. Talk about abuse of power," said Lt. A. mournfully.

"Lou, what happened after the incident with Captain Levin? It sounded as if he was fair," said Charlie.

"I don't know if he was fair. All I know is that my memo book saved my ass and your worst enemy out here is *you*. If you're not afraid of paperwork you'll get by, but if you shun it you're asking for all kinds of trouble. As long as you don't get lazy you will find you can probably cover your ass in most hairy situations."

Charlie made a mental note of what the lieutenant said and started to drive to the lieutenant's old sector in Stapleton. As they made their way through the streets of sector E-Eddie, he could see the lieutenant drifting away with his thoughts, but after a few moments of silence he suddenly started to speak again.

"You know, Charlie, after the incident with Captain Levin and Police Officer Cooke I kind of floated. I mean some days I walked a beat and others I rode in a sector, but most of the time I flew. Today I know you go on an occasional detail, whether it be a parade or demonstration, but when I was younger we had regular details that lasted for months at a time.

"The precinct sent one man alone on these flying details. I was the new kid on the block so I could count on my flying to other commands at least three times a week. It was no fun but I wouldn't trade it for all the tea in China. This is where I learned how to become a street cop."

Charlie was all ears because Lt. A. was about to embark on yet another one of his war stories, which Charlie never tired of hearing.

"Have you ever heard a man cry before? I mean, other than you. I cry sometimes so don't be ashamed to tell me that you do, too. What I'm talking about is hearing another man cry, which happened on one call I went on. I swear I had never seen or heard another human being cry so loud and hard. His sobs were so intense and thunderous that they literally shook his entire body.

"What happened?" Charlie asked.

"The guy's wife had informed him that she was going to leave him and take the kids," said Lt. A. as he stared out the window, and Charlie thought he saw a slight tear forming in the boss' eye.

"My partner Frank and I had nearly a total combination of thirty-three years of experience between us when we responded to that call. It came over as a dispute with a possible gun involved. I can honestly say today that I've frequently wished I had never responded to that one; I wish I had called out sick instead.

"It was in one of those two-story wooden frame houses on Victory Boulevard just up from Cebra Avenue, right near old Nick's barber shop. We knocked on the door and a woman immediately let us in. It was obvious that she had been crying. She told us that her husband could not stop drinking. It wasn't that he beat them when he was drunk. Instead, he spent all their money on that poison and had binges which lasted for days at a time.

"The wife told us she had finally mustered up enough courage to tell him she was leaving with the kids. I guess she hoped that her telling him would have knocked some sense into him and scare him into seeking some professional help," Lt. A. said wistfully as he took out yet another cigarette and drew heavily on it, inhaling the acrid smoke deep into his lungs. Charlie was used to his boss smoking as he told his war stories but he was worried about Lt. A. smoking too much.

"Frank and I wanted to know why she called us if her husband was a peaceful drunk, because by then she had already explained to us that he never hit her.

"She went on to tell us that she still loved him very much but was worried because he had gone down into their basement and she could hear him crying uncontrollably. She also informed us that before he really started to drink heavily he had been an avid hunter and probably still had his hunting rifles down in the basement.

"Frank and I looked at each other quietly mouthing the words, 'OH, NO!'"

"We immediately proceeded down the basement steps. Although the wife wanted to come with us, we convinced her to remain upstairs. Before we went down into the basement she asked us if we thought her husband would harm himself. We both asked her if this upcoming separation was a shock to him or if he knew it was coming. The wife told us she had just decided to tell him she was leaving but he should have expected it. As we descended the stairs, which were very narrow as well as steep, we called out his name so as not to surprise him."

"George, are you there?"_Frank called.
"I'm in the back," a male voice answered.
We both walked to the back of the cellar where a makeshift den had been created out of an old, worn, black and white TV and an ancient couch which was torn and ripped in many places. There were old newspapers scattered around everywhere as well as numerous empty bottles of vodka.

George was sitting in a worn out chair, crying. He had a bottle of Stolichnaya in his lap and a 30-gauge shotgun in his hands with his finger on the trigger. It was pointed directly at his chest. A string of Rosary beads had been strung around his head like a headache band.

Lt. A. inhaled deeply on his cigarette as he recounted his story.

"George, let's talk. Your wife loves you very much. She just wanted to put a little scare into you so you wouldn't drink all the money up. She wants you to get help because she loves you, man," I pleaded.

"He started sobbing and talking all at once, Charlie," the lieutenant said in a helpless voice, "and the blast that immediately followed scared us so much that we almost jumped out of our skins."

Lt. A. shook his head as if denying the memory then took another long drag on his cigarette before he continued.

"George lay slumped in his chair. The hole in the dead man's chest wasn't big at all but the hole in his back was several inches across. The blood quickly ran down his back and began forming a rapidly spreading puddle at our feet. His wife heard the explosion and started screaming as she ran down the stairs. She was quickly subdued by Frank and taken back upstairs, screaming and crying.

"Later on we found the slug, which had ripped through George's body, imbedded in a rear cellar beam."

The lieutenant attempted to wipe a tear from his eye as he began to describe his feelings about the suicide.

"Charlie, I still don't know to this day if I did the right thing. Maybe if I had just left him alone he might have fallen asleep and slept it off. Maybe he would have been able to come to some kind of terms with his wife and he still would be around."

The lieutenant blew his nose with an old Kleenex he found in the filthy glove compartment. As he did, Charlie wanted to say something to him but didn't know if it was his place to do so. He figured if this man was able to bare his soul and feelings in such an outpouring then perhaps he could, too.

"You know, Lou, you didn't pull the trigger. In your heart you really wanted to help that guy but he just wanted out of the picture at that time. If he had wanted to really see his wife, he would have gotten out of that chair and done it. You didn't kill him. It was his time.

"We, of all people, should know that. We're not fucking Gods, even though everyone expects us to be. We're just human beings like everyone else. We love and we want love. We hate and we are hated. We cry and we are cried for. So many of us carry around so much repressed guilt, all because we see so much shit every day of our lives. How many abused kids do we have to see before we break down ourselves? How many times do we have to go home to our kids after we've been called pigs all day? How many times do we have to be spat upon by ghetto kids and go home and take it out on our own families? We have to be super human robots, almost God-like, in order to do police work. Deviate once and make a mistake, even unintentionally, and society comes down on us like a ton of shit," said Charlie taking a deep breath and wondering what type of reaction he would glean from the lieutenant.

"Charlie, thank you," said the lieutenant softly. "Let me buy you a cup of coffee."

Charlie was curious and wanted to know what happened to George's wife but he figured tomorrow would be another day to get to the finale of that one. The lieutenant wanted to take a ride into the barn, which was the station house. Old timers on the job used terminology like that.

When they arrived at the precinct, the boss told Charlie to wait for him in the lounge, which was the basement. It had been remodeled in the early 1970's by members of the 120th precinct club. The dues provided for the lumber and the lighting while the sweat of some of the handier guys provided for the labor. There was an old couch down there as well as a pool table and cable TV. The guys had also bought an old refrigerator and microwave oven, which the entire station house used.

On the midnight tours the guys just chilled out and rested for the hour that was theirs and guys came and went all night. It gave them a place to take a break from patrol.

The lieutenant said he had some administrative work to complete and told Charlie to relax and that he would call him if he needed him. That was one of the perks of being a boss' driver. You could chill out and do it legally.

The lieutenant spent about forty five minutes on his paperwork then radioed Charlie to meet him at the RMP. When they got outside, the lieutenant reminded him to use his name if he ever got caught down there by another boss. Charlie escaped some heavy rips for doing just that. The lieutenant always said that no driver of his would ever get a complaint for driving him.

Charlie learned later on that Lt. A. had never received a complaint from any of his supervisors. He also learned that, as a boss, Lt. A. had never given a cop a complaint and he never would. He was a prince.

The two men resumed patrol and, for the most part, it was a quiet night.

Charlie couldn't help but think of Terry again and made up his mind to stop at the coffee shop later. He wanted to ask her if it was okay if could stop over in the morning to see her. Charlie drove past the Dunkin Donuts and saw Terry's car parked in the parking lot. He asked the boss if he wanted anything and then he went in. Terry saw Charlie immediately and walked right over to him. She knew enough to be discreet so she didn't kiss him or let on to anyone that she was his girlfriend. Charlie placed his order and when she came back with the coffee he softly mouthed the words, "Is tomorrow morning okay?"

Terry flashed a huge, sexy smile and nodded yes while sticking her tongue out and licking her lips as if to say, "I want to eat you up."

Charlie said goodnight and went back outside to the RMP.

The lieutenant said he wanted to drink his coffee down by the water so Charlie drove down to the end of Hylan Boulevard adjacent to Penny Beach, next to the Alice Austen House. He parked the car and both men took out their coffee and donuts and silently sat. It was fairly early and quiet for that time which meant that the remainder of the tour would also be fairly quiet.

It was the perfect time and place for the lieutenant to reminisce about coming to the 120th, and he did just that.

"When I came to this precinct I thought I would be a footman forever. I mean look what happened to me with that drunken cop who wrecked the radio car and handed it over to me. I was in the 2nd squad and I was the only footman in that squad. There was Joe Nunzio, who was the broom, but he never went out on patrol anymore. There was Police Officer Ettinger, who was out on long term disability and would probably get a three quarters pension and never come back. Then there was Police Officer Brownell and Police Officer Smull in sector Eddie as well as Police Officer Catalano and Police Officer Folder in sector Charlie. Out of all of them, I was the new kid on the block," Lt. A. explained.

Back then the lieutenant wasn't a rookie but he *was* the only footman in the squad which meant that he got all the details and dirty assignments. Whenever there was a prisoner to guard in one of the three hospitals the 120th covered, he got it. The 120th covered

Saint Vincent's Hospital on Bard Avenue, Staten Island Hospital on Castleton Avenue and Marine Hospital, which was the official United States Public Health service hospital, located on Vanderbilt Avenue.

Whenever there was a DOA to sit with, John also got it. Police procedures called for a police officer to remain with a DOA if the person died in the residence. The body was usually released to either a funeral home representative or to the medical examiner's office. Either way, one UF 95 tag (also known as a DOA tag) remained with the deceased while a second, duplicate tag, went back to the station house with the police officer along with the paperwork concerning the death.

All those various assignments made time go by, but John now knew what he wanted – a permanent assignment in a sector car. He wanted a seat. That's not to say that some of those details weren't interesting. Some were even fun sometimes. He was often sent to other commands while assigned to the 120th. He came from the "flying 1st,"_ so he was used to it by now.

One night John found himself 'flying' up to the 16th precinct in Times Square. He was assigned to a deputy inspector for the entire tour and all he had to do was carry the portable radio for the D.I.

The inspector was assigned to a detail to guard Raquel Welch at one of her movie premiers. That was a fun night and John even got to have a photo taken with Ms. Welch, although most of his other details weren't like that.

"Charlie, have you ever gone to a full-fledged riot while on the job?"_asked Lt. A.

"Can't say as I have, Lou."

"Well, my first one was in Brooklyn," Lt. A. explained. "I had been assigned to a detail in East New York and found myself at a rally at Fulton Avenue and Nostrand Avenue where a group of white racists were protesting New York City's willingness to fork over welfare money to any and all blacks who got off the bus barefoot and broke from the south. The group was called SPONGE, an acronym for the Society for the Prevention of Negroes Getting Everything. There were about one hundred of them marching in a circle with placards and banners. The white group was surrounded by a larger group of white cops who were then surrounded by a larger group of angry blacks.

"The Mayor at that time, John Lindsey, became aware of the demonstration and for some unknown reason decided to come to Brooklyn and visit during this tiny event. Mayor Lindsey foolishly decided to walk directly into the middle of the chanting demonstrators and began, unfortunately, shaking their hands.

"The first bottle flung from a nearby roof missed its designated target and struck a little black girl on the perimeter of the circle of whites. Almost immediately the word began to spread that a white cop had clubbed the little girl. The Mayor, who had started the whole thing, was whisked out of there quickly by a phalanx of plainclothes cops and it didn't take long before other bottles and debris of all shapes and sizes began to rain down on those remaining.

"The order to clear the streets was given out by a Captain using a bull horn; that's when all hell broke loose. Some of the Negroes grabbed a few of the demonstrators and began to beat and stomp them. Not surprisingly, the small and meager force of cops on hand was not enough to restore order.

"The bosses called a 10-13, assist patrolman, and soon radio cars began arriving from other nearby precincts and commands with their turret lights glaring and their sirens blasting. The chaos in the streets was cleared up quickly but reports of sporadic gun fire began popping up over the airwaves of the busy police frequency.

"I was assigned to a sergeant with five other police officers and we were sent to a nearby street corner to keep people indoors and out of harm's way. I was dog tired. My shift had begun that day at 4:00 P.M. and now it was almost 2:00 A.M. I hadn't even had a cup of coffee yet, and you know how I love my coffee!" said the lieutenant, laughing a little.

Charlie listened attentively. He had never been part of a real riot and only knew what he had been told by other cops or read in the papers. He nodded as the boss began to describe what happened the rest of the night.

"I was standing next to a sergeant from the 88th precinct in Brooklyn North when all of a sudden a shot rang out from somewhere above us. The sergeant quickly went down with a cry of pain; he had been shot in his right leg and the blood was gushing heavily. I grabbed his portable radio and called for an ambulance to respond forthwith and called in another 10-13 of shots fired at officers. At the same time, one of the other officers used a belt as a makeshift tourniquet by placing it on the sergeant's leg.

"Within ten seconds, an RMP screeched to a halt right in front of us, practically mounting the litter-filled sidewalk. Two huge cops got out and lifted the injured officer into the back of the car then they sped off with lights flashing and sirens blaring."

The lieutenant explained how he had been left on the corner with five other cops, none of whom was a supervisor. Within five minutes they all heard another shot ring out but this one was much louder. They all looked down the block and saw a huge black man running in their direction. He had what appeared to be a shotgun and it was pointed directly at them. Lt. A. described how he dove behind a parked car and attempted to get his revolver out of his holster. By the time he was able to draw his weapon, the other guys had blown the bear of a man away.

All John heard was the *pop pop pop* of 38's letting lose, and when he got up out of the gutter all he saw was the man lying on the sidewalk several car lengths away, the shotgun still in his hands. He had been shot repeatedly in the chest and was bleeding profusely. With multiple holes in him everywhere he looked like a piece of Swiss Cheese.

The next thing John heard was the wail of police sirens everywhere.

Sporadic shootings were being reported within the entire precinct as well as reports of large scale looting. The information reached the Police Commissioner who deemed the incident as an official riot, which brought massive manpower and equipment into the precinct.

The black shooter was taken to Woodhull Hospital by an RMP which had been designated as the trauma hospital for the entire incident.

Detectives as well as Emergency Service Unit cops, also known as ESU officers, stormed the shooter's apartment and came up with an arsenal of weapons and ammo. John then spent the remainder of the night on the same corner and was finally relieved at 8:00 A.M. after having spent sixteen hours of riot duty on his feet.

Lt. A. finished telling Charlie about his first experience of riot duty at 6:00 A.M. Although he was getting tired, the lieutenant now needed to go in and relieve the desk sergeant who had to leave earlier than usual. Charlie was glad because it meant that he could get a head start changing into his civilian clothes then visiting Terry. He drove back to the barn and the lieutenant took his place behind the giant wooden desk to begin the monotonous paperwork that all desk officers dread.

Charlie went upstairs to his locker and changed out of his uniform, deciding to hang out in the locker room, out of harm's way, until the end of his shift at 8:00 A.M. Before he knew it, his shift was over. He went back downstairs and signed out on the return roll call then got into his car and drove over to a phone booth, one he knew worked, on Victory Boulevard. First, he had to call Terry to make sure that everything was still on then he had to think of an excuse to tell Annette. The call to Terry went smooth and she said she was anxious to see him.

The call to Annette wasn't as easy. His wife told him she had decided to stay home from work and prepare him a big breakfast. Afterwards she said she would tuck him in, which meant that she wanted to make love.

Charlie was at a loss. He didn't know what to do.

He didn't want to call Terry and change their plans but yet he was beginning to be consumed by guilt again. His stomach was in knots and he began sweating.

He told Annette he had made a collar and had to appear in criminal court but felt that she hadn't bought his excuse. The last time he lied about making an arrest, he noticed Annette deliberately looked in the paper for any article indicating that Charlie had made a collar. She hadn't found anything.

Charlie got off the phone with Annette and swore to himself that this would be the absolute last time he was going to see Terry. He knew he had to end the affair.

He drove out to Terry's house and knocked on the door. She answered wearing black high heeled shoes with a black, French lace bra and garter belt with black silk stockings and no panties. She had so much makeup on that she almost looked like a street hustler. She was absolutely, fucking gorgeous.

"Hi, Charlie," she purred in a low, sultry voice. "I've been waiting for you."

He entered the house and couldn't take his eyes off of her. All he could think of was fucking the shit out of her. She led him directly into the bedroom, which was again lit only by candles. The dresser, with its huge mirror, had been moved closer to the bed. It was obvious that Terry had moved it because all of her cosmetics and jewelry boxes had been placed elsewhere.

"What's with the dresser?"_he asked.

"Oh, Charlie. Don't you want to watch when you make love to me? I know you like to watch when I go down on you. Now you can watch as we do everything," Terry cooed, ever so softly.

She quickly climbed onto the bed, pausing to pull down the bed spread. Her breathing was heavy as she looked up at Charlie, her breasts larger than ever. As she watched Charlie undress, she began to finger herself.

"Oh, Charlie, hurry! I need you so much," she said as she began to rub her clitoris faster and faster.

Charlie undressed as fast as possible, almost tripping when he removed his shorts. He exposed his penis, which was dripping wet with his fluids, and Terry quickly reached over and grabbed him hard, pulling him onto the bed. She did not kiss him or say any words of endearment. Instead, she roughly grabbed his cock and plunged it deep into her open mouth, engulfing his entire shaft. She began moaning, quietly at first, but soon she was emitting grunts so loud that she sounded like a bull elephant in heat. Charlie was lying on the pillow with his head back trying to hold back his impending explosion. He wanted to prolong this pure animal lust that Terry was displaying. He had never seen her filled with so much lust and need.

He decided to look up into the dresser mirror, but before he could even turn his head, she had swung her legs over him and straddled herself into a sixty nine position, exposing her vagina to his waiting mouth and tongue. He couldn't resist this gift of pure flesh being offered for his physical pleasure. He grabbed her cheeks and spread them wider, exposing all of her, and she began to moan even louder when he inserted his tongue into all of her openings. He couldn't hold back anymore and inserted his tongue deep into her anus, which drove her completely crazy. She began screaming that she was going to come so Charlie decided to let it all go and they came at the same time. He thought he was going to choke her with his huge ejaculation but she swallowed every drop and even licked his shaft clean. Afterward, he was entirely spent but knew he would recover in a few minutes for another round of whatever it was she might have in store for him.

Terry got up and walked over to her nightstand where she grabbed a tissue. She then made her way into the hallway bathroom. Charlie lit up a cigarette and waited for her to come out. When she did, she was completely nude. She had removed all the sexy lingerie she had been wearing earlier.

"Why did you take off all those sexy clothes?" he asked with a pout.

"Oh, baby, they were for me to get in a crazy mood. Didn't you enjoy it?"_

Charlie had no idea what she meant.

"First she puts on clothes to turn me on, then she takes them off," he thought, keeping the words to himself.

He was soon ready to go again but wasn't sure of what was happening. It didn't take long for Terry to notice the puzzled look on his face.

"What's the matter, honey? Don't you want to fuck me hard now? I know how much you like me to go down on you and how much you like to go down on me, but I really just want and need you inside me. Okay, Sweetheart?" she asked.

"It's just that I've never seen you like this," he responded.

"Oh, baby. You're just not used to a sexy, aggressive woman. I know what I want and I want it from you. Nothing has changed between us. I just choose not to lie there and be passive. Sometimes I like to take charge and get it when I need it. Okay?"_

He didn't know how to respond but it didn't make much of a difference. Before he knew it, Terry pushed him back onto the bed and smothered his mouth with deep wet kisses, almost sucking his tongue out of his head. It was almost as if she was telling him to shut up. She knew how to seduce a man and get what it was she needed. He got hard again but his mind was angry and reluctant even though his flesh was eager and willing. They finished making love and didn't speak much when it was over. Charlie made some small talk and then showered. He told Terry that he had to leave even though he could have stayed several hours more. He had spent only three hours with her but he sure was tired. She had drained him physically as well as emotionally.

CHAPTER FOURTEEN

W hen he arrived home it was almost 11:45 A.M. Annette was in their den when he walked in the door and he explained that the court arraignment had taken place faster than usual. She was surprised to see him but also had a look of relief on her face. Had she thought he would have spent the entire day with another woman? Arriving home early on Charlie's part probably put a damper on her thinking.

"Hi, honey. Did you have a good night?"_she asked.

"Pretty good. I made a family dispute collar so all I had to do was the paperwork with the Assistant District Attorney. I didn't even have to appear in the court room," he lied.

Annette gave him a peck on the cheek and Charlie excused himself saying he wanted to hit the sack. He really must have been tired because he slept from around noon until Annette gently roused him from his sleep at 8:00 P.M. She knew her husband didn't like to sleep beyond that time. He got up, had a light snack then showered and shaved and left for work.

When he got to the station he found a folded piece of paper in his mail slot in the sitting room which had probably been placed there by the T.S operator. He opened it quickly and found it was from Terry. She simply said, "Forgive me." He was a little upset that she had left a message so personal with the T.S operator but he also knew that the switchboard operators were the most discreet police officers anywhere.

Now he didn't know what to think. He thought he had wanted to end this affair but had Terry really meant what she wrote? Could she have surmised that Charlie had been taken back by her aggressiveness?

Could she even have assumed that Charlie had been considering ending his affair with her? Was this note the truth or was it some kind of female trickery to bend and warp his mind? Was she a Mata Hari or just a normal woman with a kid who was vulnerable and looking for love?

Charlie didn't know what to think but, more importantly, he didn't know what to do. He decided just to rid his mind of it for now and dress for work. As he did, he found himself hoping the night would be busy or that the lieutenant would have more stories to tell.

He stood roll call and soon discovered that the lieutenant had to go out immediately. There had been a hostage situation in sector K during the 4X12 tour and the lieutenant had to relieve the Platoon Commander, who was still at the scene and tying up loose ends, but who also had to get back to the station house to make his report. Those loose ends sometimes took hours, especially when the Hostage Negotiating Team had been called in.

The lieutenant and Charlie drove over to an apartment building on Bard Avenue. When they arrived they found the hostage team already on the scene and making good progress. Lt. A. conferred with the 4X12 ESU Sergeant and returned back to Charlie, who was waiting in the RMP.

"Well, hopefully this will be wrapped up within an hour or so. Why don't you go and get us some coffee? Also, if you could, get me two packs of my cigarettes," said Lt. A.

The boss explained that they were dealing with an emotionally disturbed patient who apparently had stopped taking his medication and had his mother locked up with him in his room. There had been no weapons involved so it looked as if it would be over in an hour or two.

Charlie left the Lieutenant with some of the guys from Truck 1 of the ESU unit. The Lieutenant had worked with some of them, including the ESU Sergeant before the Sergeant had been promoted to ESU, so he knew he didn't have to worry about Lt. A. while he was there. He had been on the job long enough and practically knew someone in every command in Staten Island, downtown Manhattan and most details in headquarters.

The donut shop on Victory Boulevard was only a hop, skip and a jump from Bard Avenue and Charlie made it there in less than five minutes. He parked the RMP directly in front of the shop and entered.

Terry was busy serving a customer so he waited patiently until she was finished. When she was, she walked over to Charlie with a serious look on her face and not a smile. It was almost as if she knew she had done something wrong.

Charlie silently handed her the note. He waited for her to say something but she did not. Finally he spoke and asked what the note meant. He knew it was neither the time nor the place for such a question, but he had to get it off of his chest and let Terry know that it bothered him. She read the note, acknowledging her own words, and meekly smiled at him while remaining silent.

"Look, I know we really can't speak here but we are going to have to talk, unless you tell me now that you don't want to see me anymore," he said quietly.

"Charlie, whatever gave you that idea? You know how I feel about you. Can't you stop by tomorrow morning? I promise you that we will just talk and straighten this out, okay?" she asked.

He agreed and explained that he had to get back to the hostage scene but promised he would come by early.

He knew he wasn't going to lie about a fake collar to Annette this time. He would use the hostage scene as an excuse because it would make the local paper for sure. He drove back to the scene but stopped at a local Bodega for the Lieutenant's cigarettes.

When he arrived back at the scene on Bard Avenue he joined the Lieutenant, who was bullshitting with the men from the ESU squad. They had successfully removed the mother and the emotionally disturbed son without harm to either one.

CHAPTER FIFTEEN

The next time he checked his watch, it was only 2:00 A.M. and they had six hours of the tour left. Charlie didn't want to start thinking about Terry so he asked the Lieutenant about his time in the 120th.

"Lou, how long did it take you to get a steady seat in a sector after you came to the 120th?"_

"Well, I told you I was a footman in the 2nd squad and that I wanted a steady seat and partner more than anything," said the boss.

Charlie nodded his head affirmatively as the boss began to tell him how he got his first sector assignment.

"I wanted a seat so bad I could taste it. I actually had dreams about being a cop in a radio car. Those were the days of Adam Twelve with Martin Milner. You're probably too young to remember it, but it was a show about two good cops on patrol in Los Angeles. Their car number was Adam Twelve. I watched it every week and yearned to be one of them. George Maharis played his partner and they got into some hairy situations but always managed to get out of them unscathed. Then again, this *was* television," explained the Lieutenant with a smile.

John had been in the 1st precinct for almost two years before he was transferred to the 120th. He had been in the 120th about the same amount of time when he decided it was his turn to get a seat. He was tired of filling in as a utility man wherever he was needed and he realized he had to get his summons and arrest activity up. This was when he decided to get to know the roll call man.

The position of roll call man was like God in the precinct of years ago. When John was in the 120th, the roll call man was Tom Holley.

Tom was a tough cop who had done his time in the street. As the roll call man, he decided who walked, who flew to details and who got the seats in the sectors.

Years before, Tom had been jumped by three perpetrators while walking his post on Richmond Avenue down by Richmond Terrace. Tom shot one of them, killing him instantly, and although the other two ran from the scene, they were later apprehended and arrested. Not long afterward, one was found hanging in his cell on Riker's Island, a correctional facility, while the other died when he either tripped or stumbled down a stairway in the Court House on Schermerhorn Street in Brooklyn. It never did pay to hurt a cop.

John knew that staying friendly with his roll call man meant more than saying hello and goodbye. He always made it a habit of bringing Tom and his assistants a piece of cake or a dozen donuts if he was working day tours, and he also tried to get into the precinct around lunch time so he could deliver a six pack of Schlitz beer to Tom. When he did this, John would never make an issue of it. He would simply walk into the office, deposit the six pack into the refrigerator, and walk out without saying a word. They knew he was there but it was an unwritten law not to flaunt gifts.

Sometimes John got a foot post with a vegetable stand. When he did, he would bring in all the makings of a nice salad, which the crew went wild over. Other times John would stop at Kipp's Bakery on Victory Boulevard and pick up a loaf of French bread or pumpernickel to go with the salad.

The only time a seat opened up was when the cop who held it died, was transferred, retired or got promoted. John was patient while he waited.

Frank Brownell and Dusty Smull were partners in Sector Eddie, which was the Stapleton area. John had worked with both of them when one was out sick or had been assigned to court.

The boundaries of Sector Eddie began at Bay Street and Water Street, ran along Bay Street southward to Vanderbilt Avenue, went west up Vanderbilt to Van Duzer Street, ran along Van Duzer to Water Street and then back to Bay Street. It also covered part of the waterfront.

Dusty's dad was a lieutenant and was Commanding Officer of the 123rd precinct detective squad. He wielded a lot of power as Commanding Officer and many considered his job a political plum. He was also Dusty's hook and rabbi.

One day, clear out of the blue, Dusty was promoted to Third Grade Detective Specialist. He remained on patrol and, even though he made more money than his partner for doing the same work, they remained good friends, although some of the guys did notice some resentment on Frank's part. Frank was laid back and had a very high boiling point. If he had any emotions, he controlled and hid them well. Both Frank and Dusty were hunters and spent hunting season upstate every year at a hunting lodge.

Dusty was very smart and had a talent for taking tests. He studied hard for the Sergeant's exam, which was held every two or three years and was considered one of the city's toughest.

In March of 1971, Dusty got promoted and was transferred to the 9th precinct on Manhattan's lower east side, which opened up the seat that John had been waiting for. Tom Holley called John into his office about a week after Dusty got transferred.

"Do you want the seat, kid?"_asked Tom.

"Are you kidding? Damn straight, Tom!" answered John.

"Okay. Next Monday when you swing back into days you will start working with Frank Brownell in sector Eddie," Tom said.

Even though John had worked with Frank before on a fill-in basis, he was nervous because he knew Frank had not been given any say in the matter. He had not been given the option of choosing his own partner. There were other footmen available in other squads but it would have meant squad changes. As a result, Frank was stuck with John whether he liked it or not.

Monday came quicker than usual for John and he had to remember to bring certain items with him on radio motor patrol that footmen did not have to carry or worry about. One piece of equipment required on patrol was the buxom riot gear helmet.

Occasionally radio cars had to respond to emergencies in other precincts or boroughs and there simply wasn't enough time to go back to your own precinct to pick up needed gear, so you had to be sure you had it with you. Footmen also weren't required to carry all of the forms that were needed to handle the varied and numerous jobs that radio cars responded to.

John placed an abundant supply of U.F. 61's, DOA tags, dog bite forms and a few missing person's forms into his attaché case, which he had purchased when he learned he would be assigned to sector Eddie with Frank. Thankfully, footmen could always call a car and get the forms they needed to complete the paperwork for any assignment that came their way.

John descended the stairs adjacent to his locker room and entered the muster room where he immediately availed himself to the shoe shine machine. Once his shoes had a good buffing he made his way over to the full length mirror hanging adjacent to the entry way of the muster room and gave himself the once over. After inspecting himself side to side and front to back, he was satisfied that his uniform was in good shape. His shirt and trousers were recently dry-cleaned and he had made sure that they put military creases in his shirt. He walked over to one of the empty, metal chairs and sat awaiting the arrival of the 8X4 sergeant to conduct the roll call.

He saw Frank walk in but, unlike most partners who sat with each other during roll call, Frank chose to sit with other cops in the rear of the room. A few minutes later, Sergeant Murphy entered and began the roll call. Roll call was informal because it was also part of in-service training, which meant you could sit while it was in session.

"Pape,"_called out the Sergeant.

"Here."

"Auriama," said the Sergeant.

"Present," replied Tony.

134

"Sector AB, meal at 10:00 A.M., ring 27. Give special attention to Von Briesen Park for auto stripping,"_said Sergeant Murphy.

These instructions to the sector team meant they were to take their food break at 10:00 A.M. Telling them that their ring was 27 simply meant that they had to call the switchboard every hour at 27 minutes after the hour. The ring would be recorded into a log that was maintained by the TS operator and was regularly inspected by the desk officer. Murphy also directed the sector to pay special attention to any hot spots that might be occurring in their sector.

"Brownell," Murphy continued.

"Present."

"Audenino."

"Here," answered John.

"Sector Eddie, meal at 8:00 A.M., ring 45.

"Listen up guys. When you turn out, take a ride over to St. Vinnie's Hospital. There's a footman guarding a prisoner in room A-123. One of you needs to remain with the prisoner while the other drives the footman back to the station. I'll get a day tour footman to relieve you as soon as I can," ordered the Sergeant.

John acknowledged the order and Murphy continued with the roll call. When completed, the Sergeant ordered the troops to open ranks and prepare for inspection, although it was the desk officer who usually gave the order to carry this out.

The inspection went well. Murphy walked up and down the ranks and muttered some things about haircuts and un-shined shoes, but he didn't write anyone up.

The moment John had been waiting for was upon him. He was assigned as the operator for the first four hours and Frank was to be the recorder. It would be John's responsibility to retrieve the keys from the operator of the previous tour and gas up the car as well as make all the required entries into the gas log, while Frank made sure he had the necessary forms since he would be doing all writing of the actual reports during the first four hours.

Usually the previous sector teams would be waiting outside the station house on their respective relieving points and they would not enter the station house until properly relieved. John learned right away that nobody used the relieving points. Instead, teams just pulled up anywhere that was convenient. If you did a good job no one gave a fuck but if you screwed up, the brass would shove one up your ass for not being on the relieving point.

John walked outside and saw that sector Eddie, which used RMP 1095 as its steady car, was directly in front and Officers Peterson and Molloy were getting their gear out of the vehicle.

Peterson and Molloy had been partners for five years and were good street cops. As steady partners assigned to sector Eddie they were responsible for all crimes in their area. That is why just prior to going in to sign out, steady teams shared information about crime trends as well as what was going on to the incoming team. Peterson knew John was newly assigned and spoke first.

"Welcome aboard, John," Peterson said.

"Thanks, Bob."

"Listen," Bob said. "They're stealing cars like crazy out of the parking lot next to 212 Broad Street."_

Frank had descended the stairs from the station house and was also listening to the conversation. "Any clues as to who it might be?" he asked.

"Yeah, it's probably Jeffrey Roberts. He's the kid who lives on Gordon Street near Broad Street. We grabbed him last month for grand larceny auto. He just likes to drive and steals cars to do it," Bob explained.

"I'll keep an eye out for him," answered Frank.

John was a little taken aback by Frank's remark. Instead of saying, 'We'll keep an eye out for him' he had said, 'I'll keep an eye out for him'. It was almost as if John didn't exist in Frank's eyes. John attributed this to the fact that Frank had never worked with him on a steady basis and it would just take a while for Frank to think of him as a partner.

Both Frank and John placed their attaché cases into the back seat of their patrol car and positioned their batons on the floor, wedged between their seats and doors so they would be readily accessible if they needed them in a hurry. As John adjusted his seat and rearview mirror, Frank made a notation of the car's mileage then picked up the phone from its cradle and called Central.

"120-Eddie requesting a radio check," he said into the receiver.

"I read you loud and clear. Five by five," answered Central.

"Ten-four," responded Frank.

With that, he got comfortable in his seat and fell silent. John put the vehicle in gear and pulled away from the curb, proceeding along Richmond Terrace towards Bay Street.

Out of the blue, Frank suddenly spoke.

"It's easier to get to Saint Vincent's Hospital if you turn around and go along the Terrace to Lafayette Street and then along Henderson Avenue. The faster we get there, the faster we can get relieved and head over to the sector."

"Okay," said John, smart enough to keep his mouth shut and listen and learn.

Less than five minutes later he pulled up to the emergency room entrance of the hospital and Frank got out of the car without another word. He entered the building through the emergency entrance and made his way up to room A-123 which was on the fourth floor in the old wing of the hospital. A few minutes later a cop John had never seen before came down and got into the car and John drove him back to the precinct to end his shift. John was surprised when he saw how refreshed the cop looked.

"How was your tour? Did you get many scratches from the Sergeant?" asked John.

It was customary for the patrol sergeant to visit anyone who was assigned to a detail in the precinct and to sign his memo book attesting to the fact that he had made his visits. Patrol sergeants also called various sectors during the tour and gave them a scratch.

"Sergeant Conroy came up about 1:00 A.M. but that was it. He's a real prince. I got about four good hours. I just handcuffed the guy to his bed. He wasn't going anywhere," the wide awake cop explained with a smile.

John figured the cop had about seventeen years on the job and knew the ropes. John dropped him off in front of the station house and drove back to the hospital. When he arrived at the emergency room entrance, Frank was already waiting outside. The day man had apparently driven his private car to the hospital and relieved Frank. Taking your private vehicle to post was a violation of the Rules and procedures but sometimes, if you got a desolate post or fixer, it became your only haven to sit or get warm. Most bosses knew it was common practice but only asked that the car be parked out of sight or off post so as not to cause an embarrassment.

When John pulled the RMP up to the hospital entrance, Frank got in and again did not say a word, so they headed out to Stapleton, which was their sector. He didn't know what Frank wanted and he questioned himself about whether he should get coffee first or check out the sector. John didn't want to appear like a rookie so he decided to just drive the sector until Frank said something, if anything at all. As he negotiated the turn out of the hospital's parking lot and headed down Bard Avenue to the Terrace, John hoped they would get a radio run.

Richmond Terrace ran from the Saint George Ferry terminal westward along the north shore of the entire borough of Staten Island. It bordered the body of water known as the Kill Van Kull which separated New York and New Jersey. It was a very busy water route for tankers and carriers bringing oil and cargo to Howland Hook, a drop off point for the entire north eastern seaboard.

John felt good behind the wheel and was happy he had been chosen for this seat and especially this sector which was considered one of the busiest in the precinct. He drove carefully but just a little bit below the speed limit. A radio car was supposed to observe its surroundings no matter where it was. After all, the shields that all cops wear say City of New York, not just sector Eddie of the 120th precinct. He also liked the area around Saint Vincent's Hospital, also known as Randall Manor.

Randall Manor was largely comprised of huge Victorian style homes with enormous pieces of property. In the latter part of the 19th century and the early part of the 20th century, Captains of whaling vessels lived in most of the homes.

Descendants of Cornelius Vanderbilt, a shipping magnate who was buried on Staten Island, originally owned much of the property in the area. Cornelius had been entombed in Moravian Cemetery which was in the 122nd precinct and adjoined the 120th.

The ride along the Terrace back to Stapleton took no more than ten minutes and, not surprisingly, Frank did not say a word the entire time. When John reached the intersection of Bay Street and Water Street, which was the start of Sector Eddie's boundary, Frank quickly and violently reached over to the vehicles shift lever on the steering column and threw the lever into drive.

"For Christ's sake if you're going to drive then drive the car in the right fucking gear! You've been driving in second gear ever since you left the fucking hospital," he screamed.

John felt like sliding under the seat right there.

"Maybe I'm not fit to be a sector car driver," he thought dejectedly.

With that, a transmission from Central rang out over the car's radio.

"120-David," said the female dispatcher.

"120-David standing by," Frankie Catalano's voice answered over the radio.

"David, respond to 180 Parkhill Avenue, Apt. 6C, on shots fired," the dispatcher directed.

"Ten-four," responded Catalano, acknowledging the call.

"120-Eddie," came the voice of the same dispatcher.

John's partner Frank picked the phone out of its cradle and responded back.

"120-Eddie, standing by," he answered, knowing full well that Central was going to direct them to back up sector David at the Parkhill apartment.

"Eddie, also respond with sector David to shots fired at 180 Parkhill Avenue, Apt. 6C," directed the dispatcher.

"Eddie, ten-four," Frank responded without a hint of emotion.

John felt the butterflies in his stomach rising up to his throat and wanted to ask Frank if there was anything he should do. It was common practice for partners, whose very lives depended on each other, to speak to each other while on route to a heavy job and formulate some plan of action. However, after the debacle with the shift lever, John decided to keep his mouth shut.

Both sectors arrived at the address at the same time and as John maneuvered his RMP into a parking spot directly in front of the address he noticed that Frankie Catalano had parked his car just short of the actual address. John quickly understood that Frankie had done this deliberately, as a safety precaution, just in case someone did have a gun and decided to have target practice on the boys in blue as they exited their cars.

John had just learned his first valuable lesson of the day but, sadly enough, it had not come from his own partner.

Frankie Catalano greeted Frank with a salute.

"How's your new partner working out?"_Frankie asked in an innocent tone. Not surprisingly, Frank did not respond to the question and quickly changed the subject.

"Have you ever been to this apartment before?"

"No, but they all have guns in this shithole," answered Frankie.

All four officers entered the building together. The lobby directory was a mass of broken glass and countless, glittering shards covered the floor. The letters remaining in the directory that were supposed to spell out the names of the residents had been re-arranged and used to spell out profanities of all kinds directed to one's mother. The only reliable information was that apartments A through M were on the left elevator side and N through Z were on the right side. Naturally, Murphy's Law was in effect and the elevators were both out of service.

The four cops began their trek up the flight of stairs to the sixth floor. When they got there, Frank continued on and made his way up an extra flight to the 7th floor. John looked at Frankie Catalano as if to ask what the hell was going on.

"The guy just doesn't talk to me," he reluctantly admitted to Frankie.

"Go up with him, kid," Frankie replied like a father giving advice to his son.

John followed his partner up the stairs which eventually spilled them out on the roof. A few minutes later, a black male came running up the stairwell from the other side of the roof where, appropriately enough, Frank was standing with his service revolver out, cocked and at the ready. The male stopped dead in his tracks when he saw Frank with his gun out.

"Where are you going in such a hurry?"_asked Frank.

The black dude didn't seem threatening in any way. As a matter of fact, he seemed a little bookish and nerdy. He was only about 5'8" and had short cropped hair. He didn't even have a 'fro,'_ which was the in thing for all the young brothers of the sixties. He spoke in a quiet and reserved manner.

"Good morning, Officer. I was just going to my lady's apartment on the other side of the building," the stranger said in a nonchalant tone of voice.

"Where are you coming from?"_Frank asked, never taking his eyes off the young dude.

"I live in Apt. 6C on this side of the building," the man replied as a slight bead of perspiration began forming on his brow.

141

With this information, Frank ordered the young black to turn around and spread eagle against the outside of the stairwell. John knew that as soon as the man said he lived in Apt.6C, Frank had enough information to conduct a frisk.

Frank holstered his weapon while John removed his and covered Frank as he conducted the frisk of the young turkey. He came up with a nickel bag of pot but more importantly he found a .32 caliber revolver stuffed down into the man's waistband. Frank checked the cylinder and found one shell missing. Frank quickly rear cuffed the young dude, who was now cursing at both officers.

The green metal roof door where Frank had been standing and the young black had exited from suddenly swung open and Willie Folder, Frankie Catalano's partner, came through.

"Frank, we've got a broad down in Apt.6C who said that her common-law husband fired a shot at her. She caught him fucking around with another woman on the other side of the building and confronted him with it," said Willie.

"We got both him and the gun," Frank replied.

The woman was brought to the rooftop for an on the scene identification and quickly pointed out her common-law husband.

"That be the mother-fucker. I cooks for him, I had two of his kids, and I fucks for him anytime he wants. He be thinking that I ain't good 'nough for him no more, so he gots to be fucking somebody else. Sheet, just because I got kids with two other dudes, he be thinking that all I gots to do is spread my legs and give my pussy to the neighborhood. Sheet!"_she said matter-of-factly.

Frank and John assured the woman that her husband would not be back that night but she would have to appear in criminal court when subpoenaed to testify. Both Frank and John also knew that within 24-48 hours the woman would have a change of heart and most likely have the charges dropped when she got to the complaint room at the court at 67 Targee Street.

Even though John and his partner had made the collar, Frank turned it over to Frankie and Willie because the original job belonged to sector David. Besides, Frankie wanted the collar. If the guys in sector D had been fill-ins then Frank would have kept the collar because he, in fact, was the apprehending officer. A gun collar was a good pinch, and Frankie and Willie would have done the same for sector E.

All four cops walked down the seven flights from the roof with their prisoner. Willie placed the dude in the rear seat and Frankie sat right beside him. Willie got behind the wheel and sped off to the precinct with sirens and lights all blasting on full.

CHAPTER SIXTEEN

C harlie looked at the lieutenant and frowned.
"Lou, are you telling me that even after the drive to the hospital and that gun run on Parkhill Avenue, your partner still had not spoken to you?"_

"That's what I'm saying, Charlie. I started to believe that perhaps I should go back to the squad as a footman and was afraid I would have to accept the fact that I would be a fill-in for the rest of my career in the 120ᵗʰ," Lt. A. replied.

"Did he ever speak to you, Lou? I mean, I know he eventually did but when and how did it happen?"

"I'm just about to get to that part. It's really amazing how it all came about," said Lt. A.

When we resumed patrol, Frank notified Central that we were available for assignment.

"120-Eddie to Central."

"Proceed, Eddie," Central answered back.

"120-Eddie is 10-98, K," Frank said.

I began driving back to the confines of the sector Eddie and decided to drive down Vanderbilt Avenue and make the turn northward along Tompkins Avenue, passing Public School 14 and the home for female mariners of the sea. The home was for women only who had served proudly in the Merchant Marines and was an offshoot of the famed Sailor Snug Harbor which housed the male mariners who had retired.

It was getting close to 11:00 A.M. and was time for our sector to have our meal hour. We had originally been assigned a meal time of 8:00 A.M. but had it changed because we had been assigned a job at that time. Radio car teams did not get to eat at their assigned time if it was busy. As a result, meal times had to be rescheduled. When this happened, the meal hours were staggered because a certain percentage of cars always had to be available for patrol.

Depending on the shift they were working, cops had special places they frequented. I knew sector Eddie was a good sector for eating and most places were good to us cops. We either got food on the arm or huge discounts.

Frank still had not spoken a word to me yet, so I asked him if there was any place special he wanted to go.

I realized Frank did not really know me yet and his issues with me might be as simple as a question of trust.

"Go down to Mama Rosie's on Canal Street," Frank directed.

I acknowledged then drove us down Canal Street and parked directly in front of Mama Rosie's place.

"Do you want me to go in, Frank?"_I asked.

"Stay in the car and monitor the radio. When I come out, then you can go in," he replied.

I nodded my ascent and he went in. After a few minutes Frank came back out carrying a paper bag. When he got to the car, although he did not say a word, he looked at me as if to say, "Get off your ass and go in."

I made my way into Mama Rosie's to order my food and buy a pack of Kent Kings cigarettes. As I browsed the shelves inside the small store I couldn't help but notice they carried Twinkies, which were my favorite, so I bought a package. Tuna salad on white with lettuce with mayonnaise was another one of my favorites so that is what I ordered. To top it off, I bought a container of Nestle's Quick chocolate milk. The lunch was free but I left a fifty cent tip and made my way out of the storm. When I got back into the RMP, I placed the bag on the front seat between myself and Frank then closed the door.

"Drive down to pier three. We'll eat there," Frank said. I hid my surprise that I didn't have to ask him where we should go to eat our lunch.

I drove down Canal Street to Front Street then slowly pulled into the old pier. Although this particular pier was abandoned, its location was convenient for us. Before turning off the engine, I maneuvered the car so it was facing out just in case we got a call for a heavy job.

I watched quietly while Frank took his lunch from the paper bag. He had a pack of Kent Kings cigarettes, a package of Twinkies and a Tuna salad on white with mayonnaise. He also had a container of Nestle's Quick chocolate milk, which was exactly what I had purchased for my lunch.

"What are you, a fucking wise ass?"_Frank asked me.

"What do you mean?"_

"What did you do? You asked Rosie what I ordered and you got the same fucking thing!"_growled Frank without trying to hide his irritation.

"I ordered what I like and what I wanted," I replied angrily. "I don't have to order what you get."

"I've never had anyone order the same as me. Is that your brand, too?" Frank asked, pointing at the pack of cigarettes.

"Yeah, and believe it or not, I like Twinkies, too," I said with the hint of a smile twitching the corner of my mouth.

It was an incredulous conversation for two grown men to have. Imagine this – two cops sitting in a patrol car, talking about food and cigarettes. Yet this dialogue, after having worked only a few hours together as partners, was the beginning catalyst for a relationship and partnership that would span twelve years in the same busy precinct and sector.

Although neither of us knew it yet, together we would deliver twelve babies, two of which would be named after us. We would set a precinct record for the most stolen car arrests in a single month's time. We would also rush into burning buildings and pull people to safety and we would garnish Cop of the Month honors multiple times. Finally, we would both be recognized and honored as NYC Police Officer of the year.

All who shared police experiences with us and all who were fortunate enough to be trained by us would remember our partnership. There would also be those who did not understand us and many who would hate us and seek to do us harm.

Police officers are sworn to enforce the law, but in the years that followed, Frank and I learned that even the law did not side with us in our attempts to carry out our duties.

"So you see, Charlie, Frank and I worked a long time together. We saw a lot and we did a lot. I miss him like crazy and hope and pray that he is well and happy. He has a lovely family now and I will always wish him the best," Lt. A. said with a smile.

"Lou, I knew you had a partner for a long time but I didn't know you had so many similarities between you," said Charlie.

"Yeah, we were like a Mutt and Jeff team."

He paused and glanced at Charlie, noticing immediately the quizzical expression in Charlie's eyes.

"What I mean to say is I had a low boiling point. I would fly off the handle, scream and curse, pretty easily."

"Don't I know that," said Charlie with a slight chuckle.

"On the other hand, Frank kept things inside. It took a lot for him to explode. Once he did, though, it was over," the lieutenant said with a nod.

The ESU team completed their assignments and Charlie and John resumed patrol. The remainder of the night was a smooth one and they were able to sign out on time. Charlie was glad because he wanted to stop at Terry's house to find out what was going on with her and her behavior. She had been overly aggressive the last time they had been together and he didn't like the possibility that he was being used. He was a nice guy and a family man, but instead of feeling good that perhaps Terry didn't want a closer relationship, he couldn't help but feel bad.

When he left the precinct he headed out to Terry's place and parked in his usual spot. He knocked on the door and she opened it immediately.

This time she was already dressed and had on a pair of tight jeans and a silk blouse. He stood in the doorway staring at her and couldn't help but notice she wasn't wearing a bra.

She beckoned for him to come in but before Charlie could say anything, she simply put her arms around him and held him tightly.

"Oh, Charlie, I'm so sorry. I know what must be going through your mind. Oh, honey, I don't want you to think of me as a whore or an over-sexed divorcée. I just wanted you so much and I got carried away with myself. I would do anything for you. Anything! You have to believe me. Please believe me," she begged.

"I admit I was taken back, Terry. It's mostly because I have never seen you like that before. For that matter, I've never seen any woman like that," he said quietly.

She sighed and laughed nervously, "Why are we standing in the doorway? Come into the kitchen and I'll make you a cup of coffee, then we can talk. Come on."

They made their way through the living room together and Charlie couldn't help being turned on by her beautiful ass and full breasts, which were loose inside the silky blouse. His conscience was eating at him over this affair and he was afraid he would feel guilty again, but whenever he was in this woman's presence he just could not control his emotions or animal lust. He wanted her.

He sat at the kitchen table while Terry put on a fresh pot of coffee. When she walked by him to retrieve two cups from her cupboard, Charlie grabbed her and pulled her down onto his lap.

"Don't you want your coffee first?"_she asked in surprise.

"I want you first," he responded with a husky voice.

Terry sighed and kissed him fully on the lips then ran her fingers through his hair. She drove him crazy when she darted her tongue in and out of his ear. He grasped her breasts through the silk shirt but soon stuck his hand underneath her blouse and pinched her nipples. They were as hard as rocks. She quickly removed her shirt then caressed the area below his waist. His penis was nearly bursting out of his pants.

Without a word she got off of his lap and knelt before him on the kitchen floor. With a seductive smile she unzipped his pants and took his member into her mouth. He moaned with pleasure as she began to slowly lick and suck him.

She continued playing with him, teasing him, for what felt like an eternity. When she sensed he could not hold back any longer, she took him into her hand and jerked him off right into her mouth. With a deep groan of pleasure, he exploded as she enjoyed every drop.

Charlie wanted to fuck her and he wanted to do it on the bed. With a smile of satisfaction he stood up and removed the rest of his clothes until he was stark naked. Not to be outdone, Terry quickly undressed, removing her jeans and panties. Without a shred of clothing between them, they embraced then began exploring each other's bodies while the coffee percolated somewhere far away.

Consumed with passion, Charlie picked her up and carried her into the bedroom where he gently placed her on the bed. He climbed on top of her and began covering her with slow, gentle kisses and it didn't take long for him to work himself into a frenzy. He made his way from her mouth to her awaiting breasts and began to kiss and suck on her nipples as if he were a baby requiring mother's milk. She whispered his name and clasped a swollen breast as if to feed him, quietly murmuring for him to suck on her, which he did more than willingly. In fact, he spent a good ten minutes sucking one breast before moving to the other then slowly made his way down her body, tracing his lips to her stomach then across one hip. When he began kissing her inner thighs, he gently placed his middle finger inside her.

She moaned in ecstasy.

Next, he began slowly sucking Terry's clitoris as if it was an all-day lollipop. He moved up and down on her special place as if he were a pussy cat lapping up a saucer of fresh milk. It wasn't long before she exploded over and over and the sheets beneath them were soon wet with her fluids.

Charlie repositioned himself and slowly entered her. At first their coupling was slow and sensual but soon escalated until they were both writhing with pleasure. They came at the same time, screaming of their need for each other. When it was over, they cuddled close for what seemed an eternity, drained, in each other's arms. As they enjoyed the afterglow, Charlie felt himself shrinking within her before eventually slipping out of her vagina.

As they held each other, Terry did not stir, and for a moment he wondered if she had fallen asleep. Soon she moved and turned her face to Charlie while still lying within his embrace. She had a forlorn look on her face that he picked up on immediately.

"What's wrong, honey? You look like you're going to break into tears at any moment," he said quietly.

"Oh, Charlie. You know I get like this every time you're going to leave me. I just have to get used to being the 'other woman' I guess," she said in a sarcastic tone.

"Terry, I've never lied to you. I've always been up front with you from day one. You knew I was married and I never said I was going to leave my wife."

"I know, but I can't help feeling the way I do. I think I have fallen in love with you and I can't bear the thought of losing you or sharing you with another woman," she said.

Charlie began to get cold sweats. This was exactly what he did not want to happen. These women who at first say they're not looking for a husband suddenly become so possessive that all they can think of is a wedding band. They become bitches that will go to any extent to get what they want, even if it means causing pain to innocent people and breaking up families.

He took her hand.

"Terry, you have to know that I care for you dearly and I think of you all of the time. I certainly don't ever want to hurt you. You must believe me when I say that," he pleaded.

"I know that, honey. That's what makes it so difficult for me. If you didn't call me so much or think of me so much it might be different. If you didn't say the things you do when we make love I would know that all you want is to get laid like all the rest of the guys in the precinct. But I don't feel that from you. I know you really do care for me."_

She was practically crying now.

"What do you want me to do?" he asked.

"I don't know, baby. I don't know. Maybe we shouldn't see each other for a while," she suggested.

Charlie knew it might be a good idea to cool it but he was really afraid he would hurt her by saying it.

"What exactly do you mean? Are you saying you don't want to see me for a set period of time? Will you date anyone else during that time?"_he asked.

The questions just kept forming in his mind.

"If you see someone else, how do you know you won't wind up in his bed and have the same thing happen all over again?"_he asked.

"Charlie, don't drive yourself crazy. I'm only suggesting ways that might help me during those times when I'm not with you," she said.

He could feel an unmistakable tingle of jealousy rising deep within his gut. He was actually allowing himself to think of Terry sleeping with other men! If he had not cheated on Annette in the first place these feelings would never have arisen. His jealousy soon led to shame, and the guilt of what he had done was stronger than ever.

"Terry, I'm going to leave now. There's a great deal that we both have to think about. I do know how I feel about you and I do know that every time I see you I'm consumed with such a lust for you. It fills me with an overwhelming desire to possess you and be inside you."

He sighed.

"I guess what it comes down to is this. I don't want to cause you any pain and I certainly don't want to hurt my family either," he said, his words blunt and truthful.

Terry knew he was right and nodded. They walked to the door and gently kissed, saying their goodbyes.

Charlie returned home to an empty house and went to bed, sleeping fitfully while trying not to think of what had happened earlier that morning. He figured he would be better rested after he got some sleep. Then he might be able to make some sense out of what was said between them and come to a reasonable decision as to what to do about Terry.

When he got up he was surprised that Annette hadn't arrived home yet. He opened the refrigerator and poured himself a glass of cold milk. As he sat at the kitchen table he happened to glance at the phone hanging on the wall. The red message light was flashing on it. Curious, he got up and pushed play.

"You have one message, Friday, 10:00 A.M.," a pleasant voice announced.

The message began and his wife's voice filled the room.

"Hi, Charlie. I'm sorry I missed you but as usual you didn't call so I didn't know if you made another arrest and were going to be a little late. There's some left over chili in the fridge or you can send out if you like. I will be working late so I don't know if I'll see you later on tonight. Bye."_

He felt a little concerned about Annette's message. It was very unusual for her to work late and even more unusual for her to say she wouldn't be home by 10:30 P.M. She normally got off work at 5:00 P.M. and never worked overtime. He decided to call her at her office but then had second thoughts about it. He didn't want to appear as if he didn't trust her, yet he was a little jealous. He was beginning to feel like a rubber band and he didn't like it.

In the end, he decided to just watch a little television and relax. He wasn't at all hungry and went without supper figuring he could always grab something at work. He sat on the couch, put the TV on and watched the news. Not surprisingly, it didn't take long before he got tired of seeing and listening to reports of murders and robberies. He got enough of that at work.

He began to feel tired again and shut his eyes but was smart enough to set an alarm clock just in case he overslept. Annette wasn't going to be home to wake him and he didn't want to be late. He slept soundly for almost four hours and woke up feeling rested. He shaved and showered and left for work.

Annette hadn't called again so he decided to pass by her office on his way to work. He had to go somewhat out of his way to do this but didn't mind. When he got to her building he saw that all the lights were out and there weren't any cars in the parking lot. He surmised that he had probably just missed her or perhaps she stopped with some of her friends to get a bite to eat on the way home, which was not unusual for her.

CHAPTER SEVENTEEN

When he got to work, although he was a little later than usual, Charlie still had time to have coffee in the sitting room with the guys. He was stressed out thinking about Terry and now Annette, and although it was a Friday night and he knew it would be busy, he could only hope it would be busier than usual. He noticed that Lt. A. had already changed into his uniform so Charlie dressed quickly for the street and returned to the sitting room. Once there, he took a seat and lit up a cigarette.

A few minutes later the lieutenant and sergeant entered the room and began the roll call then the lieutenant began to speak. Lt. A. always liked to impart some knowledge that would be useful to his men on patrol. Sometimes it was about some obscure law they could use to write some scumbag up or arrest someone, while other times it was just friendly advice or a scoop on some inside information.

Late tour crews often missed out on some of the dirt that was happening among them and its members were like the whores of the precinct. Nobody told them much of anything or even cared.

During the meeting, the lieutenant spoke about the bars on Bay Street which catered to the drug users and underage teens that came from New Jersey to drink. The aforementioned bars were not friends to the cops but were a source of danger because of the fights that began in them, usually over girls and watered down drinks. The lieutenant was sure to stress the importance of no one attempting anything without calling for back-up first, saying he would back anyone up who wanted to issue a summons for a disorderly premise or make a collar.

When the meeting was over the lieutenant said he wanted to go out early so Charlie grabbed the keys to the RMP from the front desk and walked out to the waiting car where it was parked directly in the rear of the station house. He knew he would have to gas it up because Officer Knobbe had been driving the 4X12 Platoon Commander earlier and he never left a radio car with gas like he was supposed to. He was a lazy son of a bitch.

After filling up the tank Charlie passed the gasoline log book over to the next operator who was waiting in line to gas up. The lieutenant was waiting for him at the pump and, as Charlie finished, Lt. A. got in and made himself comfortable. Usually they would stop and get coffee but it was busy so they decided to hold off until it quieted down. Why waste a good cup of coffee by throwing it out the window?

Charlie headed out of the side lot and down Wall Street, making a right onto the Terrace and heading towards Stapleton, the lieutenant's old sector and stomping grounds. The car's radio was busy and hummed with jobs being dispatched to even the 122nd and 123rd precincts. Usually those precincts were fairly quiet but on Friday nights they had more than their share of disorderly groups and disputes. The 122nd also had its normal number of vehicle accidents, especially since Hylan Boulevard was well liked by speeders.

On this particular night the ESU Sergeant had taken off and Lt. A. had been assigned to also cover the ESU units throughout the entire borough. Lt. A. enjoyed covering the emergency service units because it gave him greater authority to respond to all jobs that the elite units were assigned to.

Charlie was glad, too, because it offered him a change of scenery. It also meant they could drive to both of their homes in the adjoining precincts and do it legally. This was a side benefit in working in the borough in which you resided.

As they drove around the lieutenant began to tell Charlie something which was a direct result of a job they had handled together a few weeks earlier.

It had been a humid night and even though it was 2:00 A.M. the thermometer still read 87 degrees. It had been a busy night also and much busier than usual. All the sectors were either on assignment or tied up in the station house with collars already. There were two sergeants on patrol and even they had taken jobs in order to keep the precinct out of a radio backlog, which would occur whenever there were more than five assignments waiting to be answered or more than two jobs held for more than five minutes.

It was inevitable on this particular night that the lieutenant not only got called in his role as Platoon Commander, but he was also used because another car had been assigned to other jobs. As soon as the next job made it onto the radio dispatcher's screen, she called the lieutenant.

"120 Platoon Commander," the female dispatcher's voice came across the radio.

"120 Lieutenant, standing by," answered the boss.

"120 Lieutenant, respond to 375 Willow brook Road on a 10-54 cardiac arrest," she instructed.

"10-4, en route," he responded back, and they were on their way.

Willow Brook Road was in a nice section of the precinct. It was still considered part of the Westerleigh area, which consisted of one and two family homes with nicely manicured lawns and pools in the backyards. It was also situated directly behind All Saints Episcopal Church which housed daycare centers and was forever in the local paper for conducting food drives for the needier population of the precinct.

Charlie pulled up in front of 375 and noticed that the EMS ambulance had already arrived and the techs were busy carrying in their gear for cardiac cases.

The EMS technicians and Lt. A. made it to the door simultaneously and were greeted by a frantic, middle-aged woman who was crying and yelling at the same time for the care givers to hurry.

The woman wore a night coat and it was obvious that she had been sleeping and had been woken up by something or someone in the house. She led the men into her kitchen, passing through her living room which was nicely furnished with blue rugs and a matching sofa. The adjacent dining room had a huge table that could easily sit ten to twelve people. Beyond the table was a well-stocked bar with beautiful glasses and brands of every kind of liquor.

When they entered the kitchen they immediately noticed a man, wearing a white tee shirt and a pair of briefs, lying on the floor. He had likely gotten up to get something from the kitchen and simply collapsed just a few steps away from the counter. He was beginning to turn blue, which was an obvious sign of cardiac arrest.

The EMS people began to do their work in earnest. They cut a hole in the man's shirt with a pair of surgical scissors and attached the portable EKG machine. Almost immediately the machine began spewing out pieces of paper detailing the man's electrocardiogram data. Within seconds they had placed an oxygen mask over the victim's nose and mouth and began CPR. Soon the man began to regain some color and didn't appear to be blue anymore. Charlie and the lieutenant both knew that the improvement of the man's skin color simply could have resulted from the artificial stimulation by the EMS team and not necessarily been from the involuntary beating of the man's heart.

Just inside the doorway, the man's wife was holding their teenage daughter who was sobbing gently. Lt. A. walked over to them and took the woman's hands into his own. He assured her that her husband would pull through this and would be fine. After reassuring them for a moment or two, he soon had them sitting down, talking to him. He explained that as soon as they would be able to stabilize him, their loved one would be transported to the emergency room at St. Vincent's Hospital.

The EMS tech worked on the cardiac victim for a good 45 minutes more then finally signaled the lieutenant that they were ready to transport him. Right away one of the other techs grabbed the lieutenant on the side and told him to tell the victim's wife and daughter that they should be prepared for the worst. Instead of telling the family this, however, Lt. A. instructed them to grab their coats and keys and follow the ambulance to the hospital.

The wife was really upset and the lieutenant didn't think she was calm enough to drive herself. When he offered to take her to the hospital, she took him up on the offer. The daughter followed in the family car. The ride took less than five minutes and both mother and daughter followed the gurney into the emergency room.

As Lt. A. and Charlie resumed patrol, Charlie wondered why the lieutenant had brought this incident up. He knew something had happened which was a direct result of this particular call they'd been on, but he just didn't see what it was.

"Charlie, remember when I told you that some days are good and some are bad?"

Charlie nodded as the lieutenant continued.

"Well a few weeks after that incident I received a letter at the precinct from this particular family. It was signed by the man who survived that night. He was released from the hospital after two weeks, exercises every day, and was put on a special diet. He wanted to thank me personally and invited me to his house for coffee. I called him and politely declined but he insisted that he wanted to see me so I stopped by one night before coming into work.

"He took me into his kitchen and introduced me to his wife and daughter who, of course, I had already met, and he thanked me for calming them that night. He said he saw what I did when I took his wife's hands into my own and he thanked me for driving her to the hospital. I asked him what he meant and if he had spoken to his wife about that night, but he assured me he had not yet spoken to her about any of it. In fact, he said he had not spoken about it to anyone because he didn't want people to think he was crazy.

"I asked why he chose me to tell, and do you know what he said, Charlie?" the lieutenant asked. Charlie could only shake his head as

Lt. A. continued. "He said he thought that I was caring enough to share it with. Humbled, I let him speak."

"Lieutenant Audenino, I don't know where to begin. I've only been home for a few weeks but I feel as if I'm about to lose my mind if I don't tell this to somebody. What I do know is that I seem to value everything around me more. Life is so precious and beautiful," he said, holding back tears.

It was obvious to me that this guy was just happy to be alive. After all, he had been at death's door. Anyone who had been what he'd been through would be happy to be alive and appreciate everything more. I could tell he was eager to continue, so I nodded for him to go on.

"Lieutenant, on the night you came to my home with the ambulance I had gone to bed early with my wife. We had just gotten back from vacation that morning and were pretty much tuckered out. I woke up with I thought was a touch of indigestion so I went down stairs to get some Tums. We kept them in the kitchen on top of the refrigerator. I remember a burning sensation in my gullet then I immediately became dizzy and passed out. I guess I must have knocked over one of the kitchen chairs when I fell because the noise woke my wife up and she came down to check on me. She walked into the kitchen where I was, gasped and placed both hands over her mouth and then screamed. Her screams are what woke up my daughter, who then ran down the stairs and saw her mother panicking. It was my daughter who called 911," he said quietly.

"Charlie, I asked him how he knew all of this, especially since he had not discussed it with anyone in his family since that night," Lt. A. said. "He told me he knew it because he had seen every second of it. He told me after he passed out he had an experience that was really hard to describe in words but he would try.

"He said he was in a dark, black tunnel of some kind. Although he could not see anything through the darkness, he sensed he was moving very fast. He wasn't afraid but he didn't feel much of anything, either. After a few seconds, he noticed what he perceived was a dot of light in front of him and he sensed he was racing right toward it. It felt as though someone was there with him but he didn't see anyone. He just sensed that someone or something was traveling with him."

Charlie nodded as Lt. A. continued his story.

"All of a sudden I was out of the tunnel and floating above my body near the kitchen ceiling. I saw my wife crying and my daughter going to the phone. I had no sense of time and was not afraid. As a matter of fact, it was very peaceful. Then I saw you and the EMS technicians come in and I watched in a detached way when one of them cut my shirt with scissors.

"It was me down there, lying on the kitchen floor, and yet it wasn't.

"I saw you take my wife's hands and comfort her. I saw and heard the technician approach you to tell you to prepare my wife for the worst then I watched as they carried my body out to the waiting ambulance.

"The next thing I remember was being in a large field of some sort that was totally surrounded by this amazing, bright light. I looked directly at it but it did not hurt my eyes. I looked at the light and somehow felt that I was part of it. I felt this amazing, blinding light was both heaven and God, all in one.

"The next thing I knew I had become totally enveloped by a blanket of whiteness. I felt such enormous love emanating from it! I saw other beings and people there, too.

"I know this all sounds crazy but I remember it so vividly.

"I looked around and saw an old friend of mine who died at a young age due to cancer. I saw my Uncle Joe who passed away just a few months ago. When he realized I'd seen him, he approached me and said I couldn't stay there. He told me to go back because I had to finish my work on earth. Believe me when I tell you I didn't want to. It was a beautiful place, calm and filled with so much love.

"The next thing I knew I was back in my body with all kinds of people around me. I know now that it was in the hospital where I re-entered my body.

"I know you must think I'm nuts, but I just wanted to thank you in person for what you did for my family that night," the man whispered appreciatively.

"Charlie, I acknowledged him and explained that I had never met anyone who experienced what he had but had heard similar stories from others. I told him about a group I thought he should contact called IANDS, the International Association for Near Death Studies. I explained that they would direct him to groups of people who had experienced similar experiences. He was thankful and we said our goodbyes.

"So, you see, that's what I meant when I said some days are good and some are bad. The good ones always make up for the bad," said Lt. A. He always had some kind of interesting story to tell and they were all real incidents he had experienced.

It was nearing 4:00 A.M. and the lieutenant had chosen not to go into the station house on this night. There were enough sergeants on patrol and he decided to allow them to work out their own meal reliefs.

After a few minutes, the lieutenant asked Charlie to pull over to the side of the road. Once they were parked, he instructed Charlie to get out and switch places with him.

"Lou, what are you doing?"_

"I just feel like driving for a while," the lieutenant answered.

Charlie felt funny driving down the street with the lieutenant at the wheel. The guys on patrol all saw him driving and thought the boss had lost his mind. Although it took a little time, the men soon realized that their lieutenant was still a cop at heart. He knew the precinct well and he was a worker who knew that cops got tired driving bosses all night. He wouldn't hesitate to take his turn and drive part of the tour every night.

The remainder of their shift went fairly well. It was busy but most of the jobs were easy and could be handled quickly. Although many of the guys wanted to make collars, it just wasn't a collar kind of night.

The lieutenant decided to grab a quick cup of coffee and look for summonses for Charlie in order to meet his quota for the month so he drove down to Jersey Street in search of unregistered and uninspected vehicles. They were lucky. Within the space of one hour, Charlie made a good start for the month when he wrote ten parking violation summonses.

Next the boss took them down to the water's edge at the base of Jersey Street near the abandoned railway spur that used to traverse the north shore along the Kill Van Kull. It had been shut down for almost a quarter of a century and was used by either couples as a lover's lane or cops looking for a quiet place to relax out of the public eye.

CHAPTER EIGHTEEN

T he lieutenant wasn't tired and spoke of his days in the 120th as a cop while Charlie listened attentively.

"The late sixties and early seventies were the times of the Black Liberation Army, or the BLA, and Joanne Chesimard. It was the sworn duty of the BLA members to "ice" as many "pigs" as possible, so there were many attacks on cops during that time period. Often a routine call to an apartment building was an ambush in disguise. Sometimes the ambush came in the form of a car stop where one of the BLA's vehicles would deliberately violate a traffic infraction. When the cops pulled them over and got out, another car called the "hit"_ car would drive by with automatic weapons and fire upon the unsuspecting cops. It was an uneasy time knowing that you were a target and could be set upon at any moment. It was also a time when young kids who really didn't know any better would yell *"oink, oink"* at you as you rode by.

"It was nothing new that the female in the black families was the matriarch, and the mother was often both mother and father of the siblings. In those early days, the father sired his children and lived off the welfare checks of the mother, often having children with several women at the same time.

"Joanne Chesimard was both the "mother"_and leader of her "family" in terrorism. If she was not directly involved in some of the most heinous cases in the tri-state area of New York, New Jersey and Connecticut, she surely planned most of them," the lieutenant explained.

He went on to say how Joanne Chesimard had been seen in Long Island. Eventually it was reported that she was staying on Staten Island somewhere in the 120th. Frank and John would have loved to grab her ass, as would any cop in the New York Area.

She was finally captured in New Jersey in 1973 after a wild shootout on the New Jersey Turnpike in which Trooper Werner Foerster was killed and his partner James Harper was badly wounded. During her trial, she steadfastly maintained her innocence and was found guilty but denounced the verdict as racist. In 1979, Chesimard broke out of her maximum security cell with the help of four men who took a guard hostage and commandeered a prison van, making good her escape. She fled to Cuba where she was granted political asylum by Fidel Castro. She had been living ever since under the African name of Assata Shakur.

Patrol was uneasy during the time of the Black Liberation Army's all-out war on the police of the nation. It was easier for members of the BLA to target members of police departments in large cities where they could assimilate right back into black neighborhoods and even gather sympathy and support from them. The majority of blacks in low-income areas were good, decent and hardworking people who only wanted to raise their children and give them an education and a chance at the good life.

Frank and John knew this yet they felt uneasy working in these areas. As cops they had to approach all people, at first skeptically and with an open mind yet ready to react in an instant.

The seventies were times of great upheaval. There was a major conflict raging in Vietnam and the police of this country were seen as agents of the state to that portion of the populace which vehemently opposed the Asian conflict. New York City had its share of the anti-war demonstrations from the Whitehall Recruitment Center to the anti-war activities of the group known as Students for a Democratic Society, or SDS.

The SDS was basically a student activist organization that was highly organized and definitely represented the new left. Their activities culminated in the attempted takeover of Columbia University and included great demonstrations in Washington Square Park in the 6th precinct's Greenwich Village area.

Just because Frank and John were not members of those precincts did not mean they did not see any action in them. A police department is a semi-military organization. When there is a conflict in one area that requires more manpower than is normally assigned, a call for mobilization goes out and members from all precincts respond to cover it.

"Such was the case one day in September of 1969 when Frank and I as well as twenty or so other members of the 120th were called upon to respond to Washington Square Park in the 6th precinct. Supposedly members of various college organizations with ties to the SDS and ACLU were going to demonstrate peacefully against the Vietnam War," Lt. A. said.

"The uniform of the day was also reflective of what one would wear to a peaceful demonstration or parade. We were told to wear our summer hats, summer blouses and white gloves. The brass in headquarters knew that this was an anti-war demonstration, and had been informed in advance that the anti-war demonstrators from these groups had brought baseball bats and baseballs imbedded with nails to previous demonstrations. It was also well known that City Hall was behind the call for the white gloves uniform.

"The uniform you wore determined what you could carry in the form of defensive equipment. Wearing white gloves meant that no helmets could be worn or night sticks carried. It was obvious that City Hall wanted no photos of police officers raising night sticks over the heads of poor defenseless college students.

"Once again the men and women of the police department were let down by its gutless and spineless leaders at One Police Plaza," Lt. A.

explained. "When the contingent of men from the 120th arrived at the famous arch in Washington Square Park, they were ordered by the captain of the detail to stand at ease and relax until the men from the other precincts arrived. Sergeant Red O'Hara was in charge from the 120th."

Both Frank and John had a great deal of respect for Sgt. O'Hara. He was a good, hardworking boss who knew the book but was also street-wise and would stick by his men if they were in the right.

The first thing Frank and John noticed was that the demonstrators were arriving and milling around, apparently waiting for their re-enforcements. Each demonstrator wore a football type of helmet and carried a camera around his neck. It was clear that this demonstration was marked for violence and maximum media exposure.

It seemed kind of strange that what was about to happen in Washington Square Park would somehow be construed by a certain part of the population as part of the war effort. These demonstrators, some of whom had good intentions and wanted to end all the killing in Vietnam, would be seen as heroes because they refused to go to war. Some burned their draft cards in a symbolic gesture while others fled to the safety behind our northern neighbor known as Canada.

Most of the other participants were professional agitators whose only mission was to destroy property and hurt innocent bystanders. Afterward they could then place the blame squarely on the shoulders of the police department.

Nineteen sixty-eight and nineteen sixty-nine saw many events that would affect future relationships of both generations. In nineteen sixty-eight, Martin Luther King Jr. was assassinated and Senator Eugene McCarthy ran for president, basing his entire platform on anti-war issues.

For Frank and John, as well as other members of the force, the incident that touched home the most was the student take-over at Columbia University.

It was during this event that many members of the New York City Police department were seriously injured when, after days of negotiation between students and faculty, the order was given to the police to restore order and reclaim the campus. Statistically speaking, one police captain was made a vegetable for life when bricks hurled by students rained down on his head while over 100 other officers had to be treated at area hospitals. The NYC mounted unit was also assigned to the scene at Columbia for crowd control, and seven horses were injured when the lowlife students threw baseballs at them with imbedded nails.

So the same group that caused the conflagration at Columbia University was now present in Washington Square Park, directly in front of Frank and his partner, John. Sergeant O'Hara was one of the first to realize what was going to happen that day.

"These motherfuckers are going to goad us into attacking them and then take our pictures while we joyously crack their fucking skulls. Well, I'll tell you what we're going to do. How many men have their jacks with them?" asked the feisty sergeant. The jack was a piece of steel wrapped in leather on a thong that you could buy legally in a police equipment store. It differed from the police issue of a day stick which was just a piece of rubber on a thong. The jack also had a spring built into it.

Thankfully, every member of the 120th had their jacks with them. Maybe men who worked in quiet precincts didn't have to carry jacks but if you worked in an A house like the 120th, you learned quickly that your very life depended on it.

"Take your jack and insert it into your white glove. If you get attacked and physical force is used against you, knock the fucking guy's teeth out then fall down and go sick. If the fucking brass in city hall and headquarters can't back us up, we'll go sick and make them pay through their fucking teeth," said Sergeant O'Hara with a grin.

The chief inspector in charge of the entire detail could be seen giving instructions to the captains and lieutenants who soon would approach the men and render them the same instructions. After a while it was learned that this group was the largest contingent of the SDS ever formed for a single demonstration.

"All right, men, listen up! These bastards plan to rush us and try to break our ranks. They intend to rush up 5th Avenue, destroying everything they see," explained the sergeant.

Fifth Avenue began at the north end of Washington Square Park and the demonstrators planned to break store windows and set fires all along Fifth Avenue. In effect, they were going to start a small riot.

Sergeant O'Hara explained that the police department had gotten wind of their plan through some of the department's undercover officers who had infiltrated the SDS. Undercover arrest teams were already in place all along Fifth Avenue. The side streets had waiting buses and vans to carry prisoners to the central booking facility located at One Police Plaza.

There were approximately two thousand demonstrators but only five hundred cops had been assigned. The low number of officers had been chosen intentionally once again by the yellow cowards at headquarters. From the outset, police were outnumbered four to one.

The lieutenant looked at Charlie with bright, piercing eyes.

"Sergeant O'Hara's idea about concealing the jacks in our gloves was great. If photos were to be taken, all that would be captured on film would be a white glove slapping the face of a demonstrator. Again, for reasons unknown, City Hall and police brass undermanned the detail of cops in the park that day. This was the administration of Mayor John V Lindsey; the police department never was his favorite group."

Lt. A. explained to Charlie how the demonstrators were very well organized. Their leaders carried bullhorns and each demonstrator carried a camera. Their dress was conspicuously similar. They all seemed to be wearing tattered clothes and jeans, which were comprised of bits and pieces of the American flag. They knew just what to wear to antagonize a bunch of cops who were ultra conservative in their political views.

Unfortunately, the police department did not even allow the standard wooden police barriers to assist the officer in containing the demonstrators. Every cop present that day, from the lowest rookie to the most seasoned veteran, cursed the Police Commissioner and Mayor. The absence of barriers was to be the "shot"_ heard around the world in terms of the police union's hue and cry in all future demonstrations.

"At approximately 12:00 noon the demonstrators began walking toward us. Our human bodies were all that stood between them and the edge of the park where Fifth Ave began," Lt. A. explained. "Twelve noon guaranteed that the maximum amount of people would be out on the street, most of them being out on their lunch hour."

The gait of the demonstrators increased in speed. When the two groups met, there was an enormous collision of bodies. After a brief but bloody encounter, the majority of the demonstrators had broken free and was running up Fifth Avenue.

Frank, John and their group from the 120th managed to stop a few with their dainty white gloves, now soaking wet with blood. The results of their police work could be found sprawled on the ground with bloodied mouths and broken teeth. The arrest teams were busy picking up the pieces and herding the fallen demonstrators into vans for transport to arrest processing. Fifth Avenue however, was now ablaze with trash cans on fire as well as a few cars that had been torched by the vengeful mob. Several store windows had been smashed and the sound of blaring alarms could be heard up and down the avenue.

The arrest teams waiting along Fifth Avenue were plain clothes men and were the officers who normally enforced the gambling and narcotics laws for the department. Some were also members of the different detective squads from all over the city. These men were not equipped to handle the mob that was fast approaching them.

It seemed to each and every member present, from uniformed officers to plainclothes detectives, that the city fathers would have preferred the riot which was now happening instead of the media exposing the police smashing the heads of so called college anti-war protestors.

"There comes a time, Charlie, when once, just once, you hope and pray that justice could be served right there in the street. Well, believe it or not, this was that day," Lt. A. said with a smile. "Someone in police headquarters still had a pair of balls because that someone was responsible for ordering the Mounted Unit, our cavalry, to act as the backup for that day."

The New York City Mounted Unit was ahead of the protestors and galloping towards them at a fairly good gait but the protestors could not disperse down the side streets because the arrest teams were encamped there. From their rear and closing fast were the uniformed officers from the park who were picking up speed with jacks and day sticks in hand. There must have been thirty to fifty horses with riders who had their batons out and at the ready. The horses were beautiful with their blue and yellow pads beneath their leather saddles and these mounted officers were well trained in horsemanship. Each mounted officer received a minimum of three months of specialized training in every aspect of control with their mounts, which they are permanently assigned to.

As the horses approached, some of the protesters started to toss base balls and softballs imbedded with nails and spikes at them just as they had done at Columbia University. This was all the Mounted Unit had to see.

There was an old saying that ran true on this particular day, "Fuck me once, shame on you. Fuck me twice, shame on me."_

The mounted cops lay into that mob with flailing sticks and cries just like Sam Houston's troops who cried "Remember the Alamo"_ centuries before. Within five minutes that group of lowlife scum was lying scattered all over the street. Their bloodied helmets and broken cameras were strewn all over Fifth Avenue in a mute testimony to the overwhelming street justice that was meted out by New York's Finest. Then the arrest teams simply moved in and picked up the shattered bodies, a scene which was to be replayed again at the Whitehall Recruiting Station on lower Broadway in the months that followed.

On this day, the team from the 120th made it back to their command.

It was later rumored that the Commanding Officer of the First Deputy Commissioner's office was the ranking officer responsible for ordering the Mounted Unit to respond on that fateful day. He was called into the Police Commissioner's office and demoted to the rank of Captain, the highest rank that could be reached by civil service examination. He retired and kept his pension but called a press conference before he did, extolling the virtues of the patrol force as well as the lack of support they had received from City Hall and the police commissioner's office.

He was sorely missed after his departure.

The night went quickly for Charlie. He finished writing his summonses and the lieutenant finished his tale of the Washington Square Park demonstration.

While sitting at the water's edge, both men enjoyed the sight of the sun as it spread across the horizon. After a while another sector car drove down to the secluded spot where they were parked and Charlie saw that it was Police Officers O'Dell and Rizzo. Their sector covered Jersey Street and they stayed out all night looking for collars. They only took a break when things quieted down, usually around 6:00 A.M. which was when they would usually get their breakfast at The Clipper, an old Greek diner at 40 Bay Street. Eventually most guys who frequented the joint simply called it 40 Bay Street and no longer referred to it as The Clipper.

Charlie didn't want to put the lieutenant on the spot so when he saw O'Dell and Rizzo coming into the coop, he started the RMP and pulled out without asking or saying a word. The lieutenant knew the score and didn't say anything either. He knew that the men driving in were good cops and workers and they deserved a break, too.

CHAPTER NINETEEN

T he lieutenant decided to call it a night and told Charlie to take a slow ride into the barn. When they got there, Charlie grabbed all the gear and the lieutenant walked in ahead of him.

Lt. Raymond Velez, the Platoon Commander for the day tour, was already preparing the roll call. They exchanged some pleasantries then the lieutenant went up to his locker room and changed into his civvies. Charlie did the same. This was just one of the advantages of driving the boss.

When he got into his car, he wanted to call Terry but forced himself not to. Lately every time he thought about her he found himself mired down with guilt. On this morning and, after what had been a good night, he decided to go home to Annette. It was Saturday morning and he knew she would be home.

He stopped at Alfonso's Bakery on Victory Boulevard and bought a piece of apple strudel, Annette's favorite. He also purchased a piece of Baklava, a Greek delicacy consisting of filo interlaced with honey and walnuts. It was his favorite and Alfonso's only occasionally made it.

Charlie then drove the three miles to his house and was stunned when he pulled into his driveway. Annette's car was not there. He was in a state of shock but thought perhaps she had gone food shopping earlier than usual to beat the heavy Saturday crowds. He went in and walked directly into the kitchen. There he found a message held onto the refrigerator by a heart shaped magnet.

Dear Charlie, it began, *I had to work overtime today. I probably will be home late tonight so don't wait up for me. If I get a chance I'll call you. Today's work will probably have me in and out of the office all day so don't worry if I'm not there if you call or come looking for me. Love, Annette.*

Charlie felt as if she had covered all of her bases remarkably well. He really didn't want to think she was having an affair but she had never worked overtime on a Saturday before. Here he was, off all day, and he didn't know where his wife was.

He called her office frantically and got the answering machine. The recording was a general message left by most establishments when their office is closed.

"Hi, you have reached J. Blum and Sons. Our office is closed until Monday. Please leave your name, number and a brief reason why you called and someone will get back to you."

Charlie found himself going to pieces and, although it was all he could think about, he knew he couldn't continue on this way because he would cause himself to get really sick. Now he had no doubt that he and Annette needed to have a serious talk about their relationship. All of a sudden the thought of Terry didn't seem to bother him as much. He didn't want to lose his wife and couldn't help but feel that he was responsible for driving Annette into someone else's arms, or bed.

He decided to take a couple of Excedrin PMs and go to sleep, having no doubt that the little blue devils would knock him out and kill most of the day for him. He went up to his bedroom, closed the drapes and put the television on low. As he got into bed, he realized that Annette had left her lingerie drawer slightly open.

He got up to close it but stopped when his gaze focused on the items held within. As he examined some of the colorful pieces of material tucked away inside, he couldn't help but notice that her red teddy was missing. Upon further inspection, he realized there were several other pieces in the drawer that he'd never seen before. He knew Annette was not generally in the habit of buying expensive lingerie but the itty bitty panties he saw, if you could call them that, looked very expensive.

That was when he finally had to admit to himself that someone else was buying sexy outfits for her and she was probably wearing them for him.

Charlie sighed with exhaustion, knowing there was nothing he could do about it right at that moment. He was mentally weary and physically tired. He had to get some sleep. He downed his pills and concentrated on the T.V.

He finally fell asleep and dreamed of Terry. When he woke up close to 7:00 P.M., he felt like he had a hangover. He went downstairs to get some orange juice and heard Annette busy somewhere behind the kitchen door. She said hi when she heard him and gave him a nice kiss on the cheek. He didn't know how to react. He didn't want to appear as if he had no trust in her.

"Hi, honey. How was work?" he asked.

"Busy, sweetheart. Did you try to call?"_she responded.

"I gave it a shot when I walked in. I thought I might have been able to reach you before you left the office. I didn't know you worked on Saturdays," he managed to get out.

"Since when have you been interested? I have worked Saturdays quite a few times since you started making arrests on Friday nights and don't come home until 2:00 or 3:00 P.M. How would you even know I was working? I always thought that the boss' driver didn't have to make arrests? Or at least that's what you've always led me to believe."

She stared at him for several long seconds then added with a serious glare, "You know, Charlie, I just don't know what to think or believe anymore."

Charlie was tongue tied. In his heart he knew she was completely right. He was the one who had been screwing around and now perhaps his wife was as well. He was certain it was his fault for driving her further away. As he stared back at her, unable to speak, he suddenly realized he had to save his marriage. Now was the time when he had to say, or do, whatever it took.

"Annette, I'm sorry you feel the way you do, and I know I have been neglectful. I don't want it to be like this anymore. I truly want to work on our marriage and relationship. Is it too late for me to try?"_he pleaded.

She stared at him with disbelief.

"Honestly, I don't know, Charlie. I have tried so many times before with you. I have waited for you and I have dressed sexy for you, yet I don't seem to turn you on anymore. Don't you find me desirable? Don't you want me?"_she asked, but she didn't give him a chance to answer before she continued, her eyes flashing. "I want someone who is there for me 100% of the time. I want someone to want me. I want someone who finds me desirable and wants to make love to me every day."

Feeling as though his marriage was about to hit rock bottom and smash into a million pieces, he struggled to find the right words.

"Annette, I'm sorry for my behavior and I am ashamed of myself. Can you forgive me? Honey, I love you. Do you still love me?"_he asked.

"I really don't know, Charlie. To be completely honest I wish you no harm or ill will but I just don't know if I love you in that sense anymore," she said, her eyes filled with sadness.

"Annette, is there someone else?"_he asked meekly. Although he suspected what her answer would be, it was still a surprise to hear it.

"Yes, Charlie. I have been seeing someone."_

"Who is it?"_he asked, unable to hide the jealousy in his voice.

"Is it really important?"_she asked as her eyes flashed defensively.

"I guess not," he said quietly.

"How about you, Charlie? Are you seeing someone else?"_

"I was, but it's over. I realize that I love you," he replied.

Charlie knew he wasn't telling the entire truth, but he had no doubt now that he wanted to end it with Terry.

"You know, Charlie, I knew from the start. A wife can always tell. I had hoped it was just a fling like most cops have with a bar maid or waitress. Men fool around for the sex, but women are more vulnerable and cheat for more than sex," she explained.

"What are you telling me? Have you fallen in love with this guy, whoever he is? How do you know he isn't just in it for the sex, too?"_he asked.

"Charlie, we can go around and around with this all day. Let's just agree to be civil right now, okay?"_

"Yeah, I can agree with that, but before we do, I need to know if you going to end it with this guy?"_

Charlie wanted his answer and he wanted it now.

CHAPTER TWENTY

"**A**re we going to try to work this out now, Annette, or do we wait until you decide if you want me again?"_he asked.

He was full of so many questions and wanted, no *needed*, them answered.

"Charlie, no more questions, please. We'll get along better without both them and the pressure that you exert on me," she said.

He felt completely helpless. He was losing his wife to some unknown schmuck who probably just wanted to get laid like he did with Terry. As he stared at her, not knowing what to say, he suddenly realized that he was now on the other side of the fence and he didn't like it, not one bit. He decided to give Annette room and space. He would treat her better and try to woo her like he had done years before. He knew which buttons to press.

He would also contact Terry and break off their relationship. He decided not to call her because he couldn't take the chance of running out of the house to use a payphone. He was down and forlorn but he didn't want to give Annette the impression that he was not happy. He thought if he could be jovial and optimistic, maybe some of it would rub off on his wife.

He would do some chores around the house he'd been keeping on the back burner because of all the time and effort he had been giving to Terry. He needed to catch up on some painting but did not want to drive to Home Depot by himself. He also didn't want his wife to think he was running out to call his girlfriend, so he asked pleasantly,

"Annette would you like to take a ride with me over to Home Depot? I have some painting equipment I want to get."

"No thanks, Charlie. I have some house work that needs catching up."

After mentally running through his honey-do list, he headed down to his basement to tinker around. He had been wanting to organize his workshop for a long time and now seemed like a good time to do just that. He spent a few hours sorting through tools and other gadgets, happy to find that the work helped his mind to relax and kept his thoughts away from his marital problems. When he was finished, his workshop never looked better. He threw away so much junk and clutter that it took four huge garbage bags, which he promptly hauled out to the curb. Now he had a lot more room to work in, and he'd found tools and equipment he'd forgotten he had to boot!

He started to feel hunger pangs so went up to the kitchen to see what he could throw together for dinner. As he approached the top of the stairs, he found Annette already there, standing at the stove, cooking. When the scent of seafood hit his nose, he realized she was making one of his favorite meals. The table was set with some of her good china, not the best, which she reserved for company or very special occasions, but better than their everyday dishes. There was a bottle of white wine chilling in an ice bucket and two shrimp cocktails were sitting at their place settings.

The ice bucket had been a gift he had bought her years ago. It was silver and had an emblem crest on it of an old Italian winery. He also took in the unmistakable aroma of garlic and knew that she had prepared shrimp scampi to go along with the shrimp cocktails.

Charlie was elated to find that his wife seemed as if she was really trying to make things work. If she thought their marriage was a hopeless cause then why would she go through so much trouble to fix his favorite dinner?

"Is there anything I can do to help?"_he asked.

"Just go and wash up. I have everything under control," she said with a shake of her head.

After cleaning all the dirt off his hands, he joined his wife at the dinner table.

"Thank you," he said simply.

"For what?"

"For you; for all of this," he said as he waved a hand across the table before his tone turned serious. "I love you, Annette, and I always will."

"Oh, don't be so melodramatic, Charlie. Eat your food before it gets cold." Although her own voice sounded harsh, she was smiling, just a bit.

Charlie knew that inside Annette was smiling, too, and he found himself on cloud nine. He fervently hoped they could continue in this direction as the coming days turned into weeks.

After dinner he helped load the dishwasher with the dirty dishes then straightened up the rest of the kitchen. When they were finished, Annette put the Italian Espresso maker on and they took their coffee into the living room as soon as it was ready. They watched TV for a while but the entire time Charlie's head was full of questions.

"*Should I try to make love to her tonight? I wonder if she even wants me to try? Does she want me or not? What if I don't make love to her? Would she think I don't want to?*"_Endless, silent questions raced around in his head.

After the nightly news they got up and went upstairs to their bedroom. Charlie undressed, leaving his white tee shirt and boxer shorts on while Annette went into the bathroom and came out wearing a nightgown. She climbed into bed and Charlie reached over to give her a goodnight kiss, which she freely accepted. He tried to kiss her again and placed his hand on her breast.

"Charlie, we had a nice dinner but tonight is not the night for this," she said, answering his unasked questions from just seconds before. "Don't take this wrong, but I have to go slowly with this. Let's not spoil it by rushing into something sexual."

"Okay, honey. I guess you're right," he said then kissed her once more and rolled over on his side. She was right, of course.

When he finally slept, it was Terry, not Annette, in his dreams.

***

The next day Charlie was the first to wake up. He got out of bed and just stood there, watching his wife as she slept. She was beautiful. One of her breasts had become exposed and Charlie couldn't help but think that another man had not only looked at them but had probably kissed them, too. He thought of the so called double standard; he had done every imaginable sex act with Terry but the thought of another man with his wife was killing him.

He forced himself to shower and shave and left the house before Annette woke up. He went to the local bagel Bistro and bought some bagels, some cream cheese and the Sunday paper. He knew that the bagel store had a phone booth but resisted the overbearing temptation to call Terry. He returned home and found Annette up and dressed. She had on a cute outfit of jeans and a silk blouse. He immediately thought of Terry when she had greeted him at her door wearing a similar outfit but quickly forced those thoughts away.

Annette had the coffee on already and was cooking bacon.

"Good morning. I bought your favorite bagels. I even got cream cheese to go with them," he said, smiling at her.

"Sounds good. How do you want your eggs?"_

"Over easy would be fine," he answered.

Charlie poured himself a cup of coffee, sat down at the table and opened his paper.

"Looks like another suicide bomber has killed more people over in Israel," he said grimly.

"I don't think there will ever be peace over there. They're all fanatics," she said as she rotated the bacon.

"Yeah. I guess you're right."

They ate breakfast together with Charlie reading the news section and Annette reading the travel section. When he noticed what part of the paper she was perusing, he found himself a little taken aback. She never read the travel section.

"So where are you going on your vacation?"_he asked jokingly.

"Oh, I don't know. A few of the girls said they wanted to go to Puerto Rico, and it's surprisingly not expensive for an all-inclusive package," she said.

"What are you talking about? You and I never take separate vacations," he stammered.

"Oh, it's not really a vacation. They just want to get away for two or three days."

"Since when do the girls want to get away? They have never done this before, have they?"_he asked as he struggled to hide his anger and disappointment.

"There's a first time for everything, Charlie," she replied casually.

He didn't want to come across as suspicious but vacations were generally a week or more. Two or three days away was more like an office tryst with the boss.

"Are you serious, Annette? You would go someplace like that without me?"_he asked.

"Oh, don't worry. I can take care of myself," she said.

"I'm not worried about you. I'm just trying to work on us. I don't think going away without me is going to help us in any way. Is this something that has been planned already? Is it? I mean is this something that you and your friend had planned together?"_he asked, unable to contain his suspicion any longer.

"Charlie, don't do this. You're acting as if you have no faith in me."

"Annette, I love you. You tell me to go slow. You fix me a wonderful meal and then you hit me with sayonara, I'll send you a postcard from the sunny shores of Puerto Rico. What am I supposed to think?"_

"You simply have to trust me. It's plain and simple," she replied, as she carried her dishes to the sink.

Charlie knew she was right; he would have to leave off with the questions. If she were to come back to him emotionally as well as physically, he would have to pave the road to her heart with gold and not cold, black tar. He would have to win her back with confidence. Whatever was going to happen was going to happen, even if it meant that his wife, the mother of his children, was going to leave him. He dropped the subject like a hot potato and, using reverse psychology, even offered advice on some nice spots in Puerto Rico that he'd heard about. He hoped it would work.

They spent the day outside working in the yard, even taking a nap together later in the day. Although the repair of their marriage looked promising, there was still no physical intimacy between them.

As the day finally drew to an end, Charlie found himself looking forward to going back to work and seeing Lt. A. He had never asked the lieutenant for advice but this time he thought he just might.

CHAPTER TWENTY-ONE

Before he knew it, Charlie found himself once more staring into a mirror beginning his nightly ritual of showering and shaving for work. He didn't mind late tours, in fact he loved them in an eerily, sick sort of way. What he hated was getting out of bed at that time of day to prepare for them. Once he was done with his preparation he was ready to face the night. During the coming shift he was finally going to share his problem and confide in his boss, Lieutenant Audenino. Charlie knew that other men confided with their partners but this was different. Lt. A. was like a partner but so much more. Even though their lives depended upon each other when they were working, the lieutenant was also his boss.

Charlie wondered if Lt. A. would handle their conversation like a partner and keep it to himself, or like a boss and forward it upwards through the channels to the police department's early intervention unit. This unit had been set up to help cops with marital or emotional problems caused by either drinking or money woes. However it would be handled, Charlie's mind was made up. He was going to ask his boss for help.

He kissed Annette goodnight and began his drive into the 120th station house. He decided to take the Staten Island Expressway all the way down to Father Capodanno Boulevard and then along Bay Street to Saint George. He had clear sailing on the S.I.E. and exited at the South Beach exit onto Father Capodanno Boulevard.

The boulevard's namesake had been a Mary Knoll priest with the rank of lieutenant in the U.S. Navy Chaplain Corps. Father Capodanno lost his life providing comfort and assistance to marines fighting in the Quang Tin Province of Vietnam on Sept. 4, 1967 and was posthumously awarded the Medal of Honor. He was a native Staten Islander.

Charlie thought the light traffic was a fairly good sign that the night before him would be quiet. He hoped his assumption was right because he wanted to really utilize the time with his boss.

He parked his car in his usual spot behind the station house and was happy to see that the lieutenant's vehicle was already in the spot in the side lot reserved for the Platoon Commander. Charlie hurried upstairs, bypassing the sitting room. He put on his uniform as quickly as possible then grabbed his gear and lit up a cigarette before descending the back stairs to wait for roll call. As he waited Charlie engaged in a little talk with some of the guys and learned that there had been a shooting in Parkhill. The 4X12 Platoon Commander was still on the call and would need to be relieved by the midnight lieutenant. Charlie wasn't too thrilled to hear this but silently hoped it would be wrapped up by the time he got there with Lt. A.

The sergeants took the roll call and the lieutenant spoke briefly about car stops and safety factors while on patrol. There was no inspection and the troops were quickly turned out into the night. Charlie gassed up the car and picked up the lieutenant, who was waiting in front of the station house.

"We need to relieve Lieutenant Moor over at 180 Parkhill Ave first," the lieutenant told him. "They had a drive by shooting during the night and are waiting for the ESU sergeant to arrive. We're going to hold it down for about an hour because Sergeant Scott had something to do. I told her I would attend to it until she could get there, so let's get our coffee and head over to Parkhill, okay?"_

"Anything you say, Lou," Charlie agreed with a nod.

He drove them to the coffee shop in Stapleton instead of the Dunkin Donut shop on Victory Boulevard because he did not want to see Terry. Not yet anyway.

As they drove, he wondered if the lieutenant noticed how they passed the coffee shop on Victory Boulevard and was relieved when nothing was said about it. When they arrived at the coffee shop in Stapleton, Charlie went inside without asking the boss what he wanted. When it was his turn to order, he asked for a large coffee, light and sweet with half and half, and a large cinnamon bun for the lieutenant and a French Cruller for himself.

Back in the car, they drove over to Parkhill Avenue along Bay Street, passing Bayley Seton Hospital which formerly was called Marine Hospital.

Bayley Seton was named after Elizabeth Anne Bayley Seton. She was the first American born Roman Catholic saint. She used to spend summers on Staten Island at her father's residence in Saint George, and her grandfather was Rector of Saint Andrew's Episcopal Church in Richmond Town in the confines of the 122nd precinct. Elizabeth Anne converted to Catholicism in 1805, after the death of her husband, and later founded the Sisters of Charity of Saint Joseph in Baltimore, Maryland. Her order was responsible for opening numerous Catholic hospitals and orphanages and she is considered the Patroness of the parochial school system in America.

Charlie was amazed that his head held such an array of trivia about the precinct but it had been almost a hobby for him. Too many people took for granted where they lived or how the street on which they lived got its name.

He pulled up to the entrance of 180 Parkhill Avenue and put the car in park. After taking a large sip of his coffee, the boss got out and walked over to Lieutenant Moor who was standing outside of his own RMP. After a brief conversation, Lt. Moor and his driver were soon on their way back to the 120th. There was one sector car on the scene from the 4X12 tour and they were waiting to be relieved by a 12X8 unit.

Lt. A. got back in the car with Charlie, took another sip of coffee and lit a cigarette.

"Looks like it's all cleaned up here," the lieutenant explained as he exhaled a line of smoke out the window. "We just have to wait for ESU to conduct their search for the record and then we're out of here."

Charlie was relieved to hear this but didn't know whether to start his tale of woe right then or wait until a later time. After several long seconds, he finally decided now might be better.

"Lou, do you mind if I ask you a personal question?"_

The lieutenant looked at Charlie in a quizzical way and it made him feel as if Lt. A. knew what he was going to ask.

"First, are you okay?"_asked the lieutenant.

"Yeah, I'm alright, but I really need to talk to somebody and it can't be just anybody. I know how you are with everyone. It's no secret that you do the guys' write ups when they want a medal for a collar. They are always talking about how you spend your own meal hours in the back room at the word processor doing their paperwork for them," said Charlie.

"Well, I enjoy doing it for them. No one else will and no one did it for me when I was a junior cop," explained Lt. A.

"I know that, Lou. That's why I want to speak to you about a problem that I have at home."

"Okay, go ahead," Lt. A. said with a nod.

Charlie told the lieutenant how he had met Terry at the donut shop then explained how he and his wife had been slowly drifting apart, stressing how it never seemed to be as bad as it was now between them. He told Lt. A. his wife had a boyfriend and was planning to go away for a few days to Puerto Rico then admitted how he had made an ass of himself when he began questioning her.

The lieutenant did not once interrupt and allowed Charlie to vent his frustrations for one complete hour.

"Well that's it, Lou. I guess it all comes down to one thing; I'm going to lose my wife," Charlie finally said, half expecting the lieutenant to speak to him like a father and maybe even preach to him a little.

"Charlie, do you love Annette? Can you tell me the feelings you have when you are with either one of them?" asked the lieutenant.

"Well, when I'm with Terry I think of my wife and have feelings of guilt, yet when I'm with Annette, I daydream about Terry."_

"Charlie, I can't tell you what to do – no one can – but I do believe it's human nature for men to think and feel that sometimes the grass is greener on the other side of the fence. Right now, the physical intimacy you have with Terry is fresh, new and exciting. It makes you feel like a young stud again. Unfortunately, it comes with a high price of broken hearts and shattered dreams.

"I am not going to preach to you but believe me when I say I speak from experience. It comes down to this; you must simply decide want you want. How did you feel when your wife told you about Puerto Rico? How did you feel when she prepared your favorite meal? Did you perk up after that? Do you think you have a shot at saving your marriage?

"I'm sure I don't have to tell you that too many guys think with the head between their legs and not the one on their shoulders. Surely you must realize that, just as you are speaking to me now, Annette must be talking to someone close to her also. She, too, must be seeking out advice. If you want to truly save your marriage, and all that it means to you, you must do whatever it takes. Don't play games. Be honest, both with yourself and your wife. From what you are telling me she seems to be very honest with you, as painful as it may be."

The lieutenant took a drink of his coffee then added, "She hasn't actually said that she's going away, has she?"

Charlie nodded.

"Well first I think you should try to feel inside of you. Go somewhere quiet and do your best to listen to the little voices that seem to come out of nowhere and direct us. I truly believe we are guided by these voices, these *guardian angels*, if you wish. Take your time with your decision and just try to live your daily life without any negative vibes. Refrain from anything that you feel or think might be harmful to your life. I truly believe doing positive things and living in a positive way will help you make the right decision for yourself, Charlie, no matter what the outcome is."

When he looked over at Charlie, Charlie nodded.

"If you like, you can talk to me anytime you want. And of course, you know that whatever is said in this car stays in this car. Okay?"

"Thanks, lieutenant. I really appreciate this and I do feel a little better already," said Charlie.

"Is there any particular place you want to go to after we get relieved?"_asked Lt. A.

"No, Lou. To tell you the truth, I was kind of hoping that it would be a quiet night so maybe you could tell me more of your experiences here in the precinct."

"Good!" the lieutenant said as his eyes lit up. "I did want to tell you about another incident that my partner Frank and I handled back in the seventies, but I want you in good shape to hear it."

Lt. A. raised his eyebrows and looked at Charlie with feigned doubt, then they both laughed.

Charlie glanced at his watch and saw that he had been speaking for much longer than he'd suspected he would. He was happy to feel a weight lifted off his shoulders and his head had cleared.

As he lit another cigarette, he noticed another radio car pull alongside them. It was Sergeant Scott; she had finished whatever it was she'd had to do. She saluted Lt. A. and thanked him for covering for her. He nodded at her in return then motioned for Charlie to resume patrol. As they pulled away, Lt. A. notified central radio that they were back on the clock and available for assignments.

"You can drive around or you can park somewhere if you're not up to it, Charlie," Lt. A. said quietly. "I don't really have any preferences tonight."_

"If it's all the same to you, Lou, I think I'll just drive around for a little while," Charlie answered.

They headed back to the station house with the intention of heading out to Mariner's Harbor along Richmond Terrace. Although Charlie had no particular place in mind, it was an easy enough drive at 1:30 A.M. so he took them down Vanderbilt Avenue and made a left turn onto Tompkins Avenue.

"Lou, do you know how Tompkins Avenue got its name?"_

"I don't have the foggiest idea," the lieutenant admitted with a chuckle.

"It was named after Daniel D. Tompkins, who was Vice President of the United States under President James Monroe," explained Charlie. "He lived in Saint George and died on Staten Island."

The lieutenant smiled and nodded, obviously impressed with Charlie's knowledge of Staten Island.

They drove the entire length of Tompkins Avenue and headed down to Bay Street passing the ferry terminal and station house on their way out to the harbor.

"You know, Charlie, driving through Tompkinsville reminded me of when Frank and I handled a job on Targee Street right at Broad Street, just two blocks up from Tompkins Avenue," Lt. A. said wistfully. "Frank and I were assigned to sector E, as you already know. We worked a twenty squad chart back then and just happened to be in our late tour week. It was Christmas Eve and we were working with a skeleton crew, which afforded more men to be off for the holiday.

"Frank didn't have any kids yet and I was damn glad I was doing late tours because it meant I could be home during the day to be with my family. I would get home in time to see my kids open their gifts that old Saint Nick had delivered during the night, and I was also looking forward to having Christmas dinner with the family. I had planned to spend some time with the kids early then get a few hours of sleep in order to be rested enough to get up and enjoy my wife's famous ravioli dinner."

The lieutenant smiled at the memory then continued.

"Frank and I turned out and got our coffee at the all night diner on Bay St. Back in those days we didn't have any Dunkin Donut shops around. We got our coffee and drove up Broad Street and parked on the NE corner of Broad and Targee Sts. facing Van Duzer Street and Demyan's Hofbrau, which was a famous German style restaurant. Demyan was proud that he was the only restaurateur who provided all the food that was used and catered for the filming of the motion picture, *The Godfather*. It was filmed right here on Staten Island. Did you know that Charlie?" asked Lt. A.

"I knew it was filmed on Staten Island but I didn't know about the restaurant catering it," Charlie replied.

"Well, I can't blame you. Demyan's is long gone but I bet you young guys have been to the bar called 'the caves'," said Lt. A.

"Oh, yeah," Charlie said. "I've stopped there a few times. As a matter of fact, the 120th has held some of their parties there."_

"That ugly bar used to house some of the best aged steaks and German beer this side of Bavaria," Lt. A. said. "Anyway, Frank and I parked and started to drink our coffee. It started to snow around 8:00 P.M. but it was a beautiful night. The falling snow looked like innocent, glittering crystals but it was dangerously cold. The air was frigid with the temperature hovering around 8 degrees and every flake stuck to the ground. Before long, about 4" or 5" of snow covered the ground.

"While we sipped our steaming coffee, midnight mass was being celebrated in Saint Paul's Church on Targee Street. Parishioners inside were hearing the story about how baby Jesus was wrapped in swaddling clothes and left in a manger 2,000 years ago.

"It wasn't by chance that Frank and I decided to park at that particular intersection. We were assigned to the midnight mass church crossing. Can you imagine that? At the end of the mass roughly 100 or so of these church-goers would exit the building and we would have to get out of our warm radio car and help them cross the deserted street. It was more public relations than anything else."

Charlie nodded.

"Anyway, while we were having our coffee and talking about the next sergeant's exam, we both heard what we thought was glass breaking from somewhere behind us. We turned to peer through our rear window, which was pretty clear since we'd kept the heat on full blast for just this purpose because remember, we didn't have windows with heated strips back then like we have today. When we turned our attention to the rear window we both saw a figure or silhouette going into the old Romano house on Broad Street. This was an old, two-story wooden frame building that had been abandoned for years and was only used by the local junkies as a shooting gallery. It had been marked for demolition by the city for years but somehow remained standing.

"Frank said he wanted to check it out and I suggested we call for a backup unit, just in case. Although Frank agreed, he started to walk towards the Romano house. That's when the first shot was fired.

"It ricocheted off a metal garbage can that had been left at the curb. The sound was eerily melodic and seemed to linger, like a distant echo repeating itself over and over. Frank wasn't three feet out of the RMP when the second shot shattered the front windshield of a car parked at the curb just a few feet from where Frank was standing. He dove for cover and screamed at me to call in a 10-13, assist patrolman," said Lt. A.

"We got a fucking sniper somewhere in Romano's!" Frank roared.

"Now remember, Charlie, we had no portable radios in those days so I picked up the phone receiver from its cradle, attached to the dash board, and tried to remain as calm as possible. I knew that shouting into the receiver would only produce garbled transmissions on the other end so, in a calm voice, I made several attempts to reach Central but got no response.

"I watched Frank as I spoke into the radio. He was lying flat on his stomach as close to the building line as he could possibly get. I realized then that Frank must have been freezing his ass off and hoped his adrenaline would have kicked in already.

"When I continued to get no response from Central, it struck me that we must be in a radio dead zone. The fucking precinct was loaded with them. The dispatcher who everyone called 'Central' was located on the eighth floor of One Police Plaza in downtown Manhattan. Staten Island had some of the highest elevations on the entire eastern seaboard and the radio signal had to traverse the New York Lower Bay.

"I yelled to Frank that I was going to move the RMP in hopes of getting out of the dead zone and told him not to play hero. Then I drove the car south along Targee Street against traffic on the one-way street and made a left turn onto Metcalfe Street. I drove down the short block and made a left turn onto Gordon Street before finally arriving at Broad Street. Here I was just down the block from Frank and almost directly in front of the Romano house. I parked right there in the intersection because the parishioners in Saint Paul's Church would be getting out of mass soon and I knew that probably 2/3's of them would use the rear doors of the church and walk along Gordon Street right to Broad Street. I had to be in position to warn them not to approach Broad Street.

"I tried to call Central again, even saying that I had an emergency message, but I still got no response. This time though I heard other sectors trying to reach me," the lieutenant explained.

"What do you have, John?"_asked Frankie Catalano. He and Willie Folder from sector C were also working that night.

"Frank, tell Central that we have shots fired at officers. There's a sniper in the corner house at Broad and Gordon. My partner is pinned down at Broad and Targee! I'm using the RMP as cover at Broad and Gordon."

Thankfully, I immediately heard Frankie relaying my message to central radio._

"120 C to central," said Frankie.

"Proceed, sector Charlie," answered the dispatcher, finally.

196

"Central, be advised we have a 10-13 in the confines of the 120th precinct in sector Eddie at Broad and Gordon Streets. Also be advised that two shots have been fired. We need backups and ESU to respond forthwith," Frankie said, his voice calm and direct.

"10-4," replied Central, acknowledging the call.

"This was the first time that I'd heard Central speak. Whatever was broken seemed to be fixed.

"Within a few seconds the sweetest sound this side of heaven, or anywhere else for that matter, came waffling down out of the falling snow right into my ears. Sirens, lovely sirens, Charlie! My brothers in blue were answering my 10-13," said Lt. A., smiling at the memory.

Whenever a 10-13 came over the airwaves, cops stopped whatever they were doing and pressed their feet to the pedal. Many a hot cup of coffee went flying out of car windows or onto laps when a 10-13 sounded. When trouble comes their way they know that the only people they can depend on are other cops. Their very lives are dependent upon each other and their dedication to each other means the difference of going home at the end of the day, or not. Cops don't speak about it but it's there and quite evident. It's there all the time.

The lieutenant smiled and nodded as he stared out the window and continued his story.

"A third shot rang out. I was lying in the snow along the passenger's side of the car, using the vehicle as a shield. I remember feeling how wet and cold the snow was. I was wearing my hat but had it on backwards because I didn't want to give the bastard a target with my shiny, metallic hat device.

"When the fourth shot came, it blew out the driver's side front tire, and the fifth shattered the windows on the left side of the car. The scumbag was getting close. The sirens were growing louder and were music to my ears, which were now becoming uncomfortably numb from the cold.

"As I waited for my reinforcements, it didn't take long for me to realize that the sectors couldn't go all out in their attempts to get to me because the snow on the ground was accumulating and driving was all too treacherous. Any approaching cars would have to be driven with extreme caution. Anyone coming to assist us wouldn't be much use to Frank and I if they cracked up on the way to us.

"Added to our predicament was the fact that there were only five sectors working instead of the usual eight. However, it was Christmas and all of the men working agreed to do so with less coverage in order for more men to have the holiday off.

"I wanted desperately to let a shot go at the bastard but I didn't yet have a decent target. I had six rounds in my chamber and twelve extra in my ammo pouches. Remember, Charlie, we didn't have speed loaders back then like we do today.

"My mind filled with a million questions. What if I shot aimlessly? What if the bastard counted my shots? What if help didn't arrive in time? All my questions led to answers telling me that the cocksucker holed up in that house would blow my head off if I didn't use it to think straight. I didn't even know which window the prick was shooting from.

"I had to take a chance and look up so I decided to crawl on my belly to the rear of the RMP and hopefully get a glimpse of where he was. It wasn't long before I saw the flash of the sixth shot. It instantly and completely reduced Sal's barber shop front window into a million shards of glass. He was holed up in an upper window on the right side of the house. The fuck had a clear view of everything!

"The sirens faded into silence. I knew this meant either they were very close and had no reason now to use the sirens or they had gotten into a jam themselves. At the same time, the ringing of the church bells signaled that midnight mass was over. This was when I experienced something which felt as if it lasted forever but I later learned it had lasted only a few seconds."

The lieutenant paused briefly, buried in memories of a time long gone, then said, "This was when I saw my life pass before my eyes, Charlie. I saw many things that felt like forever but in reality was only a few seconds.

"I was a child again, playing with friends but then, in a split second, I was at my own wedding. I blinked and witnessed the birth of each of my children, then saw them running down the stairs on Christmas morning as they hurried to see what Santa had brought them.

"When this shootout happened on Broad and Gordon, my kids were six and seven. As my life flashed before my eyes, I saw each and every one of their Christmases and I swear to you, Charlie, just as sure as I'm sitting here with you right now, that I heard my son call to me on that night thirty years ago. He called me Daddy and told me to hurry home because he needed me. I knew I had to get home to him, no matter what. Although I didn't know if the images from my past playing through my mind were real or imagined, I had no doubt that the hot tears running down my face that night *were* real because they reached my mouth and I could taste the saltiness of them.

"I was certain that the bullshit going on that night had to end one way or another. I glanced to my right and one of my worst fears materialized right before my eyes. Some of the churchgoers were exiting through the rear door and were heading right towards me.

"Although we both know that ordinary citizens can be inquisitive, why do they have to be so stupid most of the time," the lieutenant said with a frown as he glanced at Charlie. "The crowd from the church noticed me lying in the snow then soon saw the blown out windows and glass glistening atop the cool blanket of white covering the ground. Believe it or not, I could actually hear some of them yelling that someone must be making a movie. Yeah, we were filming a movie minus the lights, cameras and actors. I had the action though, didn't I? I yelled at them to get back onto the side street but the idiots stayed right where they were and just stared."

He took a drink of coffee before he continued.

"Then another shot rang out. I can still hear the scream that followed as if it just happened yesterday. It was blood curdling, loud, and unlike anything you hear in a Hollywood movie. Screams in real life are incomparable to movie screams. This one was real and was followed by moans and murmurs. The crowd that lingered before was gone now except for one strapping young black kid who probably lived in the Stapleton houses across the street.

"I reached into the RMP and pulled the radio out of its cradle, stretching it as far towards me as it would go. I wanted to reach anybody that I could. Thankfully, Frankie in sector C heard me and I told him I had a shooting victim. I explained that I didn't know his condition or where he'd been shot but I needed an ambulance right away," Lt. A. said.

"Charlie, I crawled over to the kid, staying as low as I could. You know, if it had been just a little warmer I would have been soaked, but since it was so cold, I stayed fairly dry.

"I heard the kid moaning and was relieved to know he was still alive. Although I didn't know what the scumbag was shooting with, I knew it was powerful because of all the damage it had done.

"I grabbed the black kid by the collar of his coat and pulled him back to the cover of the RMP. Frank must have seen me dragging the boy from wherever he was hiding because he laid down a barrage of shots at the house in order to provide cover for me. Thankfully, it worked and the sick fuck didn't let any more bullets fly while I was dragging the shot victim to safety.

"I checked the kid out and as far as I could tell he had been hit in the stomach or groin area. I couldn't help but hope that since I didn't see much blood, maybe this young kid who had just finished celebrating baby Jesus' birthday would make it. I said a little prayer for both of us and started to apply pressure to the young man's wounds. a few seconds he came to a little. When he saw me, he began to pleading with me not to let him die," the lieutenant said quietly.

"'Please, Mister, don't let me die. Oh, Mommy, help me!' the boy said through tears of pain and fear. When I was trying to reassure him that he would be fine, he passed out again. I didn't know this was caused by loss of blood or shock, but I knew either one could be fatal.

"I made my way back to the rear of the car and fired two shots at the upper window. As the sound of gunfire echoed through the city, I took a chance and opened the trunk of the car, hoping my shots would keep the bastard's head inside long enough for me to retrieve a blanket from the trunk. It worked. I got the blanket, brought it over to the kid and covered him. As I did so, I glanced down Broad Street and saw the most brilliant array of colors coming towards me. The approaching sector cars had their turret and dome lights on. In the falling snow, the reds, whites and yellows cast a beautiful Christmas glow to an already white and glistening scene.

"The truck of ESU was the first to pull up. They positioned their vehicle between the Romano house and me. Frankie Catalano in sector C was next and he pulled up on my right side," Lt. A. explained.

"'Are you okay? Where's your partner?' asked Frankie. I told him I was fine and asked him to go check on Frank but before Frankie could leave, my partner appeared from the Gordon Street side of the block. When he saw all the units arriving he ran around the block and came down the side street adjacent to the church.

"Reunited once more, Frank and I didn't say anything to each other. We just smiled and shook hands," the lieutenant said with a reminiscent smile.

"The ESU rig came with their own supervisor and he gave the order to his men to suit up. This meant that the team would all don thick, protective bulletproof vests and arm themselves with heavy gauge shotguns. The ESU sergeant also directed one of the 120th units to go to the rear of the house in order to prevent the bastard from escaping.

"The ambulance for the kid also arrived and they quickly transported him to the hospital. At the same time, ESU sharpshooters had their guns trained on all the front windows as well as the roof. Before long, ESU Sergeant Joe Noturo led his men up the front stairwell of the house.

"As I'm sure you know, the ESU unit consisted of cops that other cops called when they needed help. These were the troops who climbed the spans of bridges and talked jumpers down. They were also the ones with paramedic training who could keep victims alive. Tonight they were searching for a sniper who had attempted to kill a few of their own and who just might have killed a civilian.

"Joe Noturo had been a Sergeant in ESU for almost eight years. He started out in patrol but applied and got on in his first interview. He had been trained in everything from repelling out of helicopters to walking the bottom of New York Bay in diving gear.

"Sergeant Noturo approached the 2nd floor landing of the house in question but didn't hear a sound. He held his flashlight down and to the right of his body just in case the bastard aimed for the light. He hugged the wall as he and his two men approached the first room closest to the stairs on the landing. When they reached it, they burst through the door but the room was empty. A small sink and commode, which had been smashed by vandals years before, lay on the floor. There was only one room left on the floor to search; the front room bedroom where the shots had originated from.

"All three officers approached the door. After pausing for just a second or two, Sergeant Noturo, all 200 pounds of him, kicked the door in. The room was small and had a closet in the corner. Quietly the trio approached the closet door. One of the men grabbed the handle and swung it open while the other two stood at the ready with their weapons cocked, but the tiny room was empty. They searched the bedroom and there, on the floor right below the window facing the street, was a K-tec machine gun pistol. Spent shells littered the floor around it.

"The trio completed their search of the entire house but came up short. The bastard must have gotten away through a rear entrance before the 120th sectors were able to secure it.

"The Sergeant confiscated the gun and had it delivered to the precinct for vouchering. From there it would make its way to the ballistics lab in the city in order to see if it had been used in any previous crimes. It would be dusted for prints at the precinct level to see if the shooter could be identified. Hopefully it would be linked to the shooting of the kid if, in fact, he died.

"Sergeant Murphy, the 120th patrol supervisor, had also responded. He told Frank and I to get into his car then he drove us back to the station house. He had already notified the department tow truck to come and tow the bullet riddled radio car to the department pound, which was located at the 122nd Precinct. There they would take photos of the car and collect any shells or fragments found in the car so they could be used in court at a later date.

"The crime scene unit, who constantly monitored all radio frequencies from their home base in Manhattan, also had to respond. When they heard that someone had been hit during the sniper shooting, they packed up their gear and headed out to the 120th. They had the responsibility of searching the crime scene and assisting in any way they could in the collecting of evidence.

"Sergeant Murphy sent one of the sector cars that had been on the scene to the Saint George Ferry terminal, where one of the rookies who had been assigned to the precinct earlier that month was walking a foot post in the empty but still icy cold terminal.

"There was no police room in the terminal back then, where you can get warm and even lock the door and take a nap, like there is today. The sector would pick up the kid on foot post at the terminal and transport him to the crime scene. Once there, he would guard the area until the CSU, or crime scene unit, had completed their work. Even though it meant standing outside in the snow, it still was good duty for the rookie since he got an opportunity to be part of the investigative team.

"Unlike police drama on television, where the good guys shoot the bad guys and leave bodies on every street corner, my partner and I had to face hours of both questioning and paperwork after this incident. Since we had both discharged our weapons, they had to be checked out, too.

"Finally, it was 6:00 A.M. and we were almost finished with the paperwork. Although the entire incident in the street lasted for only about an hour, the paperwork stretched out afterwards for almost six hours.

"The boss on the desk that night was Lt. Fontaine. He walked into the back room just as I was finishing up," Lt. A. explained.

"Where's Sergeant Murphy," asked the desk officer.
"He went up to his locker to get some cigarettes," I answered.

"Well, when he comes down, please tell him that he needs to amend his U.F. 49. That young black kid succumbed to his wounds a little while ago at the hospital," Lieutenant Fontaine said sadly.

"Charlie, I was totally dumbfounded. I didn't expect that kid to die. Suddenly I wanted to know anything at all about him," Lt. A. said quietly.

"He was only eighteen years old and his name was Devon Alston and, according to all accounts, he was a good kid. The squad doesn't have any previous record on him and he had no rap sheets. According to some of his neighbors, the young man was scheduled to take the next police officer exam in January. It's a fucking shame. You know, with Christmas and all that," said Lt. Fontaine.

"I'm sure I don't have to tell you that I felt like shit, Charlie. I had tried to reassure the kid that night so long ago that he would be okay. This was when I realized again why I hate fucking holidays," Lt. A. said.

I went up to my locker and changed, trying not to think of the kid who had probably gotten killed in an attempt to save my life. All I could think of was going home to my wife and kids. I said a silent prayer and went out to my car for the drive home.

I called my wife and told her I would be a little later than usual but didn't tell her what had transpired. I figured it would make the local paper and then I would explain to her what really happened. I didn't want to spoil her day and make her worry needlessly. Cops' wives worry enough just by reading the paper and listening to lies and half-truths that are printed by rag newspapers. I knew she would keep the kids on the 2nd floor landing of our house until I got home because she knew how much I wanted to see them run down those stairs. I didn't want to miss those gleaming smiles on their faces as their eyes widened with wonderment when they saw all the brightly covered presents Santa had left for them.

When I walked in the front door, I heard them on top of the landing.

"Hurry, Daddy, hurry!" my daughter squealed.

With a smile and a prayer of thanks, I told them to come down. My wife had the camera at the ready but I didn't need any camera. I had just lived that scene a few hours earlier and now I was actually home. I wanted to take those kids into my arms and squeeze them forever, but I knew they were totally enveloped in unwrapping those beautiful presents that old Saint Nick had left.

For a moment, my mind suddenly wandered and I thought about Devon Alston's family. I wondered what they might be going through. I said another silent prayer for them and thanked God for what I had as I wiped a tear from my face. My wife asked me if anything was wrong but I told her no, everything was just fine. I had made it home for another day.

Lt. A. looked at Charlie as a tear trickled down his face. "Now you know why I hate holidays," he said quietly.

"I can see," Charlie agreed.

They had been driving along Bay Street the entire time it took the lieutenant to share his story about the sniper.

"You look tired, Charlie. Pull over and I'll drive for a while."

Charlie was used to sharing driving assignments with the boss. For all he knew, Lt. A. was the only boss in the entire borough who shared the driving.

They switched seats as well as their gear. As the lieutenant pulled away from the curb, he noticed Charlie's head bobbing up and down. Although it was obvious he was fighting to stay awake, it appeared to be a losing battle.

"You want coffee, Charlie?" asked the lieutenant.

"No thanks, Lou," Charlie answered as he stifled a yawn.

The lieutenant drove to an all-night bodega on Jersey Street and got a strong cup of Tampico to go. He knew the bodega made a good cup of Spanish coffee because he'd had it from there before. With steaming cardboard cup in hand, the boss then drove out to Sailor Snug Harbor and parked on a quiet and desolate block. After turning off the engine, he opened the coffee and began sipping the hot, strong liquid.

"I thought you got the coffee for me?" asked Charlie.

"No, Charlie. Close your eyes. I'll wake you if anybody comes around," said the boss.

Here was Charlie's boss, a lieutenant, telling Charlie to sleep. Lt. A. was a good, fair boss, and when it was needed he worked his ass off. In spite of this, he didn't let anyone shit on his men and he definitely didn't let a cop fuck another cop. He cared about his troops.

Lt. A. finished his coffee and let Charlie sleep for about 45 minutes. Charlie woke up on his own and felt somewhat refreshed. All he had needed was to close his eyes for a while and take a power nap.

The rest of the tour went quickly for Charlie. Even better, he knew what he would have to do about his problem.

CHAPTER TWENTY-TWO

C harlie had no doubt now that he wanted to save his marriage. To do this, he would have to break off his relationship with Terry. He decided to call her and ask if he could come over for a cup of coffee. He would not call Annette because he knew it would only make her think he was lying again.

He and the lieutenant drove into the station house then Charlie carried in his gear and climbed the back stairs to his locker room to change. He decided to save a few minutes by signing out in his civilian clothes and figured the desk area would be so busy that no one would even notice him. He was right. He had a good head start and drove to a pay phone on Victory Boulevard where he called Terry. When she answered, she sounded happy to hear from him.

"Oh, Charlie, I've missed you these last few days! Can you come over this morning?"_

"Yeah, but I can't stay too long," he replied.

He tried his best to not sound cold but also didn't want to infer that he planned on getting laid either. His only desire was to tell the truth. Cheating and lying was a part of that whole negative trip that Lt. A. had advised him to avoid; he didn't want or need any more negativity in his life.

"I planned on making you a nice breakfast, sweetheart. Then I thought maybe we could take a nice bubble bath together and hold each other in bed. I know how you love sex in the morning and I can't help but tell you that I'm dying to put my mouth on you, honey," she murmured.

"Unfortunately, I don't think I'll have time for that this morning, Terry. I have a few things I have to do today but I did want to see you and talk to you this morning."

"Okay, Charlie. I'll put the coffee on and you can tell me whatever it is you want to tell me," she said in a questioning sort of way.

Charlie hung up the phone and made his way out to Terry's place. He wanted to get this over with as quickly and as painlessly as possible. He didn't want to hurt Terry but he also didn't want to lose Annette, even though there was a strong possibility that his wife would still leave him.

He parked in his usual place and walked up the driveway to her front door. Terry was waiting there with the door open and welcomed him inside with a big hug. When he hugged her back, it was obvious that she could sense an eerie coldness in his return embrace.

"Charlie, what's wrong?"_

"Nothing, Terry. How have you been?"_

She didn't answer. Instead, she walked straight into the kitchen and sat at the table. Charlie followed her in and did the same. He thought it strange that he noticed she was wearing the same tight jeans and silk blouse with no bra but he wasn't turned on or even thinking about sex.

"Charlie, I know something is wrong. What is it? Do you have a problem at work? Is your wife okay? What is it, Charlie? Please tell me. Please don't be like this," she begged.

"It's nothing like that, Terry. My wife has a boyfriend. When I confronted her about it she asked me if I was seeing anybody and I told her the truth," he explained.

"I see," she said coldly.

"Terry, you know how I feel about you. That hasn't changed. You're a sweet, beautiful young woman," he said as he tried to lessen the pain he knew his words were inflicting on her.

"Yeah, sure. Sweet, young, and beautiful, but you don't want me anymore, right Charlie? You've finished with your play thing and now you're moving on."

Although he wasn't surprised by her reaction, her words still stung him.

"Terry, how can you say that? I have always been open and honest with you. I've never lied to you. I gave myself to you in a very special and caring way."

She sighed as she stared at him across the table. "I'm sorry, Charlie. I just don't want to lose you. Please forgive me for saying that. What is your wife going to do? Is she really planning on leaving you?" Before he could answer, she added, "Charlie, does she still love you?"_

"I don't know. She said she needs time to think it out and honestly, I guess I do, too."

Terry realized Charlie was choosing his wife over her and he was going to try salvaging his marriage with Annette regardless of what his wife did. She also had no doubt that she had fallen in love with him and, although she was devastated by his decision, she didn't want him to know how deep her feelings were for him. Even though he was older, he was different from all the other men she had ever become involved with. There was something about Charlie that she adored. It wasn't just one thing, but a lot of little things, that put a smile on her face whenever she thought of him and a gleam in her eye whenever she desired him. She didn't want to lose him and she was prepared to do whatever it took to keep him.

"Charlie, do you love me? I know what you say when we're in bed together, but do you really love me? I would really like an answer, an honest answer, to that question, please," she said.

"I do care for you, Terry. I think of you every day and dream of you. I desire you and want you all the time, but is that love? Honestly, I don't think I know what love is anymore. What's right? What's wrong?

Do the answers to those questions matter anymore? If I left my wife, would our relationship remain the same or would it change? Would change be good or bad for us? Would I begin to blame you for my failed marriage? Would I blame myself and allow guilt to consume me and destroy any chance for happiness for either you or I? I don't know the answers to any of those questions, but I must make a decision and time has to be on my side," he explained rationally.

She sighed and remained silent for several seconds. When she finally spoke, her voice was pleading. "Okay, Charlie. What do you want me to do? Are you going to call me anymore? Will you still stop in for coffee? Do I keep telling other guys that I can't go out with them because I have a boyfriend? Please tell me what it is that you want me to do."

"I have no right to tell you to sit at home while I try to save a marriage that may already be beyond saving. If I fail then I will have to pick up the pieces to my life. I can't expect you to sit and wait for the outcome, whatever it may be," he answered.

Terry realized that Charlie was right. It wasn't what she wanted to hear but he was painfully right. She had no doubt that the next few weeks would be rough on her; she suspected it would be rough on both of them. She was tired of being nice and playing second fiddle to married guys who came and went before and after their shifts. She needed time to think and plan.

"Well Charlie, I guess we both need time to think. Could you do me a favor though? Until you know for sure what your wife is going to do, could you at least call me once in a while?" she begged. "I do care about you, you know."_

Charlie didn't want to call. He was certain that a clean break would be the best for both of them, but he couldn't deny he would want to know how she was doing. He didn't want to destroy her completely and besides, what harm could there be in an occasional phone call?

"Yeah, sure," he said. "I'll call you once in a while."_

Their discussion was over, so they hugged each other one last time then Charlie got into his car and drove home. When he got there, as he suspected, Annette had already left for work so he showered and went to bed.

He slept soundly for the entire day and, thankfully, didn't dream about Terry. He was tired from the night before. He had driven quite a bit even though the lieutenant had allowed him to grab a few winks. He couldn't wait until he told the other guys and knew some of them would be jealous.

When he got up, Annette was home and busy preparing supper. At first he thought it was nothing special. She had taken out some previously frozen Marinara sauce and was putting it in a pan. A pot of water was boiling on the stove, and a box of pasta was open on the counter, ready to be added to the water. His mouth watered when he realized Annette was making some of her delicious meatballs.

As he watched his wife bustle around the kitchen, he was dying to tell her that he had officially ended his relationship with Terry but decided not to even broach the subject. He would just go about his daily life as if the affair had never happened. He secretly hoped that Annette would be able to pick up on his feelings and emotions and also end her affair but he wasn't so sure that she would. He walked over to her and gave her a kiss on the cheek then sat at the kitchen table while she worked on supper.

"How was your day?"_he asked.

"Good. I had a real good day. I decided not to go on the trip to Puerto Rico with the girls," she added.

"Oh? How come?"_he asked, trying to keep his voice neutral.

"I know what you thought about that trip, Charlie," she said quietly. "You thought I was going to go on it with my friend, but you were totally wrong on that one."_

He was glad to hear it but did not show his joy.

"Well, maybe you and I could get away for a little trip of our own. We could go to Atlantic City or the Bahamas for a few days. We can kind of make believe it's a second honeymoon if you like," he suggested.

"We'll see, Charlie. It's been really busy at the office and I know I won't be able to get away any time in the near future."

Although he wanted to discuss it more, Charlie decided to let the subject rest and just agree to let time go by as it would.

"I'm ready anytime you are," he said with an encouraging smile.

A few minutes later Annette served dinner and they ate while she talked about her day. He really tried to listen aggressively and seemed interested in what she was saying, even though most of it was boring stuff about real estate deals and house closings. They cleaned up after dinner together and watched TV for a while. After an hour or two, Annette said she was feeling tired and went to bed. She knew Charlie would stay downstairs and use the bathroom on the first floor to prepare for work, but this time she walked over to him and kissed him nicely.

"Be careful at work," she said quietly then turned and made her way upstairs.

Charlie felt good and couldn't wait until he saw Lt. A. to tell him that he had followed his advice and everything seemed better with his marriage.

Now if only Terry felt the same way.

Charlie drove to work through heavy traffic, which wasn't a good sign. Congestion on the roadways at this hour usually indicated that the night would be a busy one.

Upon entering the station house he saw several prisoners waiting in front of the desk, each in the process of being booked. Standing directly behind them were the elite members of the Street Crime Unit, not in any uniform but wearing civilian clothes, which was expected. Most sported heavy beards and pony tails, making them appear to be perpetrators themselves.

It most assuredly looked as if it was going to be a busy night, which made Charlie happy. The busier it was, the less he would have to drive. He knew Lt. A. liked to work, but the boss also enjoyed telling his war stories, which they wouldn't have time for if it was busy.

Charlie made his way up to his locker and put on a fresh shirt. He liked to get three days out of a shirt but the one he was wearing was very much wrinkled from his nap the night before, so he decide to put on a new one. He was dying for coffee and hoped the lieutenant would turn out early. It didn't take long for him to realize he was lucky; Lt. A. wanted to go out right away.

"Did you pass the fire on your way to work?"_the lieutenant asked him.

"Was that the cause of all the traffic, Lou?"

"Yeah, the old Italian deli, Montalbano's, was going up in flames."

Montalbano's had been part of the Rosebank neighborhood for as long as he could remember. It was a small place, but walking into that store was an instant feast for your nose. There were hanging cheeses of Parmesan, sides of Prosciuto hams curing, as well as plenty of dried figs and apricots. There were rows upon rows of sun dried tomatoes as well as garlic strung up on twine, each one giving off a wonderful yet delicate aroma. The hero sandwiches, made by Mama Montalbano, were so large that even after you cut it in half you would still think it was too much to eat.

Montalbano's was good to all the cops in the precinct because the owner's son was a detective on Staten Island. It also had the respect of all the cops in the precinct and was never taken advantage of. There was a well-known yet unwritten law that only the men assigned to the sector holding this place of business could partake of their generosity, even though the owner would have fed all the cops in the precinct if given the opportunity. Other men who wanted to partake of their delicacies paid full price, just like everyone else.

"I sure hope they rebuild," the lieutenant said morosely. "My partner and I frequented the place many times years ago when we had the adjoining sector. That deli was in sector C, which belonged to Frankie Catalano and Willie Folder. I did tell you that once, didn't I?"

"Right, Lou. They backed you and Frank up on Christmas Eve, I think you said?" remembered Charlie correctly.

"Yes. Just thinking about those two guys makes me remember an incident that happened years ago and frankly, I'm surprised I didn't tell you this one sooner.

"Frank and I were working a 4X12 tour when he told me Frankie and Willie were going to make an unannounced visit to the Underground Tavern at 10:00 P.M. sharp. I knew what had happened there a few weeks back and agreed that street justice was the only form of justice street punks understood.

"My partner Frank had more time on the job than I did, but not more than Frankie or Willie. God knew that the Underground Tavern probably deserved whatever it was Frankie had in mind and then some. I told Frank I wanted to be a part of whatever was going to go down, and I didn't want to fink out," Lt. A. explained to Charlie then drifted into his story.

The Underground Tavern in Staten Island was a bar and gin mill. Although most cops called it a "Bucket of Blood" because so many fights occurred there, the place was different from many other bars that simply hosted bar fights and near riots. The Underground was a skel joint supreme, rowdy and raucous. There was always a fight going on and someone was always getting assaulted with a broken bottle or worse. It was a hangout for bikers, young toughs, local winos and just about any loser you could think of. It became even more rowdy when the Hells Angels, the infamous motorcycle club, set up their clubhouse on Jersey Street not far from the precinct itself. It was not your friendly neighborhood social club.

Of course there were plenty of bars that catered to local residents. These were for people who just wanted to stop in for a quick brew, watch a sporting event or just catch up on local gossip. Most of them had no loud rock or rap as choices in music. Instead, the jukeboxes were stacked with oldies, Sinatra and Streisand. Joints like this were also frequented by local cops and were considered safe havens. Veteran cops didn't want any trouble. They just wanted a quick and quiet beer after a 4X12 or a quick game of liar's poker.

There were also bars one could go to if one just wanted a strange piece of ass. Those were the bars frequented by teeny boppers, groupies and cop buffs.

The Underground was neither. Any music being played there consisted of heavy metal and rap. The bar itself was made of wood and many a knife-wielding patron had carved his or his mother's name into it. There were no tables and only a few booths where, it was rumored, biker girls completed their initiation into the club by giving blow jobs to all the other members. The bartenders, for the most part, were ex-convicts. It was obvious that someone in Borough Hall got paid off for allowing all this to happen.

The lighting in the place left a lot to be desired. It could best be described as early Tom Edison. There were just bare bulbs and flickering neon lights, which caused blindness after so many weeks of illumination, and the interior decor was no better. It could be classified as early dump. The floor was strewn with broken bottles, cigarette butts and roaches – and not the living kind. Not surprisingly, those who frequented this special place hated and detested cops.

Frankie and Willie had been called to The Underground on one of their 4X12 tours to handle a dispute. Imagine that, a disagreement in The Underground. When it was revealed by Central over the radio that the call was for a fight, everyone who heard the broadcast laughed a little bit inside. Any nearby sector would head in that general direction, just in case a call for assistance was requested. Usually the car assigned would find out first and if no help were needed, a "no further" would go out over the airwaves.

When Frankie and Willie got there, they walked in and found a guy lying on the floor. At first glance it looked as if he just had too much to drink and fallen off of his stool. He appeared to be out like a light, so Frankie knelt down to get a closer look. The guy's breathing was labored and Frankie soon saw that he was bleeding from the top of his skull.

While Frankie checked out the victim, Willie had his eyes glued on everyone in the place. When Frankie nodded to Willie, he knew a crime had been committed and they had a crime scene to preserve. Willie quickly made a head count of everyone in the joint. There was one bartender, six at the bar, two booths with two each and bathrooms yet to be checked.

"You all had better sit tight. No one is going anywhere until we find out what happened," Willie said with authority. Without another word, he made his way over to the door and locked it.

Frankie walked behind the bar and used the phone he found there to call Central. He told the dispatcher what he had and requested the Patrol Sergeant, an ambulance and the night watch detectives to respond.

As first responders, Frankie and Willie had the responsibility of conducting the initial investigation. They began by asking the most basic questions, but everyone clammed right up. No one had seen or heard anything, which was to be expected. There was no love lost in that skel hole between its patrons and cops.

Frankie began going through the victim's pockets in hopes of finding some identification. Assaulting someone was one thing but removing his property was robbery and that would make it a heavy. Before he was finished, Frankie was amazed at what he found.

The guy on the floor was a cop. He was either off duty or a plain clothes man on duty, but this fact had yet to be established. From the I.D. card and other papers on him, Frankie ascertained that the young cop was a member of the P.C.C.I.U., which is the Police Commissioners Confidential Investigating Unit. Those were the guys who had the nickname of Prince of the City. They were untouchable but weren't super clean like Eliot Ness' men. Instead, these guys were on the take, plain and simple. They had citywide jurisdiction and were befriended by judges and politicians alike in all boroughs. They wore diamond pinky rings and smoked expensive cigars, answering only to the Police Commissioner's office.

Frankie quickly patted down the unconscious cop and quickly realized that his ankle holster was empty.

"All right, mother fucker," he roared looking squarely at the bar tender. "What the fuck happened and where's the fucking gun?"

"I don't know, shit pig, and if I did I wouldn't tell you a fucking thing anyway," the man behind the bar spat back.

It was quite obvious that almost everyone in the place had either seen what had happened or, by now, knew something about it. Frankie knew someone in the bar had called 911 and hoped that whomever did was still there. He also realized that person who had made the call wasn't going to voluntarily come forward, at least not in front of the other patrons. As he stared at the faces around the room, Frankie began to wonder if the young, unconscious cop had stopped in this skel joint on business or pleasure, or both.

When it was clear no one was going to talk, he told Willie he was going out to the RMP to get some chalk and tape to help secure the crime scene. Frankie unlocked the door and opened the door as a biker quickly followed him outside. After they were both outside, Willie quickly relocked the door behind his partner.

When he heard the door lock, Frankie quickly grabbed the biker following him and threw him against the side of the building. He hit the bearded patron several times with the back of his hand, causing blood to flow from the scroungy, biker's lips. Frankie quickly placed handcuffs on the man and threw him into the rear seat of the RMP then opened the front door and sat down behind the wheel.

"I thought that was you, Tony. Grow a beard? Sorry I roughed you up but I didn't want to blow your cover," Frankie said to the bleeding biker.

Tony Calandritto had been a plainclothes cop assigned to gambling and narcotics and had been drafted to go undercover. He was an avid motorcycle enthusiast so they tapped him to infiltrate the Hells Angels. Frankie had broken the kid in when he was a rookie in the 60th precinct which covered Coney Island in Brooklyn. If he survived the assignment, he would be promoted to detective 3rd grade.

"Tell me what the fuck happened in there, Tony," Frankie said.

"The fucking kid came in acting like gang busters, Frankie. He started to toss everybody in there and before I knew it, he was coming up with all kinds of shit. I mean everything. Acid, PCP, hash, pot, guns, I mean the works. Then he dropped some of it on the floor at the end of the bar."

Tony caught his breath as his eyes flashed at the man in the front seat. "You know as well as I do, Frankie, that some of those guys in there are three time losers. As in, they've got to do heavy time if they get busted on weapons possession."

Frankie was all ears.

"So, like I said, the fucking kid drops some shit on the floor. When he bent down to pick it up, the bartender cold cocks him in the head with a fucking jack that he had hidden somewhere behind the bar, " Tony explained.

They both knew that this was for information only. Tony could not break his cover and Frankie couldn't use him as a witness in court. As far as Frankie was concerned, the young cop inside bleeding on the floor was stupid and overzealous but was acting like a cop and was not intent to shaking anyone down for money.

"Drive me around the block, Frankie. I'll get a cab and lay low for a while. Somebody will take care of my wheels for me. It's parked on the side. It's a Harley with black saddle bags. I'll get my C.O. to create an arrest number with my cover name on it to be generated in the 120th, " said Tony.

Frankie dropped him off at a phone booth several blocks away and drove back to the bar. He rapped on the front door with his nightstick and Willie let him in.

"Where the hell have you been?"_asked Willie.

"Tell you later, partner, " Frankie responded.

While Frankie had been en route back to the bar he put in a second call for an ambulance without letting the dispatcher know that the victim was a cop.

Now knowing what had happened, he approached the bartender.

"Tell me what the fuck happened and tell me now, scumbag, " he demanded with outrage. "If you don't, I'm going to find out anyway. "_

Frankie was hoping for some kind of admissive statement from the pimply-faced bartender, who was an ex-convict with arms that bore the unmistaken signs of tattoos indicating membership in the Aryan brother- hood. He even had the word 'evil' tattooed across his knuckles.

Frankie had no doubt that if the young cop ever regained consciousness, he wouldn't be able to identify his assailant because he was struck while he was facing downwards. He also knew he would not and could not blow Tony Calandritto's cover under any circumstances. It looked as if this was going to remain an open case with everybody beating the rap.

"So tell me now, " said Frankie.

"Eat this, " the bartender said, grabbing his crotch.

218

"When I find out, and I will, I'm coming back for you, mother fucker," said Frankie with a growl.

The bartender knew no one would be able to identify him and none of the patrons would rat on him, so he continued running off his mouth. Frankie wanted to take his own jack and smash the guy's teeth in but he heard the sirens of the approaching ambulance and was more concerned now in taking care of his young cop.

Willie unlocked the door when the paramedic team pulled up. It was EMS # 27 out of Saint Vincent's Hospital. One EMT immediately bent down and began checking the kid's vital signs.

"Looks as if he's stable enough for transport," said the older of the two paramedics.

Vic, the younger EMT, had been a paramedic for seven years, all with Saint Vincent's, so he knew all of the men assigned to the 120th. He quickly snapped open an ammonia amulet beneath the kid's nose and amazingly enough, the injured cop started to come out of it. He wasn't speaking yet but he did seem to have some awareness regarding his surroundings. Vic and his partner opened up the portable gurney they had brought in and together, with Frankie and Willie, the men hoisted the kid up onto the stretcher then wheeled him outside. After lifting him up into the rear of the ambulance they sped away with lights shining and sirens blaring to Saint Vincent's Hospital.

Before Frankie and Willie left the bar, Frankie pointed his finger ominously at the bartender.

"You and I now have a date, scumbag," he promised as he and his partner got into their radio car.

On the way to Saint Vincent's emergency room, Frankie said, "Willie, get on the radio and have the patrol sergeant re-directed to the emergency room instead of going to the bar."_

"Okay, Frankie."

"We'll just have to complete our paperwork there," Frankie added.

Neither Frankie nor Willie had told anyone that their young victim was a cop but they knew they could trust Vic, who would only do what was medically necessary for the kid. He wasn't a snoop and could be counted on 100%. They were also very careful not to put anything over the airwaves indicating that the victim was a police officer. News agencies always monitored police department frequencies looking for news. The longer they could keep the lid on the details, the better off it would be.

It was a two mile run to the hospital. The staff at Saint Vincent's had a good relationship with the men of the 120ᵗʰ precinct, unlike Doctor's Hospital over on Targee Street, which treated cops lower than whale shit.

The 120ᵗʰ precinct was a busy house and the emergency room at Saint Vincent's was a reflection of the brutality that its population inflicted upon itself. The cops were even given their own little room where they could complete paperwork out of view from visitors and outpatient psychos. The hospital staff was glad that the cops were there and the cops were glad to be there for them.

Frankie stopped on the way and picked up two coffees for himself and his partner as well as a dozen donuts for the ER crew. When they arrived, Sergeant Murphy was waiting for them.

Sergeant Murphy was one of the most highly decorated members of the police department. Before being promoted to sergeant, he had been a member of the infamous Stakeout Squad or SOS. The SOS was a team of cops, sergeants and detectives who were all hand-picked for the assignment. They would be assigned to places of business which had been the target of numerous stick ups involving weapons. Their job was simply to hide in the rear of the establishment under cover and, on a pre-arranged signal, come out blasting.

Sergeant Murphy had been in that unit for almost four years and, in that short space of time, had been involved in seventeen separate shooting incidents with twelve of the perpetrators shot fatally.

When the ACLU finally came to New York City the unit was forced to disband. Afterward, robberies and deaths skyrocketed once again.

Sergeant Murphy's chest was a virtual fruit salad. He had every medal that the department issued, from Excellent Police Duty right up to the Department Medal of Honor which most men win posthumously. He had been a street cop and now he was a street sergeant. He did not work in a detail or the ivory tower of police headquarters.

"Charlie, he was my idol," Lt. A. said with a smile. "I wanted to be like him and I wanted to stay in the street."_

Some bosses had to rely on their stripes or bars for the authority that they yielded, and some, but not most, relied on who they were and what they stood for, like Sergeant Murphy. You could have asked him anything and he would have known how to handle it. He was a cop's cop.

"You know how I drive at night when you seem a little tired? Well, the first time I saw any boss drive was right here in the 120ᵗʰ precinct. It was sergeant Murphy," Lt. A. said quietly.

"What do you have, Frankie?"_asked Murphy.
"Sarge, we have an assault and robbery," Frankie answered.
"Do you know who the victim is?"_
"Well, we know he's a member of the P.C.C.I.U. and his gun is missing," Frankie said with a frown.
"And no one saw or heard anything, right?"_asked the Sergeant.

"You got it. Except there was an undercover in there with the Angels," said Frankie.
"Shit. We can't use him. You know that, right Frankie?"_
"Yeah, I understand, Sarge."
"I'll notify operations by land line. I don't want this going over the air," Sergeant Murphy said as he headed into the cop's room to use the phone. Frankie used this time to explain to Willie what had gone down outside the bar.

The only thing they had to worry about now was the extent of the cop's injuries and the location of the missing gun. Hopefully the cop would pull through without any permanent damage. His youth was on his side but his gun was another story. It would probably surface if it was used in another crime.

While waiting for the Sarge to return, Frankie walked over to the registration desk to say hello to Julie, one of the receptionists who worked the 4X12. She was Hispanic and light-skinned to boot, divorced with a teenage daughter, and had a body to die for.

"Hi, Julie," said Frankie.

"Hello, darling!"

Julie called everybody either darling or hon, which was probably easier than trying to remember every cop's name. A lot of cops walked in and out of the ER and many of them tried to put the make on her. She seemed to be friendly with everyone and there wasn't any scuttlebutt in the precinct about her. If someone had been lucky enough to get into her panties, it would have surfaced by now.

"What happened, hon?" she asked.

"It's an assault and robbery," Frankie answered. Although he didn't lie, he didn't volunteer anything either. Julie was good people and she would find out soon enough anyway.

One of the young interns, still dressed in his green scrubs, came out of one of the treatment rooms and called Frankie over.

"Officer, are you with our young head injury inside?"_he asked.

"Yeah, Doc. How's he doing?"_

"Well, he has a pretty bad concussion and I gave him eight stitches to close his head wound, but he should be okay in a couple of weeks," said the young doctor.

"Thank you. I appreciate all you've done," said Frankie obligingly, glad the young cop was going to make it.

With that the young doctor disappeared back into the treatment room. A moment later, when Sergeant Murphy came back from the police room, Frankie told him the good news.

"We both know you have to be hung like a horse to get into the P.C.C.I.U., right Frankie?" Murphy asked.

"Yeah, that's true."

"This kid must be the fucking Mayor's son then," said Murphy.

"What do you mean, Sarge?"_asked Frankie.

"I called operations to let them know what we have over here and they put me on hold for almost ten fucking minutes. When they got back to me, there's a fucking deputy inspector on the other end who orders me not to even make out a fucking aided card on the fucking kid. No aided case, no fucking UF 61, no detectives. No nothing," Murphy replied, disgusted as all hell.

"What about the fucking gun? If someone uses it in a crime they'll trace it back to him and then what?"_Frankie asked, his voice filled with disbelief.

"I brought that up. They said they would worry about it later."

"So nothing is done. No follow up, no nothing, and the scumbag gets away with it," said Frankie with a growl.

"That's fucking bullshit. We have to deal with these cock suckers every day!" chimed in Willie.

"Well, this is what they want and this is what they're going to get," Murphy said angrily.

As far as the Sarge was concerned it was pure bullshit, but for some reason headquarters wanted to keep it hush-hush so Murphy instructed both men to get every piece of paper pertaining to the case and throw them all into the sewer instead of leaving them in the hospital waste bins. He then told his men not to discuss any of it with any hospital worker.

Murphy left and resumed patrol. While Frankie and Willie were upset that the job had let them down, they also knew that this wasn't anything new.

Every textbook ever written about police work extolled the value of the patrol force. It was forever called the backbone of the police force. Yet, when the chips fell, it was always the patrol force that bore the brunt of every politician's attack, just like it was always the patrol force that was told there was no money in the city's coffers to fund a raise in pay. Mayors and chiefs alike would visit the funerals of deceased cops, praising the virtues of the slain warrior almost as if they were their own children, but all cops knew this was just for media attention and a way to garner votes.

"Charlie, I made my wife swear to me that if I should ever die in the line of duty she would insist that no mayor or politician be allowed within ten miles of the funeral parlor, even if it meant that I would be denied the so called honor of an Inspector's Funeral," stated Lt. A.

The very idea of keeping a tight lid on this vicious attack against a cop would be tantamount of sending a message that we all surrendered to the scum bags of the earth.

Frankie knew he could not let that happen, no matter what the cost. If he did, he would lose control of the entire sector and, in time, word would spread. If it did, there was no doubt how fast he would lose the entire precinct and then the city.

Frankie knew what he had to do.

"Charlie, my partner and I had no idea about what Frankie had in mind for The Underground, even though we knew what had happened that night, down to the smallest detail. Adjoining sectors shared almost everything. We backed each other up in life and death situations almost daily and trusted each other explicitly," explained Lt. A. as he went back into his story.

On the night Frankie decided to exact street justice, Sergeant Murphy was the only patrol sergeant. Frankie didn't want to involve Murphy because if his plan backfired, Murphy would be held accountable. He was too good a cop for that to happen.

Frankie chose 10:00 P.M. because he knew Murphy would be in the station house relieving the desk for meal time.

At exactly 10:00 P.M., Frankie, Willie, Frank and I pulled up in front of The Underground. Neither of us notified the dispatcher of our location. As far as Central radio was concerned, we were all still on patrol.

The four of us approached the front door to The Underground and walked in. Heavy metal was playing on the jukebox and the sweet smell of marijuana filled the air. There were about eight people sitting at the bar and the same scumbag bartender was drawing beer from the tap. It wasn't long before every bloodshot eye was focused on the four of us. Willie went to the bathrooms and checked out every one, male and female alike. They were empty. Still not a word was said and you could hear yourself fart. Willie nodded at Frankie who quickly locked the door.

"You've got to pay the piper," Frankie said as he smiled from ear to ear.

"Go fuck your mother," said the bartender while giving him the point of his middle finger.

Frankie walked behind the bar and quickly found the jack that had been used on the young cop only weeks before.

"What's this, mother fucker?" he asked the bartender, who had finally begun to sweat and squirm.

"Never saw it before," said the bartender spitting at the object.

With that, Frankie raised the jack into the air. In less than a split second, the bartender's own weapon came down onto the side of his head, leaving a gaping hole that quickly began gushing with blood. As soon as the skel collapsed onto the floor behind the bar, the other skels at the bar started to mouth off, but we weren't finished yet. We raised our night sticks and with a battery of blows, rendered everyone at the bar incapacitated.

Blood was gushing and spewing all across the room. Teeth and pieces of teeth were lying all over. Would you believe that when we were done, some of those fuckers still had enough strength to moan? Frankie, who was still behind the bar, placed the jack into his rear pocket. Then, with his baton, he shattered the mirror on the wall behind the bar then proceeded to break every liquor bottle behind the counter as well as those in the wooden cabinets that adjoined the broken mirror. We even found more stored in cases, which we poured all over the floor.

We took out our knives and sliced every piece of upholstery in each one of the booths. Next, we went into the bathrooms and broke all the mirrors and destroyed every piece of ceramic toilet into millions of pieces. When we were done with that, Frankie cut all the lines to the taps and broke all the lines to the water supply.

Once we were finished, Frankie bent down and grabbed the bartender by the hair.

"If you report this to anybody, I'll come back and find you, then I'll kill you. You can bet your ass that's a promise," Frankie cooed as he smiled again from ear to ear.

"Then the four of us walked outside and totally destroyed all the motorcycles that were parked illegally on the sidewalk. When we were finished there was nothing left of any of them. Energized with adrenaline, we got in our cars and simply drove away. We handled a few calls but did not hear anything else that night about The Underground. As a matter of fact, Charlie, we never heard anything again until a few weeks later when The Underground closed. It never re-opened and eventually the lease was turned over to a Hispanic man and his family. They opened a bodega, much to the pleasure of the neighborhood. So you see, Charlie, that's just another reason why I love the 120th so much," Lt. A. said with a satisfied smile.

Charlie liked the story he had just heard even though it was hard for him to visualize his boss breaking the law in so many ways. That was when he understood that what he had heard from other old timers was true. The cops of the old school did hold court in the street and meted out justice brutally and savagely, but it was justice, pure and simple.

If the story he'd just heard from the lieutenant happened in today's world, it would mean certain jail time because the skels of today realize that politicians consider locking up a cop the road to promotion and advancement.

Charlie had been eager to tell the lieutenant about his decision to break off with Terry but the tour was almost over and he chose to wait until he had more time.

The lieutenant suggested they grab a couple of coffees and take a run into the station house so he could catch up on some of his paperwork. There were enough sergeants out on patrol and bedsides, if the lieutenant was needed, they could always call the house.

CHAPTER TWENTY-THREE

B ack at the station, Charlie found a comfortable chair in the lounge so he could catch a few winks. He was just about to drift off when he heard his name bellowed over the precinct intercom directing him to report to the telephone switchboard operator. He ran back up the steps and walked over to the rookie on the switchboard who handed him a folded sheet of paper.

Charlie opened it and it read, "Call me please, Terry."_

"What the hell does she want?"_he asked out loud. Then, looking at the rookie, he asked, "When did you get this?"_

"She called about twenty minutes ago," the young cop answered.

It was almost 5:30 A.M. and she was calling the precinct. Charlie didn't know if he should call her back or not. He knew she lived with her mother but he didn't want to wake up the entire household if he called. After struggling with his decision he got the key to the clerical office, where he would at least have some privacy, so he could make the call. He entered the office and found a desk with a phone. After making himself comfortable, he dialed her number. She picked it up in the middle of the first ring.

"Terry? It's Charlie. Are you okay? It's kind of unusual for you to be calling the station at 5:30 A.M.," he said quietly.

He could hear Terry blowing her nose on the other end of the line.

"Charlie, I miss you so much. I just want to see you one last time. Please, Charlie, can't you come over in the morning just for twenty minutes?"_she sobbed.

"I don't think that's a good idea, Terry," he answered as he ran a hand through his hair.

"Oh, Charlie. How am I going to get through this? Please, you have to help me get over you. I feel as if I'm losing my mind," she sobbed.

Charlie had no doubt he could have stayed on the phone with her for hours. She had lost it completely and was in so much pain that he began feeling guilty again. Against his better judgment but wanting to help her through the transition, he decided to visit her in the morning.

"I'll come over when I get off work, okay?"_

"Oh, thank you, Charlie!"_she said with a deep sigh of relief as she blew her nose again.

"I'm only going to be able to stay for a few minutes though," he cautioned as he tried to make his point quite clear.

"Okay. I'll see you later, Charlie," she said.

As he hung up the phone, Charlie knew that going there was a mistake. If he was ever going to patch things up with Annette, he had to stay away from Terry. He suddenly realized that even his wife wasn't sure if the marriage could be saved, but it did look as if she was trying. He was crazy to even think about going to Terry's house but he felt trapped and didn't want a crazed female walking into the station house looking for him in front of the desk officer. He had seen that happen before and it was embarrassing for the cop, the mistress and the wife who innocently was dragged through the quagmire. He also didn't want to be transferred and knew that the department would relocate his ass to the far reaches of the Bronx or Queens on just mere suspicion of conduct unbecoming a police officer.

He had to be strong enough to resist whatever it was that Terry had planned. Did she want to seduce him again with perfume and sexy outfits? What could she do that she hadn't done already? Most importantly, Charlie knew that he was weak in the flesh.

He hadn't made love to Annette since they both learned about each other's secrets. Although he missed having sex, he simply wanted to cool things down with Terry. His mind was in overdrive thinking of different ways in which to appease her. Maybe he could convince her just to allow them to have sex every once in a while but there would be no phone calls. Yet Charlie knew that having sex with Terry was something he swore to himself he would never do again. He didn't want to be used and he certainly didn't want to use anyone else like that.

What if Annette found about it? How on earth could he explain to his wife that he was just going there for sex when he should be going to his wife for relations?

Charlie's mind and heart were in a quandary. It was almost as if he were in an abyss and spinning out of control, sinking faster and faster with no help in sight. No matter, he was resolved to hold his ground. He would let Terry speak first when he got there.

He finished his tour, signed out and practically sped to Terry's house. He knew, and at least hoped, that Annette had left for work at her usual time but he wanted to be home roughly at the same time just in case his wife had decided to stay home.

Charlie arrived at Terry's, making good time. He parked in his usual spot and walked up to her front door. He rang the bell and Terry opened the door immediately. She was wearing a robe and her hair was wet, as if she had just stepped out of the shower. She looked tired and had dark bags under her eyes. It was easy to see that she had been crying. She beckoned for Charlie to come in and they walked into the kitchen without saying a word. Terry had two empty cups on the table and poured Charlie a cup of coffee. She sat and just looked at him for a few minutes. Finally she spoke.

"I can't do this, Charlie. I'm going crazy. I haven't slept all week and it's beginning to affect my mother and son. I feel as if I'm lost and can't find my way home," she said, her voice soft even as it broke.

"What do you want me to do?"_he asked.

"I don't know, Charlie. I swore to myself that I wasn't going to give you up or lose you but I know that I can't force myself on you. If I was like other women I know I would make you miserable just like I'm miserable," she said.

Charlie began to sweat a little at that remark. He had heard horror stories about girlfriends of cops who were scorned. They could make your hair stand on end. It was hard to believe that some women could be so bitchy and evil at the same time.

"I never lied to you or mislead you, Terry. My feelings were always what I truly felt. Life is no bowl of cherries and I'm sorry for what you are feeling now; I truly am. If I could bear the pain for you I would, but I can't. My wife is seeing someone and I don't know if she is going to leave me or not. I want to save my marriage and I have to be honest with myself, and with her, if it is going to work," he explained.

"Charlie, if your wife leaves you, do you think I want sloppy seconds?" she asked, her red-rimmed eyes glaring at him across the table. "I want you to let me know what you're intentions are if she leaves you and I want to know now!"

Charlie didn't know how to respond. "I have to be honest with you and say that I don't know what in good Christ's name I'll do. I can't expect you to stay home and sit by the phone. I'm going to try to fix things with my wife, that's all I know right now."

"How could you try to fix things with your wife? When you didn't know she had a boyfriend, you were coming here and making love to me, not her. You were holding me, not her. You were getting aroused for me, not her. You were coming inside of me, not her. Now all of a sudden you think you're going to lose something that you didn't have and you expect me to say, '*Aw*'?"

Her eyes flashed with anger.

"That's okay, Charlie. You go home and be with your wife. I understand. I understand that it's all bullshit and you know it. God damn it!"

Charlie saw Terry as he had never seen her before. She was angry and possessive and he was really beginning to think she was going off the deep end. He didn't want a psycho female on his hands or in his life, certainly not at this stage of his career.

"What can we do together? I'm open to any suggestions you might have," he said appealingly. He needed her to think rationally. He thought if he could get her to calm down then maybe they could work something out.

"I don't want to hurt you, Charlie, but I really am at my wit's end," she said gruffly as she tried to regain control of her anger.

"I know, Terry, and I don't like to see you like this. What can we do, baby?"_he asked.

"Maybe you can just see me once in a while until I get through this? Maybe we can have coffee sometimes. If I know that I have you in my life somewhere then maybe I can find the strength to go on," she suggested.

"Is that what you really want? Would you be satisfied with coffee once in a while?"_

"Yes, I would. I think that if I had you somewhere in my life then I could do it," she said, "because right now the only other option is not something I can deal with. Not yet."

"You know that I'm not going to call as much, right?"_he asked, somehow masking the doubt in his voice.

"I know, Charlie," she answered.

He was glad Terry had been the one who came up with the idea. It was better than having a crazed female on his hands. He thought he could fit her into his schedule once in a while as long as he did not succumb to her sexuality, which he suspected she would be using in the coming days. She would just get more possessive as the weeks rolled by. Of course the best way to deal with her would be a swift, clean break but Terry was not prepared emotionally to face or accept that. He vowed to remain strong.

"Terry, I'm not going to promise you or tell you when I'm going to call, but I will tell you that I will call when I can get a chance. It might mean that I'll be able to call every day, or it might only be once a week or even less. I don't want you sitting by the phone waiting for a call that might not come. If you can do that then maybe we'll be able to work things out," he said.

Terry seemed to accept Charlie's offer of a few crumbs and he could only hope that she had meant what she said. He didn't want to go into work every night and find messages left by her.

They said their goodbye at the door and he drove home, praying that Annette had already left for work. When he got home he was relieved to see that her car wasn't there and his prayer had been answered. He went in and made himself a strong cup of coffee and poured himself a shot of Sambouca to calm him down and help him relax. After a while, he went up to bed and slept soundly until Annette came home. Thankfully, he didn't dream of Terry.

CHAPTER TWENTY-FOUR

W hen he woke up, he took a quick, refreshing shower before going downstairs and heard the familiar sounds of Annette moving around in the kitchen. Even after sleeping all day he still felt tired. Late tours had their pros and cons, but feeling tired all the time was one of the cons for sure.

Annette looked somewhat down and seemed as if she might have been crying. Charlie didn't want to upset her but felt he had to say something, even if only to let her know that he was aware of her feelings.

"Are you okay?"_he asked quietly.

"I just had a bad day. There was a lot going on and it sort of took its toll on me. Thanks for noticing, though," she replied.

"Do you want to go out for dinner?" he asked. "We can always throw those chops back in the refrigerator for tomorrow." He smiled at her then added, "What do you say?"_

"Thank you, Charlie, but I think I'll take a rain check. I just need to keep busy for a while."

He hoped it was only a busy day that was causing his wife's condition even though he suspected it might have been the result of her relationship with her office beau. Maybe she made an attempt to break it off with him, or maybe she made the final decision to leave Charlie and just didn't know how to go about telling him. He decided to let it go for now and have his dinner in peace.

After they ate, they relaxed while watching a little TV. Annette really must have been tired because she soon fell fast asleep which was unusual for her. Charlie woke her up when it was time for him to leave for work. He kissed her gently on the cheek and for the first time in a long while, she kissed him back.

***

When Charlie arrived at the precinct, some of the guys were already there, sitting in the back room having coffee. They weren't talking and were all huddled in one corner of the room. There were several gangster types just walking around the back room, gazing at bulletin boards and other cop posters. Two detectives in suits from the Waterfront Commission squad were seated at the only table in the room doing what appeared to be some type of paperwork.

Charlie could only assume that the squad, or wherever these detectives came from, had made a raid somewhere and were probably waiting for transportation to night court over in Brooklyn. Curious, he walked over to his buddies.

"What the hell is all this?" he asked after greeting them with a nod.

"Looks like the Waterfront Commission made a raid on bookies down by the piers," said Tony Auriama as he took a puff of his long cigar.

"Yeah, but how come they have to sit in our room? This is OUR private area. Why don't they take them up the 120th squad room?" asked Charlie.

"Get used to it. When are you going to learn that we have no rights and no one gives a flying fuck about us or our back room?" asked Tony.

Charlie was pissed. He realized that this wasn't the first time outside agencies made collars and used the back room at the 120th precinct as the holding pen for their prisoners.

"Yeah, it's happened before. Why don't they cuff them to the fucking table instead of letting them walk around? You guys have personal information on those bulletin boards, don't you?"_asked Charlie.

His fellow officers looked at each other as if to say yeah, but what could they do about it.

As Charlie was waiting for an answer, Lt. A., who had apparently gotten to work early, entered the back room. He approached the table where the two detectives were working and slammed his attaché case down hard on the wooden surface, causing papers to scatter everywhere.

"Gentlemen, what's your command?"_he asked in a deep and demanding voice. One of the detectives pulled out a shield and identified himself as a sergeant from the Waterfront Commission's squad.

"We made a few collars tonight and we're waiting for a ride back to our office with our prisoners, Lieutenant," said the sergeant.

"Prisoners? What prisoners?" asked Lt. A.

"Fellows, come over here and stand by this table," said the sergeant to the three men, who were all smoking expensive cigars.

It was very obvious to Lieutenant Audenino that these detectives were on the pad, receiving monthly graft money from these bookies that they were treating like Gods.

"Oh, *these guys* are your prisoners?" Lt. A. asked without hiding the sarcasm in his voice. "Listen, I'm not going to ask you why they're not in cuffs, and I'm not going to ask why you haven't placed them in a secure area. That's your business. I am going to tell you that I'm the Platoon Commander of the 1st Platoon and in exactly five minutes from now they, as well as you, will become my responsibility."

He glared at the sergeant, who was still sitting at the table, then continued.

"So in five minutes I want those prisoners out of my cops' back room. That's a direct order. Do you understand, Sergeant?"_asked Lt. A., his voice stern and unwavering.

"Yeah, Lou, but where do you want me to put them?"_

"Do you really want me to answer that question?" Lt. A. asked, his eyes blazing.

"I guess not, Lieutenant," the sergeant answered in a defeated tone.

The sergeant finally understood that the lieutenant wanted the prisoners out of the sitting room. At first he didn't know where to bring them but he quickly made a wise decision and marched them up to the 120th squad detective's office on the second floor. It didn't take him long to realize this was where he should have brought them in the first place.

Lt. A. glanced at Charlie and gave him a wink then walked out to the desk.

Charlie remembered that the lieutenant had been a cop in the 120th for seventeen years. The same thing had likely happened to him and his buddies a time or two in the past, but of course, in those days, no one did anything about it. That back room was the cop's domain and those bulletin boards were used for more than just memos and orders about the job. They held personal papers containing data about cops selling cars and private information about houses for sale, including private phone numbers and addresses.

The men knew that Lt. A. did it for them because he loved them and would stick up for them as long as they were in the right. He had proved it to them time and time again.

The sergeant who led the prisoners upstairs wasn't happy that Lt. A. usurped his authority so he called his boss, who was a Captain in the Waterfront Commission squad. The Captain then called the Staten Island Duty Captain and made a bitch about Lieutenant Audenino.

The 12X8 duty captain that night was Captain Joe Turvy from the 123rd Precinct, who had no balls. It was no surprise to anyone that Lt. A. knew just how to handle him.

Captain Turvy called the 120th and had the desk sergeant direct Lt. A. to return to the station house with instruction to call the 123rd immediately, which Lt. A. did. Once there, he used the desk phone to call Captain Turvy. As soon as Turvy answered the phone he began screaming at Lt. A. and demanded to know why Lt. A. had kicked the sergeant out of the back room.

"Captain Turvy, why is it no one in your command answers the phone?"_asked Lt. A.

"What are you talking about?"_

"I tried calling your command because I needed you to respond here immediately. You're the Duty Captain, are you not? I wanted to write up a sergeant for allowing loose prisoners to walk all over my station house and I couldn't reach you for shit," bellowed the lieutenant.

The Captain knew that if he had responded when Lt. A. called, he would be writing all night. He also knew that Lt. A. was right and had the sergeant by the balls.

"Calm down, Lieutenant. I'll call the Captain at the Waterfront Commission squad and straighten it all out," said Turvy.

"Straighten what out? That asshole sergeant had prisoners walking all over my station house! What are you going to do about it, Captain?"_demanded Lt. A.

"I said that I'll take care of it and I will," Turvy replied angrily.

"Look, I'm going out on patrol and I don't want to be bothered again tonight by that fucking sergeant or I'll ream out his asshole."

"I agree with you," said Turvy, "and I'll take care of it."

Lt. A. loved to use reverse psychology on his bosses, especially the ones who were lazy and afraid to write. Turvy would call the sergeant back and convince him that the lieutenant was crazy enough to start a war, then he would suggest they should leave well enough alone. It meant, of course, that captain Turvy could return to the farm land of the 123rd Precinct and hole up in his office for the night. Then he would wait until the tour was over, hoping and praying all night that at the end of his shift he could write in his memo book, 'nothing to report.'

CHAPTER TWENTY-FIVE

C harlie and his boss got their coffee while out on patrol. The men out there had known what the lieutenant had done for them and every one of them approached him at some point during the night and offered thanks.

Charlie, wanting to keep Lt. A. abreast of what had been happening in his life, decided now was a good time to talk about it.

"Lou, do you remember what we talked about the last time we worked together?"

"Yeah, I do. How's it going, Charlie?" asked the boss.

"Well, I went to see Terry because she called me during the tour. I knew I had to see her in person rather than try to take care of it over the phone. She was falling apart and talking crazy for a while. I told her I had been honest with her but that didn't go over too well. I also told her I had decided I was going to work on saving my marriage and would call her once in a while just to see how she was doing," explained Charlie.

"Just call, Charlie?" asked the lieutenant.

"Well, I told her I would not lie or steal time from Annette but if I could, I would come over for coffee."

"That's where you have to be careful," Lt. A. replied with an understanding nod. "Terry doesn't want to lose you and she's bought time to figure out how to keep you. I don't think she realizes that, by using her female wiles to keep you, she is really turning you off and will lose you. She might just try to lure you back into her bed. She may be even talking to friends who might suggest devious ways to hold onto you even though she herself may not be devious."_

"Lou, I'm at my wit's end. I don't even know if my wife is going to stick it out with me or what. Now I have a possible female psycho on my hands who is very likely capable of turning my life as well as my career upside down," said Charlie.

"Well, I really feel that you should try to place time and distance between you and your friend. Don't call her even if you have time every day. Try to call at little as possible. Maybe she'll get the message," said the lieutenant hopefully.

"I'll try that, Lou. Thanks again for the advice."

They were finishing their coffee when yet another radio car pulled up and men from the sector team thanked the lieutenant for keeping their sitting room a sacred and hallowed ground for cops only.

"What the hell did you do, Charlie? Did you broadcast it over the air, too?"_

"Lieutenant, you're the only one who ever sticks up for us. You did the right thing and yet that sergeant had to make a phone call to his boss. Why? Because his fucking pride was hurt? Well, too fucking bad. You're always doing shit like that for us and we want you to know that we see it and appreciate it," Charlie said, his tone serious.

The lieutenant merely looked at him and nodded. After a moment, Lt. A. lit up a cigarette and cleared his throat and Charlie realized he had touched a sensitive spot deep within the lieutenant somewhere. He decided to ask the boss to tell one of his stories but wanted to hear something different, maybe upbeat.

"Lou, how about a funny story? You must have a lot of them, right?"_

The lieutenant laughed.

"How did you know I was in the mood for a funny story?"

Charlie shrugged and the lieutenant smiled.

"Some stories are funny even though they may have pain interwoven in them. What can make a sad story funny is the outcome.

"You know, Charlie, all police departments have what we refer to as steady customers. We've all seen westerns where the sheriff walks into the jail in the morning and goes back to his cells and releases the town drunk who had been sleeping one off over night. We all respond to the same locations over and over and lock up repeat offenders. We all know that the majority of them are drunks and wife beaters," said Lt. A.

"The 120th has certainly had its share of steady customers, but there was one who must have had a guardian angel over his shoulder."

And with that, he began his story.

Joe Grayson, a superintendent of a high-rise complex in sector Eddie, was a quiet, timid man when he was sober. The complex was in a middle class neighborhood and balanced both racially and ethnically. Police were not often called there for problems unless they concerned Joe.

As the super of the complex, Joe, or Joey, as we affectionately called him, lived rent-free in addition to receiving a small stipend every month. He could have done his drinking at home or even in the bars of middle class neighborhoods, but he chose the skel bars and dives of Saint George and Tompkinsville. Although he was only thirty-three years old with a full head of beautiful, jet black hair, he was a full-fledged alcoholic already.

The cops of the 120th would literally be picking him off the floor of various bars whenever he went on a binge. For some reason, he loved the bar in the Ferry terminal and would get kicked out by their bouncers almost every Friday and Saturday night.

I had him on more than one occasion. Most of the time Frank and I would just drive him to his apartment building and deposit him at his door. Somehow he always managed to retrieve his key and gain entry.

For some mysterious reason, he called all of us Willie. He also had a habit of throwing money at us. He would dig deep into his pockets and just throw all of his change at us. All the while he would be laughing like a crazed hyena.

There was one particular winter night I won't ever forget, though. It was the day we all thought he had crossed the line and wouldn't make it home alive.

I was working solo in a one-man car due to manpower shortages, and I had been assigned to sector G-George which covered Saint George and a small part of Tompkinsville. It was a bad night. It was snowing and freezing cold out.

There was about 5" of snow on the ground and it was still snowing. Traffic was light and for once the Department of Sanitation was out early in full force with salt spreaders and plows. The weatherman had predicted a warm spell to hit the Tri-State area in a few days, so we knew it would clear up soon. It was a 12X8 tour, closing on 4:00 A.M., and I was about to go on meal. That's when I was called by Central for an assignment.

"120 George," called the dispatcher.

"120 George, standing by," I replied.

"120 George, respond to the Stork's Nest Bar and Grill at Bay Street and Victory Boulevard on a report of a broken window," directed Central.

I didn't know if the broken window was a result of a burglary or an accident.

"120 Sergeant 1 to Central," said Sergeant Charlie Helmes. He was the patrol supervisor who was also riding solo and decided to back me up.

"Proceed, Sergeant 1," said the dispatcher.

"This unit will back up sector George on that possible burglary, Central," said Sergeant Helmes.

I arrived at the same time as Sergeant Helmes. He was a good boss and wasn't afraid of paperwork, either.

I advised the dispatcher that I was present on the scene. When I shone my flashlight to the front of the bar, I saw a gaping hole and broken glass shimmering in the newly fallen snow. There wasn't a soul anywhere to be found. The Sergeant arrived and we checked out the shattered glass, quickly determining that the break was initiated from inside, not from anyone trying to break in. We advised the dispatcher not to have any other units respond, saying we would investigate it further.

The bar had apparently been closed for a while because it was weeknight and colder than a witch's teat outside. Sergeant Helmes looked closer at the scene and noticed some bloodied footprints going down Bay Street. We each got into our solo cars and slowly drove down Bay Street with our driver's doors open, following the bloodied prints. Traffic was practically non-existent so we didn't have any problems on that end.

The prints led to a dead end alleyway just a few hundred feet north of Victory Boulevard and finally stopped between two houses at the end of the alley. We noticed the bloody prints only went into the alley and not out. When I wondered why this was, Sergeant Helmes said that the flow of blood usually stops when death occurs.

I saw Joey first. He was lying on his back just a few feet away. When I turned him over, I quickly saw that his face was so smeared with thick blood that he was almost unrecognizable. His hands were a mass of cuts and looked as if he had been defending himself against a knife attack. When I looked closer I could see that his palms were imbedded with shards of glass.

The sergeant contacted the radio dispatcher.

"120 Sergeant to Central."_

"Proceed, Sergeant."

"Central, have an ambulance respond to the side of 215 Bay Street. We have a heavy bleeder," said Helmes.

"10-4."

Sergeant Helmes always kept a small first aid kit in his supervisor's auto. He retrieved some moist towelettes then returned to me and cleaned some of the blood away from the victim's face. It was only after we had cleaned him up that we both saw who it was. The injured man was Joey Grayson.

"Joey, can you hear me? Are you okay?" the sergeant asked.

Joey was stewed to the gills and it didn't take long for the smell of booze and urine to reach our nostrils. He began regaining consciousness and must have realized we were cops because he began calling out the name Willie, over and over.

Within a few minutes we both heard the ambulance's sirens and saw the approaching red lights glimmering across the snow. The two technicians on board entered the alleyway and recognized Joey immediately.

"Joey, again," one of the techs said. "The last time we had him in the emergency room he attacked one of the doctors."

"We'll escort you there and stay with him until you stitch him up," offered Sergeant Helmes.

Turning to me, he said, "John, tail the ambulance closely and stay with him until they patch him up. You know Joey. He'll sign himself out as soon as they finish with him."

Sergeant Helmes then instructed me to finish my paperwork at the hospital then go to the station house. Once there, I was to inform the desk lieutenant that Sergeant Helmes had given me permission to come in and he would meet me there later. The Sergeant knew it would be easier for me to finish up in the station house and he was rewarding me for good work and giving me a break by allowing me to finish up inside instead of going back out onto patrol.

When I arrived at the hospital, I helped the attendants wheel Joey into the emergency room. On the way there, I noticed they had shackled Joey up with leather restraints.

"What gives with the restraints, guys?"_I asked.

"He started to fight us in the back of the ambulance like he normally does so we restrained him," said one of the technicians.

"How the hell are they going to patch him up if he fights us inside?"_asked the other technician.

All of a sudden, Joey noticed me again and began shouting at me.

"Willie, take me home!" he demanded with unmasked frustration.

"Joey, you need to be stitched up. Let the doctors work on you and I promise you that as soon as they finish, I'll take you home."

"No, Willie. You stitch me up," he said with breath that could kill a bull rhino.

I had an idea and walked into the nurse's station to speak to the intern on duty, Kenny Schonetube, who would be handling Joey's case. I went to high school with Kenny and had been in a few classes with him; I remembered how he was a down-to-earth kind of guy.

"Today he is a pediatrician right here on Staten Island after fulfilling some of his residency requirements at Staten Island Hospital," Lt. A. said as a smile tweaked the corners of his mouth.

Kenny always had an open handshake for me whenever he saw me.

"John, how are you?"_he asked.

"Hi, Ken. I'm fine and I have an idea on how to treat Joey that might just prevent some of his rampages," I said.

"John, at this point I'm open to anything. Last time he practically destroyed every piece of equipment in here," Kenny said with a frown.

"Why don't I stand next to you in the treatment room when you start working on him, Ken? You wear my uniform hat and I'll talk to him as if I'm the one stitching him up. What do you say?

Kenny got a kick out of my suggestion and said he was game.

Joey was wheeled into the treatment room and prepped for his suturing. His face and hands were washed and parts of his hair on his scalp had to be shaved. He was given several shots of a local anesthetic, not that he needed it. Then he was ready to be sewn up.

I gave my hat to Dr. Schoentube to wear and I put on some green scrubs just for antiseptic purposes. Kenny began to suture Joey and, just as we expected, he resisted. I started speaking to him quietly, instructing him to not move because I was sewing him up. Joey must have actually thought it was me doing the sewing because he instantly began to calm down.

"Joey, I'm going to start with your forehead and I want you to be still," I told him as Kenny worked on him, moving from Joey's forehead right down to his hands and fingers. I continued talking to Joey the whole time as if I was doing all the suturing.

The entire procedure took over an hour. When it was over, Joey had received over one hundred stitches. Kenny recommended that he stay overnight for observation but just as Sergeant Helmes had predicted, Joey signed himself out. I drove him home and once again deposited him at his front door a little after 7:00 A.M.

"What's really funny is after that, the hospital staff called me doctor every time they saw me coming in. The nickname stuck and after a while the guys in the precinct began to call me Doc. That's a true story, Charlie, and I laughed every time I told it because I actually lived it.

"This one was both funny and sad, but the story has a happy ending because Joey is still alive today. What's even better is that he is on the wagon and hasn't touched a drop in a long time. And, he still calls me Willie," Lt. A. said with a grin.

They rode around for a while then decided to take a trip into the confines of the 122nd precinct. Under normal conditions, the lieutenant had to remain within the confines of the 120th and act as Platoon Commander, but on this night he was also assigned to cover for the emergency service unit, which was based out of Patrol Boro Headquarters. Normally, the ESU had a sergeant assigned to work the midnight tour but tonight its sergeant, Shane Sullivan, had taken the night off, and neither the 122nd nor the 123rd had an available boss to cover.

Charlie headed out along Bay Street and drove up Vanderbilt Avenue passing Bayley Seton Hospital then continued to Richmond Road and into the confines of the 122nd precinct. When he reached Burgher Avenue the lieutenant told him to make a left.

The boss lived on Burgher Avenue and just wanted to make sure his house was secure. That was one of the positive perks of living within the borough where you worked. The radio car slowly passed the boss' house and all was quiet. Charlie continued down Burgher Avenue until he reached Hylan Boulevard where he made a right turn.

The 122nd was a huge precinct; it covered approximately 1/3 of Staten Island. One sector covered as much territory as an entire precinct in Manhattan or Brooklyn. It was a fairly quiet house but could erupt on weekends. Cops who needed back up sometimes had to wait as much as four or five minutes, which could be a lifetime if you really were in danger. The 120th precinct would also lend a hand in calls for assistance and were often the first cars to arrive at the scene.

Charlie continued to drive along Hylan Boulevard and soon they were passing the Hy Turkin Little League ball field, which was meticulous and well kept. Staten Islanders were very proud of their little league teams, both before and after they won a few little league world Championships.

A moment later, they finally saw the 122nd precinct station house coming up on their left.

"Lou, do you want to stop in and sign the log?"_

It was customary for visiting supervision to stop in the station house to sign in the log and do a brief inspection.

"No, I have no love lost for the brass of the 122nd," Lt. A. answered.

The 122nd Precinct had a city-wide reputation that wasn't much to be proud of. Most cops there had second jobs and didn't want to get involved with collars.

Charlie continued driving and soon came to a 7-11 convenience store on the corner of Hylan Boulevard and New Dorp Lane. The store was noted for its fresh coffee and was a gold mine of customers at all hours of both day and night. Charlie went in and got two coffees to go as well as a large cinnamon roll and the lieutenant's favorite, a French Cruller.

When he got back to the RMP he handed the lieutenant the bag and asked, "Where do you want to have this, Lou?"

"Let's head back into the 120th. If a job comes up it will likely be in the 120th anyway."

Charlie headed back north on Hylan Boulevard and made a left onto Clove Road, passing the Nissan dealer of Staten Island. He then made a right onto Howard Avenue and brought them up to one of the most spectacular views that ever existed. He brought the car to a stop near the Wagner College Campus and parked at the curb.

The scenery was breathtaking. In the distance the Verrazano Bridge was all lit up like a Christmas tree while the full moon shining above cast a reflection of peace across the water. Brooklyn was directly across the Narrows and they could see traffic blinking along the Belt Parkway.

Although it was hard to imagine now, just a few hundred years earlier Henry Hudson sailed through the Narrows on his ship, the Half Moon. Staten Island was all forest back then and home to all kinds of wild animals as well as native Indians. In the neighborhood just below Howard Avenue, numerous streets had been named after many of the tribes that had lived both on Staten Island as well as upstate New York. The lieutenant's grandfather, Giovanni Audenino, had settled on one of those streets, Tioga Street.

"Let's turn around and drive onto the campus," suggested Lt. A.

Charlie made a U-turn and steered the RMP toward Wagner College. The campus security jeep stopped them on their way in but the lieutenant explained that they were only coming in on un-official business and just wanted to look at the campus. The security force was more than happy to have them there.

Charlie drove them down a narrow roadway which led around back of the main building on the sprawling grounds. The large, brick structure housed classrooms as well as administrative offices and was also home to the Hawk's Nest, a café, malt shop and general hang out for students.

They continued to follow the winding road and soon they found themselves in front of an old house with a sign in front which read 'Cunard Hall,' home for the registrar as well as the office of the college president. Adjacent to this smaller building was an older house which served as the living quarters for the president and his family. Before the property was donated to the Wagner College Association it belonged to Sir Edward Cunard, the manager for all U.S. Operations for the Cunard Shipping Company.

It didn't take long before they arrived at a circle which would have allowed them to exit the campus. This is where most of the school's dormitories were located.

"Charlie, pull up to the edge of the grass. This is where we'll have our coffee," said Lt. A.

"Lou, aren't you worried about the students?"_

"The students?" the lieutenant asked. "Well, the way I see it, they are sleeping, studying or getting laid. They're not worrying about us and we're not going to worry about them."_

The lieutenant was right. As they made their way to the edge of the grass, the few students who were out on campus at that hour for whatever reason didn't give them a second look.

Since it was centrally located, this was a good place to have their coffee, allowing them to get to any place within the precinct quickly if they had to. As they enjoyed their steaming cups of java, the two men also enjoyed the view.

"Lou, the last time you told me one of your stories, it had a happy ending."

"Right. That was the story about Joey Grayson," replied the lieutenant.

"Did you ever meet anyone famous, like a movie star?"_asked Charlie.

The lieutenant nodded. "Actually, I have. Autographs are scattered throughout my memo books from actors I ran onto in the streets as well as different details. I have pictures taken with various bosses who posed with different Presidents of the United States, as well as photos taken with beautiful starlets from back in the day when I was assigned to opening nights on Broadway. Believe it or not, Charlie, they don't really mean that much to me.

"On the other hand, I also met a simple man who spoke broken English and made an indelible mark on me yet was not famous. He was a priest who had such enormous faith and love in his heart, and anyone he came into contact with him only benefitted from the encounter, no matter how brief."

The lieutenant took a drink of his coffee and stared out the window for a moment, lost somewhere in his memories. After several quiet minutes, he finally spoke again.

"Father Josef had been a prisoner in the Nazi death camp in Treblinka and his wrist bore the unmistakable tattooing of a Nazi prison camp. He had been interned there towards the end of the war and was involved in a democratic underground which aided Jews to escape the Nazi's and eventually, out of Poland.

"His name was Father Josef Krackowski. How could I ever forget him? He was a lover of life, of men and most of all, of humanity."

Charlie nodded as he drank his own coffee.

"After the liberation of the Nazi death camps by the allies," Lt. A. continued, "Father Josef immigrated to the United States where he settled in the community of Saint George. At the time, Saint George was a diverse community composed of Poles, Italians, Irish and blacks.

"As a priest, Father Josef was assigned to the Saint Stanislaus Kostka Church, which had served the Polish community on Staten Island since 1924. He was pastor, friend and confessor to so many people. Maybe his love of life stemmed from the fact that he had witnessed and endured so much pain and suffering during his lifetime. He told me once about how he had come very close to being transferred from Treblinka to the gas chambers of Auschwitz.

"I met this simple but endearing man in the summer of 1978. Frank and I had been partners for a few years already and were pretty much respected by all the brass in the 120th. We had made some high profile collars, but meeting Father Josef was one of the best experiences that either of us had ever hoped to have."

We were assigned to a 4X12 tour one particular Friday night and thought we would be spending the night in our sector in Stapleton. As luck would have it, however, we were re-assigned to a parking detail instead. We tried to get out of it by asking the desk officer to give it to a rookie or foot man, but there were no footmen available so we got it. The detail was at the Saint Stanislaus Kostka Church on York Avenue, deep in the confines of sector J-John. We were instructed to be at the church at 5:00 P.M. sharp and introduce ourselves to a Father Josef Krackowski.

As instructed, we arrived at 5:00 P.M. on the dot, after we had our coffee, of course. We parked directly in front of the church and walked over to the pastoral residence, an old wooden frame house that sat adjacent to the stone church. Directly next to it was another house built exactly the same way. As a matter of fact all the homes on that block looked identical except for the color of the different shingles.

When we reached the pastoral residence, we knocked on the door and a pleasant enough plump woman with a Polish accent greeted us then let us in. She escorted us into a sitting room directly off of the entrance hallway. There was a framed painting of the Last Supper hanging on one wall and a huge crucifix across the room on the opposite wall. The painting looked like it had been created a million years ago. It was faded and lacked any brightness or color. The crucifix looked just as old. It was made out of wood and had so many chips in it that it appeared to have been made out of the wood right from Jesus' cross. The carpet which covered the floor was tattered but clean.

I noticed right away that this was not a wealthy parish. The walls were clean but were in desperate need of a fresh coat of paint. The unmistakable smell of sauerkraut and Polish kielbasa hung heavy in the air and caused both Frank and I to smack our lips.

The round, Polish woman asked us to sit then informed us that Father Krackowski would be with us momentarily.

"Frank have you ever been here on a parking detail?"_I asked as we waited.

"Never."

"What's with all this introduction stuff? Don't we just stay outside and do what we're supposed to do? Why do we have to meet the priest? What's he going to do? Tell us how to do our jobs?"_I asked, feeling as though I was bubbling over with at least a thousand questions.

"I don't have a clue," replied Frank with a shrug.

No sooner had we fallen silent, a huge bear of a man walked slowly into the room.

"Hello! Hello, my friends! Welcome to my home and to Saint Stanislaus Church," bellowed Father Josef.

I was amazed at the size of the man. He was at least 6'3" and had to weigh in at a good 230 lbs. Since he was wearing a New York Yankees T-shirt, it was easy to see he had no beer belly and appeared to be in great shape. He spoke with a fairly heavy Polish accent and his hair was silver gray, thinning a bit on top. He had a contagious, opulent smile and I just felt like I had to smile back.

The burly priest began to sit down on a brown couch opposite where Frank and I had been seated but rose immediately, almost before he made contact with the couch. Without a word, he walked over to a well-stocked liquor cabinet where he pulled out a bottle of Chivas Regal and three glasses. With a smile, he set the bottle down on a small table separating the two sofas and spoke in broken English.

"Gentlemen, if you would please to join me in a toast to this wonderful night and celebration."

We were both stunned that this priest was asking us to drink with him, and so early in the evening!

"If it's alright with you, Father, we'll take a rain check on that until we finish our work outside," Frank answered with a smile and a nod.

Looking at Charlie, Lt. A. said, "What purpose would it have served to greet a church-going crowd with booze on our breaths?"

Charlie smiled, picturing such a scene in his imagination, and the lieutenant continued.

"Exactly what is it that's going on here tonight, Father?"_asked Frank.

"Well, we have the pod luck supper in our Church hall," replied Father Josef.

Although Frank and I realized he meant pot luck supper, neither of us corrected him.

"Every family, they bring in something from home. Nothing is bought outside. Everything comes from my people. We are a poor parish but everyone's generosity makes us feel rich! My people will come at 6:00 P.M. and will set up the hall. Then, we begin at 7:00 P.M.!" he said, smiling as he gestured with his hands.

As we talked, we found out that Father Josef had spoken to our Commanding Officer earlier in the week and gotten permission for his parishioners to park their cars perpendicular to the curb instead of parallel.

"You fine men please to handle it anyway you like," he said as he grinned from ear to ear. "I want you to know that you come in to my home anytime

you want. Just open door. If you use bathroom, it's down hallway at the end. Remember, my home is your home."_

"Thank you, Father. We'll take care of everything," said Frank.

We got up and went outside to our RMP. We had roughly a half hour before any guests were to arrive so Frank took the car and went to get us more coffee. We both couldn't go because it was a fixed post so one of us had to stay behind.

The first family arrived just after we finished our coffee and last cigarette for a while. We both got out of our car and started to work.

The driver of the first car began parking his car in the normal manner in front of the church but we re-directed him to park perpendicular. After that, all we had to do was remain there and make sure that the rest of the drivers followed suit, which they did.

Every one of those families either thanked us or said good evening and it seemed as if it was going to be a pleasant enough tour. After about thirty five minutes, the last of the arriving cars were parked. All of the guests parked and entered the church hall knowing that New York's finest was going to be watching their cars for the night. That's what Father Josef told them, anyway. Frank and I had no doubt that this would be an all-night detail.

"Frank, why don't you go and get us a couple of cups of coffee? And while you're at it, get me a copy of the Staten Island Advance?" I asked.

"Do you want anything else besides the coffee?"

"Yeah, could you get me a tuna salad on white with lettuce and mayonnaise and make sure you get some of those garlic pickles?"_

Frank nodded. "Be right back."_

With that I got out of the RMP and Frank drove to the diner at 40 Bay Street. It was barely 8:00 P.M. and just starting to get dark. Thankfully it wasn't too humid and I started to think that once in a while it was good to get a relaxing tour. It was nice to get away from the 'shots fired'_of sector Eddie.

Frank came back after about twenty-five minutes and parked on the opposite side of the street where we had a good view of all the parked cars. We opened our coffees but saved the lids. Just because we were on a fixed detail in front of a church didn't mean that we wouldn't respond to a 10-13 if it came over the

*radio. All street-wise cops saved their coffee lids. It was a good waste of both cof-
fee and money if you had to throw out your food every time you got a hot run.*

*The tuna salad was good and fresh and the pickles were crunchy. We settled
down for a peaceful albeit boring night. About 45 minutes later Father Josef
came out of the church hall and walked over to our car. Frank and I had
our windows rolled down because there was a nice breeze coming right up York
Avenue off of the Kill Van Kull. He approached Frank's side of the car with a
smile.*

"My friends! Please to come with me into the church?"_

"Is everything okay in there, Father?"_asked Frank.

*We both thought maybe there was a dispute or someone had gotten sick, but
Father Josef smiled again and said, "Everything is good. I want for you to join
with me for a while."_*

*We got out of the RMP after rolling up the windows and locking the doors
then followed the priest through the front door of the church. The vestibule area
of the beautiful building was enormous. There was a literature rack to the right
of the entrance filled with daily and weekly schedules of events as well as the
schedule of masses. To the right of the vestibule and just before the main door
that led to the center aisle of the church was another door that the portly priest
opened and walked through. Next he led us down a set of stairs which took us to
the basement hall. As we reached the bottom of the stairs, we heard the distinct
sounds of polka music.*

*We followed Father Josef into a great hall where couples were dancing and
accordion music seemed to be coming from everywhere. There were tables set
up that were mostly occupied by women, while groups of men stood everywhere
engaged in conversation. Children played in groups but were not loud or overly
boisterous. The smell of Polish food seemed to waif over everyone's head and
went straight to our noses. We were enticed with the familiar scents of sauerkraut and Kielbasa. I wasn't surprised when the pungent aroma of potato latkes
drove me wild and made my stomach rumble.*

*At first Frank and I thought the priest was going to seat us somewhere and
feed us. After all, we had told him earlier that we were going to take a rain check*

on the drink he offered. We quietly followed him up to a raised platform which doubled as the stage and soon saw a small table with two fresh place settings where no one else was seated. The priest walked beyond the table and made his way up to a set of stairs that led to the stage itself. He walked over to a podium and grabbed the microphone tightly between his hands.

"My friends, my friends," he began loudly before he cleared his throat and patiently paused. Within thirty to forty seconds, as if Jesus was about to give the Sermon on the Mount, silence blanketed the room as everyone waited attentively to hear his words. Even the kids who were playing stopped without being told by their parents.

"First, I hope that you have good time tonight," said Father Josef, smiling at the faces staring up at him as the crowd applauded and showed their satisfaction. "When you arrive tonight, you see that you park your cars in different way so you could be closer to our holy church. These two police officers who you see outside have been watching your cars for you so you do not have to worry about their safety."

We weren't sure if Father Josef meant the car's safety or ours, but we kept silent as he continued.

"They would be outside now but I brought them in so we can show them your wonderful cooking food. I want them to sit with me at my table to toast this night and to thank God that we are all safe together," he said with deep emotion.

Applause filled the room for several long seconds, then the priest introduced us by our first names. As the entire audience clapped again, loud cries of thank you could be heard both in English as well as Polish. Humbled, Frank and I sat down as women brought us a little bit of everything.

"Now you will sit down and drink with me, no?"_asked the priest.

"Now we will drink with you, yes!" said Frank emphatically.

While Frank and I ate, we shared stories with Father Josef, and he did the same with us.

He described how he had been in a concentration camp in Treblinka then shared stories about the camp commandant who had a passion for using Jews and the elderly as targets for his sharp-shooting practice. He told us of many atrocities and explained how the Germans used to take small children away from their mothers, never to be seen again.

For some reason, Father Josef took a liking to Frank and I that night and invited us to visit him at any time. I found him to be a man of such great compassion that I began to stop in and see him in the days and weeks following that first assignment, even in my off duty time. I would call ahead and he would tell me the time was perfect and to come right on over. That first visit was the start of many in which I would learn about life's sufferings as seen through the eyes of Father Josef.

Frank, on the other hand, never took Father Josef up on his invitation.

Perhaps I was drawn to him because he reminded me of another great priest. I had been married by a Mary Knoll missionary who had served in the Army during the war. He was nicknamed Fighting Father Dunne and had been portrayed in the movies by Pat O'Brien.

The first time I visited Father Josef after our initial trip was after an 8X4 on a Saturday afternoon. When I arrived, the priest took me into his kitchen where he offered me a seat and a cold drink, then asked me what it was I had on my mind._

"Father, I couldn't help but notice the number tattooed on your wrist. Were you a prisoner in a concentration camp?"_I asked.

"Yes, I was," he said quietly, "and if you wish, I will tell you about it."_

"If it's okay with you, Father, I would certainly like to hear it."

After getting us each a glass of iced water, Father Josef began his story.

"I was in the Treblinka camp for a short time in 1943. It was in operation for one year only. During that time, 850,000 murders were committed against my people. When I say 'people' I mean the Jews of Poland.

"Before World War Two, three million Jews lived in Poland. They made 10% of population of thirty three million people. Hitler's Army invaded Poland in September, 1939. It was start of Second World War. By end of month our government fled into exile to Romania. When they regrouped, they operate out of London, sending support to the underground groups which were in existence. They start to round up my colleagues and fellow priests, and many were shot in

street. That is when I join underground to help in any way I can. They killed not only priest but also teacher as well. The Germans regarded my Polish brothers as sub human and Polish Jew beneath that."

Lt. A. paused and looked at Charlie.
"I'm sure you're not surprised when I tell you I listened to Father's story in utter stillness. This man had endured such obvious brutality and harshness of life, yet he was sharing it with me.'"
Charlie nodded with understanding as the lieutenant continued.

"My friend, the German program for Polish Jews was one of concentration, isolation and eventually, annihilation. By 1942, Poland was the Nazi regime's dumping ground for Jews from all over Europe. By the end of the war, over three million Polish Jews were dead with only fifty to seventy thousand surviving. It was my job as part of underground to hide Jews whenever I could until the time I could sneak them into other part of underground that would take them out of country. I did this for a few years but was eventually captured.

"To this day, I do not know why I was not summarily shot on the spot. Instead, I was transported to Treblinka. It was amazing the way the Germans led us to believe we were only going on a temporary journey instead of being led to our deaths.

"I know that always some ask the question of why the Jewish people did not fight back or resist. Well, there was the small pocket of resistance, but why would anyone offer to fight if they thought the journey was only temporary? They believed the end of the trip offered an opportunity to be re-introduced into society as a productive member," Father Josef said as he paused to take a drink of water.

"Father, you mentioned that the Jews did not resist because the Germans gave them hope that they would be returned to their homelands. Is this true?"_I asked.

"My friend, the Germans took care to send the message that those who were about to die would be given the impression that they had arrived at a transit camp from which they would be sent on to a work camp. Before they were herded onto the freight trains and put in box cars like so many cattle, they were given

*very explicit and detailed instructions on how to mark their luggage and belong-
ings so they would be able to identify them later at their journey's end. Of course,
we now know that each piece of luggage was collected and sifted through, any
usable items taken by the Nazi regime. Books, photos, shoes, jewelry, clothing
and absolutely everything else was put into piles and inventoried.*

*"My camp was situated in the north eastern end of the province, not far
from Malkinia, a town with a railroad station which was built in a heavily
wooded area making it naturally concealed. The Germans even tried to hide
the gas chambers in Treblinka from the rest of the camp. It was totally separated
from the camp by barbed wire and high fences, with the barbed wire intertwined
by tree branch limbs to conceal it even further. The entrances to this area of the
camp were then hidden behind special partitions and a tube in which the victims were led through, delivering them directly into the crematoriums.*

"The SS men of the Treblinka camp called this tube 'the street to heaven.'"

*Father Josef paused, took a deep breath then continued in a quiet voice
trembling with grief and anger.*

*"The gas chambers were lined with white tile and installed with shower
heads which led to the realism of the showers. The water pipes, running across
the full length of the ceiling, did not carry water but the horrible gas which took
its victim's lives. When the doors were closed the room became pitch black, adding to the terrifying horror of the moment.*

*"To the east of the gas chambers lay huge ditches where the countless bodies
were tossed away like garbage. Many of the victims were still alive but met their
fate after being buried alive."*

*The priest sighed, his eyes filled with sadness. I could see that the retelling of
this story was starting to take its toll on this burly, yet angelic man, so I decided
this was enough for one day.*

*"Father, maybe I should come back another day," I said as I moved to stand
up. Before I could get very far, he placed a warm, wrinkled hand on top of mine.
Understanding he was not yet ready for me to go, I sat back in my seat.*

*"Do you think I cannot finish telling you my story?" he asked quietly. "I
have lived this and seen so much more that I have not even begun to tell you
yet. I sometimes speak of this to my congregation and they listen in awe and*

wonderment but are also shocked. I know they cannot comprehend such brutality and cruelty unless they have also experienced it for themselves.

"An entire race of people was almost entirely snuffed out and people everywhere are beginning to forget it ever happened. There are those among us who go around and say that it never happened at all. Instead of embracing and believing the stories they have been told, they insist it was an exaggeration."

He shook his head, patted my hand, and said, "I know that, as police officer, you see and experience things the average person does not witness or cannot even imagine. We both know that man's own inhumanity to man is the totality of all evil on this earth. This is why I will tell you in the weeks ahead everything I saw and felt and experienced. You are younger than me, but it is my hope that you will also know, not forget, and believe what I say. I, and other survivors like me, need to keep the memory alive by having you tell others who would also believe," the old priest said with a tear in his eye.

"I swear to you, Father, I will," I said.

"Charlie, I swore I would do whatever it took to do what this man wanted. As I sat there with him, listening to his countless memories of a time long gone, I couldn't help but wonder how it was possible that he could be filled with such love and wonder after all the pain and misery he had experienced in his life," said Lt. A.

"Father, how did you finally get out of the camp?"_I asked, hungry for any information he was willing to share.

"My son, I told you before about the scattered resistance in my camp. There were one hundred prisoners who devised a plan for escape. A locksmith who had worked on the Nazi arsenal first created a wax impression, then a key for a lock.

"The planned escape was to take place in the summer of 1943, but it wasn't totally successful. The phone lines were never cut and many of the prisoners were not told what was happening. Of the 800 people who partook in the uprising, more than 400 were killed in the camp while the other half escaped to the forest where 300 of them died.

"Surprisingly, there were only about forty soldiers killed in the battle. When it was over, the Germans took 100 prisoners and shot them all in the head in front of the remaining prisoners as retribution. It wasn't long after this that the camp was completely dismantled. I was one of the lucky ones who made it to the forest and escaped. I knew if I wanted to survive the war, I had to go into hiding. I continued to work with the resistance units and was eventually joined by three fellow human beings that I shall never forget.

"The first was Father Urbanowicz of Brzec-on-bul, and he had been helping Jews long before I ever met him. The second was Roman Archutowski, the rector of the clerical academy in Warsaw. He was also tortured to death by the Germans in a camp somewhere that I still do not know the location of, even to this day. The third became the best of my friends and we still keep in touch as long as we live. His name is Karol Joseph Wojtyla," explained the priest.

Although I recognized the name, I could not place it at the time.

"Karol was, and still is, a lover of life. Maybe that is why I am the way I am today. He was a wonderful mentor to me. To this day I have never met anyone in my life such as that man," the priest went on.

"Karol wanted to be a professional actor but the Nazi occupation of our homeland changed all of that. Instead, he became very active in the Christian Democratic Underground, aiding Jews to escape the Nazis. Before World War Two ended he decided to become a priest like me."

"I think that maybe your friend Karol learned to love life and took after you," I said. "Where is he today, Father?"

"Karol is in Rome. He has been elevated to Cardinal and is assigned to Vatican City. In fact, in just a few weeks I will be flying there to partake in the celebration of Mass which will elevate my friend Karol to Pope," the priest said with a smile.

It was then that I realized this priest's best friend was soon to become Pope John Paul 2nd.

"That's amazing, Father," I said. "Your best friend is going to become the Pope!"

Father Josef nodded with pride as I added, "That's like my partner becoming the Police Commissioner! Do you think you will want to serve in another capacity now that you're going to have a Rabbi?"

"What other capacity? I serve God here and with the people that need me and love me, as I love them and God. No, I shall remain here," the priest answered simply.

Somehow I knew Father Josef would give me this answer. I also suspected that he was the main reason the Pope had become a priest in the first place.

On my way out I told him I would stop by to say goodbye before he embarked on his journey to Rome.

The weeks that followed were busy ones for the men of the 120th. It was also a time when my partner Frank called out sick more than he had ever done in his career. He decided to take a few weeks off and came back fit as a fiddle.

Frank and I did manage to visit Father Josef before he flew to Rome to attend the celebration Mass for his friend, Cardinal Karol Wojtyla. However, our plans to visit him socially were interrupted by a police call which sent us instead to the rectory of Father Josef's church. Our orders were to respond to a past robbery where the victim was a priest.

Although neither of us knew which one of Father Josef's staff had been robbed, we responded there at break neck speed with lights flashing and sirens blaring. When we arrived we knocked on the front door of the rectory and, to our surprise, Father Josef greeted us sporting a bump on his forehead the size of a golf ball.

"Father what happened?" asked Frank.

"Come in, my friends. Let me get you a drink," said the priest.

Neither Frank nor I could believe that this man who had just been mugged was more concerned with getting us a drink than attending to his bleeding head.

"Father, sit down. I'm going to call for an ambulance," I insisted.

"No, I will be alright, but I do have a favor to ask of you, if you don't mind," he said quietly, practically pleading.

"Anything, Father. Just name it," said Frank.

"I promise you that I will be alright. Mrs. Powerski, my caretaker, said she called her brother to come look at my head. He is a doctor and I promise you that I will do whatever he tells me," Father Josef said.

"Tell us what happened, Father," said Frank with a nod of his head.

"Well, I was walking down York Avenue just a short time ago. I had gone to visit Mrs. Dziergowski who has not been able to come to mass lately because she has been ill. I went to her house to give her the sacraments of the mass.

"I carry the Lord's Host in my attaché case and as I was walking home, a young man hit me and grabbed the case then ran down the hill towards Jersey Street. I want to know if you can help me look for the case," he pleaded.

Both Frank and I knew the chances of recovering the case were slim, if at all. If a young, black punk from the Jersey Street projects stole it, the case would probably wind up going down the garbage chute. We had no doubt that whoever took it would go through it looking for cash, checks or whatever could be fenced for easy cash. The thief would then dump it as soon as possible so he wouldn't be caught with it on him.

"Why do you want the case back, Father? Were there any other Lord's Hosts in it?"_I asked.

"No. It's not that. My plane tickets for tomorrow's flight are in the case. I also placed my special gift to Karol inside," Father Josef explained.

So that was it. This priest is going to Rome and his tickets and gift get stolen the day before.

"We'll do the best we can, Father," my partner said.

Both Frank and I made every effort to assure this man that we would do the best we could do in recovering his property, even though we felt it was a lost cause.

First we went back to the station house and spoke to the boss who was working the 3ʳᵈ platoon with us.

Michael Delehanty, a young Captain, was considered to be a rising star in the department. He had worked busy houses both as a sergeant and lieutenant before getting promoted to captain and transferring into the 120ʰ. He had a good working relationship with the men and knew the job. Frank and I decided to visit him and explain our dilemma, or rather Father Josef's dilemma, to him.

The Captain listened attentively and seemed very much interested in the story of this miraculous priest.

"What suggestions do you fellows have?"_he asked.

"We would like to change into our civilian clothes so we can search the entire wooded area around the church and Jersey Street," said Frank.

"I'll tell you what. It's almost 6:00 P.M. now. I'll give you the rest of the 4X12 tour to see what you can come up with. I wish you and Father Josef luck. Please give him my regards," said Captain Delehanty.

With that, Frank and I changed into our civvies and notified the desk officer that sector Eddie would be out of service for the remainder of the tour. Then we went back to the church and began our search. It began to rain and all we had were our flashlights and cigarettes.

"We have to find that briefcase. If we don't find it, that man will think we never even tried to find it," I said.

"Look, John. It's not as if he won't be able to get another ticket for Christ's sake."

"It's not the fucking ticket but the gift he wanted to give his friend," I argued.

"Well, what the hell is it that's so important and valuable?"_asked Frank.

"You know that every once in a while I have been going to visit Father Josef, right?" I asked.

"Yeah, so what about it?"

"It was Father Josef, and the kind of human being that he is, that probably led to the new Pope becoming a priest in the first place. They both worked together in Poland aiding Jews to help them escape from the Nazi regime. When Father Karol was ordained, Father Josef gave him a gift, which remained in Poland for a while but somehow found its way back into Father Josef's hands. That gift was Father Karol's first Holy Grail and now Father Josef is going to return it to him. You can't place a value on something like that. The Holy Grail is in his briefcase and out there waiting for us to find it," I explained.

"And what if it's in the furnace of 80 Jersey Street?"_asked Frank. "What then, John?"

"What's the matter? No faith? We're going to find it. I feel it,"I said, offering him a confident smile.

We began our search where the young kid first approached the priest on the street. There were older houses on this section of York Avenue and on the same side of the road as the church. The other side was a very steep and grassy hill which led up to back yards belonging to houses on the street above. The homes on the church side of the road also had back yards but were separated from Jersey Street below by a section of extremely dense woods. It would be much easier for a mugger making his getaway to run down the hill instead of up.

We started on the street level. We inspected every hedge and searched every yard between the mugging location and the church. Not surprisingly, we had to fend off dogs and identify ourselves in almost every yard we searched. We often forgot that we were in plainclothes and just entered yards without getting permission first. It wasn't long before we were soaking wet and really beginning to feel chilly and miserable. We finally reached the wooded area where we split up and worked opposite ends. Soon it was also getting dark which made our task even tougher.

At the beginning of our independent searches, Frank came up with a purse in the woods that contained keys and some miscellaneous papers which probably had been stolen in a purse snatching. We both agreed that we would voucher it at the end of our shift. We crisscrossed the woods then switched sides with still no luck. Before we knew it, it was almost 9:00 P.M. and we had been searching for about three hours.

"What do you say, partner?"_asked Frank.

"I'm not quitting. You want to quit, go ahead. I'll meet you back at the precinct,"I said, my voice filled with determination.

"Don't be so fucking stubborn!"

"Look, I'm staying until I find it,"I said adamantly.

"And what if it's not there? God damn it, John, you know better than anyone that sometimes these things wind up in the chutes of the projects!"

"It's here. I'm telling you, Frank, it's here. I know it. I feel it!"

264

"Well, then I'm staying with you, partner."

I was glad he decided to stay. I knew this wasn't a choking baby or a build-ing on fire, but my partner decided to stick it out with me, which is just what partners were supposed to do. As we stood there in the chilly air, a sudden surge of pride came over me because of this bond that only true police partners could forge between them. We often entrusted each other with our very lives, but it was so much more than that. It was the small things, too, like this act of faith on my part and my partner's acquiescence of it.

We were both wet and chilled to the bone but began our search again with renewed vigor. I truly believed that Father Josef's attaché case was somewhere in this wooded area. We combed the woody hill in grids from left to right and up and down, but still we found no case. Before long we realized it was nearing 11:00 P.M. and we had to have the RMP back at the station house within the hour.

I had decided to canvass the lower part of the hill one last time when all of a sudden I saw the huge shape of a man approaching me from the York Avenue side of the hill. At first I couldn't make out who it was but as the figure loomed closer, I recognized Father Josef, sporting a bandaged head.

"Father, what the heck are you doing out in this weather and at this time of night?"_I scolded.

"I am very lucky, my friend," said the bandaged priest. "This bandage only covers a mild contusion and not a concussion. The doctor said I will be able to travel tomorrow as planned." Then, as his gaze shifted from me to Frank, he added, "Have you had any luck?"

"Sorry to say so, Father, but no luck yet. It's okay though, because we haven't given up hope. I just feel that it's here somewhere," I said quietly.

"Please, I brought you both some coffee. I even put some of my special 'sugar'_ in it, okay?"_he asked.

I could smell the special 'sugar'_ even before we removed the lids from the styrofoam containers. The unmistaken odor of Anisette was emanating out of the steaming cup. I carefully took one from Father Josef's hand but, because it was so hot, I dropped it immediately. The cup fell to the rain soaked ground and burst open, splashing coffee every which way. With a cry of frustration,

I trained my flashlight on the fallen cup. As I did, my eyes fell upon a brown attaché case that could have been no more than two feet away from where I was standing.

"Oh, my God! Is that it, Father?"_I exclaimed.

"Jesus, Mary and Joseph. That's it!" shouted the priest with jubilation.

The bandaged and burly priest leaned down and, in one scoop, had the attaché case in both hands. He stared at it for several long seconds with tears streaming down his rain soaked face.

"Maybe we had better open it first, Father. We don't know if anything is missing just yet," I suggested.

Frank had heard the shouting and joined us from the other side of the woods. Father Josef was beaming as if nothing had happened yet somehow, magically, we all knew that everything would be as he last saw it.

"Father, let's just open it and check the contents. Sometimes the bad guys steal things like this and just toss aside whatever they don't want or are not sure of the value of what they have," I said.

"My son, my son, where is your faith? Do you not see with your hearts as surely as you see with your eyes? As I sat inside I thought of you both and how wet and cold you must be after all these hours so I came out here to comfort you. My thoughts and prayers were with you to give you strength and perseverance. I hand you your coffee and you drop it. When was the last time you dropped a cup of coffee, my friend?"_Father Josef asked, his eyes lit up by a small smile.

"I don't remember, Father, but I'm sure I must have dropped one along the line at some point," I answered.

"Okay, and you drop it at your feet. You drop it right in front of you and we look down and there is my attaché case. Why did we not see it before this? Why then, when the coffee spilled? It is called faith, plain and simple. I knew you would find it. More importantly, you knew and felt you would find it.

"God works His wonders in mysterious ways, my friends. Sometimes we seek answers to life's puzzles and the answers are right in front of us. It is called faith. Let us go back to the rectory and we will open the case there," the priest suggested.

Without another word, the three of us, rain soaked to the bone, worked our way up the worn path back to York Avenue. When we reached the church we entered the rectory and were welcomed into Father Josef's parlor. The housekeeper, Mrs. Powerski, was a nervous wreck.

"Father, where have you been?"_she asked, her tone a combination of worry and scorn.

"Do not worry, my dear lady. I am well, and as you can plainly see, my two friends have found my attaché case," said Father Josef.

"No, Father, we found it together," I gently corrected.

"I disagree. It was you and your faith, my friend. If you had not stayed in the woods for as long as you did, I would not have brought you your coffee," said the thankful priest.

"Well, what are we waiting for? Let's open it up!" Frank suggested, anxious to see what was, or wasn't, inside.

The priest placed the case on top of the dining room table and pushed the two release tabs on either side. The top popped open and, after raising the lid all the way, Father Josef began to fumble through the contents. The first object he felt below some folded handkerchiefs was the Holy Grail, the gift for his friend. The priest continued his inspection of the case and soon located the tickets in an upper slot where he had placed them the day before. Although Father Josef didn't seem very surprised, Frank and I were both amazed to learn everything was there.

"My friends, there is absolutely nothing missing," said Father Josef.

"Sometimes that happens, Father. It's possible that when you were mugged, your assailant didn't realize you were a priest. When he opened the case and saw the Grail, he was probably overcome with guilt and decided to leave it alone. Or maybe he realized he wouldn't be able to sell it to anyone. He couldn't return it out of fear that he might get arrested, so he just dropped it and ran," I suggested.

"My friends, please allow me to hold your hands," said Father Josef.

I gave him one of my hands and so did Frank. With a nod, the priest then asked Frank to take my other hand into his other hand. Once the three of us formed a closed circle and with a contented smile, Father Josef bowed his head and began to pray aloud.

"My Heavenly Father, thank you for this day. Thank you for my life and for the love that you have brought into my life. Thank you for John and for Frank. It was you who brought these two men, these two policemen, into my life only a few short weeks ago so that they might be with me here tonight. Thank you for their faith. May you always be with them and watch over them in their lives. May you bless them and their loved ones and all good and decent people everywhere. Amen."_

Both Frank and I repeated the priest's final word then released each other's hands while I silently said an additional prayer for having Father Josef in my life.

Father Josef's was scheduled to fly to Rome out of Kennedy Airport in Queens. I knew it would be an evening flight, as were most European flights out of JFK. The next day I stopped by the rectory before going in for my 4X12 to say goodbye to him. I knocked on the rectory door and was welcomed in by Mrs. Powerski.

"Come in, John!" As the door closed behind me, she added, "You want to know something funny? Father Josef was expecting you. Go on upstairs to his room. It's the second door on the right."

I made my way up the stairs and approached his door, prepared to knock once I got there. Just before I reached the room, however, the door swung open and there stood Father Josef, dressed in his Sunday best, literally.

"Father, how are you? I don't want to interrupt but I just stopped by to wish you a pleasant flight. Say hello to the new Pope for me," I said as I shook his hand.

"My friend, there is nothing you could ever do that would be an interruption for me. If it were not for you, I would not be going with the full and happy heart as I am now," said the jubilant priest.

We walked down the stairs together but as I headed toward the door, Father Josef called for me to come back. When I reached him, he wrapped me up in a tight embrace.

"I love you, John," Father Josef said as tears streamed down his cheeks.

"I love you, too, Father," I replied, trying not to choke on my own tears.

"So you see, Charlie, Father Josef WAS the most famous man I have ever met," Lt. A. said. "He wasn't a movie star or a sports figure. He wasn't even a president.

"What he was, however, was an ordinary man with extraordinary faith and love, which left you no choice but to love him right back."

"Is he still down at the same church, Lou?"

"Believe it or not, Charlie, he is. He is older but still has such zeal! He also continues to go out and about in the community visiting the sick and infirm."

The time spent with the lieutenant on the campus was relaxing for Charlie, especially hearing such a positive tale. Before long, dawn began to break on the horizon and the view of the morning sun rising over the Atlantic Ocean was breathtaking.

"Charlie, what do you say we get out of here before the morning shift comes in? Those daytime security forces are sticklers when it comes to the rule book. Before we know it, they'll want us to sign their log books attesting to the fact that we were here," suggested Lt. A.

"Okay, Lou, whatever you say. Why don't we get two cups and go back to the house?" asked Charlie.

They got their morning coffee and took a slow ride back to the barn. Although Charlie had an opportunity to call Terry, he decided to take the lieutenant's advice and not call. He prayed there wouldn't be a message waiting for him at the switchboard when he returned from their tour.

When they arrived at the precinct, Charlie went in and purposely made his way by the switchboard operator on his way to the mail slots. Thankfully there weren't any messages waiting for him.

Feeling ecstatic as well as relieved, he made his way down to the lounge and dozed for his allotted hour. He knew he had to be ready to go afterward but if he reasoned correctly, the lieutenant would prob-ably stay at the desk and bullshit with the incoming lieutenant.

The end of the tour came quickly. Charlie got a jump start on changing his clothes and was out the door at 8:00 A.M. He stopped to get his daily newspaper then drove home. When he arrived he immediately noticed Annette's car still in the driveway and he couldn't help but wonder if she had just decided to stay home or if she was running late. He entered and found her sitting at the kitchen table. He could see she had been crying and felt his stomach reaching up into his throat.

"Annette, honey, what's wrong?"_he asked as he went to her.

"Charlie, sit down. I just don't know what to do anymore. I've been trying so hard to make a go of it with you. You know I have. You could see that, right?"

"Why, of course I have. I thought we were doing okay. We haven't been intimate yet but I guessed that was because you wanted to proceed slowly. Sweetheart, I ended my affair. I told you that. I want to save our marriage so I ended it, and I did so with no regrets.

"If you say you've been trying, does that mean you've ended your relationship with your friend at work? If you still see him there, doesn't it make it more difficult for you? I'm sure the bastard doesn't want you to save your marriage and leave him, but if you still see him, Annette, how will you ever know what you really want?"_Charlie asked.

"I don't know, Charlie. I just don't know," she sobbed.

"Look, if you work with this guy, you're going to have to make a decision to either leave your job or leave me. That's the only way you're going to get your mind straight," said Charlie.

Annette started to cry even harder. She grabbed a Kleenex from her purse and loudly blew her nose then threw the tissue into the kitchen garbage can which was already full to the brim with discarded tissues. She must have been crying for some time.

"Annette, are you willing to try a marriage counselor? Maybe just talking to someone will make you feel better," he suggested.

"I don't know, Charlie. I just feel so lost!"

"Look, honey, I just want you to feel better. I want you to be happy, even if it means you don't love me anymore. Why don't you go to a psychologist or counselor by yourself," he suggested quietly.

"Okay, Charlie, I'll try," she agreed.

"I'll back you up on whatever it is you choose to do, Annette, and we will always be friends no matter what you decide. I love you and always will be here for you."

"Charlie, I want you to know something," she said with slight hesitation. "I... I chose not to go to work today because I didn't want to see my friend. I have been trying to avoid him but it's so hard because we work together. When I see him I feel that I should break it off but when I don't see him, I miss him."

"I understand how you feel. It's as if you're burning candles at both ends, right? You feel like you're a rubber band that's being stretched to its limits."

"That's exactly how I feel," she nodded, "but how did you know?"

"Because you're human, honey, and we weren't built to handle two relationships at once. That's why you must seek professional help and prioritize your life," he said.

"I feel a little better, thanks to you," she said, straining to smile. "Do you want some breakfast?"_

"No thanks, I think I'll have a cup of tea for a change, then just sit out on the deck and read my paper before I go to bed for the day."

"Okay. Then I'm going to keep busy doing some chores. If I go anywhere I will leave you a note," she offered.

Charlie made his tea and read his paper, glad he hadn't blown up in a jealous rage. He knew it would have served no legitimate purpose other than to drive Annette back into her lover's arms. He was resolved to think positive and was ready to accept her decision no matter what it was. He did love her and wanted her to be happy.

After a while he went to bed and slept soundly. He was tired and slept most of the day, getting up at 6:00 P.M. when his alarm went off.

Hungry, he made his way downstairs and found Annette finishing up dinner. Even though she hadn't made anything special other than a pot of stew, he wolfed it down then helped her clean up. They made small talk and didn't speak about what had transpired between them earlier that morning.

He showered and shaved then kissed his wife goodnight. During his drive in to work the realization that he was losing her struck him hard. There was an aching emptiness deep within the pit of his stomach and he began to have cold sweats, feeling as though he was a failure and totally responsible for the tears he had seen his wife shed only hours before.

As he navigated his way through the familiar streets he became filled with dread about going to work. He desperately wanted to speak to his wife but what else could he say? They were beyond the talking stage. He had told her he loved her and would be there for her. What more could he do? The ball was in her court now and he just had to try to be patient and maintain control. He hoped that going to work was the right thing to do.

He parked his car and entered the station house through the rear door. When he checked his mail slot, he was relieved to find it empty. He scanned the roll call and saw that he was the lieutenant's driver, as usual.

There were three sergeants working, which was a luxury for the boss because one would be assigned to the desk while the other two went out on patrol. They would handle their own meal reliefs so the lieutenant acting as Platoon Commander could do whatever it was that he wanted or needed to do. He could stay in the house and do administrative work or go out and get some activity.

Charlie hoped the boss would go out. He didn't want to stay in the house on this particular night. He went up to his locker and changed for the street. Opening it wasn't easy; the pictures of Annette and his kids inside made his eyes fill up, but he didn't want to start crying with all the other guys around. He had to make it to the street.

He took a tissue from a box in his locker, grabbed his gear, and headed out of the locker room. When he made it down stairs he saw that Lt. A. was already in uniform behind the desk, conversing with the three sergeants. The lieutenant saw him and gave him a wave and Charlie waved back.

Roll call, either conducted by the desk officer or the sergeant who was assigned as sergeant #1, started right on the dot by the sergeant. Lt. A. could speak after the roll call but usually didn't unless he had desk duty. He chose not to speak on this night and Charlie was grateful. He wanted to hit the street as quickly as possible.

He approached the desk and scanned the keys that had been deposited by the incoming shift. He found the ones to the Platoon Commander's auto and grabbed them so fast that you would think they were made out of gold. He drove the car to the side lot and gassed it up, making all the required entries in the gasoline log book. When he was finished he passed the log book to the sector next in line at the pump then drove to the front of the station house and waited for the lieutenant to come out. Although he knew the lieutenant could choose to stay and bullshit for a while since there were so many sergeants working, he still hoped the boss would remain consistent and choose to go out early as usual. Just when he thought they would have a routine for their shift, he saw Lt. A. walking out to the awaiting car with his gear.

As he got in the car, the boss placed his attaché case into the back seat, jammed his nightstick between the seat and the door, then said, "How about some coffee, Charlie?"

"Sure, Lou."

***

The radio began crackling with jobs that were picked up by the answering units. Most nights the 120th was the busiest house, but sometimes the 122nd could get crazy, too.

Charlie drove along Bay Street, deliberately passing the Dunkin Donuts shop on Victory Boulevard where Terry worked. The lieutenant noticed but let it go without remarking about it. At the next coffee shop Charlie went in and got their usual then he drove the RMP down along Front Street to the piers where they could share their ritual in peace, away from traffic and nosy night pedestrians.

Charlie removed his lid and placed it on the dash board, then lit his cigarette.

"I've been working with you now for almost two years, Charlie, and I think I can safely say that I know you and your moods," the lieutenant began. "Am I right?"_

"Yeah, you've got me pegged, Lou. I found Annette crying yesterday morning and it was over the fucking mess that we're in. She doesn't know what to do. It sounds as if she just might be in love with this guy and yet, I think she still feels something towards me. She says she's torn."

"It sounds as if she is trying to be honest with you, Charlie."

"Yeah, it does. Too bad honesty sucks when it comes to feelings. I think I'm going to lose her, Lou," admitted Charlie.

"Well, she might make that choice. What happens if she wants to move out? Will you be able to handle it? Have you asked yourself any of these questions yet? Will you sell your house if she wants a divorce?" asked the boss.

"I don't know, Lou. I haven't really had a chance to ask myself any questions. I'm still feeling miserable about the whole fucking mess. I hate to say it, but I've failed at my marriage."

"Whoa, step back a bit before you go saying something like that. It takes two people to make a marriage and two people to make it fail. People react to other people, and you know as well as I do that none of us are perfect.

"Annette is probably feeling the same thing as you are right now. Neither of you wanted this scenario but you got stuck with it. Now you both have to make an important decision," said the lieutenant.

"What's that Lou?"_

"You both have to decide whether the marriage is worth saving, Charlie. If you decide that it is then you both need to work at it, whatever the cost. If you can't agree to do that then it's time to call it quits and spare both of you any further anguish," explained the lieutenant.

Charlie knew Lt. A. was right but he couldn't face the possibility that he could and, probably would, lose his wife. He had some important decisions to make and he had to make them soon. He began to accept his situation and knew he had to have another talk with Annette about their marriage to see if it was worth the effort to be saved. He knew he wanted to save it and would do anything needed to achieve that goal, but, even after all these years, he wasn't sure how she felt.

They fell into silence as they drank their coffee and ate their coffee house treats.

Charlie had the rest of the night ahead of him and wanted it to go as quickly as possible. Since there were three sergeants on duty, Lt. A. probably would not have to respond on any jobs other than really serious ones where the Platoon Commander was required.

"Lou, you've told me sad stories, funny stories and even stories about great faith. You've told me about justice meted out in the street and how you met your partner. Do you have any stories that are really evil? You must have handled some cases that were really horrible. If you do, and wouldn't mind, I'd like to hear one if you are willing to share it with me," Charlie said.

The lieutenant looked at Charlie skeptically then said, "I know your mind is foggy right now with what is happening in your life."

"It is, Lou, but I think listening to your experiences will help take my mind off things; at least, they always have in the past."

"Okay, Charlie," said Lt. A. with a nod.

CHAPTER TWENTY-SIX

Evil takes many forms and wears many faces. Bleeding heart liberals will say that evil in man is a sickness to be forgiven, while conservatives say it should be exorcized with a noose. Either way, no one ever comes up with a solution for the victim or the victim's family.

Lt. A. saw evil many times in his career, but nothing compared to the evil he witnessed personified in the body of one man named Wilbur.

Wilbur Hartmill was a drifter and an alcoholic and had more addresses and aliases than anyone could ever imagine. He had outstanding warrants from multiple states when he was arrested by John and his partner Frank on one fateful Easter Sunday in 1977. When running a check on him they found he had traffic tickets from every state, all part of his journey from New Mexico to Staten Island.

Only God knew why Wilbur showed up on Broad Street in sector Eddie on Staten Island.

***

John dreaded Easter Sundays. Some of his worst experiences as a cop had occurred on Easter Sundays.

Frank and I were on routine patrol in sector Eddie in the Stapleton section of the 120th. After we had turned out and gassed up our car, we headed to Raymond's Bakery on Targee Street to get some hot cross buns as only Raymond's could make them. Raymond's was one of the last authentic German bakeries and had been on Targee Street for a very long time.

Once our fresh, baked goods were in our hands, we would drive out to our Sunday church crossing and have our coffee while people inside were celebrating Easter Sunday Mass as well as the resurrection of Jesus. This was the same block where, a few years earlier, we had been shot at by a sniper during the Christmas midnight mass.

We had just started our drive up Broad Street towards our final location when we spotted Hartmill. He was wearing a button down white shirt and blue denim jeans. His hair was long, brown and almost shoulder length. He was unshaven and his face covered with about a week's growth. On his feet he wore very soiled white sneakers. He dragged his feet as he walked, almost seeming to shuffle.

Frank and I eyed him suspiciously, especially the unidentified object slung over one of his shoulders.

"What the fuck does he have?"_Frank wondered out loud.

"Not sure. I can't make it out."

We made a U turn and pulled alongside Hartmill on the other side of the street, now facing traffic in the wrong direction. We passed him and came to a stop twenty feet away then we both got out of the car and approached him. Seeming not to notice us, Hartmill kept walking in our direction.

Frank saw it first.

"Jesus Christ," he screamed in disgust.

Hartmill was holding a newborn baby by its ankles. The infant was only clad in a diaper and seemed to be just a month or two old, judging by its size. It was white, which was unusual since Stapleton was mostly populated with blacks and Hispanics.

As he reached us, I grabbed Hartmill by the throat and ordered him to release the infant. Surprisingly, he did what he was told and did not resist or try to flee. Frank threw the cuffs on him while I held the baby. Hartmill was quickly placed in the rear of the RMP then Frank got behind the wheel and headed for Saint Vincent's hospital. In the passenger seat, I administered mouth to mouth resuscitation on the innocent child.

Who was this monster? Whose baby was this? As I continued mouth to mouth, Frank picked up the radio while driving with lights and sirens.

"120 Eddie to Central," he said into the receiver.

"Proceed, sector Eddie," answered the dispatcher.

"Central, be advised that this unit is transporting one infant, not breathing at this time, to Saint Vincent's Hospital. Have the ER standing by. The infant is approximately one to two months old. Also have the patrol sergeant 10-85 us at that location. Notify the 120th detective squad that we have the possible perpetrator in the car," Frank said calmly.

"120th Sergeant, read direct," said Sergeant Knobbe who had overheard the transmission and would meet us at the hospital.

"120 C-Charlie to Central," said Frankie Catalano.

"Proceed, sector Charlie."

"Central, sector Charlie will also respond to the hospital to ascertain if we can be of any assistance," said Frankie.

When we arrived at the hospital, Frank maneuvered the RMP directly into the ambulance loading dock. Doctors as well as nurses were standing ready with portable oxygen canisters and resuscitation equipment. As soon as I opened my door, the baby was in the hands of the doctors and nurses. I followed them in while Frank moved the RMP to the police vehicle parking area.

Frankie and Willie pulled up while Frank was parking the car.

"What do you have, Frank?"_asked Willie inquisitively.

"I'm not sure yet. This guy was walking down Broad Street carrying a baby over his shoulder like it was a fucking chicken," said Frank incredulously.

"Who is he?" asked Frankie.

"I don't know. He's not from around here, that's for sure. We just gave him a quick toss before we put him in the car but we haven't searched him yet," said Frank.

"This is definitely one for the squad. I mean, who the hell does that baby belong to? Is it his? We have to turn this one over to the pinky rings," said Willie.

The squad and Sgt. Knobbe, the patrol sergeant, arrived roughly at the same time. Sgt. Knobbe was close to retirement and did not want to get involved in anything that might jeopardize his pension.

In actuality, Sergeant Knobbe was a poor supervisor because he was afraid to make decisions. When he did, they were based on emotions and not the facts at hand.

Frank frowned when he realized Knobbe was the responding Sergeant. "Jesus fucking Christ! Why him? Why now?" he yelled.

"What do you have, Brownell," asked Knobbe.

Sergeant Knobbe never used first names and he never backed up anyone on heavy runs. Not surprisingly, he wasn't well liked. Out of all the sergeants in the entire precinct, he was the only one without a steady driver assigned to him because no one wanted to drive him. It was considered a punishment tour to be assigned to Sergeant Knobbe.

I had been assigned to him once before I got my steady seat with Frank, and although I had anticipated my tour with Knobbe to be rough, it went better than expected. On my first tour with him I waited in the car for him to get in. When he finally did, Knobbe spoke first.

"Don't smoke, don't chew gum and don't speak until I tell you to or ask you a question, got it?"

"I smoke, I chew gum and I don't give a damn if I never speak to you," I said with unhindered sarcasm.

"Get the fuck out of this car, now!" the sergeant screamed.

I lasted all of 45 seconds with the infamous Sergeant Knobbe, which was unheard of. The rest of the guys could not believe how I had gotten out of driving him.

✳✳✳

Glancing at the man in the back seat of the RMP, Frank told Sergeant Knobbe what he had. As luck would have it, the timid sergeant simply directed Frank to turn him over to the squad.

Detective Bobby Rizzo was the day watch detective that fateful Easter Sunday. He had been a cop in the 1ˢᵗ Precinct and worked with me when I was assigned there after my graduation from the police academy. Bobby remained in the 1st after my transfer to the 120th. He made some great collars and it wasn't long before he was promoted to detective 3rd grade.

While a detective in the 1st squad, Rizzo was assigned to a task force which was assigned a job uncovering corruption in the Fulton Fish Market. He had been in the midst of that investigation when he spotted a young female who was locked in a car on one of the deserted streets adjacent to the fish market. He investigated and found that she was a runaway from New Jersey who had been picked up by a pedophile in midtown and was about to be shipped overseas to the Mideast to become a sex slave to the rich and famous. This was a common occurrence and something you never read about but all cops knew it went on. This particular sixteen-year old just happened to be the daughter of a U.S. Congressman from New Jersey. Needless to say, Bobby made 2nd grade detective out of that discovery. It was then that he also transferred to the 120th squad.

Bobby knew most of the sector teams in the 120th, at least the busy ones. Frank and I had given him good tips and leads we got from our squeals in the street. In turn, Bobby gave us some minor cases where the patrol force was allowed to make arrests.

"Hi, Frank. Where's John?"_Bobby asked.

"He's inside with the baby and the doctors," answered Frank as he filled Bobby in on everything he had.

"We did a preliminary with missing persons when we heard you had a baby with this perpetrator," said Bobby.

"And?"_Frank asked back hoping for an answer.

"Zero, zilch, nada," said Rizzo ruefully.

Nobody had reported a baby missing anywhere in the entire city in the past twenty-four hours. Rizzo had checked all the hospitals to see if a baby had been stolen out of one of the nurseries, but no luck. Where the baby had come from was a total mystery and the only person who could come up with an answer was Hartmill.

"Let me talk to him alone, okay, Frank?"_asked Bobby.

"You got it."_

Frank walked over to where he had parked the RMP, opened the door and reached over the visor where he kept his cigarettes. He took one of the Kents out *of his pack and lit it with his Zippo lighter then drew in heavily on the cigarette and repeated the process. Whether it was imaginary or not, it had a calming effect on him.*

He finished his cigarette and walked back to the black squad car where Bobby had been speaking to Hartmill. Frank almost bumped into me as I emerged from the emergency room doors. Frank just had to gaze at the expression on my face to realize the baby didn't make it.

My eyes must have looked like two oceans about to open the flood gates. Frank immediately offered me a cigarette, which I took willingly.

"The baby is dead. It was probably dead while I was giving it mouth to mouth. The doctors said it was about six to eight weeks old. It sure looked younger to me but they're the doctors. Two months old and it's on its fucking journey to dust. Where's the prisoner?" I asked angrily.

"He's in the squad's car with Bobby Rizzo," Frank answered.

"Any bosses show up yet?"_

"Yeah, Sergeant Knobbe came and left," replied Frank.

"Thank Christ," I said.

We smoked our cigarettes in silence while we waited for Bobby to finish with Hartmill. He must have spent at least forty five minutes with him. We saw Bobby pass cigarettes to the prisoner, probably in an attempt to butter him up so he would talk.

"Jesus Christ, Frank. He's had him for almost a God damned hour! He must have found out something by now," I said impatiently.

"It takes time, partner. Bobby is a good detective but you have to approach people in a certain way. First, he has to get to know who he is and where his head is at. If Hartmill is an out and out lunatic, it just makes Bobby's job all the harder," Frank said in response to my question.

After a few more minutes, Bobby Rizzo finally exited from the car. He slammed the door and threw his cigarettes down to the pavement as if in disgust then made his way over to where Frank and I were waiting. We didn't really know what to expect judging by his actions. I was the first to speak.

"What did you find out, Bobby?"

"Not a fucking thing! The guy's mouth is tighter than an aardvark's asshole! I'll tell you what though; this guy's been around the judicial system before. He knows his rights and wants his lawyer, and I mean now.

"I have enough to hold him on, so I'll take him back to the precinct and put him in a cell for a while. Later I'll let him make his phone call. How is the baby doing?"_

"The baby is DOA," I said quietly.

"Did the doctors give you a cause of death or time yet?"_he asked.

"Not yet, but we'll hang around and get it. As soon as we do, we'll call you," said Frank.

"Okay, talk to you later then. I'll get busy putting out an all-points bulletin on the baby. All the radio divisions in all the boroughs will get the APB," Bobby said.

"See you later, Bobby," I said.

Frank and I waited outside the emergency room for someone to let us know the cause of death. The case was now a homicide and as such, warranted top priority.

We both knew that the rest of the day would now be filled with police work dealing with finding the parents of the dead baby. Once we did that, we knew we would be faced with the hardest job any patrol officer could encounter – notifying the loved ones of their terrible loss. After a short time, a young man dressed in green scrubs exited through the emergency entrance and lit a cigarette as he approached Frank and I.

"Are you the officers who brought the baby in?"_

"Yes, Doctor," Frank quickly answered.

The man in the scrubs nodded then said, "The baby died of blunt trauma to the head and sternum. The trauma could have come from either dropping the child or slamming its head against a hard object. The trauma to the chest was the result of a thrust of strong force to the area."

"In other words, the baby was either punched in the chest or an object was used," said Frank inquisitively.

283

"In my opinion, the baby was punched. I can see what appears to be the outline of knuckles in the rib cage area. The ribs are broken and pierced the lungs but death preceded the lungs being pierced."

"Thanks, Doctor. Do you have a time of death?" asked Frank.

The young man nodded. "I saw the report that stated you arrived at 8:00 A.M. I would say that death occurred at approximately 7:00 A.M."

"Thank you for all you've done," said Frank.

The doctor returned back to his emergency room as Frank and I remained silent. Eventually we got back into the RMP and rode to the station house, also in silence.

Here was a baby, barely two months old, whose life had been snuffed out without a thought. Here was a child who would never say the words mama or dada. Here was an infant who would never know who its parents were. It was a tiny life whose eyes would never gaze upon the blue sky of daylight or a dark sea above filled with glittering stars. Its tiny hands and fingers would never feel the texture of its mother's hair or icy, cold snow on a wintry morning.

I soon realized that I didn't even know the sex of the baby and, somehow, this made me feel even more horrible. What if we couldn't locate the parents? Would the baby have to be buried in Potter's Field on Randall's Island? I swore to myself then that, if the parents were not located, I would petition to have the right to give the baby a proper Christian burial and purchase the tombstone myself.

All I could think of were my own two kids at home. I would be getting off at 4:00 P.M. and would be able to catch the latter part of the Easter Sunday dinner with my family. My son, Richard, was in second grade while my daughter, Diana, was in first grade, both at St. Anne's Parochial School in Dongan Hills. They were good kids and I wanted nothing more than to see them right at that very moment. Thinking of that innocent child, I thanked God for what I had.

I was a decent guy, but if Hartmill would have been before me right then, I would have killed him without any hesitation. I didn't just think it; I knew it, and the very thought scared me.

Frank was quiet, too, but in his silence he did not think of kids. He had a habit of hiding his emotions and did not easily express sorrow or anger. If he ever did, it was done in solitude.

When we arrived at the precinct, Frank double parked the car in front of the station house and remained in the vehicle while I ran inside. I saluted the desk then ran up the stairs to the detective's offices. A sign on the door read knock before entering so I did so and opened the door. Upon entering I saw several detectives sitting at typewriters, each of them busy poking away at the keys with two fingers. The lone cell in the room contained Hartmill, who was sitting silently on the narrow bench.

Across the room I saw Bobby Rizzo speaking with Lieutenant Mcshane, the Commanding Officer of the 120th Precinct squad. Captains usually commanded precincts but lieutenants commanded the detective squads. Lt. McShane had over twenty-five years on the job with twenty of those spent in the detective division. With a name like Mike McShane, he was destined to become a cop or detective.

I stood silently by the detention cell housing Hartmill. The interior of his enclosure was painted green which was typical of all the cells found in squad rooms throughout the city. It had a single open toilet and a wooden bench but there were no pillows or blankets. His space was roughly 12' by 8', not a holding cell for overnight prisoners.

The precinct cells were the smallest types of cells and built for single occupants, used to hold prisoners while the detectives did their paperwork or further investigative work. When a detective finished his paperwork on a prisoner, he would transport him or her to court for pre-arraignment. If court was not in session, he would lodge his prisoner downstairs in the precinct's detention facility.

Holding cells had blankets. If the prisoner was lodged before super or breakfast, the precinct would provide a sandwich and drink, free of charge. If the prisoner had his own money, he would be allowed to purchase something more substantial. It was a common sight throughout the city to see multiple prisoners walking out of station houses in the morning, shackled together and stepping into paddy wagons.

Of course, not too many new cops refer to the patrol wagons as paddy wagons anymore. The term 'paddy wagon' was a reference to the turn of the century when the majority of immigrants were Irish and therefore the majority of arrests were Irish people. Soon thereafter the police force consisted of mostly Irish and the term stuck.

Hartmill was sitting on the hardwood bench. His eyes were closed but I did not know if he was just dozing or faking it. Lt. McShane finished talking with Bobby and returned to his office in the rear of the squad room where he closed the door behind him. The words Commanding Officer *were painted in green at eye level across the opaque glass section of the door.*

This squad room was illustrative of all NYPD squad rooms throughout the city. There were six to eight desks spaced evenly apart with a typewriter in the middle of each desk. Just a few inches away from each typewriter was an in and out basket, of which the in rack was always more full than the out one.

Some of these baskets contained DD 5's, open cases, pending interviews and *to be filed. There were large metal file cabinets all around the circumference of the room and bulletin boards hung everywhere. There were clipboards with papers hanging on a nail anywhere a nail could safely be hammered into the wall. Some held labels, such as Legal Division bulletins, Operations Orders and precinct memos.*

One section of one wall housed a slim, enclosed glass cabinet which measured roughly 10' by 2". It contained photos of criminals filed by crime and modus operandi. The way a criminal committed his crime was also important and thus the study of his method of operation also important. The photos within were hidden by a large green shade which was torn and tattered. A speaker on the wall next to the cabinet, precariously hanging from yet another nail, was tuned in to the Richmond Radio dispatcher as well as the RMP's in the field.

Some detectives were seated at their desks, others were speaking on the phone, and still others either had victims or potential prisoners seated beside them in heavy, metal chairs.

The scene was reminiscent of an old movie called Detective Story I had seen on TV, starring Kirk Douglas and directed by William Wyler. It was a realistic

account of detective police work in any major city and was even more realistic than Barney Miller or Kojack.

After Lt. McShane's door closed I walked over to where Bobby was standing.

"What did you find out at the hospital?" he asked.

"The baby died around 7:00 A.M. or thereabouts. The doctor said it was blunt trauma to the head and chest area," I answered with a frown. "How about you? Anything?"

"Hartmill called a few numbers but no answers on any of his calls. He didn't even ask for a God damned phone book. I took an inventory search on him. All he has are traffic tickets from all over the country; some are issued in the name of Hartmill while others are in names he gave to the police who stopped him. It looks like the tickets were issued without any verification by the cops who wrote them. I have some from New Mexico, Texas, the Carolinas, and even a few from Florida," said Bobby disgustedly.

"Okay, so he's a drifter. If that's the case then where the hell is his car? Don't forget that when Frank and I first spotted him, he was on foot," I said.

"I really don't think the car is important," said Rizzo, "at least not right now. I had a talk with Lieutenant McShane and I'm going to book Hartmill as a John Doe for now and wait to see what his prints bring back. If he was printed before, we'll know it."

Both Bobby and I knew it was going to be a lengthy process.

The first step would be Hartmill's finger printing in the detective squad office. Three cards were required for this – a New York City card, a New York state card and finally an FBI card. The information required would have to be typed onto these cards. Detective Rizzo would then have to drive into the city and deliver them to the Bureau of Criminal Identification, located in police headquarters.

It was common for the wait at B.C.I. for Hartmill's prior arrest records, which were called "rap" sheets, to take as long as four to six hours. When the results were finally obtained, they would contain a record of Hartmill's prior arrests and incarcerations from all over the United States.

"Well, Bobby, let me know if you need anything."

"Thanks, John. I will, and I'll let you know if we come up with anything," said Detective Rizzo.

I made my way out of the squad room and back down the stairs to the main floor, where the lieutenant on the desk called me over.

*"Audenino, Sergeant Knobbe told me about the baby. Do we have any identification on it yet?"*_

"Nothing yet, Sir. I was just about to go back on patrol to see what I could come up with," I answered.

*"Okay. I want you to answer your jobs, though. You need to be available and not out of service, understand?"*_

*"Yes, Sir."*_

With that I walked through the front doors and rejoined Frank, who was waiting for me in the RMP where he had been passing the time working on the NY Daily News crossword puzzle. If it had been a typical Sunday morning, we would have had our coffee and donuts, checked our sector for broken glass and past unreported burglaries. Then we would have settled in somewhere and Frank would have attacked his puzzles before the midday crunch of family disputes and auto accidents, which were always in abundance. People in sector Eddie slept late on Sundays, even Easter Sunday, but afternoons were another story. They were always busy.

*"Any word over the radio on the missing baby, Frank?"*_I asked.

"Nothing. The radio has been dead."

CHAPTER TWENTY-SEVEN

*F*rank put the car in gear and the Chevy V-8 engine strained to tear off down the street. RMP 1095 was one of only four V-8 engines in our precinct's fleet of cars; all the others were six cylinders. Our baby really flew.

Frank drove down Bay Street and stopped in front of Paul's Sweet Shop, an old fashioned and small confectionary store with a wide, red counter and a line of old fashioned stools. Paul, the owner, was a local known gambler, or KG. He was one of many KG's who worked and lived in the confines of the 120th precinct, but he made the best egg cream on Staten Island. Some local old timers boasted that Paul made them even better than the ones they had in Brooklyn as young boys. As a KG, Paul's was off limits to cops whether they were on or off duty. However, Frank and John frequented the place on Sundays when a lot of other stores were closed in their sector. They realized they could be caught on tape at any time either entering or leaving but they paid for anything they bought and never stayed in the joint. The place was known to have been bugged on more than one occasion.

"Do you want anything?"_asked Frank.

"Two packs of Kent Kings, please," I answered with a nod.

We both knew what the remainder of the day might have in store for us and they didn't want to run out of cigarettes. As soon as he made his purchase, Frank came right out and handed me the pack of Kents and looked at his watch. It was almost 10:30 A.M.

"We have a 1:00 P.M. meal. Do you want to wait until then or do you want to grab a bite now?"_he asked.

"I'm not really in the mood to eat now."

"Neither am I, but I have a feeling in my gut that we're not going to get a chance later on," he said.

"Why don't we give Frankie over in sector C a 10-85 and have him meet us? This way we'll have an idea of what's going on," I suggested.

"Good idea."_

With that, Frank drove over to Vanderbilt Avenue and Bay Street which was the dividing line between sector E and sector C. He parked in an old, abandoned gas station on the corner then plucked the radio handset out of its cradle and spoke softly into it.

"Frankie, B&V," he said softly, bypassing the radio dispatcher.

"10-4," Frankie acknowledged.

Most adjoining sectors had codes for meeting locations because they didn't want the brass or shoo flies to know what they were up to. Frank also didn't want Sergeant Knobbe snooping around. He didn't need the ballless fuck, today of all days.

After a few moments, Frankie Catalano and Willie Folder pulled up and parked parallel alongside our RMP.

"We heard that the baby died. Tough break, guys," said Willie sympathetically.

"Yeah, have you guys heard anything yet out here?"_asked Frank.

"Nah, it's dead as a doornail. People are either in church or are sleeping in," answered Frankie.

Since Hartmill had been caught walking, we reasoned that the baby had to be local. Frank and I had first seen Hartmill at 8:00 A.M. and it was now almost 11:00 A.M. Although nearly three hours had passed since we'd found the heartless man lugging the innocent child over his shoulder like a sack of potatoes, no one had reported a missing infant.

Both of our teams began coming up with our own theories as we talked about the case. Maybe Hartmill had driven with the baby from another state, which would explain why no one on Staten Island had reported a missing baby? If this was the case then where was the car? We also considered the possibility that Hartmill may have also kidnapped the infant's mother, which would explain why there was not yet a report of a missing baby. Hartmill was a drifter and we all knew he was aware of the legal system.

There were a few flop houses in the 120ᵗʰ and one fleabag hotel. There were also a few welfare motels but, judging by the dates on the tickets found in Hartmill's pockets, he would not have had enough time to qualify for any kind of state assistance.

Frankie, Willie, Frank and I decided to work in tandem and check out the flop houses in our respective sectors. We then agreed to meet back at this same location in one hour. Frank and I took the Saint George Hotel and some daily/ weekly flop houses right around the corner from the Saint George on Central Avenue, while Frankie and Willie would check out a Salvation Army Center on Clove Road near the Grasmere Train Station, which took in transients who were down and out.

The Salvation Army Center was a huge, white stucco building and had been in operation for many years. The only requirement to stay there was sobriety and if you were caught drinking or drunk, you were ejected immediately. If you had any money, it was suggested that you donate part of it towards your room and board. If you didn't, the staff would allow you to do odd jobs in lieu of your room and board.

Frankie pulled up in front of the stucco building and Willie ran inside. Two minutes later he emerged, shaking his head.

"No one has checked in for a least a week. The last person was a southerner who left last Sunday," he said. He hadn't checked to see if there had been any female boarders because this particular center housed only males.

Frank and I, who were checking out the flops in our sector, didn't have any luck either. Both sectors returned to Bay Street and Vanderbilt Avenue at noon.

It was amazing to us that no one had called the local precinct or 911. A dead baby lay in the refrigerated vault of Saint Vincent's Hospital with no name and no one coming forward. Surely this child of God would wind up with more than the kind thoughts of a middle class police officer who was willing to give it a Christian burial and a tombstone. Its existence and death needed to have more meaning than a simple end to life.

Was that all there was to life? Simple extinction? Was there any purpose to life at all? Could there be something beyond the clouded veil?

I knew all too well that cynicism was a cop's worst enemy. To see life's worst on a daily basis broke down a cop's vision of joy, happiness and hope. People suffer every day in ways that the vast majority of the public do not see and are never made aware of. It is not the cop's fault that people suffer. It is not their fault when society does not provide remedies for their suffering or fails to rescue its own.

What does a cop do when he finishes his tour of duty and still has the freshly imbedded vision in his mind of a two-month old baby who has just gasped its last breath? What does a cop do when he awakens at night and sees in his mind the battle scars of a three-year old who has been physically abused for the past two years of its life? How much can one man cry? Should he start drinking to forget? Should he transfer those suppressed feelings onto his own family or maybe onto other members of the community to which he serves? Should he try to forget them or force them deeper into his own mind?

I didn't seek solace in drinking. I also didn't want to grapple with the existence of God and life, at least not at that moment.

Lt. A. was in no hurry to finish his story of Hartmill and the baby. "Lou, if you don't want to finish it now, I understand," Charlie said. It was obvious that Lt. A. was reliving his feelings of helplessness while telling the story of that fateful day. Charlie could see the frustration in the lieutenant's body language as he wrenched his hands and clenched his fists. The lieutenant was also chain smoking at this point.

He glanced at Charlie as he took out another Vantage regular and lit it up.

"Lou, I thought you said you smoked Kent Kings when you worked with Frank?"_asked Charlie.

"Oh, I did. Frank and I both quit smoking at the same time, years later. I had quit for twelve years but when I got promoted to lieutenant they transferred me to the police communication division and I started smoking again my first day there. The only brand available in the cigarette machine on the ninth floor, other than menthols, was Vantage regulars. That's how I got hooked on them."

He took a drag of his newly lit cigarette then continued telling Charlie about the Hartmill case.

The two teams had completed their canvass of the flops and flea bag spots in their sectors, and neither of them wanted to run the risk of driving all the way out to Mariner's Harbor to check out the last flea bag joint. If a job came up they wouldn't be able to respond as quickly as they would have liked. Of course there were other transient hotels but they were in the confines of the 122nd precinct. Both sectors decided to resume patrol and put the problem into God's hands; God and Detective Rizzo's.

Detective Rizzo had really gotten lucky. He had delivered his prints to B.C.I. and they were returned in less than two hours.

The fiend's real name was Wilbur Hartmill and he was originally from Memphis, Tennessee. He had prior arrests for burglary, assault with intent to kill, and endangering the welfare of a child, and this was just in Tennessee. He had served a ten-year stretch in a federal prison for the manslaughter of a teenager who had made the unforgivable mistake of calling him a bum. He was also wanted on a minor traffic violation, which escalated into an arrest warrant when Hartmill failed to show up in court.

This information made Detective Rizzo extremely happy. It was all he needed to hold Wilbur, until, hopefully, someone came forward to claim the baby.

Bobby also planned to contact the local paper, the Staten Island Advance, and ask for their assistance in seeking someone related to the baby. In times of need the paper did assist the police, but overall was considered liberal in its views. Most Staten Islander's read it to see which of their neighbors got arrested, who died and the times of the movie showings in their local neighborhoods.

John and his partner headed back to sector Eddie to resume patrol but still declined to eat. It was roughly 12:30 P.M. when they arrived there and Frank was driving up Broad Street at almost the same spot where they first spotted Hartmill.

Then it happened.

"120 C-Charlie," called the radio dispatcher.
"Charlie standing by Central," answered Frankie.
"120 Charlie, respond to 185 Parkhill Avenue, apartment L David. See the
complainant on a missing child," directed the radio dispatcher.
"120 Charlie, 10-4. Message received."
"Central, do you have anything further on that assignment?"_asked
Frankie.
"Negative, sector Charlie. Just see the complainant on a missing child."
"Do you have a call back number?"_asked Frankie.
"That's affirmative," responded Central.

"120 Charlie is requesting that you call back the complainant via land
line. Please ascertain if the missing child is an infant. If it is, please notify the
120 squad to also respond."
"Will do," responded Central.
Sector Charlie, with Frankie and Willie, was en route to the Parkhill com-
plex. This was the first break in the case, but it was still not known if the missing
child was an infant. Missing kids were common occurrences in the 120ʰ and
the majority of them were runaways. Some were kids who just lost track of the
time and stayed out later than usual, worrying their parents to death. It was
Easter Sunday and most kids were hunting for Easter eggs or involved in eating
their chocolate bunnies.
Frank and I had been monitoring the conversation between the dispatcher
and sector Charlie.
"What do you think Frank?"_I asked my partner as he drove us towards
the Parkhill address.
"I think we're probably going to be meeting some frantic parents."
"Yeah, I think this is the job we've been waiting for all day," I said with a
sigh.
When Frank pulled up to the front of the building he double parked the
RMP and notified the radio dispatcher that sector Eddie was also on the scene.
Frankie and Willie had arrived only a few minutes earlier and were waiting

in the lobby for us. After a nod from Frankie, we all walked down the hall and passed the bank of elevators to apartment Lobby David.

"I don't like the fact that it's on the ground floor," said Frankie.

"Why not?"_I asked.

"Ground level affords burglars easier entry, unless you have steel bars on the windows," Frank chimed in.

We reached the apartment and Frankie pushed the buzzer on the door. It was opened immediately and we were greeted by a man and a woman in their late twenties.

The woman had a bathrobe on and was crying softly. The man was wearing an old sweat shirt and a pair of denim jeans covered in dried paint. They invited us in.

Frankie was the senior officer of our group and also the recorder in sector Charlie so he began by asking what the problem was. The rest of us all knew not to interrupt him. This was his job and he would handle it his way.

"Please come into the kitchen," suggested the man.

We followed him through a hallway and into the kitchen, unable to avoid the smell of fresh paint. Gesturing toward the chairs around the small table, he invited us to sit down.

"Normally, I would have invited you all into the living room but my wife and I were up all night painting it. We just moved in two weeks ago and we've been busy painting and buying furniture," said the husband.

"Our baby has been kidnapped," he added, barely getting the words out.

As he said this, his wife broke down into deep sobs which caused her husband to start crying as well, wide, ragged tears streaming down his cheeks. After a long moment, the husband struggled to compose himself and finally spoke again.

"We spent most of the night up painting. Forgive me, officers. My name is Robert Jenkins and this is my wife, Gloria."

"Mr. Jenkins, how old is the baby?"_Frankie asked him, making certain to keep the baby's age in the present tense and not the past.

"Our baby is two months old. Why would anyone want to take him?"_Mrs. Jenkins' voice broke as she struggled to control her sobs.

"How long do you think it will take before you find our baby, officer?"_asked the distraught father. While he waited for an answer, he wrapped one of his large hands around the woman's smaller ones.

Frankie was at a loss for words because he knew that very shortly he would have to ask one or both to go with him to Saint Vincent's Hospital to view the baby's body and make a positive identification.

"Mr. And Mrs. Jenkins, I must tell you that a baby was found earlier this morning. He was being carried by a drifter not too far from here. We took the baby to the hospital for treatment," explained Frankie as calmly as possible.

It was obvious that he was trying to break the news to them as slowly and gently as possible.

"Our baby is alright, isn't he?"_asked Mrs. Jenkins.

"He's alive, isn't he? Please tell me that he's okay," demanded Mr. Jenkins.

Death notifications were the hardest task that any cop, anywhere, faces.

At that moment, each of us would rather have been walking the toughest foot beat in the toughest precinct than to be there with these two parents.

"Mr. And Mrs. Jenkins, I have to ask you to come with me to Saint Vincent's Hospital," said Frankie.

"For the love of heaven, why? Are you telling me that our son is dead?"_ asked the father.

Frank could not hedge anymore. He had to come out and be brutally honest. It was cruel and inhuman to keep them dangling any longer.

"If the baby is yours, if it is yours, then yes, it is deceased. We need you to view the baby and make a positive identification." Frankie paused for only a second then added, "Do you want to call anyone at this time?"_

"No. Let's just go and see the baby. Maybe it's not ours," said the grieving father, still stunned with disbelief.

We waited while the young parents grabbed their jackets and keys then followed them outside. Mr. Jenkins led his wife to the rear parking lot but Frankie said it would be better if they rode with him in the RMP.

Except for the soft sobs coming from Mrs. Jenkins, the ride to the hospital was dead silent. Frankie radioed Central to let them know he and Willie were en route to the hospital then requested that the radio dispatcher contact the

120th *squad and let them know they were going there for identification purposes. Before arriving at the hospital the radio dispatcher directed Frankie to notify the squad room if the parents made a positive identification.*

Frankie pulled into the hospital's parking lot and stopped the RMP between two ambulances that were parked and out of service. While Willie escorted Mr. and Mrs. Jenkins through the entrance, Frankie let Central know that they had arrived and would be out of service for the remainder of the tour.

Willie had made a good choice by leading Mr. and Mrs. Jenkins through a delivery doorway instead of any of the main doors or even the emergency entryway. The media were already encamped near those entrances and had practically had encircled the hospital like Indians surrounding a wagon train. They had no mercy.

Although it was Easter Sunday, the delivery door was open. Both Frankie and Willie knew it would be because the hospital workers often used it as a point of exit and entrance. They even took smoking breaks on the loading dock.

The news media had converged on the hospital when they heard that a family had finally reported a missing child. It was also apparent that some reporters had telephoned the precinct and spoken to Lieutenant McShane.

Tensions were frequently high between the media and the police. It had always been the police department's perception that the media dealt solely in sensationalism and only worried about headlines and selling papers. On the other hand, the media's perception of the police was that they prevented them from their first amendment privileges. In any event, Frankie had never heard of a cameraman putting down his camera to lend assistance at any emergency scene.

The four officers and the distraught parents made their way through the hospital kitchen which adjoined the loading dock and delivery entrance and was just a single, huge room with a conveyor belt parting it down the middle. On either side of the long belt were stacks of dishes, glasses, trays of plastic spoons and knives and a few chafing dishes.

It was almost 1:00 P.M. and lunch was being prepared for delivery to every patient in the hospital. The first kitchen worker on the line placed an empty tray on the belt. Then, as the tray made its way along the belt from beginning to end, other kitchen workers and dietary aides were at various stations along its entire length. Each tray had a room number, the patient's name and type of diet. Some specified a low calorie diet while others read regular or 1800 calories. Each worker at his or her respective station knew exactly what to place on or what to withhold from the tray.

As each completed tray finished its journey along the belt, other workers placed them on portable delivery carts. It was amazing to see that the entire process of feeding every patient was completed in less than one hour.

After passing through the kitchen, Frankie led the group to the sub-basement, which was also utilized as a temporary morgue where bodies could be kept until claimed either by a licensed mortuary or the medical examiner's office. This baby's death had been ruled a homicide and therefore would have to undergo an autopsy by the NYC Medical examiner. The results would then be added to the death certificate and its contents would be subsequently used by the prosecutor in any criminal proceedings.

Frankie directed the parents to wait in the narrow hallway with the other three officers while he went in to speak to the orderly on duty. When he found him, Frankie explained that he was going to bring in the parents of the baby brought in earlier for identification purposes. He requested that the orderly have the body prepared so the process could be completed as quickly as possible.

Preparation of a corpse, especially one as small as the one in question, was neither a big deal nor an entailed process. It simply meant pulling open the drawer of the refrigerated vault where the body was being kept, removing the corpse from its black body bag, and placing a plain sheet over it.

Frankie wanted to prevent the parents from observing the drawer being opened. It was heart wrenching enough to view the remains held within, but to see your loved one being slid out of a cold drawer was just too much sometimes. He simply wanted to spare them any additional pain and agony.

The orderly prepared the baby in Frankie's presence and nodded signifying it was okay to allow the parents to enter. Frankie went back out into the hallway and rejoined the parents as well as his fellow officers. He gestured the parents over to a bench, then sat down next to them and quietly explained in detail what was to follow.

"Mr. And Mrs. Jenkins, both of you will walk inside with me, unless you decide now that just one of you will do this," he began as tactfully as possible. *"Thank you, officer, but we've decided to do it together,"* the father responded quietly as he held his wife's hand.

"Okay. You will follow me into the anteroom. When we get inside, you will be required to sign into a log book, which will indicate the time of your visit and the person who is being viewed. Just sign your names and I'll take care of the rest," Frankie explained. He wanted them in and out as quickly as possible and was trying to spare them the administrative paperwork that would gobble up time.

"After you sign your names, the orderly will escort us into the viewing area. This is simply a small room at the rear of the office. There is no heat in there and certain areas of the room are refrigerated, so don't be disturbed by the cold," Frankie reassured. The other officers weren't surprised when he avoided telling them that the only parts of the room that were refrigerated were the drawers where the cadavers were kept.

*"When we get into the viewing area, I want both of you to stand on my right side. The orderly will look at me and wait until I nod. I will only do this when I see you nod to me telling me that you are ready, okay?"*_

"We understand," said the father.

"When I nod back to the orderly, he will pull back the sheet and expose the baby from the shoulder area up."

Frankie knew there had been blunt trauma to the chest and that Hartmill's knuckles had been imprinted there. He wanted to spare the parents this additional heartache.

"I want you to look at the child's face. If you identify it as yours, please nod to me. The orderly will then pull the sheet back up."

Frankie's voice was quiet and his eyes filled with empathy as his gaze moved from the young father to the mother. When they stated that they were ready, although the steps to the process seemed simple and easy to follow, Frankie suspected it would not go as smoothly as he had described. The parents would very likely stare and want to hold their baby one last time, but he had no doubt that if he allowed that to happen, their pain would be infinitely worse.

Frankie stood up gave them a nod. They followed him into the anteroom, where Mr. and Mrs. Jenkins signed into the log book. With this done and arms around each other for support, the young couple walked together into the back room.

The floor here was made out of stained concrete and was just as cold as Frankie had described. Numerous attempts at washing it had failed to remove some of the old blood stains which were deeply imbedded into it, and the room smelled strongly of antiseptic, making it impersonal and totally unfriendly.

Frankie walked over to where the orderly had prepared the baby for viewing then motioned to both parents to stand to his right. He had done this many times before but it never got any easier.

There were certain experiences in life which you could never prepare for or get accustomed to. Death was the night visitor. It was the topic we wanted to avoid at any cost, coming and going in an instant. It was bearable as long it didn't come for us.

For cops everywhere, death was as much a part of the job as life and birth. For as many DOAs that Frankie had handled and for as many death notifications he'd had to deliver, there were the lives saved by good, swift police action to think of. And, of course, there were the babies.

He was part of a scene that was the saddest and most tragic event any parent could face, but he had also brought life into the world. Any cop who had done time in a residential precinct long enough and been in the right place at the right time has had the wonderful and glorious opportunity to attend a birth delivery. The four cops present this day with the sad, nervous couple were no exception.

While the orderly kept his eyes focused on the cop standing before him, Frankie looked intently at the parents. He quietly mouthed the words, "are you ready," and they both nodded. Frankie then gave the signal to the orderly, who gently pulled the sheet back exposing the infant's head and shoulder area.

The baby's eyes were closed and its face was ashen white but not blue. Although he had been dirty when he was brought into the hospital earlier that morning, the nurses in the emergency room had cleaned him up before tagging him for the morgue. The infant looked like a porcelain doll.

Mrs. Jenkins cried out first, and her heartrending screams could be heard two flights up.

"Oh, my baby! My baby! They've killed my baby!" she screamed as her body became wracked with anguished, heart wrenching sobs. Mr. Jenkins placed his arm around his wife in a vain attempt to console her, but he, too, was now crying loudly.

Frankie nodded at the orderly, who quickly pulled the sheet back up over the infant, then quietly led the distraught parents back into the anteroom. For several minutes he had them sit there rather than go out into the hallway.

Frank, Willie and I had been waiting in the hallway, but when we heard the lamenting, we also entered the anteroom. Frankie called me over to the side and asked me to call the 120[h] squad to inform Detective Rizzo that the parents had made a positive identification on the baby.

As their first onslaught of tears abated a little, the parents became filled with questions.

"Who could have done this?"_cried Mr. Jenkins.

"Did he suffer?"_sobbed the mother.

How, why, when? So many questions and so few answers. Frankie did not want to lay a guilt trip on the parents but he remembered they had told him that they had been up most of the night painting their apartment. When Mr. Jenkins had led the officers into his kitchen, they had walked past the baby's nursery. Frankie had noticed that the window in the baby's room was up a little bit, probably to get the paint smell out of the apartment. It was obvious to Frankie that Hartmill had seen the light on in the apartment as well as the windows open. When the Jenkins' turned off the light and went to bed, Hartmill had likely climbed in through that window, probably in an attempt to burglarize them. For some reason, he had taken the baby. Only Hartmill knew why. Perhaps the baby had started to cry and, in an attempt to silence him, he punched the infant and mortally wounded it.

Why he had taken the child with him at all was the question of the ages. Frankie had heard of weird actions by burglars defecating on people's floors and in their beds, but the act of taking a baby which was probably dead already was tantamount to taking a trophy at a turkey shoot. It was sick and depraved.

Frankie acknowledged their questions as he began speaking to the parents.

"Mr. and Mrs. Jenkins, we speculate that the person who took your child is, in fact, someone we have in custody. This person was apprehended with your child in his possession."

"You mean you caught someone who had our baby with him?"_asked the father incredulously.

"Yes," I answered.

"Was he alive when you found him?"_asked the mother as she clenched a Kleenex tightly in her hand.

The officers all realized that the mother and father were only trying to retrace their child's last moments of life on earth, which was a normal action for them to be undertaking. Before the grieving process could begin they would have to vent anger and answer as many of the unanswered questions as possible.

"We now believe that the person who took your baby probably saw your light on and made a decision to burglarize your home. There could have been no way for him to know you had a baby in there until he had entered the room," said Frankie.

"Once he was inside, he likely saw your son. At that point, only God knows what possessed him to take the baby and harm it," added Willie.

"It's our thoughts and feelings that death came swiftly for your child," I said.

Both parents were now sobbing softly.

"Whenever you are ready, we will drive you back to your apartment," said Frankie.

I pulled him to the side and told him that Detective Rizzo wanted to sit down with the anguished couple to explain to them what would be happening next and where they would have to go for the upcoming pre- arraignment. Frankie nodded, and after a moment, Frank, Frankie, Willie and I, as well as the parents, made our way out of the anteroom and into the hallway, retracing our steps back through the kitchen and out onto the delivery loading dock. Before we knew it, we were back at the RMP, which was still hidden out of view between two ambulances.

Frankie notified the radio dispatcher that the civilians were entering the car and requested a time check from Central. With that done, he then headed out to the Parkhill Avenue complex.

"My son was so beautiful. He had such deep blue eyes. I had so many plans for him," Mrs. Jenkins said quietly in the back seat as she broke down in loud gasps again. As she cried, all her husband could do was hold her and try to console her.

Frankie made the turn onto Parkhill Avenue from Osgood Avenue. As soon as he had negotiated the turn, he could see that news media vans had converged in front of the Jenkins' apartment building. He also saw the detective's blue, unmarked car parked roughly 200 feet in front of the blood-sucking media.

He pulled the RMP right in back of Rizzo's car. The mother and father got out but Frankie waited until Frank and I also arrived on the scene.

"Frank, we're going to go up with the family. John, stay here and keep a watch on our vehicles," Frankie directed.

I acknowledged him as the rest of my team began to escort the Jenkins couple to the front entrance. As they got closer to Detective Rizzo's car, the other officers realized that Hartmill was inside the back of the squad car. Thankfully, neither the parents nor the media saw him there.

Rizzo approached me and asked if I would guard Hartmill. I agreed but requested that the prisoner be rear cuffed and placed in my car. Rizzo cuffed him and placed him in the front seat with me.

Near the entrance to the building, Frankie, Frank and Willie were now trying to form some sort of protective wedge for the parents in an attempt to get them through the crowd of reporters and cameramen who were blocking the lobby of the apartment building. Detective Rizzo caught up with the group and simply pushed his way through the throng of media people, pretending that he lived there. Reporters and cameramen were falling everywhere; it was a beautiful sight. When Rizzo finally caught up with the other officers, he explained that he had placed Hartmill in the car with me.

When he heard those words spoken, it was as if something snapped inside the father's brain.

Mr. Jenkins tore through the lobby doors and pushed his way through the crowd of reporters, actually knocking several of them to the ground. When he reached the street, he looked to his left and saw the RMP with the man who had murdered his son sitting in the front seat. Without pausing, he ran towards the cruiser with fury and hatred in his eyes.

The window on Hartmill's side was closed and the door was locked. My door was unlocked but when I saw the father racing toward our vehicle, I quickly locked it. My window was partially down, however, and I didn't have time to roll it up completely. The grieving father didn't hesitate as he reached into the partially opened window in an attempt to grab Hartmill from outside the vehicle. He was blind with rage.

"You fucking murderer! I'll kill you! You son of a bitch!"

The crazed father continued to reach further and further into the window and I was afraid he was going to break the glass with the force of his body.

In an instant, Mr. Jenkins grabbed my left hand and began pulling it up and over the pane of glass. The pain was excruciating and I truly believed that my arm would be pulled completely out of its socket. With my free hand, I unlocked the door and pushed it open with the left side of my body. The opening door caused Jenkins to release my arm and I fell to the pavement. The enraged father then tried to climb over my body in an attempt to get to his baby's killer.

I was in a lot of pain and had lost the use of my left arm. Although I did not want to intentionally harm Mr. Jenkins, I could not allow him to kill Hartmill, no matter how much the son of a bitch deserved it. I also didn't want the grieving father to get into any real trouble. He already had enough sorrow and heartache. No matter how bad it was, I knew I would not pursue any charges against Mr. Jenkins for my arm injury.

I grabbed him around the waist with my free arm but Jenkins turned around and lifted me high into the air. The photographer for the New York daily News was there and the front cover photo the next day was of this image, Jenkins raising me over his head. This was when the rest of my team reached us and restrained the grieving father as gently as possible. After a slight struggle, they escorted him back to the lobby and the safety of his apartment.

304

An ambulance responded to the scene and I was treated for the injury to my arm. Thankfully, it was determined that my arm only needed to be in a sling, for which I was out for the next few days. Although my injury gave me a good reason for staying home to recuperate, I dreaded being out and wanted to get back to be with my partner.

Detective Rizzo finally made it up to the Jenkins apartment and, after offering his sympathies, quietly explained what their next steps would entail. While he did this, Frankie, Willie, Frank and I resumed patrol.

Eventually Hartmill was indicted by the Staten Island Grand Jury and faced trial. He was sentenced to 25 years to life and, to this day, sits in solitary confinement in the Sing Sing Prison in Ossining, NY.

"So you see, Charlie, this was how I met evil, face to face, in the form of Wilbur Hartmill. Now you know the main reason why I detest working Easter Sundays in the 120th. When I sit back and look at the entire picture, I can't even begin to imagine what pain those parents must still be enduring. You always hear people speaking about closure in cases like this. Closure my ass! Mr. and Mrs. Jenkins will have a hole in their hearts for as long as they live. Hopefully they had another child and eventually got on with their lives, but no one will ever know the pain they felt and endured that fateful day.

"So, if there is any lesson to this story, it is simply this; while there is life, there is hope. With life, all things are possible. We have the power to heal, to change our ways and to make peace with our God and with our loved ones," said Lt. A. stoically.

"I guess you're right, boss," Charlie said with a nod.

He was going to take advantage of the lieutenant's mood and tell him what was going on in his life between Annette and himself. He had been following the lieutenant's advice and avoided all contact with Terry. Even though he had been brutally honest with her, it seemed she could not accept the fact that she had not won him over.

It was only after Charlie had made the difficult decision to make the clean break between them that he had painfully discovered she had been lying to him. She had always said she would never hurt him or cause him pain, but the opposite soon became clear through blatantly truth.

"Right after I told Terry that I was going to try to reconcile with my wife, Annette received a large manila envelope in the mail. It contained every card and written love letter I'd ever sent Terry," Charlie said as he shook his head.

"Lou, when a man sleeps with a woman, it's a very personal and intimate time spent together. The words spoken to each other during these moments are the deepest and most intimate, reserved only for their ears. I wrote those very thoughts and feelings in my letters and cards to Terry. I used to speak and write of my burning desire for her and tell her how I wanted and needed her so much. I very vividly described what I wanted to do to her. You can imagine how Annette felt when she read those words. Her pain must have been horrendous."

He paused and shook his head, still having a hard time believing Terry could do something so cold and heartless after all they'd shared.

"Annette and I were really trying very hard to work out our problems. She was happily aware that I had severed all ties with Terry and I knew she was no longer seeing her boyfriend from work. As a matter of fact, she transferred to another branch of her firm on the north shore, without my asking her to do so. We had been going out to romantic dinners and I truly believed we were really getting close again, but when she received that envelope from Terry, it all fell apart.

"I tried to explain that, yes, I had said those things but it was during the relationship which was now over. Unfortunately, it didn't seem to matter to her at that point.

"Just two days later a second envelope arrived. This one contained every piece of jewelry I had ever bought for Terry. There were charms in the shape of little handcuffs, a miniature shield and a little police baton. Everything was police oriented.

"Also included in the envelope was a letter, hand-written this time, where she explained to Annette that she would win me back or die trying.

"Annette's response was that she'd had enough and wanted nothing more to do with me. She said she was completely drained and it was over between us, once and for all. I tried to be honest and told her I had done all those things because, at the time, I truly believed that I loved Terry and was not just using her for sex.

"In any event, we haven't been sleeping in the same bed or speaking for almost a week now. I feel completely lost, Lieutenant," Charlie said, his eyes filled with regret and his voice barely a whisper.

"I really feel for you, Charlie, and I have a suggestion. Remember when I told you about Father Krackowski on York Avenue? He was that wonderful priest who had been mugged and his gift for his best friend, Pope John Paul 2nd had been stolen."

Charlie nodded.

"Well, I never told you this, but my wife and I had gone through a little marital problem around that time and we both agreed together to go and see Father Krackowski. I had spoken to him countless times over the years while I was still a cop in the precinct. He was a man so full of love and infinite wisdom. He loved people so much that his love just spilled over in so many caring ways.

"I think if you could convince Annette to go with you and see him, he might be able to help you both reconnect. He knows how to find the real you, if you know what I mean."

Charlie nodded again as the lieutenant continued.

"I met another priest like him years before I became a cop when I was married in Saint Anne's Parish in Dongan Hills. The regular priest was ill at the time so we got married by one who was temporarily staying at the Franciscan Brother's Friary up on Todt Hill. My wife and I were required to go see him as part of the marriage process. We only stayed an hour with him, Charlie, but I was completely enthralled by him. He was on a sort of hiatus from his missionary duties in Asia and had been a Chaplain during World War Two. He had also been portrayed in the movies by actor Pat O'Brien. They made a movie of his exploits, titled *Fighting Father Dunne.*

"I have always been in awe of these men of the cloth whose belief enabled them to overcome insurmountable barriers and whose faith and love moved mountains, just as the scriptures say.

"Remember that I was present at the miracle of Father Krackowski when we recovered his gift for Pope John Paul 2nd? Now my faith is telling me now that what you and Annette truly need is the special love and attention that Father Krackowski has to offer. He is older now but he is still the pastor over at St. Stanislaus Kostka Church on York Avenue. If you would like I can give him a call and ask him first, of course, if he is up to it," explained Lt. A.

"Lou, I would really appreciate that. When I get home I'll try and speak to Annette and see what she says," Charlie agreed without hiding the hope in his voice.

When the tour was over, he signed out and drove straight home. On the way, Charlie decided to stop in front of Saint Anne's Church. This was where he had been married as well as the place where his kids had gone to parochial grade school. He remained in his car and said a silent prayer to St. Anne, the patron saint of Christian mothers. Annette had always been a good mother, if not a great mother. She sacrificed for them when they were younger by giving up her career so she could be a stay-at-home mom. She had volunteered for their children's classes at school and had been involved in all their school trips and projects. She had also been there for them when they started dating.

He said a silent prayer for her, no matter which direction fate and life took her. He loved her and prayed that he could convince her to go with him to see the priest. He also hoped, more than anything, that Father Krackowski would be up for the task.

Charlie drove home, parked his car and went into the house. Annette was still there and looked so very depressed. She had not even gotten dressed for work and it was obvious that she had been crying.

"Annette, please don't cry. I know how you must feel after receiving all those cards and jewelry. After I broke off the relationship, Terry told me she would do something like that. She said if she could not have me, no one would. Sending you the cards and jewelry was her way of trying to accomplish that. All I can say is that we are working on it and I feel so happy, happier even, in working with you now than I ever have at any other time in my life. I want us to be victorious in this, honey. Let's not let her win. Please," he begged.

"I'm just so down right now, Charlie, and I don't know whether or not it will pass."

"Annette, you know I have been talking to Lt. A. about this for a while. He really cares about us and listens to every word I say. He suggested we go see someone that he also went to years ago when he was having a similar problem with his wife," he explained.

"Who is it, Charlie?" she asked.

"It's the priest he became close with when he was a cop years ago in the 120th, the one who was in the concentration camp in Poland. I don't know if I ever told you about it, but Lt. A. says the man is truly special and thinks we should go see him."

"I don't know, Charlie. A priest?" she asked quizzically.

"Lt. A. says he is more than a priest, honey," Charlie replied. "He believes Father Josef is a very special human being.

"I've made the decision that I want to save our marriage and have a life with you, Annette, and I am willing to do all that I can in order to achieve this. I know you did, too. You proved it by getting the transfer to another branch of your firm."

He paused as he took her hands in his.

"Annette, honey, please don't let these gifts I sent Terry during that time ruin our chances now. I think we *can* save our marriage and rekindle our romance, but if we are going to do it, we have to both try and work at it."

He was sure to remember to neither speak of nor mention whether or not his wife had ever received any gifts. He was sure she had but was smart enough not even to broach the topic with her.

"Charlie, just give me a few days, okay?" she asked quietly.

"Okay, sweetheart, whatever you need," he answered lovingly then he kissed her on the cheek and made his way to their bedroom. He had just enough time to recharge his mind to be ready for whatever the night ahead would bring, so he lay down and slept for a few hours. When he woke up, he showered, shaved went downstairs, where he found Annette, sound asleep on the couch. Although he wanted to kiss her goodbye, he decided it was best to not disturb her and left without waking her.

He arrived at the precinct at his usual time and climbed the rear stairs to his locker. It was becoming increasingly difficult for him to gaze at Annette's picture, which still hung inside the metal door, night after night knowing if she didn't go to Father Krackowski with him it meant she had made the decision not to even try to save their marriage. He had to remain positive, though, just as Lt. A. had advised him to do weeks before.

After roll call Charlie and Lt. A. hit the streets. The boss had to make a few visits to the cooping prone locations, which he did early in the tour.

"How about some coffee, Charlie?" Lt. A. asked as they headed out. "You look like you could use a cup; maybe even something even stronger."_

Charlie nodded and said, "I do, Lou. I brought up Father Krackowski to my wife earlier."_

"And?"

"And she said she wanted to give it a few days."

"Okay, well that's not a 'no,' Charlie. Just give her time and stay positive. And remember, a sulking man is not very attractive," said Lt. A with an encouraging smile.

"I know you're right, Lou, but it's still hard to do," Charlie answered honestly. "I just feel so helpless right now."

The lieutenant nodded. "How's it going with Terry?"

Charlie ran a hand through his hair.

"Well, the last contact was her mailing the envelopes. I guess she figured my wife would consider it the last straw. She probably figured if Annette left me, I would go running back to her, but I swear, Lou, if my wife left me tomorrow, Terry would not be on my list to people to contact. Not ever. I don't want any part of her or of anyone who would go out of their way to harm an innocent person."

"That's a big decision on your part, Charlie, but I think you made the right choice based upon what you said she's done. Terry knew you were married. You both acted as adults at the time and made choices, right or wrong. Your wife was always the innocent victim. For Terry to hurt her after the fact was mean and cold-hearted," Lt. A. explained.

"I totally agree, Lou."

After a moment of quiet, the radio dispatcher's voice suddenly broke the silence in the car.

"120 Lieutenant."

"120 Lieutenant, standing by," responded Lt. A.

"120 Lieutenant, please respond back to the station house on a 10-2," directed the dispatcher.

"10-4, message acknowledged."

When the lieutenant arrived back at the station house he was informed that the desk sergeant had reported sick and went home. This meant the lieutenant would have to assume desk duty, and since there wasn't any other sergeant on patrol, the 122nd patrol sergeant would now cover both precincts. Charlie was silently glad this had happened because the boss would silently allow him to go down to the police officer's lounge to watch TV or grab a few winks of sleep.

Every once in a while, Charlie would come up to make a coffee run for the house brigade. Of course, when he did he bypassed the Dunkin Donuts shop where Terry worked. He didn't even drive by because he didn't want to risk seeing her. It wasn't a question of temptation on his part; he truly didn't want anything more to do with her.

The night was a beautiful one and Charlie even managed to get a few good, solid hours on his back. As his shift came to an end, he was in a hurry to get home so he changed into his civvies before sign out time in order to get a good head start. He drove home not knowing what to expect from Annette but hoped with all his heart that she had come to some kind of decision. She wasn't the type to mope about for days at a time when she had something on her mind.

A soon as his house came into view, the first thing he saw was his wife's car still parked in the driveway. He parked his own car next to hers then walked in and found her sitting at the kitchen table, drinking a cup of tea. He greeted her by simply saying good morning. She said hi and asked how his night went. Normally he would have said it was busy or rough but this morning he said he had a great night, thanks to Lt. A., and could take advantage of it by staying up longer with her than he normally would.

"Charlie, tell me some more about the priest," she said as he sat down at the table.

"Well, Lt. A. met him years ago when he worked with his partner, Frank. After that initial meeting, the lieutenant would regularly visit Father Josef because he was a man of pure love and joy who had suffered and endured so much when he was a young priest in Poland. He had been interred in a concentration camp but escaped and finally immigrated to the United States. Lt. A. also described how he and his wife had some of their own marital problems and went to see the priest. He told me those visits were better than any marriage counselor –

they worked wonders for he and his wife. He encouraged us to go and said if we do, he would happily call the priest to set up a meeting," explained Charlie.

"Okay. I'll try it once, Charlie."

He was suddenly on top of the world. She *did* want to save her marriage! If not, she would have never agreed to go to see Father Krackowski. Charlie silently said a prayer of thanks, then said one more, asking for the priest to still have a little bit of magic to spare for he and Annette.

As he sat there looking at his wife, Charlie realized he had never felt as alive as he did at that very moment. He wanted to grab Annette and just hold her in his arms, but he didn't want to scare her away and seem overly optimistic. She had agreed to go with him but she had also said, quite clearly, that she would try it once. One shot at this might make or break that final straw.

Charlie felt well rested and as high as a kite because of her decision and willingness to go with him to see Father Josef. Although he was a bit tired, he had no doubt that if he did go up and lay down, he would just toss and turn, so he decided to stay up and complete some chores around the house, which he had been procrastinating about for weeks. He needed to replace some loose tile in the bathroom as well as some caulking around the tub. He figured he might get tired by doing some of his tasks then could lay down for a while before he had to go back to work.

It was about 2:00 P.M. when he finished and decided to lie down for a few hours. As he was walking out of his downstairs bathroom to go up to his bedroom on the second floor, he caught sight of the mailman walking up his driveway to place their mail in the mailbox. The uniformed man was carrying not only the mail but also a huge, manila envelope. When he saw it, Charlie's stomach dropped.

"What is she sending me now?"_he said aloud.

He ran to the front door and opened it as the mailman was just about to drop the mail into the mailbox. When he saw Charlie, the uniformed man handed him the huge envelope, said, "Good afternoon!" Then, with a parting smile and a nod, he turned and walked back down the walkway.

Charlie looked for a return address on the envelope and was relieved to see it was from the Patrolmen's Benevolent Association, which routinely sent out pamphlets on all kinds of helpful information.

He didn't even bother to open it. Instead, he climbed the stairs and went into his bathroom and showered. While he got ready for work, all he could do was continually gasp sighs of relief and say silent prayers, thanking God that the package hadn't been anything sent by Terry. He reminded himself that he had to remain positive and keep negative thoughts out of his mind. After his shower, he went in to the bedroom and pulled down the room-darkening shades then turned the TV on low but loud enough to drown out any street noise. He slept soundly until 8:00 P.M. then went downstairs, he found Annette sitting on the couch watching TV.

"If you're hungry, I made some broiled scallops with broccoli and rice. It's on a dish in the microwave," she said.

"Thank you. That sounds delicious."_

He went into the kitchen and heated his dinner then took his plate back into the living room on a tray where he sat and ate in Annette's company. She seemed pleased that he chose to be nearby and not alone in the kitchen. She gave him a slight, silent smile and continued watching television.

"It's delicious. Did you have some, too?"_he asked.

"Yeah, all of a sudden I got hungry. I had to make them before they went bad anyway and I know how much you love scallops. Remember, that's what you always ordered when we used to go to Atlantic City."

Charlie was simply beaming. In fact, he was ecstatic. When he finished his dinner he got up and put his plate in the dishwasher then walked back into the living room. He moved slowly towards her, as if to wait for her permission to kiss her goodnight or be ready for a hand in his face that would tell him, "Not now!" He bent over to her and quietly said goodnight then moved to give her a kiss, which she did return, although hesitantly.

"Charlie, be careful, okay?"_

"Thanks, I will," he answered.

He walked out to his car and couldn't wait to tell Lt. A. about his progress with Annette. He drove down Burgher Avenue, but this time chose a different route to take him into the precinct. He made a left onto Hylan Boulevard and drove about a half mile to Reid Avenue to McClean Avenue then made a left onto Father Capodanno Boulevard. For some inexplicable reason he wanted to take a scenic route. He knew it was a little bit out of the way but traffic was light and he thought he might have been able to take in the scene of the full moon over the Verrazano Bridge. His luck and timing were perfect. The round, white orb in the dark sky shone directly over the bridge and its bright reflection shimmered in the Narrows below. It was like a shot of energy for his soul.

He arrived at work and changed quickly. When he was almost fully dressed he overheard a group of officers talking in the next aisle.

"So Ben, I heard you met a nice piece of ass the other night," came the voice of Officer Mike Bertucci.

"Yeah, I met a nice girl, if that's what you mean," replied Officer Ben Morano.

"Well, you should speak to Charlie about her because he's spent a lot of time with her. Maybe he could give you some pointers on how to score," teased Bertucci.

"I don't need pointers from anyone."

Charlie was shocked as well as surprised. He didn't believe what he was hearing. How did these guys know he had been seeing Terry? If they knew, the whole precinct knew. He thought he had been discreet and wondered who had let the cat out of the bag?

He didn't want to start asking a million questions because it would appear that he might be jealous and was still interested in her. He had broken off the relationship and secretly hoped she would find someone else so she could get over her obsession with him and move on with her life. He decided to speak to Ben on the side and just engage him in conversation without coming out and admitting to anything.

Charlie quickly descended the front stairs which led out to the desk area. Lt. A. was busy instructing the sergeants on the latest patrol guide amendments concerning the new Stop and Frisk Form. Most cops were against it but Lt. A. believed it could be used as a tool to support all officers as long as the paperwork was filled out properly.

Glancing around, he saw Ben sitting in the SP-10 room opposite the telephone switchboard. Charlie had used the very same phone several times when calling Terry from the station house. He walked in under the pretext of looking for some extra forms and couldn't help but overhear part of the conversation that Ben was having. It was obvious he was speaking to a female.

"Hi. How have you been? I just thought I would give you a ring before it got too late. I didn't want to call you later knowing your son has to get up to go to school in the morning," said Ben.

Charlie could only assume what the other party was saying but it was obvious they were terms of endearment coming from the other end of the phone.

"I don't know about that. I don't think I can come over in the morning because I have an early class at the College of Staten Island. Remember I told you I'm studying nursing? I figured it's the best way to get into the Emergency Service Unit. Unfortunately, I don't have any hooks or Rabbi's to call to get me in," Ben said.

Surprisingly, Charlie didn't feel jealous. If it was Terry on the other end, he felt thankful that maybe she was beginning to get over him and get on with her life.

"Okay, I'll stop in and see you tomorrow night before I go in. You know how I like my coffee, right?" asked Ben.

If it was Terry on the other end of the phone, and Charlie was now almost 100% sure that it was based upon the conversation, he truly hoped she was happy. She was a good kid even though her jealousy caused Annette to experience so much unnecessary pain and heartache. Charlie knew Ben was a single guy but he wasn't the type to kiss and tell then boast of his conquests with women like so many other cops did. Ben also had solid goals about rising within the police department.

Charlie felt pretty good and could hardly wait to talk to Lt. A. about it all.

He went into the muster room and stood roll call. After the sergeants addressed the troops, Lt. A. spoke briefly about the new Stop Frisk Report. He made it clear to the men that it was not meant to handcuff cops in their duties like so many other decisions that came down from the ivory towers of One Police Plaza.

After roll call, Charlie walked out to the front desk and retrieved the keys to the RMP. He grabbed his gear and made his way through the double set of glass doors and down the front steps to the street where the 4X12 operator had securely parked the car. He stowed his gear in the back seat and jammed his night stick in its usual place, then waited for Lt. A. to come out. The lieutenant joined him several minutes later and placed his night stick next to Charlie's then lit up the first of the many cigarettes he would smoke that night.

"Charlie, let's drive down to Canal Street. We can get our coffee at the new Bodega next to the Staten Island savings bank. They make a strong cup of bustello there and I think I need one of those right now."

"Okay, Lou. Sounds good."

They drove along Richmond Terrace, passing the entrance to the Saint George Ferry terminal. The clipper at 40 Bay Street was packed with passengers who took the ride over from Manhattan as they searched for a place to eat. He continued driving past Victory Boulevard to Bay Street towards Stapleton then made a right at Tappen Park and pulled into an empty space in front of the bodega.

Charlie went in and ordered two cups of the steaming coffee as well as two hot, buttered Portuguese rolls. He was happy when he learned they had just come out of the oven. Without a word, he gave the young, Spanish clerk $2.00 dollars cash and got back eight quarters in change.

The guy was good and Charlie made a mental note to tell the other guys to give the place special attention. A good cop always watched over the places that took care of the cops. One hand always washed the other.

After getting back in the RMP, he drove down to the end of Canal Street to the water's edge and parked next to one of the abandoned piers. Both men opened their cups of the Bustello and, of course, lit up their cigarettes.

"Well, Charlie. How's it going? Did you ever talk to your wife?"_ asked Lt. A., remembering he had advised Charlie to speak to his Annette about Father Krackowski.

"Yes, Lou, and she said she would try it once!"

"That's great, Charlie! How soon do you want to go?"

"Whenever you can set it up, Lou," said Charlie with obvious relief in his voice.

"I'll call Father Krackowski in the morning," the lieutenant said with a small smile. "Better still, I'll drop in on him personally."

"I really appreciate that, Lou, and I have no doubt that whatever I tell you stays in the RMP."

"That goes without saying, Charlie."

After hesitating for several seconds, Charlie blurted out, "Lou, I overheard Ben Morano speaking to a female on the phone tonight, and I'm pretty sure it was Terry."_

"What makes you think it was Terry?"

"Well, I also overheard Mike Bertucci talking to Ben in the locker room before the phone call, but I don't think they knew I was there. From what they were saying, I'm almost certain they were talking about her," said Charlie.

"How did that make you feel, Charlie?"_

"Well, I'm happy to say that I didn't feel jealous. As a matter of fact, from what I hear about Ben he seems to be a pretty good kid. At least, he's not married," said Charlie with a chuckle.

"Ben is in my squad and under my Span of Support. I have always rated him high," said the lieutenant. "He seems like he's got a good head on his shoulders and is one of the few men in my squad who has a definite career plan mapped out for himself."

The lieutenant fell silent for a moment, taking his time drinking his coffee and smoking his cigarette. Eventually he continued.

"We all move on, Charlie, every one of us. Life goes on. You have a large task in front of you. Cheating is one thing but the real question is why did you stray in the first place? That's what you have to find out about yourself, and I think Father Krackowski can help."

Both men finished their coffee, lost deep in their own thoughts. The night flew by and it was fairly quiet as far as the lieutenant's duties went. He even allowed Charlie to hunt for a few moving violations to meet his monthly quota of summonses. He was scheduled for an upcoming vacation and didn't need the Commanding Officer to deny him his time because of the dreaded quota that existed everywhere except in the minds of the brass at One Police Plaza and City Hall.

CHAPTER TWENTY-EIGHT

Morning came quickly and Lt. A. signed out, completely bypassing the usual bullshit session at the desk because he wanted to drive over to the church on York Avenue to see Father Krackowski.

The drive to York Avenue from the station house took less than five minutes and was a straight run along Richmond Terrace to York Avenue. John made the left and drove up the steep hill then parked directly across the street from the church. He found it strange that every time he parked near this church he recalled the first time he and his partner Frank had been assigned there all those years ago. It had led to his long-time friendship with Father Krackowski, of which he was very thankful.

Lt. A. walked up the flowered walkway and knocked on the rectory door. After a few minutes it was opened and he was greeted by a woman who appeared to be in her early forties. She was about 5'8", had blond hair and was wearing a colorful, flowered apron.

"May I help you?"_she asked in perfect English. Although she had no accent, she definitely looked Polish.

"Good morning. My name is John Audenino. I'm a friend of Father Krackowski's. I was wondering if I could see him for just a few moments, if it's at all possible."

"What did you say your name was?"_she asked.

"It's John Audenino. I'm a lieutenant here in this precinct."

"John, oh my God! My mother used to speak about you all the time! She told me that you and Father Josef used to sit for hours at a time and talk," she said.

"What was your mother's name?"_he asked.

"Her name was Anna Powerski. She was the caretaker here for many years," said the young woman.

"Wow, I remember her. How is she?"

"My mom passed on several years ago," she said quietly. "I used to help her here when she wasn't feeling well. Then, when she died, I just kind of took over."_

"I'm sorry to hear about your mom," he said. "She was a real nice lady."_

"Please, come on in and sit. I'll get Father Josef. Oh, by the way, my name is Katrina."

Katrina led Lt. A. into the small parlor where he and his partner Frank had been all those years earlier. Gone was the pale painting and the wooden crucifix which hung on the opposite wall. In its place were framed photos of Pope John Paul 2nd and Father Krackowski, taken at the Pope's ordination in Rome in the late 1970's.

After a few moments the door to the parlor opened and there stood Father Krackowski. He was wearing a NY Giant's t-shirt and glasses, which John had never seen him wear before. He still looked trim but seemed to be a slightly smaller man than he had been. He still had a smile that seemed infectious, however. John quickly rose up and both men embraced.

"John, my son! You look wonderful! It has been so long since we last met. How have you been? How is your wonderful wife?"_

"Hello, Father. I'm good, thank you, and so is my wife, and I am eternally grateful to you for it."

The priest nodded as John added, "And it was so good to see Anna's daughter!"

"Yes, Katrina is such a beautiful person, and she is an even better cook than her mother was," said Father Josef with a boisterous laugh.

The door opened and Katrina walked in, carrying a tray which held a pot of espresso coffee and a small plate of croissants. She placed the tray on the table in front of both men and did not say a word, leaving the room as quietly as she had entered.

"John, sit please," the priest said with a gesture to a nearby chair as he reached into a cabinet and took out a bottle of Sambouca.

"I know you are not in uniform, so we will drink with our coffee," Father Josef said with a smile.

"Okay, Father. I'm glad you remembered how much I like Sambouca with my espresso!"

Father Josef poured the Italian liquor into little shot glasses and handed one to John.

"To life and joy," the priest said, toasting the moment.

"To life and joy!"

Both men spent some precious moments reminiscing their time spent together as well as times yet to come. John felt totally relaxed with Father Josef and, after a while, began to explain the real purpose of the visit.

"Father, years ago you helped my wife and I when we were going through some pretty rocky times in our marriage. You are the only person I have ever spoken to about my problems and I have always valued your discretion."

Father Josef nodded as John continued.

"I'm here today because of a young man that I work with. He, too, is going through a tough time with his wife. He had an affair and his wife found out about it. She also began seeing someone where she worked. They both faced their situation head on and have made a decision to come and see you as I did, if you are willing to help them."

"My son, what is life all about? Why am I alive? As long as there is life, there is always hope. You know the pain I saw and endured in my past, yet, for some reason, God has allowed me to go on. My only purpose in this life is to love and help all of my children, as I am proud to say I helped you. Have you told him anything about why you came to me?"_asked Father Josef.

"No, Father. I just told him that I came to you because my wife and I were going through a bad period in our marriage. I really didn't want to tell him any more than that. He kind of looks up to me and I just couldn't tell him that I had an affair, too."

"Well, my son, I won't say anything about you. If the young man looks up to you it is because you have changed your ways and live your life the way our good Lord meant for you to live," the priest said, offering John a reassuring smile.

Lt. A. had never told anyone about his previous relationship with another woman. He had ended his affair long before he even met Father Josef, but afterward his marriage was never the same.

He had made a routine of visiting Father Krackowski and finally decided to truly confess to this man because he knew the priest would not look down upon him for his sins. Father Krackowski met with Lt. A. and his wife over the course of several months and, thankfully, the result was a stronger marriage that was based on love, respect and honesty. The relationship he had with his wife after talking to the priest was better than it had ever been before, and he hoped the same would be true for Charlie and Annette.

"So, my son, when do you think your young man will want to come and see me?"_asked Father Josef.

"He seemed like he wanted to start as soon as possible. He did tell me that his wife, Annette, has only agreed to try it once, saying she seemed a little doubtful because she would be talking to a priest and not a regular marriage counselor."_

"Are they regular church-goers?"_

"I'm not sure, Father, but if I had to take a guess, I would say no, although both of their children went to Saint Anne's School. After that, his daughter went to Saint John's Villa Academy and his son went to Monsignor Farrell High School."_

"That's good. I always can fall back on why they chose to send them to Catholic schools. Remember, I did that with you," the priest said with a smile.

"You know, Father, it's been so long that I had forgotten."

"Well then, my son, it is settled. You tell Charlie to stop in after work tomorrow. I will see him after my 8:00 A.M. mass," said Father Josef.

"Okay, Father, I will do that. Charlie goes on his swing now for his regular days off. I'll call him when I get home so he can tell Annette. She may have to take a day off as she works Monday through Friday," said Lt. A.

Both men stood and gave each other a long embrace. Lt. A. felt so at ease and at peace with this man whenever he was in his presence. He knew that Father Josef, a simple priest who had endured so much, had all the trappings of a saint, and he would never understand how the priest had suffered so much yet still had such a capacity for love and forgiveness.

"Father, all I can say is thank you and give you my solemn promise that I will not let so much time elapse before we see each other again," said the lieutenant.

"John, you know me. I am going to hold you to that promise, even if it means that I have to come knocking on your police station's door," said Father Josef, his tone serious but his eyes bright with mischief.

"You won't have to do that, Father, I promise!"

Both men said their final goodbyes at the door then John walked to his car. He couldn't wait to call Charlie because it was early yet and he had no doubt Charlie would be up still, sitting by his phone, anxiously waiting for it to ring.

The phone booths surrounding the Jersey Street projects were no more than portable bathrooms with urine soaked floors and feces smeared on the receivers, if they even had them still attached. Lt. A. drove to the nearest one, which was in the Randall manor area and on his way home. Eventually he stopped in front of a known working phone on Forest Avenue near Oakland Avenue in front of LiGreci's restaurant.

The booth was unoccupied, so he got out of his car and called Charlie, who answered in one ring.

"Hello?"

"Charlie, it's Lt. A. Listen, your meeting with the priest is all set up. Father Krackowski said he would be more than happy to see you both. He would like you and Annette to come at 9:00 a.m. tomorrow, which will be after he finishes his 8:00 A.M. mass," said Lt. A. "Will that work for you?"

"Oh, Lou, that's fantastic! We'll be there. I don't know what to say or how to thank you."

"You don't have to thank me, Charlie. I just want you to be honest. Sometimes it's difficult to admit certain things, but if you are going to save your marriage, you have to be honest; sometimes brutally honest."

"You're right, of course, and that's just what I intend to do. Thanks again, Lou. I'll tell Annette right away."_

"Good luck, Charlie, and I'll see you when you come back to work in a few days. Remember you can always call me at home if you need to."

"I really appreciate that. You know, Lieutenant, you've been a good friend to me. Probably better than any other friends that I have. I'll never forget what you've done for me," said Charlie candidly.

"Thanks, Charlie. I'll see you at work in a few days," said Lt. A. and hung up with a smile.

As the lieutenant headed home to his own wife, Charlie told Annette about their upcoming appointment with Father Josef.

Thankfully, Annette agreed to the time and said she would simply call in sick. The next morning Charlie was a bundle of nerves and it almost felt as though he were going to a major dental appointment. As a matter of fact, he almost wished it *was* a dental appointment. He was nervous that he had agreed to be brutally honest, but he was going to keep his word.

Annette and Charlie climbed into his car and drove the same route he went each night for years on his way to work. However, when he reached the precinct on Richmond Terrace he continued driving the extra few blocks to York Avenue then made the left turn up the hill. He parked in one of several spots he found available then both he and Annette walked up the steps and knocked on the rectory door. This time, Father Krackowski personally answered. Instead of wearing his usual sport t-shirt, the Father had on his priestly black coat and stiff white collar. He definitely looked the part.

"My children, please come into my home. I am Father Krackowski but you may call me Father Josef," he said amicably.

"Good morning, Father Josef. I'm Charlie Goodheart and this is my wife, Annette," Charlie said nervously.

"Please, come with me," the priest said as he led them through a hallway and into his parlor.

Father Josef had placed three comfortable chairs in the room and there was a box of tissues on a small wooden table between two of them. There was also a pitcher of water and two glasses on a tray on another table as well as a carafe of ice. He beckoned them to sit down.

The photos of the newly ordained Pope John Paul 2nd were still on the wall. However, the priest had added something after John had said his goodbyes just the day before. Now hung on the inside of the parlor door was a carved wooden plaque that his friend Pope John Paul had given him when Father Josef had gone to Rome. On it was an original quote which had been attributed to Pope John Paul. Once the door was closed, the quote could be easily read by both Charlie and Annette since Father Josef had positioned their chairs facing the inner door.

It simply read, "The future starts today, not tomorrow."_

For Charlie and Annette, it did.

32200184R00189

Made in the USA
Lexington, KY
11 May 2014